Vixen

Catherine Labadie

To my husband

In this era science gave us something it had not yet shown the human race: the successful blending of human and animal DNA. The early years of Century 22 brought the creation of what is currently titled the M-DNA (Mixed DNA) race of humanity.

MASAEO HEIGHTS, the leading research scientist and chairman of Progressions University, has been credited with the origin of the mixed DNA race. For many years not much was known about this enigmatic individual, nor were any connections between him and the M-DNA people made until years after his death. Chairman Height's goal with DNA manipulation was simply to heal the host human race which was adapting poorly to a changing globe. Little else is known of his aims, but sometime in the early days of the century he succeeded in blending carefully selected animal DNA with human embryos. The results of his success could not be calculated at the time since the astronomical number of embryos he altered both legally and illegally remains unknown.

Even so, there were enough M-DNA infants to fuel the start of a new, highly adaptable human race. Whether or not the changed children would be accepted by the rest of an unwitting humanity, Chairman Heights would never know. He was murdered by a colleague, his wife of fifteen years, because of his work at the age of 58.

1

Foxes, thanks to Aesop's fables, are known for their cunning. Since my family has a good amount of fox DNA in our biology, I've always liked to think we have the same admirable traits as the fox. Many other people in the human and half-breed community may not view our cunning as profitable, but in my experience it's been nothing but helpful.

I'm sitting at the breakfast table in our government issued townhouse, exchanging morning greetings with my family of M-DNA fox half-breeds. The government has given us a lot over the past few years: our lower cost townhouse in a decent neighbourhood, better jobs for all my brothers, and more access to places our kind used to be banned from. We're still banned from a lot of common traffic areas, but something is better than nothing. Harold says it's because they're trying to follow through with the desegregation laws laid down after the war. Wade, closest to my age at twenty, says it's because they're terrified of starting another war with a stronger, more adaptable race, but Harold always whacks him upside the head when he says this. Eisen—blond, almost human Eisen with his straw-colored fox ears—laughs at them both and says he appreciates any free goodies the government gives out.

"How do you feel about school today, little sister?" Eisen asks snidely, splitting a pop tart unevenly with me since Wade stole the other one.

"Thank god the good people of Region 5 passed the law *after* I graduated from our prestigious M-DNA institution," Wade says with relief in his voice. "Mandatory attendance at a public high school would be a nightmare."

"Thanks for cheering me up," I say. "This conversation has made me anticipate my first day at a reluctantly desegregated human school even more." Wade snorts, and Eisen's gold fox ears twitch with either amusement or irritation as he smiles with straight white teeth and cleverly slanted blue eyes. I sigh inwardly, wondering why my twenty-two year old brother got the striking good looks of the family.

We all have fox features, which can be unusual in a mixed-breed family: blended DNA is unpredictable, although in recent years it seems like the patterns have finally evened out. Out of our family unit Eisen is the most human with only his fox ears revealing his half-breed nature.

"Gloating over your escape hardly seems like the

best way to cheer Sierra up before being cast to the..." Harold, my scholarly brother who is rapidly approaching the age of thirty-three, pauses and lifts his eyes from his SMARTpad. "Well, saying 'cast to the wolves' seems inappropriate since there won't be any wolves there, only humans who outnumber the few M-DNA students." I grimace and throw a crumpled up napkin towards Harold, but he evades the missile and returns to his crisp notes with a careless swivel of one tufty black fox ear. Normally he's too serious, since being an underpaid lawyer for half-breeds in a court dominated by humans can be very sobering, and it's ironic that today is the day he chooses to have a sense of humor.

"I don't think any of you should talk, since you got lucky and avoided this mess," I say as I bare my teeth in Harold's direction. Eisen and Wade ignore me as they laugh, but Harold shrugs, guilty about his humor. Maybe it's part of being a lawyer, but Harold beats himself up about his role in the well-being of others, especially my siblings and me. I don't know for sure if he regrets his joke, though, because he doesn't lift his grey eyes from his SMARTpad.

The smell of my breakfast—Eisen dragged himself out of bed for once to make toast and eggs for us all—wafts towards my nose and for a moment I think I'm hungry. Then I imagine where I'll be in a couple of hours and my appetite dissipates.

"You'll be fine, S...humans are still secretly scared of our kind," Wade interjects, clapping Harold on the back with a paw-like hand covered in auburn fur."Well, maybe not *specifically* scared of fox-kind. It would be better if you were a tiger-breed or something *sick* like a dragon..." He trails off before returning to the present and smiling at me.

"Dragon half-breeds don't exist, so I guess I'm stuck as a fox," I say, briefly savoring the idea of dragon DNA infiltrating the gene pool for my kind. Perhaps luckily, the idiot that tampered with animal and human DNA wasn't such a moron after all: he stuck to a certain class of "perfect" animals like cats, canines, birds, and other, more attractive kinds instead of branching out to insects and deep sea creatures, which would have made for some hideous, vaguely people-shaped creations.

Wade is the most accepting of what we are because he has the most animalistic mixed DNA of anyone I've ever known. Fuller fox ears with stronger hearing—placed where our human ears would have been—a truly fox-like face with actual rusty-brown fur markings, bright yellow eyes, hands and feet that, though human in function, resemble paws, and a long fluffy tail that any ordinary fox would covet. Eisen used to tease him about it a little, but now Eisen is the most forward with telling us not to be ashamed of what we are. I respect him for this more because he could pass as a full human if he wore a hat, which he regularly refuses to do on principle.

"Regardless, no one's going to be afraid of you: you're too *cutesy*," Eisen chortles and steals my untouched toast without asking.

"Shut up, Eisen," I retort, "If anyone is 'cutesy' it's you. Imagine how the girls at the coffee shop would eat up the story of how you designed a little home for

6

your stuffed panda with a shoe box." Wade makes a loud *OOO* noise to emphasize my burn; in response, Eisen leans over and lazily tugs his tail.

"You can spread stories all you want, but the ladies will never stop loving my—"

"Shouldn't you be getting to work, Wade?" Harold interrupts what might have been another one of Eisen's ego-feeding monologues and/or innuendos. "If you're late to the factory again your boss might write you up." Harold stands and takes his plate to the sink to dump it in with a pile of other dirty breakfast dishes; I sigh internally as I consider what I'll be doing when I get home from school. Because my brothers work to pay for the house, furnishings, and virtually anything else I need or sometimes want, I do the house chores as a way to balance the scales. Harold turns around and meets my eyes before gifting me with a small encouraging smile.

"Wade will be fine; the boss loves him and the SMART industry would collapse without its best worker," Eisen says, taking his cue from Harold and rising from the table. "The prince of the SMARTpad must dole out his work hours with loving care, lest the union suffer the consequences of technology too advanced for our feeble minds—" Wade, standing as well, agile as he leans over and pinches Eisen's right fox ear, tugging it down to cut off any more sarcasm.

"Sure enough, the 'prince of the SMARTpad' has to go assemble more teeny tiny mechanical parts," Wade says, releasing Eisen after a few seconds and checking his wire thin silver watch. Then he turns and grins at me. "Don't stress, Sierra. You'll be fine. The first day in a human dominated environment is always bad, but everyone gets used to you after a while."

"Thanks," I reply, not in the least reassured. "How long does the process of people getting used to me last?" Wade's grin expands to show teeth as sharp as mine before he saunters through our living room and out the front door, grabbing his vehicle key from a chipped bowl by the sink on his way.

"And you, Eisen?" Harold addresses Eisen right as my smartass brother opens his mouth to speak. "The coffee shop opens early, as you remind us every morning when you have to get out of bed before noon."

"Don't worry, Mother. We'll be out the door soon." I watch the two of them interact, amused by Eisen's wry smile; I'm still considering if it would be safe to consume food while feeling so nauseous when I catch Eisen giving me a shifty, mischievous look. "In fact, Sierra and I were just leaving!"

"Are you—" I don't hear whatever else Harold was saying because Eisen has seized my arm, and I have just enough time to grab my schoolbag before he tugs me out the door. I'm just clambering into the passenger seat when I see Harold looming in the doorway of the garage, watching us with mild disapproval on his face as if an unpleasant idea just dawned on him.

"You'd better not make her late on her first day, Eisen!" He calls, looking very like a masculine version of our mother before sickness altered her appearance. Eisen laughs, grinning at me from the driver's seat with the jagged half of my pop tart between his teeth; it's when he does stuff like this that he resembles a wayward fox invading an unguarded chicken coop. I wave resignedly at a glowering Harold as we pull out of the garage and begin the drive to my new school.

At least it's sunny, I think as we drive out of our tiny garage. I hope looking around will relax or distract me, but no such luck: the sun gleams bright this morning, and I squeeze my eyes shut tight. Eisen speaks again before we even reach the highway, and I can tell he's not paying attention to the road: we're speeding before we even get out of the driveway of our townhouse community.

"I thought you would feel better if I got you out of there," he says, manfully polishing off the pop tart he stole in two bites. "Harry's babying can get exhausting if you just want to grit your teeth and get something over with."

"You make school sound awful," I reply, grateful for Eisen's thoughtfulness even if it gets me to school faster than I would like. "It's almost like you don't want me to go."

"Well, going to any kind of high school is awful, honestly, but I'm not worried about your academic struggles. You'll be fine in that area. Public school teachers are a little less dedicated than private school ones." He snorts, probably reminiscing about his days as universally proclaimed king of the class and self-proclaimed class clown back when he was a senior in our old M-DNA high school. I ruminate over a few memories as well: I had my struggles, but I did have friends I spent time with. I know for a fact that none of them will attend the school I'm going to, since they were assigned elsewhere.

"I remember, Eisen. It was only last year that I went," I tell him.

"Right. Well this is a brave new world, Sierra, and it is unlikely anything will be the same where you're going," he replies, unusually serious.

"I know. I have to be careful not to offend the DNA purists," I snort.

"It's not just that, S." Eisen zips past a lumbering SMARTvan as he clutches the steering wheel; I doubt it will take us more than ten minutes to get to school at this rate. "I'm just a barista at a quirky coffee shop, but I hear things."

"Okay?" The anxiety resting uncomfortably in my stomach deepens. Flippant as my brother is, when he turns serious it's disturbing and ominous. His expression is stern now with his cerulean eyes narrowed.

"The pure DNA humans are restless and very... unsettled about the desegregation laws. This one about underage half-breeds attending schools formerly meant for pure DNA students has everyone in uproar about our kind." His expression changes to something more like a snarl of disgust. "I don't say this lightly, because if you do this and it's not serious I'll get written up at work, but if there's any trouble today, you call me or call Wade and we'll come get you.

"Why?" I ask, but I can guess why he would say that, and it scares me. Eisen and Wade work long hours most of the time because we need the funds to keep up with the harsh taxes, and they would never leave work for anything small. Very little work leniency is given to half-breeds; Wade's wildness is excused now and then, but he's one of the lucky ones.

"Harold was against me telling you this, even though he would've been the best one to inform you because of his job. He knows how bad things are turning for our kind...but I expect the students and probably the establishment will do everything possible to get you to leave school before the week is out. Some might...go farther than just bullying and threats." He frowns. It must take a lot out of him to keep driving me to a place where I won't be protected. Because we are closest as siblings, part of that feeling is probably protective brother behavior. But another part is animal instinct, and fighting that off is difficult. My worry festers because now I fear for my brothers as well.

If they're just now telling me this and Eisen is going against Harold's wishes, how much have they not said? I think. *How bad is it really?*

Harold sees himself as a father figure to all three of us because he is almost ten years older. Our father died in the M-DNA against pure DNA war several years ago, and my mother passed away when I was seven from a an "accidental" outbreak of one of the biological weapons meant for the war; humans died too, but half-breeds got the worst of the sickness.

Ordinarily, Harold is very open with me in a didactic sort of way. But Eisen...his secretiveness means current events are worse than he'll say.

"It may have been nicer to tell me this during the summer so I could prepare better," I say, forcing my voice to be steady as a tremor threatens to weaken it.

"We—that is, Harold—decided it was better to wait for the aggressiveness caused by the new laws to calm down over time...but it hasn't, not really. He still didn't want to tell you, but I didn't want you going in there blind. You're tough, Sierra, but I don't want you walking in there like nobody means you harm." He looks at me with his fox ears angled down from anxiety, the same as my red ears; if he had a tail it would be as droopy as mine is. For an instant, he looks so defeated it makes my heart pause. But then he straightens up in his seat with a determined set to his mouth.

"I'll be okay, Eisen," I tell him before he can speak again, my voice softer than I'd intended. "I *am* tough. I can handle whatever temper tantrum the humans decide to throw."

"Yeah, baking in the back of a bird lady's café all summer *really* taught you all you need to know about working and living alongside humans," he snorts.

"Customer service can do that to a girl," I quip, relieved to see he's back to being my cocky older brother.

I glance out my window, startled that I can already see the school on my right. Despite all I've read in fluffy teen books about high school, the actual building of the school doesn't seem horribly foreboding or gloomy. If my mood wasn't in such turmoil, I might be able to appreciate the modern vibe emanating from it.

Eisen must have been driving faster than I thought, I think. All I can do now is feel the panic of not wanting to approach this building.

Eisen is silent as he pulls into the car line, and we wait to get to the doors where he can drop me off. In the past I've wished I was allowed to drive, cursing the legal age of twenty required solely for half-breeds. (Racist, right?) Now, though, I'm glad my brother is here.

Eisen pulls to a stop as close as we can get to the main entrance. "They just updated Hostetler High this past summer," he says as I reluctantly gather my school bag into my arms in preparation to leave the safety of the vehicle. "It looks much better than the pictures you found on the SMARTspace last week."

"It does look...new," I say, my voice unintentionally higher; "New" is the kindest word I can come up with in my current state of mind. *At least I'm a senior now*, I remind myself. *Just one year of school then I'm done. One year.*

"I'll see you later, I guess," I say to Eisen, stepping out of his car and briefly choosing to ignore the growing line behind him. "Thanks for the ride." I want to add more or just hug him...but there's really nothing else to say.

"Seriously Sierra, call me if anything...well, just call me as soon as you get out today." He avoids meeting my eyes as he pulls away and leaves me on front of the steps leading up to my new school. I try not to stare after his car like an abandoned pup, but now I'm here I need to have some backbone.

He said I was tough. I know what Eisen probably guessed already as he pulled away: I won't call him to come get me. Escaping would make my life worse the next day when I'd have to drag myself back to school. Leaving early would be admitting defeat, and I absolutely refuse to let a pack of greasy DNA purists beat me.

I walk up to the main doors with my head held high, slinging my messenger bag over my head and across my body. I already sense many eyes watching my progress.

Nothing has happened yet, I reassure myself as I walk without taking in much of my surroundings. I do notice, however, that no M-DNA students mingle and loiter around the front steps of the school. My stride doesn't falter, but my heart oozes down to the seething mass of unrest in my stomach. Imagined laughter fills both my fox ears as I reach the main doors.

They all took the back entrances, my mind informs me as heat rises to my cheeks. *That explains part of all of the staring.* I wonder if it was a rule for my kind to use the other entryways.

Abruptly, I'm staring into my own eyes: they slant at the edges like Eisen's, and they're wide with fear. I blink and my reflection disappears for a moment. Every single door down the line has been fitted with mirror glass so shiny it would be blinding if the entrance hadn't been engineered with an overhead cover to block straight sunlight. I catch another glimpse of my features and my attire in the reflections, my red fox ears up and alert and my bottom lip pink from my nervous biting. I took extra care with my appearance this morning, attempting to fit in more with the cute, pretty girls with their tight jeans or short skirts and body-hugging shirts. Now I can see that the effort was probably a waste. The only features the humans will notice about me are my fox ones; distinctive ears, red-brown fur on the back of my hands and forearms, the ridge of fur I have running down my spine—not that that's visible—and the long, sleek red fox tail that curls up behind me and sways as I walk. I've only been standing here a second, but I see my hair—reminiscent of my mother's, golden brown and shot through with some of my red fox fur color—remains adequately curled, and my skin is pale except for two points of pink in my cheeks. My face is almost strictly human, except for my eyes: the pupils slant in a distinctly fox-like way, and their shade is golden yellow.

I banish my reflection again with a determined shake of my head. Someone bumps my shoulder roughly as they shove past me to get inside, so I follow the current of people pouring inside and enter the school.

2

Eisen wasn't lying when he said the school board had spent the summer renovating Hostetler High. The impractical mirror glass on the doors is an ostentatious show of hefty financial backing, but other than that the building doesn't seem so bad. I move to the side of the hallway as I enter, keeping out of the way so I can shuffle through my bag for the paper with my locker information on it. Looking around as I search, I observe how the simplistic silver-and-white color scheme makes the locker-lined hallway feel bright, as if the fluorescent lights on the ceiling were meant to be spotlights. Those spotlights feel like they're focused on me, highlighting a glaringly obvious target for any rudeness the humans might want to dish out.

Finally my fingertips brush the folded up paper in

the front pocket of my denim bag, and I tug it out, glancing at it as I proceed with the search for my locker. My heart races as my eyes dart around in what I imagine is the unmistakable manner of a frightened animal.

So many people! My mind works furiously to process all the surrounding stimuli, making me thankful that half-breeds have the ability to minimize their animal senses, making them fade to the background of consciousness. I've never been around so many humans at one time, even in a school setting. I grew up on the outskirts of a big city and travelled around with my family when necessary. However, my brothers are protective, especially since my mother asked them to take care of me right before she passed away. Harold moved us to a predominantly M-DNA populated area around when I turned eight. I know he was relieved that the scarcity of people in his line of work gave him more choice about where to live and more options even though he was only twenty-four at the time.

Thanks to the latest series of desegregation laws, here I am ten years later, lost amidst a crowd of judgmental humans.

I'm almost to the end of the hallway now, but thankfully the worst anyone has done is whisper as they stare.

"See her?"

"Walked in the front door like she owns this place. What a skank."

"Don't you mean *skunk*? She's a half-breed, could be anything..."

"Don't act more stupid than you look, she's

obviously part fox! Ha, I bet that tail of hers gets in the way of any interesting—"

"I don't care *what* she is, isn't the first day of school stressful enough without shipping in a bunch of jumped-up *animals* as well?" I almost stop walking as I hear this from one especially petulant girl, wanting to see exactly who spoke. It would be a pointless effort, though; amidst all the noise and in the crowd I wouldn't be able to pick out the speaker. Besides, what would I do, challenge her to a duel for the honor of my people? I'm sure *that* would go over well with the school committee.

Instead I keep walking, albeit more slowly, reciting my locker combination in my head to keep my thoughts in my control.

Two, fifty-three, seventeen...isn't attending a new school stressful enough for us without being mocked and belittled by a bunch of racist, spoiled, silver-spoon brats? I suppose I should be grateful the students are avoiding physical contact with me so I'm not pressed uncomfortably in the crowd.

I pause in front of locker 60, checking the not-so-crisp yellow paper in my hand to see if I have the right number; I do. Shifting the strap of my bag on my shoulder I test out the combination. From what I can smell there are still only humans around—where are my fellow half-breeds?—but I hide my anxiety so my hands are steady on the lock.

The combination doesn't work. I press in the code again on the tiny gel buttons. Suddenly, something human brushes against my tail and I jump, whirling around so my back is to the locker.

"What the hell do you think you're doing, mutt?" A tall, muscularly built boy poses right in front of me and the locker, looking down his nose with an arrogance that makes me believe he's a senior. My face heats at being called a mutt, but my embarrassment is more from the implied *this isn't your place* undertone. Or, let's be real, overtone. This is exactly the type of "red-blooded male" I tended to avoid even at my old school where I only had M-DNA peers to concern myself with. People are standing around like they were before, but now many students in the hallway tune in to this scene with expressions of either amusement or distaste.

"These aren't the senior lockers?" I ask as I look up into the blue eyes—colder than Eisen's—glaring down at me. *He called you a mutt,* my thoughts whisper in indignation as anger morphs my own look into a glare.

"Yeah, they are. *Human* senior lockers, bitch," he says, and I can hear in his voice he was the one mocking my tail as I came down the hallway. I smell his ocean-y cologne in a whiff, and the aroma is so deceptively wholesome I want to slap him for wearing it...and for calling me a bitch.

Hush, I tell myself sternly. I've been told I'm feisty by several people in my lifetime, but even I know that now is not the time for an outburst.

"My locker number is 60," I say, purposefully speaking like I'm talking to an idiot as I hold up the paper with my information on it. "This is locker 60, so obviously—"

"It's not yours, actually," a new voice intervenes,

another boy. Before I even turn to look at him I catch a feline musk, something only an M-DNA person could pick up on.

Cougar DNA? I wonder, and I'm not wrong: the boy standing in between me and the human student has an apologetic look on his leonine face. Even though he's wearing a baseball cap I can see his eyes are the color of a mountain lion's. Everything else non-human must be hidden, because I don't see ears or a tail, just a physically fit boy about my height in a baseball t-shirt and slightly oversized jeans.

"Not mine?" I ask the mountain lion boy, hoping he's wrong so I can save face. But he's staring at the human boy now, and they glare at each other. A quick thought flits across my mind, wondering if school will be this hostile all the time.

The human boy drags his eyes back to me and he looks even more furious. "Are you deaf? I already said it wasn't yours," he says. He may have continued his verbal abuse, but I've stopped listening. Instead, I wonder how much trouble I would get in with the school—and with Harold—if raked my claws across someone's face my first day at school.

The establishment really would think we were animals if we didn't show them any different, Harold would probably say in that annoyingly wise way of his.

"The lockers for us are downstairs," Lion boy says, and his voice is mild and as relaxed as his casual clothes. He's ignoring the human now, but I doubt it's from fear; I have a feeling that he is just as disgusted with this situation as me.

"Okay, thanks," I reply casually, pretending I'm

discussing the mildness of the weather. "Show me where?" I realize as soon as the words are out of my mouth that they sound needy, but I don't regret saying them. I don't want anyone to think I'm alone and friendless here, even if I actually am. My eyes meet those of the boy who is helping me out, and he nods. I step around the imbecile who called me a mutt.

"Sorry to get in your way," I say acidly, and I can feel my tail trembling slightly. "But people who can barely string a sentence together without an insult or profanity probably shouldn't be here. It sends the wrong message about this *wonderful* school, I think," I add, quietly but so others will hear me. My new friend laughs, but he's the only one. I walk away, but as expected the human gets the last word.

"*Freak.*"

I'm still angry enough to slash the eyes off this boy's stupid face with my sharp nails. But...I can't. I pause, close my eyes, open them again...

...and I keep walking after the lion boy. My fox ears droop, and my heart won't stop racing. People still watch me go, and I taste the hostility in the air.

"Don't worry about him. He's a dick," I hear someone say as I pass. I'm so comforted by the sign that at least one human sides with me that my ears prick up again. I whirl around, look for the speaker, but just like before when I overheard that one girl calling my kind a bunch of jumped-up animals, I can't find the person who spoke.

Lion boy and I reach the end of the hallway and begin heading down the stairs. He breaks the silence before I can, speaking as soon as our feet touch the stairs.

"I thought I'd have to pull you off that guy when he said that, honestly," he begins with a winning smile; his voice sounds rugged, not just deep, but gravelly. "You've got guts, Vixen. Coming in at the top and walking down the senior hallway like that."

"Oh," I say, not sure how to reply. "Were we not supposed to do that?

"Clearly *someone* didn't read the official information brochure sent to our student SMARTnote accounts last week," he says, and I feel stupid for not knowing what he—and apparently everyone else—knows.

Damn the SMARTfactory for not giving out freebies to employees, I think, annoyed. Harold is the only one who has a higher level SMARTpad—which he allows me to use on occasion—since they're so expensive, and my crappy SMARTcall device isn't good at accessing anything without freezing and sputtering out error messages.

"What did the brochure say?" I ask, resigned. "I didn't have my school SMARTpad sent to my house, so I had to wait to get it from my locker today."

"There are certain rules for us while we go here," Lion boy says, "Rules for *our* kind, not really for the humans. Mostly it's a bunch of junk about special entrances for us, and human monitors for every M-DNA student." I wonder which human student is supposed to be monitoring me, and fervently hope it's not beach-cologne boy. My companion's voice dips into something like a growl, and my own lips curl with involuntary distaste as we reach the last step.

It's not just what he said, though. We've entered the dilapidated hallway for students like me, and it's painfully obvious that we walked into the un-remodeled section of the building reserved for half-breeds.

"My name is Lyle, by the way," Lion boy tells me.

"Sierra," I return a little absently. I'm too busy looking at my surroundings and thinking about what I've just been told to respond with more than my name. This hallway and the few classrooms I can see down here take after that gritty, old-fashioned style which goes with any dreaded institutional building. The steel lockers with their dinky ancient padlocks and the chipped paint on the walls emit an aura of antiquity and industrial decay. Because the hall is filled with about thirty of my kind, though, the space holds more color than the gleaming white hall upstairs. A few faces look vaguely familiar, if not necessarily friendly: a bright bird girl with feathers covering the back of her neck and arching down over her collarbone on both sides, and a cat boy with grey whiskers twitching by his nose are just two of the many.

No one makes eye contact with me. Embarrassment heats my skin as I wonder if it's because I ventured upstairs through the front door like I was better than anyone downstairs.

All in all, the entire atmosphere is tense and... weird. Something is off but I can't place it yet.

"So if I had read the SMARTnote, would I know who my monitor is?" I ask Lyle as I finally head the right way to find my locker; I don't have to talk very loud because the tension in the hallway doesn't lend itself to

24

much idle conversation. *You're not the only one who's nervous,* I remind myself.

"No, probably not. We're not supposed to know until later this morning...probably to prevent us from harassing the humans assigned to us beforehand," he replies disdainfully, following me and glancing around at the other students. Somehow I get the feeling he's the leader of this group already. "The school is supposedly trying to integrate the M-DNA students with the pure DNA students in a safe, friendly way. The human students will watch over the half-breed ones and make sure they find their way and integrate into the school atmosphere well." It sounds like he's quoting the SMARTnote, and I infer from his tone that he thinks the entire letter was pompous trash.

I find my locker and struggle with the lock for a moment before opening the door to a dismally small storage space. Lyle leans on the closed locker next to me, casual with the loping grace of the cat he shares DNA with. I assume he's going to be my locker buddy for the year.

The five minute bell rings for our homeroom session of the day, and I hurry to shove my lunch and other unnecessary items into my locker. With the invention of SMARTpads for textbooks and notes for classes, lockers seemed a little outdated to me in the past, but now I'm glad I have something in this place to use for storage purposes. My school-issued SMARTpad rests on the shelf inside, looking like it will barely last a year in my care.

Not to mention the establishment probably has the devices wired so they'll track everything I look up.

"It doesn't sound like you believed the SMARTnote," I say to him, hoping that the intense look he's giving me will fade as our acquaintanceship grows.

"I don't, and I don't think you do either. I'm sure the monitors will abandon us as soon as humanly possible. Not that we want them around us anyway," he says. Holding my SMARTpad, I look into Lyle's eyes briefly, trying to read him.

"HI!" A chipper voice sings right behind my head and I jump, startled. "So you're my locker buddy!"

"I guess so," I say, wary as I turn around. *There's no way anyone could be that happy this morning,* I think, prepared for a gush of fake nice chatter or try-hard friendliness.

"That's great! Someone told me as I came in that you're the girl who came in upstairs...so cool!" The girl standing in front me is short, except for the gorgeous ebony antlers curving out from either side of her head.

She smiles up at me with wide brown eyes that have faint doe like spots beneath them; a sheet of chestnut colored hair falls straight as silk down to her waist. The bag she carries is a third the size of mine, and she doesn't even bother with her locker.

"Hello?" I say. Her exuberance catches me off guard, but not so much that I'm disgusted with it. I'm not sure what else to say, and I can't help glancing at her antlers more than once.

"It's okay to look, people ask me about my antlers all the time. I know they're more of a male trait, but they really suit me, I think," she says quickly, still smiling. I feel bad for staring so obviously, and my nod is awkward as I introduce myself.

"I'm Sierra. And the antlers do look good. I bet all

26

the humans are jealous." Lyle chuckles—probably because I'm an uneasy conversationalist—but doe-girl blushes and looks down. Her antlers give her a unique grace, and I feel a little shame for thinking my fox ears were so conspicuous.

"Thanks. I'm Morgan, and since Lyle was the one who went upstairs to find you, I'm sure you guys know each other by now," she says. I nod again.

"Are you in our homeroom, Morgan?" Lyle asks politely, easing the silence into a more comfortable arena.

"Yes! I think we're all in the same one...It's ridiculous how they keep trying to separate us from the humans. Cramming thirty half-breeds with different grade levels into one room for half an hour isn't smart," Morgan says, rolling her eyes as she leads the way to our homeroom. "I'm glad I'm a senior and only have to put up with this for a year."

I follow her and Lyle, assuming they know where they're going.

"Is it really legal to separate us from the human students like this? I thought the whole point of forcing us to go to school with humans was to accomplish desegregation," I say, looking around the dull place where I'm supposed to attend classes for a year.

"That may be the point some of the senators were trying to make, but I don't think it'll work like they planned. Or maybe it will...this school is prestigious, supposedly 'above reproach,' so the administration can get away with more," Lyle informs me as he surveys everyone in the hall with his lion eyes from under his red baseball cap. "That's just fine though;

27

we're a tough group."

As he finishes speaking I realize what I was missing and what seemed wrong with this whole scene. I'm really looking now, confirming what I'm thinking.

Most of the concealable aspects that we half-breed students possess have been hidden. Tails tucked into pants—which can work surprisingly well, although I've rarely bothered with the effort—ears covered by scarves and hats, paws and talons covered by gloves, and wings covered by jackets.

Only Morgan and I haven't bothered to conceal anything, she because her antlers defy any type of secrecy, and me because apparently I didn't get the memo for concealment. Even Lyle, bold enough to break the rules and venture upstairs to save the ignorant vixen M-DNA student, has hidden some of his animal features as well. But perhaps that's because he enjoys wearing a baseball cap, if he even has animal ears at all.

Why are we hiding? I think, confused. *Since when have we hidden from humans?*

"What room are we supposed to be heading to? I forgot to download the file on my SMARTpad last night," Morgan rifles through her small leather handbag as the one minute bell rings. "We need to hurry!"

"It's okay, I wrote my information down since I didn't get my SMARTpad until just now," I say. "Since we're both seniors, and since we all apparently have the same room at the start of the day, I think you won't need your information sheet as much if we share. Maybe you can read the catalog names better anyway." She gives me a grateful smile, and I'm glad that she didn't try to hide what she was. *Maybe this was what Harold was keeping from me...Eisen too,* I think,

Abruptly, an androgynous voice sounds over the intercom, cool and crisp. The sound is scratchy and distorted but still clear enough to convey information. *ALL STUDENTS PLEASE REPORT TO THE ASSEMBLY HALL FOR ORIENTATION.* As the voice is speaking I wonder if the intercom system upstairs sounds as desperately worn as this one.

"Okay then. Was that in the SMARTnote?" I ask Lyle as the crowd of students like me looks up at the ceiling towards the dusty intercom speakers.

"No, it wasn't. The number for the assembly room wasn't given on our information sheets, and orientation wasn't announced." He doesn't seem pleased with the new development.

"I assumed our teachers would keep track of our attendance and report it to the office?' Morgan says, forming her words like a question. "It *is* the first day of school, orientation is normal." The three of us are nudged along by our fellow students as they mutter and begin heading for the stairs as a nearly solid unit.

"We'll find out, I guess." I shrug, trying to keep my cool. The day has barely begun, and I'm already exhausted from the tension cascading in waves through the entire school.

3

The bell for class has already rung by the time we get upstairs. We are a gaggle of half-breed teenagers spilling into the hallway with no idea where the assembly room is or how to get there. There aren't even any signs up on this floor, aside from numbered plates on the classroom doors. Ordinarily, any one of us might have taken this opportunity to explore the place without supervision, but the oppressive atmosphere is too intimidating for games.

Also, we are a gaggle of *late* half-breed teenagers. Lyle and Morgan stand beside me, him with a frown and her with a politely confused look on her sweet doe face.

"They probably won't count us *all* late," I reason, "We were all here on time, we just didn't know where we were supposed to go." The students around me are noticing what I perceived earlier when I first came in through the front doors: the remodeled part of the building was made for the *human* students, not the M-DNA ones. Some scan the area with mild interest, mostly the younger ones that look like underclassmen. Morgan and others of the older students look as disgusted as I was when I had to go downstairs to find my locker.

"Or maybe that's what they want," Lyle says in a stage whisper that sets the entire group buzzing. He reminds me of Wade as he continues; opinionated, clever, a born instigator. "What better way to show our differences than to make us walk in late like we're too dumb to watch the time!" I nod along with some of the others. I don't want to be a mindless sheep following a leader, but what Lyle is saying does make sense. *Desegregation is a fairytale if this is how they treat us,* I think.

"We should at least *try* to get to the assembly room, though," Morgan points out, frowning. She's the least angry-looking person present. I see the bewildered half-breed freshmen glancing around and making noises of assent with everyone else in an attempt to blend in. *Isn't high school complicated enough without adding petty humans to the list?* I think.

"So what if they think we're different?" I find myself saying, latching onto the tail end of Morgan's statement. "We are: we're mature enough to not play silly games like this. We shouldn't give them the satisfaction of making us feel like freaks. We belong here as much as they do now, so shouldn't we act like today is normal?"

Most of these students probably grew up in more human environments than I did, so they would know more about how to behave around purists. The only two people in this group I know, Lyle and Morgan, have a distinct inner-city feel about them as well as a more industrial smell. Yet people agree with my words too, thoughtful frowns becoming wry grins.

"Should piss them off at least," a boy with some definite bear DNA speaks up, pulling off a wool beanie to scratch one of the black bear ears perched comically atop his large head. "Good idea, Vixen," he adds politely.

"Sierra," I correct him. I'm too anxious to smile, but I try to form my face into a friendly expression anyway.

"Then I guess we'd better look around," Lyle says, his contribution adding solidity to the idea. He grins at me, curiosity all over his face. I sort of smile back, wondering if this is a friendship building experience.

Suddenly I hear the sound of someone awkwardly clearing his throat, and the hall quiets as we turn to the source of the noise.

"Hey," It was a human boy who coughed to get our attention; he stands in the entrance to the administration hallway with an uncomfortable expression. I don't blame him; the tension is so thick a butter knife could slice it.

"The orientation meeting is about to start, and they're waiting for all of you."

His eyes scan the group of us, every eye staring at him. Well, *I'm* staring anyway. He's tall, almost as tall as the bear boy, with ginger hair and pale skin adorned with a jamboree of freckles. Light green eyes shine above a long, faintly crooked nose, and he has a surprising but acceptable amount of red stubble along his jaw; I didn't think young humans could grow a good amount of facial hair this young, but it suits him and makes him look more like a man instead of a student boy. I try to calculate why he's here: he must be an upperclassman in a leadership program, trying to do the right thing by showing us where to go. Or maybe he was sent here to make sure all the half-breeds found the right room...eventually.

Something about his voice makes me think he's the one who called the boy bothering me a dick, though. I'm good with voice recognition, enough to nearly always know which voice belongs to whom. I hope this boy is my monitor if I have to have one, even if I doubt the likelihood of such a coincidence.

"Let's go then," Lyle says, a bit pompously. The human boy's eyes drift over me once before he turns and leads the way to the assembly room, and I wonder if he'll remember me again after today. We all file down the hallway in small groups, muttering to one another.

"I'm glad someone thought to come get us," Morgan says to me, her voice low and her eyes on the back of Lyle's and the human boy's heads. "That will make it less awkward, hopefully."

"Yeah," I agree with her. "But I wonder if he came to get us on his own?" Normally only my brothers can make me feel suspicion, but the events of this morning have already made me question the general trust in people I maintained while growing up in an M-DNA community.

We're not far from the assembly room now; I hear the chatter and noise from where I am as Morgan speaks again. "I've known Duncan for a few years now, not well of course, but enough to know that he's not one of the purist bigots we normally have to put up with."

"Duncan?" I repeat his name to her and save it in my new mental bank of information. "How do you know him?" My eyes scan his wide shoulders as she answers.

"He lives in my neighborhood a few houses down, in the human section. I've seen him sometimes and exchanged greetings. He doesn't mind talking to us, which is surprising considering the attitudes of the rest of my neighbors." She shrugs as we enter. "Lyle lives in the same neighborhood as well, so we've known each other for a while," she adds. I'm not surprised; she and Lyle did seem to have previous knowledge of each other.

The assembly room appears as white and pristine as the rest of the upper wing. A steel minimalist podium has been erected on the modest stage at the front of the room, and lines of white plastic benches—pews, really—are filled with the Hostetler student body. I expected a section of seats would be reserved for us at the very front so we could awkwardly file in and make our way forward, but that's not what I see. I spot several empty seats dispersed throughout the room, always near the middle of the rows so people needing to get to the seats have to clamber over other students in a way that is unavoidably disruptive.

"Come in and join the rest of the students!" the figure at the podium, a woman dressed in a muted plum pantsuit with dark hair curling around a startlingly pretty face, calls to us.

Duncan leaves our group and strides over to the left corner of the room to sit with a group of people I assume are his friends. My face is hot, and I feel the stares focused on me since I'm at the very front of the half-breed group. Many of these students witnessed the debacle of my entrance earlier.

I don't want to loiter here any longer; Lyle has begun hunting down a seat, so I follow his lead and somehow manage to snag a chair only five seats into a row. Of course, the five students I have to squeeze past grumble and almost trip me, but I manage to sit without drawing extra attention to myself. Eventually, everyone else has found a seat and they look towards the podium with some interest.

"Welcome, students!" The woman at the front hasn't broken the tense silence since her first welcome, but the delighted tone of her voice and the sparkle in her dark eyes almost makes me feel like she's sincerely glad to have all of us at her school. "For those of you who don't know, I am the principal of Hostetler High. I was hired to replace Dr. Bell after his early retirement, so I am new here as well. My name is Belinda Harper." She smiles like her name is a gift we are lucky to have received.

It's news to me that the principal is new to this establishment as well, which makes me wish I'd read the introductory brochure even more. I look around at everyone else to gauge their reactions: half the humans aren't listening, and my kind is too flustered to pay attention.

"I'll keep this brief because you all have classes to attend and check-in to focus on. A check-in station has been set up in each of your homerooms. After this assembly you will go to your homeroom to key in your identification code before your first class," Belinda says, still smiling. "I wanted to address a few matters with you this morning instead of homeroom today. Sometimes we will have meetings like this throughout the year. 'Family' meetings, if you would like to call them that," she chortles.

I'm listening and her friendliness becomes an increasing irritation. *She thinks with a few smiles and soft words we can all be friends?* I think incredulously. Someone in the back graces the room with a ridiculously loud snort and I have to stifle a stress-induced giggle.

"First, I would like to welcome our newest students

to this school. We are all glad to have you here with the rest of us. Let's give them a proper welcome, shall we?" Belinda begins to clap and I cringe for her and for my comrades. One or two people clap politely, perhaps missing the memo that the only new students here are half-breeds like me. Everyone else sits in apparent disbelief without moving their hands at all. My tail curves around to rest in my lap so no one can mess with it, and I smooth down the bristled fur. I keep my gaze fixed ahead as the human students on either side of me give me dark looks. Finally the room falls totally silent again.

"Our next matter of business is orienting the new students to the Hostetler way of life. All of you more experienced students have been informed of the helpful measures regarding our special new students, but I'd like to refresh everyone else on the rules and standards we are adopting in compliance with the desegregation laws," the principal says. *It just keeps getting worse*, I think despairingly, wanting to melt into my chair as Belinda makes my kind seem incredibly stupid with her motherly voice. I'm not sure if she's doing this on purpose, but I know my brothers would assume her offensiveness was deliberate, and I'm beginning to agree.

The principal continues her speech. "There are about thirty M-DNA students attending Hostetler High this academic year. While this is a small figure in comparison to the rest of the student body, this number makes us the only school in this city with this quantity of alternate students."

"Like they could choose whether or not they're animals," the boy student on my right snorts. I take a deep breath to keep from "accidentally" stomping on his foot.

"Since these students are a mix of all high school ages, the school board and I decided they—that is, those of you who are in this M-DNA type—could use mentoring and leadership from the most experienced students present: the senior class. Will all of the seniors rise, please?" Belinda beams as the human seniors stand. I don't make a motion to stand because I know she didn't mean an "alternate" senior.

'Thank you! These students have been entrusted with the task of assisting the acclimation of our M-DNA students into the student body. This means escorting the students to classes and making sure they don't lose their way this week, as well as being a role model and an available ally so they can inform the school board if any monitored student is having difficulties."

Spies. The word hits me in a flash. Judging by the expressions—ranging from displeased to furious—on my comrades' faces, I'm not the only one. I don't know why I'm surprised, but I know I'm disappointed. *Why did I expect better?*

I see Lyle's face in the crowd; he slouches with his hat low on his head, shielding his glare from all but those looking for one. From this distance I see his lips pressed so tightly together that they're white. Morgan sits near his general area, and the determinedly pleasant look on her doe-like features has become rather pasty and fixed. I observe the standing students now, dispersed as they are amongst the huge room. More than thirty are standing, so I can't tell who among the group will be the monitors.

"The students among the senior class who volunteered will remain anonymous until after check-in, but they will receive extra credit for their efforts. For those of you who were not selected for this program, I'm sure all of the monitors will welcome any help you are willing to offer," Belinda says, and I can hear in her voice that this meeting is nearly done. The seniors sit and she goes on to mention a few more standard rules about dress code—blessedly, they don't require uniforms—and minor things that no one pays attention to. I tune her out while other students carry on their own conversations and the general attention span minimizes to individual interactions.

"Who would want to volunteer for something like that?" someone near me whispers, and I cringe again.

"Don't know, probably a mutt lover," a girl answers, and some snickering—accompanied by a distasteful innuendo or two—spreads through my section of the room. I stare determinedly ahead, willing the principal to speak faster.

Perhaps it was friendly, non-racist people who signed up, or simple overachievers who would do anything for extra credit, I think. My gaze falls on the back of a boy's head, the boy who harassed me earlier. Eisen's warning about them trying to get me to leave school echoes ominously in my head.

I think of Duncan again, the boy Morgan knows, and a thought occurs to me. *Maybe the ones who weren't "selected" for this program are less supportive of this regime than the humans think they should be.* I wish that were true.

Belinda, after mentioning nothing about why semi-illegal segregation is going on or why the entire lower wing wasn't remodeled using the government funds meant for expanding the school for M-DNA students, draws the meeting to a close. My eyes dart around the room trying to memorize the faces of all the seniors so I will recognize my monitor when he or she is revealed. Movement catches my eye, a flash of red hair. I see Duncan shifting his weight in his chair, looking straight ahead with a long-suffering expression. His eyes have glazed over from boredom, but because the sun is shining through a window close to the ceiling, I note the exact hue of the peridot irises from where I am. If he was a monitor, at least there would be one person who didn't aggressively hate half-breeds.

"Off to your first day of classes!" the principal says at last, beaming. "Here's to a wonderful school year!"

"I hope she smiles so hard her face splits like her ass crack," the boy next to me mutters to his friend and I find myself agreeing with them in spite of their crudeness.

One of the more severely dressed faculty members, an older woman who was seated in the front row of the room, rises with a pinched look on her gaunt

41

face. She ascends the small stairway to the podium and whispers something to Belinda, who nods and leans into the microphone once more.

"Sierra Maurell needs to stop by my office before her first class. The monitor assigned to her needs to wait outside my office so you two can get acquainted after her visit with me," she says. Her tone is so casual it sounds like she's merely inviting me for a coffee, but my heart dips into my stomach all the same. I'm grateful for the fact that a lot of people don't know my name yet, because the few who do whip their heads around to stare at me inquisitively. The principal confirms the dismissal, and I hurry to the exit along with everyone else.

Unlike earlier when I entered the school, people jostle me as I pass—some with unnecessary force—making me miss my old school with the friendly faces and basic same-species camaraderie. I'm not totally sure where I'm going, but I head back to the front of the school with a vague idea of the administration offices being in that general direction.

"Sierra!" Someone calls my name, and a body nearly crashes into me. An instant later I recognize Morgan, and I'm thankful that her antlers didn't jab me during her rush.

"If you have Business Math for this class period I'll save you a seat!" She speaks quickly, her face flushed pink from racing to catch me; I'm grateful she decided to include me, especially when she adds more information I don't know about. "The seniors aren't required to eat lunch in the cafeteria, which is great because the one for us downstairs is awful, so I hear. If I miss you in classes this morning do you want to join me and some friends outside on the back field?"

"Sure," I say. Smiling comes easier for a few seconds as she grins at me, but then I have to leave her to find where the principal's office is.

People watch me as I pass, but no one tries to intercept or help me. I survey the numbers on the doors I walk by and recognize a few from what I noticed on my schedule. The thought of spending my entire day in that dungeon they call the lower level makes me shudder. *It might be pushing the segregation issue a little too far if they separate us for actual classes,* I hope.

A student with curly blonde hair and a sickeningly potent perfume brushes past me with a very dirty look, and I resist the urge to snarl at her. Instead I think of my brother Harold, the strategic one, the only one in my family who would excel in this kind of subtly hostile environment. I direct an acidly slow smile with all of my white teeth exposed towards her, purposefully looking like a savage. Her eyes widen, and she moves on hastily. Apparently she wasn't the only one who saw because the rest of my fellow students let me pass with no more "clumsy" bumping into me.

I pass by the senior hall again as the seniors file into their homerooms to check in. My eyes fall on a redheaded boy I recognize as Duncan right as he's looking up. I want to look away so I don't see his reaction to my yellow-eyed gaze, but instead of avoiding my notice he smiles faintly and points to the doorway on my left.

Directions? I think, and when I turn I see he pointed me in the right direction.

At first I wonder how he knows I'm Sierra, but then I remember I introduced myself to the bear-boy right before we all noticed Duncan's presence in the hallway. That must have been when he overheard my name.

I smile back at him and turn to the administration area. *So as far as I know, three people in the school don't hate me: Lyle, Morgan and...Duncan,* I think. One human and two half-breeds.

I try to take that as a positive sign.

4

When I enter the administration area I'm nearly overpowered by the scent of cleaning solution. The fur along my spine stiffens but I force myself to relax. People who might be able to read animal body language might freak out if they saw my flat ears and bristled fur right now. The chilly, fashionably dressed receptionist doesn't notice my distress; she waves me through after a perfunctory glance. My monitor is supposed to be here too, but no one is present but me and the distracted receptionist with her pink polished nails and ridiculously high hairstyle.

And of course, the principal is here behind her shiny metal-plated white door. I stare at the door briefly, wondering why it looks sturdy enough to withstand a bombing.

Belinda clicks open the door right as I'm about to knock. I study her face to try and read how she feels about my presence. She's smiling, polite rather than cheerful, although an aura of motherliness still lingers at the corners of her almond eyes and perfect bow mouth.

"Hello Sierra," she says, ushering me in and closing the door. "I'm glad we have this opportunity to talk."

I can't imagine why she would be happy about having a half-breed student in her office before classes even get underway, especially after how she was talking about my kind during the orientation meeting. When she gestures for me to take a seat, I obey wordlessly.

"I have already entered your ID number into the system, so you don't need to worry about checking in once we finish here," she says.

"Neat," I reply as she pauses, clearly expecting thanks. "Why am I here?" Perhaps I'm falling into the clichéd category of surly teenagers who have no desire whatsoever to communicate with authority figures, but I can't help it. It's how I was raised, besides the fact that I am in no mood to cater to anyone in charge at this school. Also, she's staring right into my eyes, going against a few well-known instincts wired into my brain. Prolonged eye contact can mean a challenge, and I'm not in much doubt here as to who has dominance.

Occasionally I catch her gaze drifting up to my fox ears, but I reserve comment and wish harder that this will be a short conference.

"Well, part of the reason is your unusual upbringing. I wanted to speak with you anyway to make sure you understood how a pure DNA student high school functions."

"Unusual upbringing?" I ask.

"It is fairly irregular even for these changing times for a student from a predominately M-DNA community to attend this type of school. Desegregation laws aside, many students in your situation might have opted for a smaller school," she says.

"My guardian wanted me to have an education from one of the better schools in our area, chiefly because this will be my graduation year." I'm still wondering where she's going with this, but I'm also pretty positive I don't want to bring up the fact that my oldest brother is my guardian instead of my parents. Sharing this information might not make a difference, especially since she might know already, but I have a bad feeling about this meeting already. I don't want to add fuel to the fire.

"Hm," Belinda says with a flavor of disapproval strong enough to aggravate my temper again. "Tell me, Sierra, do you have any learning disabilities?" *What?* I think, startled.

"No, why?" I ask.

"Do you have access to a SMART communication device, or does someone in your family have access to a device where you can receive messages?" she asks.

I stare at her, thinking these questions are both

random and ridiculous. Her phrasing and her tone makes it sound like she's talking to an idiot, which I don't appreciate. She's still smiling, but her fine-boned face is tight and her tan skin suddenly seems uncomfortably flawless. I almost giggle as I realize she has a pretty face because of extensive modification surgery, but I manage to stifle my ill-placed humor. It dawns on me that she's probably asking about the SMARTnote that was sent out that I didn't see.

"I have been unable to fully set up my SMARTnote account on the school page since I didn't get my school issue SMARTpad until this morning. I didn't receive the welcome letter with the instructions and rules," I say truthfully. *Why is everyone obsessed with this damn SMARTnote?* I think, wishing I could voice my real thoughts instead of picking over the words I say like a diplomat.

"Because you did not read the letter we sent to your student account, Sierra, you may not realize you already committed a few infractions that must be addressed." Her smile is *finally* gone, replaced by a serious expression that she must be thinking makes her look stern but kind.

It isn't working, and I wonder why she bothers with the fake behavior: everything she says is unfriendly to my kind, however politically correct her wording.

"As I said, I was unable to set up my account," I say. "I can't have committed any drastic offenses yet because classes haven't even started. I can fully set up my account properly tonight, now that I have my school SMARTpad."

She shakes her head with a similar deliberate movement as when she nodded. "I will print the SMARTnote for you, and you can focus on setting up your account this afternoon, but it is not advisable for me to ignore your infractions so early in the school year," she says, then adds: "I must be fair to my students, after all." I grimace as she speaks. It takes a little more effort to reform my face into something more pleasant.

"Could you specify what my infractions are then?" I ask, concentrating on making my voice meek.

"I asked M-DNA students to use the secondary and back entrances to avoid clogging the main entrance for students who are accustomed to coming in that way." She says this with a little too much glee, but maybe I'm imagining that part. "I have been informed that you were dropped off at the primary entrance and arrived at school by the main doors." I get the sense that she is watching my face closely, observing any responses I might make.

What is she looking for? I think. I want to ask why the hell she thinks she can get away with such obviously racist behavior, but I don't. I'd be forced to answer my own question: desegregation laws do not automatically dismiss racism.

My mouth had opened to spout whatever popped into my head, but I force it to close; my teeth click together, perhaps revealing my irritation. *It won't do any good to argue,* I think. *She knows she can get away with the bare minimum of the desegregation laws.*

"Was there something you wanted to say?" The encouraging smile is back, painted on her face. I shake my head, not trusting myself to speak. One curved edge of her smile falters, slipping like a crack in a painting before she continues. "Secondly...well, this is a more *delicate* issue. One of the students approached me before orientation to address a few concerns he had about you. I believe they are legitimate, but it is only fair to follow up on situations like these." If I wasn't angry before, I am now. I resist the urge to drop her gaze to look down at my clenched hands. The russet-brown fur covering the top is stiff and straight, a product of my tension.

"This student seemed to believe that you were attempting to break into his locker and, according to him, when he confronted you, you insulted him," she concludes her summary of the erroneous version of events the boy bullying me earlier must have told her. Her voice is lowered, as if in sensitivity for the situation.

I have no clue how to respond to such willful bias. I already know she won't take my word for what actually happened. I could call on witnesses, of course, but who would actually take the side of a little-known fox girl? Lyle could probably back me up...but he is my kind, and clearly the word of half-breeds is not accepted here.

I try to explain anyway. "That isn't what happened." I'm trying to stay calm but I'm not sure if it's working; this has already been a long day. Belinda stares at me dubiously, but she remains silent and her smile is more thoughtful than plastic at this particular moment. "Because I did not receive the SMARTnote, I was not aware that separate entrances were mandatory for me to use, just as I was not aware that there were two lockers with the same number in this building. The boy whose locker I assumed was mine informed me of my mistake." This too kind, bare minimum version of events turns my stomach, and the formality of my words disgusts me.

She's still watching me, and I'm learning to read her expressions a little better. "Well, given the circumstances and the reality of both stories being very different, I think I will—"

"Principal?" Someone is rapping at the door, a brisk knock with three taps. I recognize a female voice, so when a girl peeks her head in I'm not surprised to see a petite white face and a mass of brunette hair tied up in a messy bun peek around the currently open door. Belinda doesn't seem surprised to see her either but, admittedly, surprise can be hard to communicate on a plastic face.

"I'm in a meeting now, dear." The principal's voice sounds warmer but at the same time more businesslike when it is directed at a student who is obviously and totally human. M-DNA students don't wear glasses, and this girl has a chunky pair of black specs—very fashionable of course—resting on a turned up nose. *Snooty* is an adjective that readily pops into my mind.

"I know," the girl says. "I'm the assigned monitor for Sierra Maurell and I just wanted to let you know she'll be too late to her first class to catch up if you keep her here much longer." Her eyes are brown and sharp, similar to Belinda's but definitely more natural. I'm surprised this girl stood up for me, but something about her voice throws me off a bit. I'm not thrilled she's my monitor.

"Thank you for the reminder. I will be finished shortly. If you could just wait in the hall I would greatly appreciate it," Belinda says and the girl frowns before abandoning the door. It automatically glides shut, and I'm alone with the principal, who continues like there was no interruption.

"Sierra. I am not unforgiving. I wish to be fair to my students, however, so I will compromise with you: you will accept the demerits I give you for failing to keep up with your student account, and I will consider the confusion you had over where your locker was as a part of that problem."

"Okay," I say slowly, wondering how many demerits I'm going to get at the same time as I'm wishing I'd clawed the face of the boy who had harassed me, and shortly after lied about me. She looks at me like she expects me to object more, but I won't give her the satisfaction, just as I'm not going to quibble over how many demerits I get. "May I go?"

"Yes," she says after a very long pause. "Yes, I think you should. Katrina should be waiting just outside to make sure you don't get lost again."

I'm out of my seat before she can finish her sentence; my school bag thumps against the edge of the chair, but I don't turn back. I've never been much of a rebel, but I'm starting to remind myself of Wade back when we were in high school together. *Thanks for the influence, brothers,* I direct this thought towards them as the door closes behind me.

"Certainly took you long enough," Katrina perches stiffly in a faux leather chair close to the receptionist desk. I was kind of hoping she would have been too impatient to stay, but her voice brings back why I wanted her gone in the first place. *Isn't school stressful enough without shipping in a bunch of jumped-up animals as well?* I remember what she was telling her friends back when I first walked in by the wrong doors.

"It's not like I wanted to be there at all," I grumble, already disliking this short, skinny teenager as she stands up. "If you want you can just show me to my next class and then leave us *animals* to take care of our own."

Her eyes narrow and she looks me up and down, assessing. This day has already worn me out, and I want nothing to do with someone who won't see past my animal characteristics. I understand why the other half-breeds hid what they could to escape the burning looks from narrow-minded people like my monitor.

"I might if you don't watch yourself," Katrina snaps, her voice petulant. Everything about her is sharp, angular; she fits into this place well. Her clothes are chic, almost too businesslike for high school, and if she was less cold she might have a sort of interesting librarian vibe about her.

"What class do you have?" she asks me as I wait for her to lead the way. She also talks to me like I'm a fool, and I'm getting less and less in the mood to put up with this behavior, least of all from someone like her.

"Business Math," I say. I begin walking in the general direction of senior hallway, and after a few steps she follows. I'm sure I can feel her staring at my fox ears and most certainly at my tail as I walk.

"I only signed up for this for the extra credit," she blurts as we turn the corner and leave the administration wing. "I don't actually enjoy hanging out with *mutts*."

"Don't worry, I would never mistake you for a decent person," I say, resisting the urge to say any more. *You already have who-knows-how-many demerits for something stupid,* I think.

"What is *that* supposed to mean?" Katrina splutters.

"You're smart. If you're this worried about extra credit you must be on some sort of honor roll. I'm sure you'll figure it out...eventually."

"Know what? I'm thinking this whole monitor thing is a waste of time. It's bad enough we're forced to attend school every day with people like *you*," she says the words to me like they're supposed to wound me. "*Your* kind has been getting above themselves for ages, and I don't think I want to be a part of this after all."

"Fine," I sigh. "Just let me know where my classes are, and you can go back to your little nerd clique and discuss the evils of M-DNA people all you want." *Good riddance*, I add in my head.

Katrina lags again; I don't hear her steps behind me. I pause and wait for her to catch up but when she doesn't I turn and face her.

"Well?" I ask. She glares at me as she shifts her weight from one foot to the other, appearing conflicted about something.

"You're in a human school. You should learn to function on your own...you think you're so smart, after all," she begins, and I feel the familiar pangs of frustration as she continues. "I have things to do and *you* are not part of them...the only thing I really needed to do as a monitor was pick you up from the principal's office."

"So why are you still here?" I say. Katrina blinks at me, rather startled I'm not following her train of thought.

"I need to make sure I still get the extra credit. If I tell Harper you were rude to me and how I worry about your hostile reaction to my helpful tips she'll understand, and I'll still get the extra credit I need."

"Never mind that it's a lie," I add, knowing she won't care.

"Who cares? The odds are more in my favor if you look at it from any *reasonable* perspective," she smiles, and her expression clears. "I think I'll do that. Have a good day with classes, Sierra. Watch your tail in the doorways!" This time I'm the one who just blinks at her as she disappears around a corner.

Favorable conditions, a longevity of roughly 120 years, and the hardiness of the new race led to a massive increase in population for M-DNA people over most of the 22nd century. Over time, M-DNA people grew too numerous for the government to conceal. In fact, the reach of Chairman Heights proved it was long enough to have made sure his experiments with mutation stretched across the globe and across decades. M-DNA people, informally called half-breeds, reached a quantity that would have required their own small continent. The humans, concerned about the purity of their own gene pool, the survival of their current way of life, and dwindling resources rejected these people outright. After much unrest and racial antagonism against half-breeds, global war broke out: humans against half-breeds.

This war became, perhaps, the most controversial and most devastating war in history. Many humans were on the side of treating the half-breeds as equals, which led to countless wasted casualties in the biological and urban warfare that took place for almost ten years. As the war dragged on and took countless lives, change surged ahead as the planet, resource quantities, science, and the half-breed race altered forever. Humanity was on the brink of either extinction or a total revolution of everything it had known at the time.

5

Before coming to a human school I thought I'd have to worry more about the pretty, popular girls making fun of me. It's an old high school drama cliché, after all, and not something I'm wholly unused to; even my M-DNA school had stereotypes. But for the people who are supposed to be on the higher education level to reject me simply because I don't have pure human DNA? This day has been so unfair that I want to call Eisen and leave. I feel the warm weight of the SMARTcall telephone in my bag, the round and silver device a comforting link to people who actually care about my life.

You can't just leave, Sierra, I think, trying to encourage myself with a positive thought. *The first day of school is always difficult.* But the fact remains I'm still standing alone in a hallway with nothing but a list of confusing catalog digits and room numbers to help me find my classes. I could always wait until the bell rings and just miss my first class, but I'd rather not do that. Or, I could try to smell my way to find Lyle or Morgan, but I don't want to wander the halls sniffing around like a weirdo either.

Dejectedly, I look up from the list I pulled out of my bag and glimpse the red hair before I recognize Duncan approaching me from around the same corner Katrina disappeared down. There's an awkward pause as he comes to a halt and notices my presence.

"Uh...hey," he says. I'm not sure what to think of him yet, since I only know what I've observed and what I heard from Morgan. I'm thankful he broke the silence first.

"Hi," I say in reply. "Escape from class already?" The effort it's taking for me to be pleasant is considerably less than what I'd have to make for some other human. He nods as he takes a few steps forward; he seems wary, but I try not to blame him for it.

"Yeah...I mean, I have a free hour first period, and I was just getting a snack," Duncan says.

"You're Sierra, right?" He goes to his locker, and I tentatively take a step or two closer. Whatever developing conversation we have doesn't need to be shouted down the hallway.

"Yes I am. And you?" I ask his name even though I already heard it from Morgan.

"Duncan Ledford," he tells me. "So you had the

meeting with the principal?"

"Yes, I did. And it was not the best conversation of my life, that's for sure." I should be asking him how to get to my class; I shouldn't be dawdling. But he's actually having a polite conversation with me, which is very refreshing after the annoyance of the past hour. Duncan smiles; even if it's a small gesture it makes me feel better.

"Yeah, it seemed like Harper could be really passive aggressive and—" He lets the sentence die before he can complete it. I blink, my tail twitching nervously as my fox ears perk up to listen better. I'm relieved Belinda is new here so there's no previous history of positive behavior with even the human students...they only know what they've read on the school SMARTspace page.

"Anyway... where is your monitor?" he asks.

"She kind of...had to go. I'm pretty sure I go to Business Math next, so that's something," I say lamely. Duncan finishes grabbing food from his locker and shuts the door; it doesn't seem like he

regrets talking to me, and he's frowning at what I said.

"Before getting you where you needed to go?" he asks. We're closer now, and I can observe more of his features. "Who was it?"

"She really wanted to get going with her own stuff, so I only know her name is Katrina." An expression of understanding crosses his face.

"Yeah, that sounds like something she'd do," he grimaces, shaking his head and slipping a bag of some unhealthy variety of snack into the pocket of his dark wash jeans.

"You know her?"

"We've gone to the same school for a few years. Eventually you get to recognize faces," he says.

Speaking of faces, I study Duncan's further. He's better looking than I thought at first, even with the flaw of a previously broken nose. His skin is entirely clear—except of freckles—and his eyes are...nice. Pleasant. Honestly, he's more attractive than I would generally admit about a human boy.

I'm not sure where to go with this conversation as it's deteriorating to an awkward finale. More small talk related questions drift around my mind, but my shyness interferes with the words reaching my mouth. I'm suddenly self-conscious of my ears and my tail and the obvious gold hue to my irises as
a second or two passes.

He may be one of the only people here willing to talk to you like a person, but don't get carried away, I think.

"If you need to get to class I can show you where it is," Duncan offers, breaking into my reverie.

"That would be great...thanks," I say. He steps closer and takes my class list out of my hand. I'm momentarily glad that our skin didn't make contact; rather, I'm glad the fur on my hands didn't touch his skin. I don't want to deal with a human reacting to touching a half-breed; depending on the human, it's not pleasant, and I can't handle that after this lousy morning.

"You said you have Business Math. That's down this hall way on the right," Duncan says. I nod, taking back the list as he hands it to me; I look at the catalog number listed. "Not that you would have gotten all that lost, but finding your way is easier if you have help."

"Yeah they assigned monitors just for the purpose of showing us around," I say, a little more sarcastically than I intended. He looks at me as we begin walking in the direction he indicates, smiling a little.

"Your first day hasn't been much of a welcome, then?" he queries. I nod, not wanting to voice my other feelings on the topic of school- assigned monitors. He doesn't say anything for a few seconds.

"Not really. I mean, I know some of...of my people already, but aside from them—" I say.

"Everyone else here hasn't been friendly. I get that," Duncan says, his tone understanding. "Especially with that scene earlier...you're pretty cool, fox girl." My shyness intensifies at the compliment. My lips curve into a smile, but all I do is murmur a thank-you so I don't embarrass myself with anything else.

We walk a few steps in silence until we're right outside the class door. I see through the rectangular window in the door that class is well under way; this makes me want to enter even less, since I don't want any more needless attention today.

"Thanks for your help, Duncan," I tell him, my hand on the door knob. I've resigned myself to the awkwardness of the next few moments already.

"No problem. I...I guess I'll see you around," He smiles politely again. "Try not to let the crap from the other students get to you." I smile back and then he leaves, heading down the hallway and retrieving his snack from his pocket.

They'll get used to you...eventually. I finish his sentence with the missing phrase in my head.

I enter the classroom, shoving the class list back into my bag so I don't have to look up and into the faces of my classmates for as long as possible.

When I do look up, the teacher is *blessedly* ignoring my presence, and he doesn't choose to make an issue of my lateness. The more important issue is finding a place to sit, but there seems to be an obvious line drawn between the two halves of the room: humans on the left, half-breeds on the right. Morgan has chosen a seat next to the window; her tall antlers make a statement without any conscious effort on her part. I don't know why I was self-conscious about my fox traits around Duncan, but I'm glad now that I didn't hide my vixen traits like the majority of my half-breed classmates. Lyle slouches behind Morgan, appearing very cat-like as he stares at the teacher with glassy eyes.

I hurry over to the two of them and slide into the seat in front of Morgan. She taps my shoulder, and I turn around.

"How did it go?" she whispers. "And your walk is very graceful, by the way," she slips the compliment in with her original question like it's a natural thing for her to do. Which, for her, it probably is.

"It sucked royally, and I hope I never have to talk to Belinda Harper again," I inform her, the injustice of the entire meeting striking me again. She murmurs sympathetically and sits back. Lyle leans around her and speaks next, his whisper a little more carrying than Morgan's.

"Did you get into any trouble?" he asks.

"I got some demerits, but she didn't tell me how many. It wasn't worth staying longer to ask," I say.

"You'll probably get a SMARTnote telling you how many, right?" Morgan asks, twirling some of her long hair around her delicate fingers.

"I still have to set up my SMARTnote account for school...and I'm not sure I want to know, really," I say. "Now let's be quiet, I don't want to
get into any more trouble for the rest of the morning."

"We'll talk at lunch, then," Morgan says, sitting back again. Lyle hasn't contributed any more to the conversation, so his silence continues, and I face the front to try and find out how useful this math class is going to be.

"This is so much better than that lousy cafeteria,"

Morgan declares as we walk outside and into the bright early afternoon sun. Our last class felt extremely long; Sociology is definitely not my favorite subject.

"It is nice to be out in the sun," I agree; I haven't seen our cafeteria, but I'm sure it's revolting. We sat beside each other in our last few classes, since it turns out our schedules coincide for the most part. Lyle also shares some classes with me, and I've been told he'd be joining us for lunch along with a couple other people I haven't met yet.

Morgan carries her lunch in her small bag, and she pulls out a small bag of deep purple grapes to munch on as she walks.

"I hope we're heading to the right athletic field...it would be so awkward to run into a pre-season football practice or something."

"Aren't practices after school?" I ask her, and she shrugs. "At any rate, this field looks empty, so we might as well stay here."

"Okay!" Morgan smiles and plops down with a surprising lack of grace under a tree. I join her, choosing my spot on the ground a little more carefully. The lunch from my bag is more substantial than hers; Harold can actually cook when he's in the mood, and he made me a grilled smoked sausage sandwich I plan to enjoy.

Morgan and I exchange casual words about the events of the day as we begin eating. We're about to discuss what happened during my meeting with the principal when we see Lyle and two other half-breeds coming our direction from over the hill. Behind them, other stragglers from our misfit senior class wander the grounds of the school looking for different spots to take lunch.

I recognize the boy with the bear traits from earlier. There's another girl with him and Lyle, but I don't recognize her.

"Hi!" Morgan greets them like we're all old friends already. The tan-skinned girl I don't recognize looks like she has some cute poodle-like features from some canine DNA; she seems startled by Morgan's cheerfulness.

"How were your classes?" I ask the group in general, further attempting to break the ice. The poodle girl's eyes widen a little as she notices me, and she grabs the thick arm of the bear boy in a "look there!" gesture. I picture the two as a couple and have to stifle a laugh.

Good thing half-breed offspring doesn't blend the animal DNA of the parents...bear and poodle would be an odd mix, I think.

"Classes were normal, aside from all the dirty looks and insults," Lyle says nonchalantly, shrugging. "Annoying, but it's bearable."

"Yeah," the bear DNA boy grunts in amusement. "*Bearable* is exactly the word I would have chosen." He flashes me a grin and poodle girl giggles at his pun. "Hello, Vixen," he says.

"Sierra," I correct him again.

"Ivar," he tells me. "This is Shelby, my girlfriend."

"As of four months today," she adds, smiling up at Ivar with reflective dark eyes. Morgan and I exchange amused glances as she speaks.

"Have an extra sandwich, Morg?" Lyle says, throwing himself down on the grassy ground and, somehow, a sandwich is already in his hand. I realize it came from Morgan's bag, but she has her own lunch in her hand so I assume they have an arrangement. *That's interesting*...I file that information away for later.

"How did the talk with the principal go, Sierra?" Morgan asks me as the others sit beside us and pull out their food.

"You're the girl who came in the main entrance, aren't you?" Shelby asks, intercepting Morgan's question with one of her own. I nod warily, not sure what her reaction will be.

"That was one of the reasons Belinda wanted to talk to me...*at* me, rather," I say. Shelby squeaks, and I observe her wild black curls almost trembling with emotion.

"That's so cool! You braving the main entrance with all the crazy humans around, I mean...not the principal giving you crap about it..." She trails off and whispers something to Ivar, who is busy manfully demolishing a sub sandwich about the size of my head. My liking for the pair of them increases—even if it's still weird to think of them as a couple—because that's two more people on my side.

"You said you got demerits...what for and how many?" Lyle asks. I explain everything that took place.

By the time I finish, my irritation with the situation has passed on to my new friends.

"The whole thing is foolish," Ivar says in his deep voice, shaking his head ponderously. Morgan is frowning, Lyle looks angry, and Shelby watches Ivar as she quietly eats her food.

"The ridiculous thing is forcing us to go to this school," I say.

"You've had a hard day, and it's barely noon," Morgan observes with a measure of sympathy in her voice.

"You're telling me," I say. "I wasn't expecting rainbows and sunshine when I walked in here, but..." I let the words die. *I don't know what I expected.*

"I'm all for desegregation and equality, but this?" Lyle says as he waves his hand in a dismissive gesture towards the school building. I'm getting the impression that he's an angry person, alongside his more admirable leadership traits. *Just the kind of thing you'd expect from a mountain lion, too,* I think, catching the irony.

I want to forget the drama, move on to find out more about the people I'm with. I'd like to ask what their stories are, and it would be great if I could find out why they and all the other half-breeds—with the exception of Morgan and me—feel the need to hide their animal traits. Besides the obvious reason of hiding out, that is...it's not like half-breeds to be so submissive. Ivar is lucky with that goal: his grand size, his bear ears, and certain blunt features of his face give away his mixed DNA, but all of that is concealable. Shelby has a poodle tail—not ridiculously trimmed like a retro human pet—but she's masked it well so only someone looking for signs would see it. Lyle has already proved himself an expert at human camouflage.

As I open my mouth to ask about the concealment, I notice another group of high school seniors exiting the building. Judging from the size and gender diversity of the group, as well as the well-dressed appearance of the clique, I assume these are the popular kids.

"Oh great, feels like I'm in junior high again," Shelby mutters, shoveling a bite of salad into her petite mouth and scooting closer to her boyfriend. Our conversation falls into a temporary lull as the group approaches; I don't want to stare, but I do.

I'm the only one in my group that appreciates the irony of glimpsing my "monitor" latched onto the arm of the ocean-cologne boy. *Of course they would be together,* I muse with a little bitterness. *Of course someone like her would be in a relationship while I'm still single and besieged by the establishment.*

"Just in case you wanted to know who my monitor was, look at the girl with the big glasses hanging off the athletic looking kid," I tell Morgan. She frowns and makes a very immature face in Katrina's direction, which tugs a smile out of me.

"I would like to inform you all that the dude next to Sierra's monitor was my monitor," Lyle says, flipping the bird in their general direction and flashing me a sharp-toothed grin. "Note the past tense."

"Isn't that the jerk who bothered you earlier?" Ivar asks.

"Yeah," I reply, resigned to the fact the whole school knows all the details to that scene by now.

"Let's hope they decide to be adults and move on without bothering us," Morgan says, dismissing the popular clique with ease. "My monitor is in that group too, but she kind of—"

"—took one look at you and ran," Shelby says. "I saw that little episode in the hall before our first class."

"It's the antlers...they scare humans sometimes," Morgan admits self-consciously as she lifts her delicate hands to smooth down her dark hair. "It's not my fault my hormones made the mutation unbalanced," she mutters as a barely audible after thought. Her words set off Ivar's head shaking again.

"Little antlers aren't scary. My monitor...well, they assigned me someone a lot smaller. He bailed too," he says. I'm enjoying the conversation a little more, enjoying hating on the people who don't give a damn about us.

"So essentially the monitors are just people who signed up for the chance to bully half-breeds?" Morgan asks. She's finished her food now and is watching Lyle fidget with the brim of his baseball cap.

"I guess so," I tell her. My eyes linger helplessly on Katrina and the group of people she's with. They're all laughing and joking, which is surprising because my former monitor came across as more of an overachieving nerd than anything else. I watch as their group converges on another, a small group of senior guys lounging more in the sun than the rest of the people who are opting for more shade. I catch a glimpse of red-hair on one of the guys...

"Who are you looking at, Sierra?" Shelby asks me curiously. I return my gaze to the people with me, my fox ears pricking up.

"No one," I say. I don't turn my eyes back in the direction of the humans.

6

By the time school is over I'm almost ready to sprint all the way home to burn off the frustration I've accumulated over the afternoon. I'm trying to be positive about the year ahead, but it's very difficult to maintain optimism. Thankfully Eisen is waiting to pick me up as soon as I gather my belongings from my locker and exit the building.

"How'd it go?" Eisen asks as I slide into the passenger seat. The fabric seats of the car have picked up his scent of coffee and the flavor oils baristas use to spice up the beverages they serve.
He looks about as tired as I feel.

"Where do I start?" I reply, crumpling into a slouch. "The teachers were either rude or inattentive, no one wants me there, and half-breeds are treated like a public nuisance to everyone."

"As I expected, then," Eisen mutters to himself as he drives. "It's reverting back to a pre-war atmosphere around here." I don't know what to say to that so I change the subject.

"How was your day? Was the beanery busy?" I ask.

Eisen's shoulders hunch up closer to his ears and I see his eyes narrow. He looks like a fox now: unmistakably up to something.

"What happened?" I ask, suspicious.

"Well...an, ah, *incident* took place today," he tells me, selecting his words with obvious care. My anxiety returns with a side order of exasperation.

"What happened, Eisen?" I ask again. "Please don't say you got fired." My brother's eyes watch me from their corners, and I see his ears droop a little.

"I didn't get fired. It's about Wade." He sighs heavily.

"Wade?" As children, Wade and I were polar opposites: Eisen and I were the ones who were stealthy about getting into trouble. My mother had a handful dealing with us growing up because it was hard to catch us doing wrong until the last minute; this pattern of behavior did not change when Harold shouldered responsibility for the family. Wade always liked to show off his ability to get into a spectacular amount of trouble, so while he always got caught first, Eisen and I were the most devious.

"Is he okay? Was he hurt at the factory?" I interrogate. My fingers clench into a fist, wrapped around the strap of my bag like it's a life preserver. Eisen shakes his head as we come to a red light, and I take a moment to appreciate the growing distance between me and the school.

"He's fine…he just did something wild. Again," Eisen says, tapping his long fingers on the steering wheel with an air of impatience. I groan, sinking further into my seat.

"How illegal was it? Is there a cop at our house this time?" I ask.

"Not when I left, but there might be at some point. The dudes we beat up might involve the law if we didn't scare them enough, plus the neighbors did see a lot of the fight—"

"We? You're in trouble too?" My voice rises in pitch as we speak.

"Some humans—older ones, not idiot teenagers like last time—were hanging around our part of the neighborhood and harassing Mrs. Chirza and her granddaughter. They must've celebrated happy hour early, since they don't seem the type to be caught sober in a half-breed area," Eisen mutters; none of my brothers like when I get upset. Mrs. Chirza is an elderly woman with a mix of canine DNA who lives a house or two down from us with her young, pretty granddaughter.

"This is the granddaughter Wade…" I leave the sentence be, knowing Eisen understands what I'm saying.

"Yeah, his crush. He was furious about what they were saying to her: even if her DNA literally makes her a mutt, the humans weren't calling her that in a scientific sense," he says. "Emilee was very grateful for the rescue and will be announcing her undying love for our brother any day now."

"Damn, that's the last thing we need: Wade in a relationship," I snort. Eisen chuckles; his laugh is one of my favorite sounds.

"Poor kid needs to get a girl sometime. As you know, our kind marry young...look at our parents, wedded and bouncing little Harry around before they were twenty-one."

"What about you, then? Where's your girl?" I ask, joking. Eisen waggles his eyebrows devilishly at me, but doesn't say anything else; then he's back to being more serious.

"He was doing pretty well on his own in the fight, but I saw one of the human guys had a knife, and I had to get in there and help him out." He's explaining himself even though he doesn't need to. I've been a part of this family long enough to know that my brothers will always help each other in fights.

"It's fine. I'm glad you both are okay," I say. I hope no legal trouble comes from this situation, but I keep that train of thought to myself. Harold probably has or probably will lecture Wade and Eisen about the fight.

"Harold is home, right?" I ask.

"He will be soon. I made Wade call him after he managed to tear himself away from Emilee, so he knows already," Eisen says. He looks a little troubled still, but apparently he's at ease: he rolls down the window, and I notice his smile as the breeze ruffles his hair and fur. I try to relax too, also ignoring the approaching heated lecture Harold is going to give my brothers when he gets home.

"How was today, S? Really," Eisen asks after a few

minutes. We're almost home now and the combination of the afternoon sun and the breeze flowing in through the partially opened windows has lulled me into the lightest of cat naps.

"It...it's nothing I can't handle, Eisen," I respond carefully as my body tenses up again.

"Sure, it was peachy, wasn't it?" he scoffs. "I'm driving slow, so if you start spilling the story now you can finish before I get home."

"Normally it's my girl friends who insist on details," I grumble, and he laughs. The mood sufficiently lightened, I summarize the events of my

day for my brother. For some reason, however, I exclude Duncan Ledford from my monologue. I don't know how Eisen would respond to that part of the story and right now I don't particularly want to find out.

By the time I finish, we've pulled into the small, narrow driveway outside of our grim little townhouse. One of the reasons I love my brother is for his silence whenever I have something serious to tell him. Wade always interrupts with bizarre questions, and it's hard to get Harold to focus on the broader picture instead of little details. My golden fox brother has remained silent, but not un-reactive. His fingers are white on the steering wheel, and his blank face is one that used to make me shut up when we were kids.

"It could be worse," I conclude my tale, feeling my ears begin to droop from his lack of response. "Eisen?"

The silence lingers for two or three seconds, then he shakes his head as if distracted. "I'm just glad you're okay," he says anticlimactically.

"That's it?" I ask, surprised. It's not like Eisen to be

quiet once I finish telling a story, even if he usually pays me the courtesy of silence while I'm talking.

"Nothing else to add," he says as he exits the car. I also get out, observing him warily.

"All of that and you don't have anything to say?" I ask again.

"Yeah, S. Go call Hayley if you want more," he says, blithely mentioning my best friend in his comment. He sounds annoyed, and it dawns on me what must be going through his head.

He's waiting to tell Harold what went on, I realize. *He's planning something.* My brother has always been quick on his feet, so hatching devious plans is one of his fortes. I'm curious about what he might be planning— maybe another "secret" conference with Harold, trying to find a way to get me transferred out of my school situation last minute—but I decide not to ask. It won't do much good anyway.

Just when we're about to reach the door, Eisen taps my shoulder. "Wade got Emilees's number, by the way. It won't do any good to lecture him about fighting with humans...he won't hear you," he says.

"His ears are too full of Emilee's gratitude, most likely," I reply.

"Pity he only has fox ears: if he had human ears too, he might actually catch a word or two," Eisen says wryly.

"Yes, pity he missed out on that particular mutation," I add. We enter our house and I shake my head again, marveling at the moodiness of my brothers.

The first thing I see when I walk in is Wade standing

at the sink, his hands coated with what looks like blood. The next thing I notice as my gaze flies up to view his face is the magnificently blooming black eye and the gleaming white smile he's sporting.

"Wade, what—" I drop my bag on the table and rush up to him. He laughs and shoves his sticky hands under the hot water running from the faucet before I can grab them.

"Relax, Sierra. It's just juice from the burgers," Wade says, his smile widening so his bruised eye closes completely. Eisen laughs as I huff and lift my hand to Wade's fur covered face.

"He's fine, S. I checked him for injuries before I left to pick you up," Eisen tells me as he walks to the counter by the stove to snack on the hamburger trimmings I assume Wade set out earlier.

"He doesn't look fine," I say, gingerly examining Wade's discolored eye with my fingertips. Wade rubs his face and the tip of his nose against my hand once or twice in a reassuring nuzzle before he pulls away to undoubtedly preserve his "manliness."

"You made dinner?" I ask as Eisen shoves what looks to my peripheral vision like an entire block of cheddar cheese into his mouth. Wade shrugs.

"My work shift wasn't as long as normal today and I knew Eisen would be home earlier than usual. Harold had a big case at work...plus you had school. I didn't think you'd feel up to cooking tonight," he says. The emotional turmoil of the day must be catching up with me because I feel a growing danger of approaching tears lurking in the corners of my suddenly moist eyes. I also notice that the dirty dishes piled in the sink from this morning are nowhere in sight.

"How was...*that*, by the way?" Wade grunts. Eisen, still attempting to swallow the huge piece of cheese in his mouth, chokes a little and waves his hands frantically at his brother. I laugh, but a weird sort of sniffle escapes me, and my eyes feel even more in danger of shedding tears. Wade exchanges a look with Eisen, who is now endeavoring and failing to speak.

"Damn, S, it was that bad?" he asks, more sympathetic than incredulous. I try to master the lump in my throat so I don't start crying. Harold raised us all to be tough, and even if I was babied sometimes I still have enough grit in me to stop crying when I need to.

Eisen finally clears his mouth so he can speak. "Don't make her tell you right now, I already heard it. Wait until Harold gets home, otherwise if she has to say it all a third time she might be hysterical by that point," he says. I give him the customary glare that he usually receives whenever he implies that I am weepy, but my heart isn't in it.

"It wasn't terrible, really," I say, my voice beginning to warble. "It could have been a lot worse—"

"All right," Wade cuts in hurriedly, nodding before resting his wet hands on my shoulders.

"Eisen and I are going to finish making dinner, so you can go upstairs and...er...freshen up before then. Maybe you can call Hayley." The water from Wade's freshly cleaned hands seeps through my shirt, but I don't mind.

"Okay," I say. I want to hug Wade, but I don't want to be more of a baby than I already am right now. My brothers hate when I cry, but they genuinely care about me and don't like seeing me hurt.

My brothers exchange information in low voices as I leave, and even though I could eavesdrop if I wanted, I decide not to. By the time I'm up the stairs the tight feeling in my throat is disappearing. *Nothing you can't handle,* I think, reassuring my subconscious in the same way I would comfort an irritable animal. It's not much, but it helps.

Now that I can focus, my mind wanders to other topics. Hayley is my best friend since childhood; her large family has Persian cat DNA mixed into the bloodline. Her mother took interest in my damaged family when my mother died. We haven't gone to the same school for years because they don't live very close to us anymore, but Hayley and I remain friends.

I tug my SMARTcall out of my pocket and weigh it in my hand, taking a moment to organize my thoughts. Unlike Eisen, Hayley won't be satisfied with the bare detail version of events. Plus, she home schools and has done so for years, which is why the government generously let her out of the mandatory public school attendance law. Earlier in the summer when we saw each other more, she asked me to keep in contact about what my new school would be like, since she's curious about public school.

I key in her number and listen to the *trip-trip-click* of the SMARTcall connecting tone. I hear her talking right when she picks up.

"Sierra." She speaks my name like it's a proclamation of doom. *"How are you?"* I'm smiling a little bit already, and it hasn't even been ten seconds into our conversation.

"I'm good, Hayley," I tell her, picturing her clutching the device to her head, her cat whiskers twitching with excitement. "What's happening over there?" A strange yowling sound transmits through the speaker of my device.

"Nothing worth speaking of. My sisters planned a sleepover for tonight, and they're upset because I want no part of the little hellion fest they're summoning," she replies dismissively. *"But never mind that! I want to know everything that happened with you today. All of it!"*

"You sure about that?" I sigh, knowing I'll probably have to tell the story of my day at the human school at least two more times today. "It's not really a good story."

"That doesn't matter!" Hayley squawks into the phone. *"I live vicariously through you...sort of...well, I wouldn't want to go to a human school, but I do want to know how it was for you,"* she concludes.

"Basically all the humans are jerks, I got in a spot of bother with the principal, and all of my half-breed classmates hide their animal features to stay as much under the human radar as possible," I say in summary. This time the yowling noise I hear comes from Hayley herself. I launch into the full details of the story, knowing how to convey the details in a way that will interest her. By the time I finish, she's just as silent as Eisen was when he heard my story.

"Well?" I ask. I wonder why everyone I talk to is so stunned by the behavior of humans towards M-DNA people...but then, I remember how shocked and angry I was as events developed this morning, and I understand.

"*Wow, Sierra, I don't know what to say,*" Hayley says at last. I can almost hear her thinking.

"You and both of my brothers. Eisen hasn't told me what he thinks about all of this, Harold won't know until he comes home from work, and Wade might only know what Eisen is probably telling him as we speak." I say before sighing again. "Honestly, I don't want to go back. It's too much trouble, and I have a feeling it's going to get worse. Maybe transferring would help..."

"*Aw, don't be that way honey! Trust me, from what I hear, transferring is going to be hell for anyone who tries,*" Hayley exclaims, trying to soothe me. "*Besides, not all the humans disliked you...and even if most of them did, who gives a bother? The Duncan kid seems normal, at least.*"

"Yeah...that's one out of many," I tell her. I'm no longer really upset; I simply feel...tired. Worn out from the bigoted attitudes of the humans I encountered today. I'm about to convey these feelings to my best friend, but suddenly the yowling noise from the other end of the phone increases and Hayley's voice drifts out of the speaker again.

"*Sorry, Sierra, I've gotta go,*" she grumbles. "*There seems to be a family issue here, and much as I'd love to keep talking to you—*"

"It's fine. We can talk tomorrow, or maybe hang out soon?" I say, resigned to her departure from our conversation.

"Sure," she says. "I'll talk to you later—*ARABELLA, IF YOU PULL MY TAIL ONCE MORE—*"

The line goes dead and I'm left alone my room.

7

If I thought getting out of bed yesterday morning was hard, I had no idea how little motivation I would have to get up today.

I managed it well enough, though, and my brothers didn't tease me as much as yesterday morning. Maybe their minimal banter was a product of Harold's irritated lecture, or perhaps it was the conversation we had last night over our slightly underdone hamburger dinner.

Eisen drives me to school again, and I think over what advice Harold gave me last night once he was apprised of my day.

We all have our battles to fight, Sierra, he'd said once we'd finished eating. I remember his posture: elbows on the table, tense posture, and fingers steepled as he considered me with his grey eyes. I expected the ebony fur lining his hands to be raised as a sign of his anxiety, but as usual Harold was professional and cool.

Life is becoming more difficult for our kind, even after the war that took father...the things that happen in court are turning barbaric, and I know Mother wouldn't have wanted you, Wade, or Eisen involved with any of the trouble.

That's what Harold wants too: me out of trouble.

"You'll be okay, kiddo," Eisen tells me, breaking in to my reverie as we pull up to the school. This time we both know better than to stop by the front entrance, and since I set up my school SMARTnote account last night without any trouble, I can follow the rules better so no more drama follows me around.

I hope.

"Thanks, Eisen," I say weakly, gazing into my foggy reflection in the car window. I didn't take as much effort today with how I looked: a little make-up, jeans, my hair curled, and a flowy yellow peasant shirt. But I didn't hide my ears or my tail. I don't understand why the others hide their non-human attributes, and I adamantly refuse to do the same.

I exit with more of Harold's advice rattling around my head. *I know it's frustrating... believe me, I do. But for you right now, the best thing is to blend in as much as possible. We can't afford to piss off the authorities, and you...I don't want you to get hurt.*

I respect Harold's opinion, but even I can see that sticking my head in the sand won't stop whatever battle might be looming on the horizon. I'm going to keep under the radar, but I don't know how much strength I'll need to bite my tongue and play it safe.

Entering the school feels akin to returning to prison, more so because the dilapidated lower wing possesses a distinctly institutional vibe. I see a group of all the half-breed students congregating near the doors. I look for Morgan right away, and she's not hard to spot: her antlers tower over the heads of a few of the other students, and I make my way to her directly.

I can tell something is wrong the minute I reach the doors. These doors aren't mirrored or shiny; they're made of chipping, creaking metal and smudged, finger-printed glass. All of the students are still hiding their half-breed traits with their clothes and accessories, but it's too...quiet. *Weirdly quiet,* I think.

"Hi Sierra," Morgan greets me once I reach her, but her focus is somewhere else.

"What's wrong?" I ask. Her smile is missing. I follow her line of vision and see Lyle standing in the open doorway, talking to a well-dressed teacher. I recognize the teacher as the prune-ish one who whispered to Belinda after the assembly meeting yesterday.

"Is Lyle in trouble?" I ask, taking a few steps forward.

Morgan grabs my elbow and pulls me back.

"No, but...you might want to wait until they're finished to go in there. Just in case," she says, her forehead crinkling up from serious thought.

"Why?" I ask. The other students around Morgan and me mutter amongst themselves, and I absorb the angry, hostile atmosphere lingering in the air. "What happened?"

"Some genius decided it would be a good idea to vandalize the M-DNA wing last night," someone close to me says and I jump, startled by Ivar's booming voice. He stands behind me with his arms crossed, glaring at the doors as if they personally offended him. Right as I open my mouth to ask for more details, the faculty member consulting with Lyle—who looks even surlier after their conversation—turns and addresses our group of half-breed students.

"You all may proceed to check-in now," she says; her thin voice rasps like a smoker's. "This boy has informed me of the mess in your hall, and it will be dealt with after class hours. Until then, carry on as best you can until the custodial staff can clean up the mess." Concluding her speech, she walks away with a soldier-like gait, not through the obvious entrance leading into the half-breed hall, but up and around the hill.

Because it would definitely kill her to breathe the same air as us, I think. Lyle looks as grumpy as I feel, perhaps because he was just called a boy like he was an errant toddler, but I'm still a little confused as to what is going on.

"Someone really trashed our hall?" I ask Ivar and Morgan as he approaches and rejoins our group. It's unbelievable; the situation sounds like something that would come out of a shallow teenage book. Ivar suddenly looks uncomfortable, which is funny because a bear who seems afraid of being rude is a comical sight. The crowd slowly files into the hall.

"Yeah...humans trying to get rid of us," Lyle growls. I'm beginning to see he has a knack for stating the obvious, but he's right and it does make me think. I want to see the damage before I judge too harshly, though.

Somehow I'm still surprised about how bad the mess ends up being. The entire row of lockers on both sides has been coated with thick, tar-like paint in thick layers of uneven lines that look like dirt tracks. Red paint appears in splatters on top of the black, and various scrawny feathers of different shades and types have been smashed into the paint. Some of the lockers have obscene worlds scrawled on them in more red paint, and patches of mangy-looking faux fur have been glued on along with the feathers.

"This is pretty intense for school vandalism," I muse aloud, watching other students attempt to clean off their lockers with paper towels from the bathroom. One locker draws my attention though, because it has far more damage done to it than the others. I walk up to it, my nose wrinkling in disgust. Someone has scrawled the word *BITCH* at the top of the locker in orange paint, and an orange fox tail—hopefully also faux fur—has been glued right underneath the barely visible locker number. *60.*

I slowly turn around to face my friends.

"Guess this is me, then," I say. My voice sounds different, unnatural. I feel more numb than angry, but the underlying fury surfaces in the form of angry tears in my eyes.

Damn it, I think. *Why is it you're surprised?* It's not even a real mystery to wonder who targeted me for the focus of this prank: it must be the boy who harassed me yesterday. Not that I could get anyone else—anyone *human*—to support my claim. I clench my fists as my gaze inevitably goes back to the mess coating the entire surface of my locker.

"At least it doesn't look like it was broken into," Ivar says helpfully. I examine the door, gingerly brushing my fingers over the stiff paint so I don't have any more contact with the graffiti than I need to. He's right, but the tight feeling in my throat keeps me silent.

"Was that your brother who dropped you off, Sierra?" Morgan asks a bit shrilly, obviously trying to distract me so I won't fly off the handle. Perhaps she thinks I'll cry if I think about what I'm seeing for too long, but I'm more angry than sad.

"Yeah, that was Eisen," I say. My silence must have made the others uncomfortable; awkwardness clutters the air. These people may be my friends, but we met only yesterday.

Come on girl, keep it together, I tell myself.

"We should probably go check in now," I say, satisfied I can speak normally again. "The last thing we need is to be late."

"Right," Ivar says. I shrug my shoulders, distancing myself from the event so I can move on reasonably well with my day.

We all head towards the check-in station in our homeroom. I rely on the others for direction, since yesterday we had the assembly meeting instead of gathering in our homeroom, and after that I had to meet with the principal instead of checking in like everyone else.

"Thanks for the save," I say to Morgan, lowering my voice so the others don't have to hear our dialogue.

She smiles at me.

"Don't mention it," she says, patting my arm. "Most of us freaked out too after our first experience with human pranks."

"This stuff happens normally?" I ask, then feel stupid for voicing that thought. *Of course it happens regularly because it's always tolerated,* I think. Morgan echoes my thoughts as we enter our dingy and tiny-windowed class room to check in.

"Yes, most of the time the humans aren't too subtle about how much they dislike us," she says, and I marvel at her nonchalant tone. "This actually isn't all that bad...one time my mom and I were coming home from a weekend vacation with my grandparents, and our house had been *totally* trashed. It looked like a group of kids had broken in and had a crazy party, but it wasn't just a random breaking-and-entering deal. People they smeared food and mud and spray painted awful names and things all over the house."

"That sucks...did you guys have to move?" I ask her.

She shrugs, and her blasé attitude makes her story worse.

"We didn't have the money to move, and the insurance wouldn't cover our repair costs. Lyle's parents and my grandparents and a few other families like us helped out, so we still live there," she tells me. "But you'd never know someone had wrecked the place. We did a good job fixing up." She smiles at me again, perhaps a bit sadly, but I could be imagining that. She enters her ID number into the neat electronic box resting on the teacher's desk while I stand in line behind her.

My anger over the situation with the vandalism on my locker hasn't diminished, but now I feel sympathy for Morgan and pity for everyone else in this room. I'm not ashamed of being a half-breed, but I think my views toward the situation are an anomaly. Everyone else here who is like me is in hiding or, if they can't hide, resigned to being persecuted for what they are. *I don't think life is supposed to be like this, even for us,* I think, suddenly very tired.

The check-in system is easy enough to use, taking no longer than a few seconds. I abandon the machine before the approved screen finishes flashing and hunt for my assigned, alphabetize seat. I notice there's no sign of our teacher as I talk to a few students and find my place between two freshman boys with the last names Larson and Miller. They're tiny for freshman, and they keep giving me sideways glances. I overhear them quietly discussing my episode with the human bully upstairs yesterday and grimace. Thankfully, however, Shelby is nearby so I don't have to make much conversation with them.

"Where's the teacher for this period?" I ask her. She shrugs and shakes her head; she's wearing pink today, which inexplicably enhances her poodle-like aspects. Shelby must just be one of those girly-girls, or maybe her poodle traits subconsciously encourage her to look more feminine.

"He didn't show up yesterday, but I understand that because we weren't in here for more than five minutes," she says. I nod and turn around in my seat, looking for people I know.

As I see Morgan making conversation with Ivar and another girl with bird features and parrot feathers in her short, blond hair, my mind wanders upstairs to where the humans are. Something about the red in the parrot-girl's hair reminds me of another redhead: Duncan Ledford. I don't know why he pops into my head, but I wonder what he'll think of the mess on the half-breed lockers. *I don't think he'd be the type to condone that behavior,* I assume.

Part of me is setting up caution signs in my brain telling me not to idolize him, especially because he's a human. I'm not trying to, and I'm fully aware that a friendship with a human would be risky. But somehow…I don't think Duncan Ledford feels what all the other humans feel about half-breeds.

I run my fingers through the waves of my hair as if this would manually remove any thoughts I don't want. Just as I look up, the room goes quiet as our homeroom teacher enters. The freshmen around me struggle to hide the sudden fit of laughter that sweeps over them, and some of the other students titter nervously as our teacher strides over to the desk. He sways as he walks, and his bloodshot, bleary red eyes scan us with a dull stare.

My gaze meets Lyle's—he's in the back of the room—and we make wry faces at each other. This teacher, whoever he is, looks like he just crawled out of one of those seedy bars adults warn wild kids to stay away from.

"Hi, class," the teacher sighs once he situates himself behind the desk. He doesn't look dangerous, but he tilts around like he's going to pass out, and that appears hazardous. All of us students let out a collective sigh of relief when he plops down onto the antique stool behind the desk. I wonder what this perfectionist, high-level school was thinking when they hired this youth with messy black curls and sloppy clothes to be in charge of a mixed grade half-breed class.

"You'd think they'd *try* to make a good impression, just in case someone came around to check on the desegregation stuff," Shelby snarks from her seat, and I hope the teacher didn't hear. It doesn't look like he did; he stares at the desk now, his thin, pale lips moving slowly over the syllables of all our names on a list. I agree with her even if I keep
my thoughts to myself.

"Right...my name is Marlow Hynes," the teacher begins suddenly; his voice is far too loud for the size of the room, and the words slur together. "I am in charge here, so any class events must be approved by me, and...well, I'm sure you all know the drill when it comes to homeroom," he chuckles in a dazed sort of way.

Everyone incredulously scrutinizes this hung-over, boyish teacher with the glazed blue eyes. My gaze wanders again, landing on Lyle; he squints thoughtfully at our "instructor," but he glances at me again and his eyes become a little less annoyed. I guess our thoughts flow in the same direction.

Only the best for M-DNA students, of course, I think with bitter sarcasm. Marlow Hynes reads through the roll again, and the room quiets except for the low chatter of the students. He seems like a drunk and a total idiot, and he hasn't even been in the room five minutes.

From what I've seen of the other aspects of this school, the administration would only hire someone like Marlow if they wanted to chase away current or potential students.

Finally, the bell rings at the half-hour mark and there's a mad rush to the door. I'm glad when I escape the calamity in the M-DNA student hall for my math class upstairs. Perhaps I'm too paranoid now, but it seems to me that Hostetler is doing everything in its power to chase me and my classmates away.

Which makes me want to fight to stay all the more.

My mind keeps going back over the events of the morning during my last class before lunch. I sit in between Morgan and Lyle in Sociology, and thankfully I know for a fact that I'm not the only distracted one. Morgan fidgets more and more—perhaps because she's hungry; she told me earlier she doesn't have time to eat breakfast in the mornings—and I hear Lyle drumming his SMARTpad stylus on the desk behind me. In fact, the entire half-breed section of this class, all six of us seniors, regards the other side of the room with varying degrees of suspicion.

The same question they must be asking silently has been rattling around my brain for hours as well: who trashed our hall? I have my own ideas about the perpetrators, but even if I decided to share them, I know they wouldn't do any good. Belinda Harper is not the kind of principal to deal fairly with M-DNA students, as I learned yesterday when I checked my school SMARTnote account for the first time. I discovered exactly how many demerits she'd given me for my small "offense." I cringe again just thinking about it. *10 demerits just for entering the building by the wrong set of doors... and 45 means expulsion!*

I'm glad I'm surrounded by a few people who would call themselves my friends. The human seniors in this class generally ignore us half-breeds, but at random I notice the nerd girl Katrina and her boyfriend on the other side of the room. I don't know her boyfriend's name, but I recognize him, and I certainly don't want to know him any better. Their presence makes me restless, and the boy in particular makes my fur stand on end from the creepy vibes. He's been watching me for at least fifteen minutes, and I'm even more certain he was involved with the vandalism that went on here at school last night.

Mutt, my thoughts whisper as a reminder of what he called me.

I feel like a freak, and part of me is reconsidering my decision to not hide my animal features. I give in to the bad habit of clutching my tail too tight as it rests in my lap; Harold always laughed at me for doing that, and said one day I'd have bald patches on my tail if I kept squeezing it so tightly. *It wouldn't make any difference if you did start hiding,* I think as a bleak

encouragement. *They'd recognize you anywa*
y.

Class draws to a close. My eyes drift towards the digital clock hovering at the top of my SMARTpad; I concentrate on the time so intently that someone's sneeze startles me. Out of idle curiosity, I turn around to find who sneezed, and my eyes catch a glimpse of red hair and freckles on a long nose at the back-middle of the room. Somehow I know those features belong to Duncan, and I wish I hadn't turned around. I slowly face the front of the room again, hoping he won't look up to catch me staring at him. It's ironic to me that the one human I like is in this class with me alongside two of the people here I want to stay away from.

At least he's not a monitor, I reassure myself, telling my brain the only reason I'm glad to see Duncan is because he seems like a decent guy. During the discussion with my friends about monitors yesterday at lunch—and whatever else I've picked up on during the morning—I heard no mention of any monitor named Duncan. Somehow I find this reassuring.

Finally, the bell rings, and I'm up and heading towards the door before the shrill tone ceases to echo in my ears. Almost against my will, my eyes follow Duncan as he exits the room; he's joined another small group of friends, and from this distance their conversation looks easy, carefree.

"Sierra, wait!" Morgan calls right as the other students pour out of classrooms and into the hallways in pursuit of lunch. She and Lyle are right behind me, although Lyle loiters to talk to Ivar and one other senior half-breed who has what appears to be crocodile DNA. "I thought we could try a slightly different spot for lunch today, since it rained last night and the ground will probably be soaked and muddy where we were yesterday," she tells me. I shrug, shouldering my school bag and continuing with her out of the classroom.

My mind is still on Duncan, and we're barely out of the classroom door leading into the pristine human senior hallway before another voice calls my name.

"Hello, *Sierra*." I could recognize Katrina's snide tone anywhere, and I don't acknowledge her presence. However, I see her and her boyfriend and their "popular" group of friends leaning up against their lockers with an air of casual, predatory glee.

"What did *you* bring for lunch, Morgan?" I ask my antlered friend as we pass them. I'm nervous, and my voice sounds too loud. Morgan drops her gaze and nearly stumbles, clearly very uncomfortable with this situation. Thankfully she plays along.

"Oh, the usual: sandwiches for me and Lyle, and a nice, tart salad with tangerine slices—" Her descriptions are nice under pressure, but I don't wait for her to continue.

"Come on, Lyle! Let's go!" I sound needier than I'd like, but I want Lyle and the guys to catch up with us.

But Lyle isn't paying attention.

"Lyle? Is that your boyfriend?" Katrina laughs cuttingly, peering around behind us until she sees the rest of the senior half-breeds catching up. Lyle, responding to the sound of his name, looks up. "You mutts breed without having the same DNA mutations? That's disgusting!" Katrina's smile is toxic as she laughs, and the temperature in the hallway seems to rise.

Several replies pop into my head, all of them extremely amusing to me and very unwise to actually say. *Bullies like attention,* I remind myself as I grit my teeth and keep walking.

The boy speaks next. "What did you think of the new decorations in your hall?" I don't know his name, but I hate him. I stop before I can remind myself again to ignore anything these petty humans say.

"If I said it was lovely or that you are an excellent interior decorator, would you leave me alone?" I ask him, sighing as if I'm bored with his jibes. It's hard to believe he'd all but admit to being part of the graffiti fest last night...but then I remember who I'm talking to, and I'm no longer surprised. Morgan's vice-tight grip suddenly clamps onto my arm, and I resist the urge to shrug her off. *She's smart, back off,* my thoughts urge me.

"Careful with that attitude, Vixen," he says, glaring at me. Katrina grins, too amused for this scene, and suddenly I realize that everyone else in the hall is observing this scene too.

Not again! I think, annoyed. I can't believe I got caught up in more drama. I turn away without saying anything. It takes a lot more strength of will to back off than I imagined it would.

There you go, Harold, I send my brother a

disgruntled mental message. Morgan follows me, a little tentatively, and I sense Lyle and the others following too. *That's right, come on, let's get out of here...*I encourage them in my mind.

"Mutts like that don't actually hate humans, which is part of the problem," I hear Katrina's boyfriend begin telling; I resist the urge to turn around because I don't need to see them to know they're following me and my friends. I satisfy myself by picturing a volcanic crater opening up between me and my enemies, and it does make me feel better for a split second to imagine them tripping spectacularly before falling into the abyss. My ears swivel backwards, twitching from all the hostility. This must be the part in movies where the audience urges the person to keep walking, to ignore the trash talk and not get in trouble. I can already tell I'm not going to listen.

"Really, Bryan?" Why?" Katrina asks. I want to gag at the bland spite in her sugary tone.

"I've heard fox bitches in heat can be a little feisty, so Sierra must be ready for—" I warn the human— *Bryan*—to stop, but my warnings remain trapped in my head. They dissolve into red fury as he finishes the statement with a vulgar description of what he thinks "fox bitches" want when they're in heat.

I'm so disgusted and so angry I think I could spit fire, and I stalk back up to Bryan before I can clear my head and return to being cold and distant. More sarcastic, burning replies queue up at the corners of my lips, pressing to be said, but I'm too angry to choose among them.

The half-breed boys nearby who heard what he said growl with unmistakable animal snarls...and also approach Bryan. One of them is a very young half-breed, but he's growling and actually rolling up his sleeves in preparation for a fight. I'd be touched by their willing defense of my honor, however old-fashioned, but my focus is elsewhere.

Smacking Bryan with all the strength in my arm is a surprisingly therapeutic feeling; it's a back-hand, too, not some weak, girly slap that this incredibly stupid human would laugh at. Bryan staggers, falling against the lockers behind him, his head turned and a red mark blooming on his face. I take satisfaction in knowing my superior animal strength hurt him.

I can't imagine what my expression looks like, but it must terrify Katrina because she backs off, placing Bryan between me and herself. Bryan, to his credit, didn't cry out when I slapped him, but he flexes his jaw tightly, and I know I left a mark.

I hope his face swells up like a balloon, my mind whispers savagely.

"Not even us 'fox bitches' would pay attention to a creep like you," I say icily. He seems surprised, *very* surprised I hit him; his shallow blue eyes glare up at me, but there's something else in there besides anger and heat. It makes me shudder, and I turn away.

"Sierra!" Morgan yells at me as she grabs hold of my arm again. Her brown eyes, deep and caring, are worried as she tugs on me, trying to pull me away.

"Let's go, he's not worth it..."

"Fine," I say. My voice sounds colder than my flushed cheeks, and I don't even realize I answered her. My hands clench into fists at my side, there's a ringing in my ears, and it's only at her instruction that I walk away, my tail straight and bristled. Everyone around me is frozen, even the half-breeds who were so keen to attack Bryan just a few moments ago. The tension still boils in the air, but I stalled it for a few moments by acting first. This hallway scene feels like it's gone on for days, but the bell only rang a few minutes ago.

Only Morgan and I hurry out of the hallway and down the stairs to get outside, and suddenly my clarity comes back. I can't wait to get away, outside of this horrible place.

I hear people yelling upstairs, a signal of the dam breaking to release a few good minutes of violence. My heart, still racing from the adrenaline, stutters erratically as I hear the sounds of feet running and the THUD of a body slamming into one of the lockers upstairs. Morgan glances at the ceiling before her eyes flicker back down to me. I know who she's worried about.

"It's okay. Go...I'll be fine," I manage to say, my face folding into the familiar lines of a false smile.

"Try to keep everyone out of trouble; it's not worth it. And by everyone, I mean Lyle." She smiles back at me gratefully, and I appreciate her friendliness even though I might have caused a whole pile of trouble for all of us.

She departs, and I'm left standing in the mess of the downstairs hall wondering what the hell I got myself into.

I don't want to eat anymore because my stomach churns from what happened upstairs. I can't believe I snapped like that, especially after all the warnings for caution from my brothers and friends. I wander around the school grounds, completely alone and hoping to stay that way. I'm glad I'm outside, at least, because I don't want to know what I caused back in the school.

At least my claws weren't out, I think as I roam across the school grounds. *There wasn't any blood.* Some of the students who probably missed the drama are outside, eating their lunch and talking without paying attention to me. At first I was planning to head towards the area where I ate lunch with my new friends yesterday, but I remember what Morgan said about the mud, so I change my mind and head in a new direction.

The new soccer field—fixed up and made presentable with a shiny green lawn—looks promising...rather, the tiny forest around the field looks like a promising destination. I avoid the realization that me going for this little secluded area seems a lot like running and hiding, but I don't know what else to do.

Eisen would come get me if I called him, I recall. I love the idea of calling my brother, especially since he would be the most understanding of the situation. It would be wonderful to leave, and leave on my own terms instead of waiting for the principal to expel me without bothering to hear the entire story. I shouldn't have hit Bryan, but a normal principal might understand events in a fairer light and I could get away with a few detentions or something. Belinda won't be so sympathetic to a half-breed she already dislikes; plus, it's unlikely Bryan will get any punishment at all for provoking me.

But I won't leave or transfer. I know I won't even if I'm entertaining the happy idea of Eisen coming to pick me up, my big brother defending me from the stupid humans and their ridiculous system. I need to stay, mostly because Harold would be so disappointed if I didn't at least try to stick it out.

But you did *try,* my thoughts hum in dissatisfaction.

"Sierra?" Someone calls my name right as I reach the edge of the little forested area. Only when I stop do I realize how rapidly I've been power walking. *That probably didn't look at all suspicious,* I think sarcastically. Sighing, I slowly turn around to see who followed me.

"Yeah?" I ask with more hostility than I intended, and I regret it when I whirl around and see Duncan Ledford was concerned enough to follow me. "Oh...hi," I add lamely.

"Hi," he says, standing aloof with his long legs poised to step back; he holds his hands out, and I look away from his curious green eyes down to the few calluses lining his palms. It's an odd but weirdly reassuring thought at the moment, but his hands look gentle as well as strong. He's warier than yesterday, I can sense, but that's probably because I snapped at him...or because I almost knocked Bryan out. I still feel like running away; Duncan wouldn't find me if I didn't want to be found, not once I got into the trees. Then again, I don't really want to leave without giving him a chance.

"Um..." I say when the silence drags on a second or two longer than necessary. "Do you...need something?" I feel awkward because we're just standing here, and he hasn't said anything else. He starts, and I realize he was staring at me; the realization is confusing. I think of how I must look right now: slicked back fox ears, flushed cheeks, rigidly tense posture except for the swishing of my bristled tail...everything about me screams UNWELCOME. Why wouldn't he stare? I think.

"Sorry...I just saw you running away from the building by yourself and wondered what was up," he says.

"I wasn't running!" I exclaim, but then I notice the flush of pink creeping up to his face from his neck. I feel bad for snapping again; he wasn't involved with that horrendous scene inside. "Sorry. This has been a bad morning," I say. I feel like I should move towards him a little more, but I don't; my instincts are still on overdrive, and I don't want to shock him with any more animalistic behavior.

"I could tell...you seem to have a habit of ending up alone after bad stuff happens," Duncan says. His hands rest in the pockets of his well-fitting, if fairly worn jeans; his jeans, in fact, fit so well in the right places that I automatically draw my eyes elsewhere and catalog the impression for a later pondering. I wonder how much he knows about what happened. Word spreads quickly, especially in a high school, but I'm not sure if he was at the scene or not.

"I guess so...I handle stuff better on my own," I say. I wonder why I'm bothering to talk to him at all, why I'm investing anything other than generic conversation material.

"I saw what happened with Bryan," Duncan says. He's still watching me without directing his gaze away, but he takes a cautious step forward, perhaps waiting to see how I'll react. Maybe he's expecting me to lash out again, or just explode with an invective against humans. Both options sound pretty appealing, despite the inappropriateness of such an interaction between me and a guy who isn't anything but an acquaintance yet. If I was with Hayley or one of my brothers I would just let the anger out. But this situation is totally different, and I don't really feel any kind of anger or frustration with this one human.

"Oh?" I say. "Not my best moment." I remember the brief feeling that jarred through my wrist when I hit

Bryan, and suddenly I really wish Duncan hadn't seen any of that. *He looks like he's too kind to say it, but he probably does view me as more of an animal now,* I think. My spirits crumple slightly.

"It wasn't his either. He didn't used to be such an ass, but bad choices and old-fashioned American sports can screw anyone up," Duncan says, surprising me. He takes another step closer, moving towards me slowly but surely. Respecting his effort, I inch forward as well, my tail rebelliously switching back and forth a couple of times. We're close enough so we're an arm's length from each other. My head cocks a little to the side as I study him, and my tail relaxes slightly as some instinct within me decides that Duncan Ledford is not a threat. My brain shortly follows what my body is telling me by relaxing, and I hum too softly for a human to hear.

It's not much, but it's a wonderful feeling: knowing that in a world of humans who despise my kind, here's one who won't try to threaten or mock me.

"I guess you've known him for as long as Katrina?" I ask. Duncan smiles, a small thing a lot of people might not entirely notice.

"Katrina's always been in this town, however much she'll want to talk about leaving and getting a high-end job in the city. Bryan is one of those star football players you won't hear much about after the graduation ceremony," he says. "Despite how it looks with all of my loyal fans crowding around me, I try not to get too connected with this place. The people here can be...toxic." I surprise myself by laughing after he speaks; he spread his arms out a little as he mentioned loyal fans, enhancing the sarcasm.

"So it's not just me? The people here really are, um—"

"—bat-shit crazy, yeah." Duncan bluntly finishes my sentence. "But not all of us are that bad...even the ones who don't like...um..." He pauses, abashed. I'm still not in the mood to fully smile yet, but I try to look somewhat encouraging.

"We call ourselves half-breeds too. It's okay to call us that; or M-DNA people, we're not picky about those names," I say. His smile grows stronger, and I come to the realization that I kind of like the way his smiles light up his face. His eyes crinkle a little at the edges pleasantly as the expression reaches his eyes.

"Even the ones who don't like half-breeds aren't as bad as people like Bryan. He's one of the extreme ones," he concludes.

"That was very politically correct of you," I say, giving him a break.

"What?" He looks taken aback slightly.

"The gist of what you said...you basically excused me for hitting a human while at the same time defending your own kind," I explain. He blinks, as if trying to figure out where I'm going with this. I'm enjoying my new aura of mystery; I grew up in a small area where all of my half-breed associates knew who I was, so it's a new experience for me to be the object of scrutiny.

"Why did you follow me? Out of all the chaos going on upstairs, you came after me?" I don't know what answer I expect to hear, and I feel awkward for making him sound like a stalker, but I want to know.

Duncan reflects a moment, and I get a first glimpse of what he looks like when he's concentrating. Furrowed eyebrows and the trademarks of thoughtfulness are there, sure, but he has a strangely peaceful expression aside from that. I haven't seen anyone mellow like him anywhere else.

"I wasn't really following you, exactly...or, if I was, I was more just leaving after the whole scene happened," he begins. "But then I saw you, and I noticed your friend with the antlers wasn't with you...plus you were kind of running away."

"I wasn't running," I remind him again, less harshly than I did the first time.

"Whatever," he concedes with another smile. "It just didn't seem right for you to be alone after a scene like that. I know my presence might not be the most welcome right now because technically I'm one of them, but...I guess I'm trying to prove that not all of us are terrible." He finishes with a shrug.

"Well..." I don't know what to say. "I probably shouldn't assume or make generalities...thanks, Duncan."

"Don't mention it. I like being different," he says. Then he looks a little bashful again. "You...you're okay, then? You're not going to..." he trails off, his gaze flickering once between me and the forested area nearby.

"Yes, I'm fine. No fleeing to the hills for me," I say reassuringly. "We vixens are pretty resilient creatures." *Too much!* I chastise myself. I keep forgetting Duncan isn't someone I can bond with in the same way I would any other half-breed acquaintance.

His reaction isn't instant revulsion, though. "Good to know...my hair is the same color as fox fur, so I should know these things already. Honorary fox club membership and all that," he says. I'm laughing now, a real laugh that I don't have to reach down deep for. Whatever else happens today, this human kid tried to connect with me on a half-breed level, and that at least is something worth remembering. I hope I get to know him better, however unlikely that is.

Suddenly the sound of a stomach loudly growling like an angry beast disrupts the air. I'm startled, and I worry that it's my stomach that decided to star in the opera, but Duncan grins up at me sheepishly.

"Sorry...lunchtime," he says. "I gave my lunch bag to one of my friends already...do you want to walk back with me to get it?" I'm surprised he offered, and a little flattered. I don't know what to think of this kid.

"Sure, if it's not a problem," I say. "Where do you guys normally eat?"

"Since it's a good day, outside closer to the ledge under the main entrance," he tells me. He begins walking back towards that destination, and I follow at a marginally slower pace. I'm nervous to meet more people, especially now, but I'm relieved he doesn't say anything else about his friends or bring it up.

We walk in silence for a few paces; my lunch is still in my locker, but I definitely don't feel like running back to fetch it. My smile from chatting with Duncan threatens to disappear as I think about the storm waiting for me back in the school. After all the fighting that probably broke out after my confrontation with Bryan, eventually someone is going to remember who caused the trouble.

But then I look at Duncan's ginger red hair waving in the very faint breeze and the freckles under his eyes, and I don't care as much.

What's gotten into me? I think curiously. I'm not normally this moody, but I'm also not this easy to appease after I cause some sort of dramatic upset that might affect a lot of people.

It's almost as if Duncan can read the train of my thoughts passing through the air above my head. "What are you going to do if you get in trouble with the school?" he asks me. I groan and shake my head, covering my face with my hands.

"If? I don't know...I was trying to not think about that," I say, taking a deep breath before lowering my hands.

"Was I helping? I'm normally good at being a distraction," Duncan says.

"Yeah, you were doing great for a little while," I say, smiling. "You talking to me at all is a distraction, honestly." Shortly after those words pass my lips, I wish I hadn't said them. Duncan blinks at me, perhaps misunderstanding what I meant.

"Why? Do you not talk to...people like me very much?" he asks. He's doing it again, avoiding names of certain people groups; I appreciate the effort. I shake my head in a negative, relieved that he didn't comment on what I actually meant and didn't intend to say out loud.

"I kind of grew up in...well, let's call it a really small town with not many humans wandering around," I inform him, trying to be casual. He looks like he wants to ask more, but our moderate walking pace—since we've slowed down for conversation—has finally carried us close to our destination. I realize we took the long way: over the athletic field and around the buildings, all the way to the right side of the building which will take us to the main entrance.

"Well, it was nice talking to you, Duncan," I say. Not that it matters, but just in case half-breed students are never allowed to use the main doors for any reason, I don't want to anger the principal or the powers that be any further. Or encounter any of my enemies here.

Basically the only human I'm okay talking to right now is the redhead in front of me. He's staring at me again, but this time it's a little more subtle, and less dazed looking.

"It...was nice talking to you too. Sierra," he says. He seems embarrassed now as he rubs his hand on the back of his neck once or twice. I feel awkward too now, and I look down at the ground; my ears angle down, and the tip of my tail sweeps the ground. I take a few steps back, showing that I'm leaving.

"See you around, I guess," I say, hoping my voice sounds casual. I'm really angry with myself for feeling at all down about this farewell in the first place; he's just a human, after all, and even if he had the decency to check up on me when I was in distress, it doesn't mean we're friends.

It might be dangerous to be friends with me anyway, so if I respect him, I should leave him be, I instruct myself firmly while at the same time feeling ridiculous for the necessity of having this internal dialogue in the first place.

"Hey!" Duncan calls once I'm a few feet away; I don't know where I'm going, but I was aiming for the back entrance just to have somewhere to go. "I do hope to see you again. Around here, I guess," he says. He looks like he feels a little nervous still, but then he smiles and that looks pretty genuine. I smile back.

"Okay...thanks for the memo," I say. "Enjoy your lunch!"

I walk away fast before I can say anything else...or before he can. My emotions are still haywire, and I feel frazzled in more ways than one.

The rest of my day is incredibly, abominably tense. I keep waiting for the principal to call for me over the intercom system, but she never does. At first I'm confused; Belinda did not give me the impression of being haphazard or lax with "justice,"
so I wonder why she's taking so long to suspend or expel me. Is she trying to hold my wrongdoing over my head, making me feel anxious as part of the punishment?

As the day continues, I understand better what's going on. Morgan and Shelby explained a good part of it; they were waiting by my vandalized locker in the M-DNA student hall when I returned from my encounter with Duncan. It seems I served as the catalyst for breaking all the tension building between the students. A lot of fights broke out, mostly between the males on both sides, and a good portion of the half-breeds have been called into the office. Many of them don't reappear in their later classes, and throughout the day I imagine them standing disheveled—some with bloody knuckles and bruised faces—in front of Belinda's desk as they try to explain what happened. Some of the humans are gone too, but I notice Katrina and Bryan hanging around and attending their classes like normal.

"Probably because Bryan doesn't want to admit he got his fat lip from a half-breed girl," Shelby snorted contemptuously once his presence came to her attention before our last class. She's been worried about Ivar being gone most of the day, so this is the most she's spoken in a couple of hours. According to her, Ivar was one of the ones most involved in the fighting besides Lyle, and he's most likely going to get into a lot of trouble.

"And Katrina?" I ask as we take our seats right before my last and least favorite class—Government—starts. "Why isn't she spilling her guts to the principal?"

"She might have already," Morgan interjects. "If she could get past the crowd of people not allowed to leave Belinda's office—"

"—and if Bryan allowed her to tell Belinda about Sierra beating him up," Shelby says, unwilling to let go of this idea. "He looks like he's a controlling sort of boyfriend."

"Okay, we get that Bryan is a scumbag...he already lied to Belinda about me yesterday. But surely she should have the whole story by now? She can't have spent all this time suspending everyone who got into a fight," I say, trying to get back to the real issue. I'm watching the teacher—another middle-aged, stereotypical history geek lecturing on how Chairman Heights polluted the gene pool with animal DNA and started the M-DNA war—so I'll notice if he sends any hostile glares in our direction, but he doesn't seem to care if we talk. Nor does it seem to bother him if a few of his M-DNA students are missing.

"You're right. It doesn't make sense," Morgan says. "I don't want you to get called into the office, Sierra, but if Belinda already has it out for you, why hasn't she called you in to punish you yet? What's the hold up?" Instead of taking notes, she's making a long, fish-tail plait with her hair; her nails are painted the same color as the red baseball hat Lyle was wearing yesterday. (Half-breeds generally don't prefer the smell of nail polish, but there are natural varieties of human products available that don't offend our sensitive noses.)

"You look like you have an idea about what's going on," I say to Morgan. "Share?"

"It's not much, really. I think...I think that maybe only a few people know you were at the start of all the drama. The ones who are half-breeds who did know won't sell you out to any human, especially because they think you're cool and daring. The humans who got involved...well, there simply aren't as many in the office, and with all the conflicting reports..." Morgan releases the river of her thoughts, then pauses. "Sorry, I'm rambling."

"No you're not," Shelby assures her. "Basically,

Belinda has to clear through all that rubbish before she can call Sierra in. She has to keep up a *little* semblance of fairness, after all. Students aren't allowed to fight in school, human or half-breed."

"People think I'm cool and daring?" I ask, side-tracked by one of Morgan's comments; I totally picked up on the rest of that dialogue, but the concept of those two words Morgan used applying to me is a novelty. Especially because anything I've done that could be considered daring has been purely accidental. Shelby releases a naturally breathy giggle, and Morgan smiles.

"Yeah. The incident with your fabulous entrance yesterday...and you hitting Bryan...it kind of all added up and you're a bit of a rebel leader among us now," she tells me with that same smile flowing into her eyes. "Or so I'm told. Lyle told me this yesterday, and I assume he's even more right after today."

"Huh," I reply wittily. Shelby giggles again. I watch Morgan as she talks about Lyle, and my curiosity stirs again. I'm about to open my mouth to ask if her and Lyle are together, but then our teacher frowns in my direction. I decide my question can wait until a later date.

Until then, I have more important questions on my mind. Like what I'm going to do once Belind gets down to the fact that I was the catalyst for the drama in the hall during lunchtime. Sure, she has a lot of conflicting reports to sort through, but in spite of my friends' reassurances, I know that eventually Belinda will get to the original story.

Still, I'm more worried about what Harold is going to do to me once he discovers that I flouted our agreement to avoid trouble at all costs.

The toll the war took on the world is considered incredible by all historical standards, and many thought this war would be the one to end the civilization as we knew it. However, an end to the conflict came in sight once SMART Industries came into play.

CARTER BOWMAN, the founder of S.M.A.R.T.— **S**cience, **M**edicine, **A**rt, **R**elationships, and **T**echnology—*INDUSTRIES set himself and the thousands of employees working for his company to the task of finding a solution that would satisfy the pure DNA and M-DNA factions on either side of the war. The solution came in the form of a vaccine which, if given to every human child between the ages of 2-5, would protect their DNA strain from being contaminated with anything animal. The battles did not end instantly, but the vaccine began the peace talks that took three years to adequately discuss.*

The end of the war and following peace brought billions of credits into SMART accounts thanks to the popularity of the vaccine, and Mr. Bowman became the richest man in the world.

Due to his and his company's efforts, new resources and methods of cleansing our planet were discovered, and humanity began adapting to this new version of Earth. SMART industries became a household name, and since the peace they have brought about most of the latest medical, scientific, and technical advances.

Unfortunately, SMART industries could not halt all aspects of the war. Even after the peace, rogue factions of the former pure DNA side of the conflict continued to attack concentrated M-DNA areas with great cost on both sides. Biological warfare was their method of choice to perpetuate their extremist cleansing of the gene pool, and it took until the end of Century 22 to capture, imprison, or execute all of these rogue units.

9

I lose my nerve. I don't tell any of my brothers what happened once I get home. Eisen picked me up like normal, and I intended to tell him what happened. But I can't, even though I know it will be worse later if Belinda ends up suspending me—or expelling me, which is just as likely—and I have to call someone in my family to come pick me up. I scheme to avoid this as Eisen drives in silence, caught up in the events of his own day at the beanery. I could always call Hayley, and someone from her family would come get me, in spite of the long drive....but that would get back to my brothers eventually, and Harold would be disappointed in me for willfully deceiving him.

My evening is quiet but internally stressful, and I have a hard time sitting still. At least I can make dinner, although it requires some effort to not slam pots and pans around as I make chicken spaghetti. My brothers notice my tension but don't ask for more details.

By the time I finally clean up and go to bed, I'm a nervous wreck, and I don't think I'll be getting much sleep. For a while, my mind runs around in circles like a deranged fox chasing an invisible chicken; but eventually I do fall asleep.

I wake up the next morning with the same thoughts as before rattling around my tired brain. *Day three of this insanity,* I think. The last thing I want to do is get up and go to school, but I'm hoping, at the very least, that the custodial crew for the school cleaned up the M-DNA hall and my poor abused locker.

Sure they did. And they remodeled the lower wing overnight too, my mind scoffs.

"Sierra!" Wade hollers for me as he thumps up the stairs, probably on all fours with his fluffy russet tail waving in the air. I'm not sure why, but my entire family has this habit of running up the stairs at home on all fours. Even Harold occasionally gives in to this impulse as he races up the stairs.

"Don't you dare bust in here, Wade!" I call to my brother. I hear him barely stop himself from colliding with my bedroom door; I've learned to keep it shut in the mornings for the simple reason that I like my privacy when I'm getting ready in the morning. Solitude is hard to come by in a house full of half-breed men who don't think to knock.

"No need to snap, S. Hurry up! It's important," Wade huffs outside my door. His tone worries me, and I hurry to finish tugging on my stone-washed jeans and my green V-neck tee. I didn't do much with my hair today, just a brush through and a loose side ponytail. Cosmetics can't help the purple circles under my eyes.

Wade grabs my hand as soon as I open the door, and begins tugging me down the stairs. "What did you do now, little sister? It sounds like you beat up a student!" he says. I could feign ignorance about the situation, but my brothers are smarter than that, especially my wildest sibling Wade.

"I didn't beat up anyone," I say firmly. "Please tell me you answered that call and not—"

"Too late. They got Harold's SMARTcall, and he's talking to someone on your school board right now. They probably used the number listed in the legal guardian section of the paperwork," Wade informs me. He was trying to be serious, but it must have cost too much effort. "You really busted up a human boy? That's great, sis, we'll make a fighting Maurell out of you yet!"

Eisen meets us at the bottom of the stairs with his lean arms crossed over his slender chest. He has yet to put a shirt on, so he's wandering the house with little but his work pants on. "Wade, I absolutely forbid you to refer to our family as the fighting Maurells. It makes us sound like Irish wrestlers, and if anything, I insist upon us being Italian," he says.

"I dunno...Emilee might like it..." Wade says thoughtfully.

I sigh and yank my arm out of Wade's grip. The three of us dawdle in our tiny living room, and I strain to decipher Harold's words in the kitchen.

"Guys, this isn't relevant!" I huff.

"What's relevant is the fact that you didn't tell us you got into a fight, Sierra!" Wade says indignantly.

"The true relevant question for this situation is *how* you reacted in this fight," Eisen says contemplatively. "According to all reports, you clawed this silly human and ran away. However, I know your fighting style much better than anyone else: a little hasty, and more offense than defense..." He loses his train of thought for a second, and I know all of us remember the days when he and Harold took a few weekends to train Wade and me in self-defense. "Anyway, I think you probably punched his lights out?"

"I back-handed him," I mutter, resigned to humoring my brothers' more violent side. Wade claps me on the back so hard I almost fall over, and Eisen grins with his sharp, white teeth.

"*Excellent,* S. That's how a woman should fight that brand of douchebag: a back-hand says your opponent isn't man enough to handle a fist to the nose," he says gleefully. I open my mouth to let the sarcasm flow, but suddenly all three of us hear Harold's raised voice in the other room.

"*—and I don't care if she knocked every single one of that idiot boy's teeth out, he provoked her with his witless vulgarity! If you try to tell me or anyone else my sister is a rabble-rouser in your school again, I'm going to use every connection in my power to take legal action against your school!*"

I haven't heard Harold shout like that in a long time; the last time had to be when our landlord tried to instruct Wade on how to use the plumbing in our townhouse. Eisen and Wade are equally shocked; the three of us stand completely stunned as the other person squawks at the other end of Harold's conversation.

"He's shouting...he's actually pissed..." Wade, who is usually on the receiving end of Harold's traditionally reasonable argument sessions, seems dazed and happy with the realization that our eldest brother does, in fact, have the fiery Maurell temper. Eisen claps a hand over his own mouth, stuffing in the gales of laughter he'd usually produce in such a situation.

"My sister is as decent a kid as I am a good lawyer, and so help me *if you push me I will* make sure *your school gets so much heat from the media that you'll be up to your eyeballs in desegregation committee shit! Your government funding will cease to exist!"*

"He's cussing!" Wade says too loudly, punching the air with a triumphant raised fist, and I give his tail a sharp tug to make him shut up. There is another moment of the person on the other end of the line squawking rapidly, and next time Harold speaks he's no longer shouting.

"Thank you for your understanding," he speaks in cold tones that are still too loud for any inside voices rule. "Sierra will be coming to school today, after I discuss the situation with her. Your request should be fulfilled by this afternoon. Thank you for your time." He barely finishes ending the call before...

"Sierra. Get in here *now."* I cringe at the tone of his voice, and Eisen sympathetically pats me on the back.

"Just keep your ears back and wait it out, it'll be over soon," Wade tries to encourage me.

Harold is standing at the sink when I enter the

kitchen, his ears perked up and his tail twitching erratically as he leans on the counter. The Thursday sun shines gently through the window, and it gleams on Harold's black hair and the equally dark fur on his ears.

"So..." I begin after he's silent for a moment too long. "I can explain—"

"Do not let that happen again, Sierra. Next time you get in trouble with school I want to hear about it *before* I get a surprise phone call before eight a.m.," he says. I hear the fatigue in his voice; Harold's constantly overworked weariness never fails to bring me sadness.

"Okay," I say softly, feeling the teeth of guilt bite down uncomfortably hard into the lining of my stomach. Harold turns around, and I observe the sadness and frustration in his eyes, eyes so very like my mother's.

"I understand how hard this is for you, Sierra. I do. When I asked you yesterday morning to try to stay out of trouble, I realized it wouldn't be easy. We are the fighting Maurells, after all," he smiles, and it looks so painful an effort that I want to run up and hug him. I take a few steps forward before I stop myself; I should let him finish speaking first. Wade and Eisen shuffle into the kitchen now; I sense their sheepishness by their hanging heads, now they know Harold heard us eavesdropping from the living room.

"I don't blame you for what happened with that human, Sierra. I wish you hadn't done it, but I also know I taught you to never let anyone disrespect you. I'm glad you can defend yourself," he says. I assume by his words that Belinda really got down to it to find the whole story, and communicated it to my brother...with

128

probable embellishments, of course. "However, you've been put into a very sticky situation now. *Wade, if you make an innuendo out of what I just said, I will rip your tail off.*" Harold is trying to be reasonable with me, but he snaps at Wade so quickly that I realize he is all but calm right now. Wade, who was about to stay something to Eisen, goes quiet, and I hear him mutter something that sounds like "man-period."

"Does the school want to suspend me?" I ask.

"Yes. Well, part of the vote was to expel you, but the more...'merciful' voters in this circumstance voted for either a two week suspension or a written apology to the human boy," Harold informs me, and every single one of us standing in the kitchen cringes. I'm more surprised than anything else, but still horrified and angered all the same.

"That's it? Those are my choices? Either suspension, or groveling to the kid who actually caused the entire situation? What happened to the rest of the students involved in the fighting?" I ask, furious. Harold sighs heavily, leaning back against the counter and crossing his arms; he looks like Eisen when he does this.

"Part of the deal is that if you do this, all the other half-breed students won't be punished. Don't you see the strategy in this, Sierra?" he asks; he's in lawyer mode now. "Belinda Harper is making a power play as the new principal of a very prestigious institution, and she wants to make an example of you, while at the same time showing what she sees as mercy. This is day three of your attendance at this school, and already you have been the source of or a relating factor in more than one dramatic situation. She sees you as a rebel; she thinks you won't do it, but if you write an apology to this ridiculous human, it is certain that he will show the document off, and the rest of the half-breeds who were starting to look up to you for being a dissenter will lose interest and back off."

"Because I groveled like everyone else," I realize bitterly. I'm so disgusted with everyone in charge at my new school I'm almost tempted to take the suspension. But I know if I leave school even for a day or two, I won't be willing to go back. Waiting a year to transfer and falling behind isn't an option I'm willing to consider.

"You can't expect her to write an apology to this little puke, Harry," Eisen bursts out angrily. "It's not in the fighting Maurell code!"

"I thought you said we weren't calling ourselves that," Wade says as he punches Eisen's arm.

"I'm resigned to it sticking around now," Eisen sighs, slapping Wade on the back of his shaggy-haired head. I half expect them to be rolling around the floor the next minute, fighting like fox pups do.

"I don't expect her to write the apology, Eisen," Harold interjects before the familial violence can get out of hand. "Because I wrote it myself while I was on the phone. I think you three will find it satisfactory," he says. He strides over to the kitchen table and picks up a sheet of standard recycled paper. I recognize the elegantly slanted, thin writing decorating it from where I'm standing. I take it from him when he hands it to me, and begin reading. Eisen and Wade come up behind me to read over my shoulder.

I'm blessing Harold repeatedly in my head by the time I finish reading. Every word somehow drips with the deepest sarcasm, and only an idiot wouldn't pick up on the total lack of repentance in this document. Yet, the plain words *do* express an apology, so the basic task has been taken care of. The wattage emitting from Eisen's and Wade's grins as we finish reading is palpable.

"Wow, Harold!" I say, immensely encouraged, although I still feel guilty for involving Harold in any of this in the first place.

"That's quite the way to obey the letter of the law, if not the spirit," Eisen comments, taking the letter from me to admire it on his own.

"You could have done just as well, Sierra, but I didn't want you to do it. There's also a very good chance all of the...content in the note might go over the boy's head—"

"It's enough, Harold," I say gratefully. "It's enough to keep me out of suspension, and the likelihood is that someone will understand the meaning of this letter, so even if the human does show it off like a trophy it won't be a good thing for him. I won't lose my pride."

"Exactly," Harold says, smiling again. "Not that I want you to be a total rebel, but I don't mind people looking up to you." His smile looks less painful, but it's still tired. This time when I feel the urge to hug him, I give in; Harold knows me well, and he's already prepared to receive my embrace before I even get to him.

"Sorry," I mutter into his neck, breathing in his familiar smell of fresh laundry and mild, dusky cologne. He pats my back comfortingly.

"I know...just *really* try to stay out of any more drama next time. I don't know if I can save you like this again; it's a miracle they believed my influence was as powerful as I said it was, and it's miraculous they settled for such an unorthodox punishment," he says. After a moment we release each other, and I hurriedly wipe away any moisture leaking from the faintly slanted corners of my eyes before Eisen or Wade can comment on my tears.

"We should probably go, Eisen," I say to my golden brother as I take back the letter he and Wade finally finished appreciating. "While you're going to put a shirt on, grab me a pop tart, will you? The cherry kind, not maple and cinnamon."

"I'm taking you today, not Eisen. His shift changed times today, so I'm heading to work first," Harold says. I smile at my eldest brother, nearly missing the pop tart package Eisen chucks at me from the other side of the kitchen. One of the tarts is already missing. Eisen blesses me with a parting wave, my other pop tart between his teeth, and I stick my tongue out at him as he goes to leave the kitchen area.

"A few parting words, guys," Harold speaks again. He's left both lawyer and brother mode behind, and now he's entering into father mode. This side scares me a little because he so rarely uses it. Eisen comes back into the kitchen as he begins scarfing down his stolen breakfast.

"I don't want to cause unnecessary worry, but some things are happening that I think you all should be aware of as you go through your days," he says with a tinge of darkness in his voice. "Tensions rise high where I work, and because I'm a lawyer I know about things. I take care of cases that give me an exclusive look at what's going on between M-DNA people and the purists."

"Yes, we know, Superman," Eisen mutters through a mouthful of food.

"Eisen," Harold says in his special why-can't-you-be-serious-for-three-seconds voice. Eisen doesn't speak again.

"I want you to know—especially you, Wade—times are changing. Very few people are happy with the desegregation laws, mostly because they've caused an unprecedented raise in taxes. We half-breeds may be happy with a few of the changes taking place, like the government funding and the equality movements, but the humans outnumber us, and next to none of them are pleased with the changes. Some privileges are in danger of being taken away already."

"Why warn *me* to be more careful?" Wade asks with a touch of defensiveness.

"Because you...well, Wade you are simply a more obvious target because your animalistic features are more prominent than anyone else in our half-breed community," Harold says.

"And you're a more violent person anyway," Eisen adds. Wade glares angrily at the ceiling, growling quietly as he perhaps prays for patience. He's clearly trying not to voice what he's thinking, but I can't help but agree with Harold.

The best thing to do is to keep Wade out of the public eye...but that's hardly possible, I think. I still feel for my brother though...after the past two days, I completely understand why blending in without trouble is so difficult.

"I want you all...there's no one thing you can do to stay safe, but I'm asking all three of you to *keep out of trouble*. It's hard, I know it is. But I've been doing it for years, and now is the time to pursue caution over equality. At least until everything calms down again," Harold says.

He doesn't say anything to conclude the conversation, but all of us know there's nothing else to say, so we depart to go about our business. My ride to school with Harold is quiet, but one thought has taken the place of the older ones tromping the paths of my mind last night.

If. If everything calms down again.

10

The first thing I notice when I walk in to school is Lyle standing in front of my locker. None of my other friends have arrived yet, since Harold dropped me off earlier than Eisen normally does. Other half-breed students meander about the hallway; most of the lockers have been cleaned off, but I also notice that it was not the janitorial squad who took care of the mess. Grubby paper towels soaked in water and covered with paint streaks litter the floor in what I recognize as a responsive rebellion to our predicament being ignored.

In the excitement of the fighting yesterday, I forgot to tell my brothers about this particular incident...but I'm not sorry. They don't need any extra drama from my side at this point.

"Hey," I say to Lyle as I approach my locker; he's

wearing another baseball cap, this one plain but bright blue. "What's up?"

He turns around, and I wince strongly. Half-breeds heal fast, but not so quickly that two black eyes, a fat lip, and a scraped face go away overnight.

"It's not as bad as it looks," he assures me as he lifts a hand to touch one of the scrapes on his face; bruises decorate his knuckles as well. "Besides—"

"—the other guy looks worse?" I say quickly. I don't want Lyle to think I'm having a girly freak-out; I've seen worse scars on my brothers from all of their fights—most of which they won, as long as they fought on the same side—and I expect to see a lot of battered looking people today.

"Exactly." Lyle smiles, and I wish he hadn't; I'm worried the scab on his lip is going to crack open and bleed. "You're okay? That guy was a total ass with you yesterday."

"I'm fine. I'm more worried about the aftermath of everything else..." I say; I'll tell him about the whole apology letter and my sacrifice to get everyone out of trouble once Morgan, Shelby, and Ivar show up so I don't have to explain more than once. "Hey, how did you get out of trouble?"

Lyle shrugs. "The principal didn't seem as interested in all of us who were fighting as a whole...not that she didn't care. I think most of us might have detentions coming up, and the humans just have to take notes home to their parents..."

"Which is grossly unfair!" I interrupt, outraged. The parents who send their kids here won't get their kids in trouble, that's for sure. Hopefully my letter will take care of the half-breed detentions at least.

Lyle nods in acknowledgement and continues. "Harper was definitely more interested in the original sin, as it were. I didn't tell her anything condemning about you, but I know someone did. I'm sure it didn't take her very long to get the whole story after that."

"Hello!" I hear Shelby's breathy voice before I see her, along with Ivar's lumbering steps reverberating through the ground as both of them approach me and Lyle. I expected Ivar to look as beat up as Lyle, but I guess Ivar is the safer fighter. The sheer size of him must be advantageous: he only has scraped up hands.

"How are you guys?" I ask them both.

Ivar smiles at me fondly. "Fine and dandy, thanks."

Shelby ogles my locker. "Wow, that was a fast clean-up," she says in a surprised tone. I follow her gaze, and it surprises me when I see only a few black paint smudges left on the surface of my locker.

"I thought the custodial crew was supposed to take care of this mess?" I phrase my thought as a question. I look down and see the bucket full of dirty water on the floor, as well as the mountain of paper towels on the ground, and I know why Lyle was standing in front of my locker.

"Wow, thanks Lyle," I say, really touched that my friend got here early to clean up a mess I probably wouldn't have time to get to until after school. He grunts something that sounds like a "you're welcome" and gazes at me with leonine intensity.

"I helped!" Morgan sashays around the corner, cheerfully inserting herself into the conversation. Her eyes fall on Lyle first before switching over to me, and I observe how Lyle's eyes don't shift in her direction away from me. "I was just taking some of the used towels to the garbage," Morgan says, amping up the power on her cheerfulness.

"Thanks to both of you, then," I say as Ivar puts his arm around Shelby, and whispers something in her ear. She murmurs something back, and they say their temporary farewells before heading off to class early.

"Well, that was abrupt," Lyle remarks curiously. "I guess they have a scheduled make-out time or something now." Morgan giggles, blushing attractively.

"Wouldn't surprise me," she says, shaking her head so her long, dark hair sways with the movement. I feel awkward with where this conversation is going, but I don't want to bring up my news and drag the mood down.

Plus, I'm starting to get a few vibes from Morgan that she wants me to back off from Lyle. I don't want to test our budding friendship over her semi-obvious crush on someone I'm not interested in.

"Well, the rest of this trash won't take care of itself. I'll see you guys in class," Lyle says. He and Morgan exchange some banter as he wrestles with the heap of disposable towels, but eventually he departs. Morgan and I stand in the hallway, watching him walk away.

"Wow, he has such a crush on you!" she blurts gleefully as soon as he's out of earshot.

"Wait, what?" I blink at her, totally surprised by her gusto. *Did I read the vibes wrong?* "I've only known him, like, three days," I say blandly, watching her face for an indication of where she's going with this. She shakes her head hurriedly, mocking my lack of romanticism.

"I know how Lyle acts when he's interested," Morgan tells me confidently.

"I...I kind of thought, you know, you and Lyle had a thing..." I don't know where I'm taking that thread of conversation; I trail off and leave it to her interpretation.

"You thought me and Lyle were an item? Oh, *heck* no!" she says brightly; I want to ask why, but she doesn't give me a chance to speak. "Anyway, listen, I have proof! Yesterday when you ran off and I went upstairs to check on...things, I saw Lyle fighting with Bryan. When I caught up with him later last night, he said Bryan tried to go after you when you walked away, and Lyle stopped him. Isn't that proof enough?"

"Well—" I begin.

"*And* he cleaned your locker! That's double proof!" she says. I don't know why she looks so triumphant, with her gleaming dark antlers tall
over her sleek hair, but she does. Meanwhile, I'm confused. The information she's feeding me seems too extraordinary for my emotions to digest...Lyle as an admirer?

"You said you helped too," I say. *Can we please talk about something else now?* I think desperately as Morgan waves one slender hand in the air dismissively.

As if on cue from the gods of luck, a half-breed girl walks up to us with a big smile on her face. I recognize her by her hair first; she's the girl I saw across the room, the one with the scarlet parrot feathers in her hair. This time another girl is with her; she has tiny scales on her face the color of gleaming silver. Both of them have a bronze-like hue to their skin that makes them look

Egyptian.

"Hello, ladies," parrot girl says; her voice is deep and throaty, but her eyes seem jovial and friendly in spite of their bird-like perception. "My name is Femi, and my sister here is—"

"—Hasida. Wonderful to meet you," the girl with the scales finishes her sister's sentence.

"This is my friend Morgan, and I'm—" I get cut off by Femi, who laughs airily.

"I know Morgan, and we already know who you are, Sierra. You're kind of hard to miss when you march in through the front doors and back-hand a human into a locker," she says, her yellow eyes scanning my face. She makes it sound like both of those events occurred simultaneously, like I marched into the school ready for combat. Hasida watches me too, though her reflective, metallic eyes occasionally flick over to a silent Morgan.

"Why is everyone so impressed with the back-hand?" I mutter, wondering aloud. Then my manners come back to me, and I try to be polite again. "Well, most of that wasn't exactly stuff I was intending to do, so..."

"It was still brilliant," Hasida says, smiling. I notice how fashionably dressed she and her sister are, with their slim fit jeans and their colorful tops with the cut-out sleeves. I feel a mildly unpleasant wave of regret regarding my apparel choices this morning; I am a common woodland animal standing between two exotic, interesting creatures.

"Um...thanks," I say, feeling awkward.

"No problem," Femi says, laughing a little as she

brushes some of her hair out of her eyes with a surprisingly talon-less hand. "Anyway, school sucks, so my sister and I are throwing a party tomorrow night."

"Not tons of people, just all the upperclassmen and some people we know from around here," Hasida says. It's a given that when she mentions "upperclassmen" and "people," she means exclusively half-breeds. Femi continues her original thought.

"We'd love it if you could come, Sierra. I think you'd enjoy this party," she says.

"Really?" I say before I catch myself; I probably sound like such a dork. The people I'm typically friends with never hosted parties, so a real high school party is going to be a new experience for me.

"She means both of us will be there," Morgan says for me, smiling at Femi and Hasida. "Sounds awesome...just call me later and you can give us the details!"

"Wonderful!" Femi burbles. "We'll see you there, then."

The two minute bell before we all have to be in homeroom rings in the hall, as obnoxious in volume as ever. As abruptly as they came, the two sisters wave a farewell as they walk to the end of the hallway where I assume their lockers are. I glance over at Morgan, a slow smile creeping onto my face.

"Did we just get invited to a real high school party?" I ask her. She smiles too, something that looks happier than when she was talking to me before Femi and Hasida showed up.

"You've never been to one?" she asks curiously as we begin walking up the hall to the half-breed room. I shake my head.

"I didn't get the chance to go to many parties," I tell her. "Harold was lenient with me and my brothers growing up, but one of his rules was no unsupervised parties until I'm a junior in high school. He was worried about the drinking and too many animals in the menagerie, let's say."

"Wow...I bet that was annoying. But now you're a senior, so it doesn't matter," Morgan says. "But do you know what this means?"

"I actually have fun plans this Friday?" I ask sarcastically. She laughs and nudges my shoulder with hers.

"No, it means that you've been accepted as one of the leaders here!" she says. "How does it feel to be popular?"

"Um, where are you getting any of that information?" I say; I almost add something about this information being as crazy as her idea that Lyle fancies me, but my brain-to-mouth filter kicks back into gear in time for me to keep that thought to myself.

"I already got the invite and so did Lyle, Ivar, and Shelby...over SMARTtext. It's not a big deal, really, but I knew Femi and Hasida back in junior high, and they always have epic parties. They made a point to invite anyone they saw as important in person," she tells me. I wrinkle my nose, not sure if I like that idea.

"That's very...elitist of them," I say. "Not that I'm looking down on them, it's just—"

"—yeah, I know. What can I say? They've always been that way," Morgan shrugs; I'm glad she agrees with me. "Something about how they were raised, I guess. Their parents are politicians in the half-breed community, so that must be a contributing factor. Anyway, their parties are worth it, trust me."

"We'll see," I reply. "Why do they think I'm popular?" We're in our homeroom now, and Marlow Hynes is actually present before the bell rings. He appears a little more presentable, but not much; at least he shaved, and he's not weaving quite as obviously. Morgan checks in, and then leans against the counter the machine rests on as I enter my ID into the humming machine.

"You are going to come, right? It's going to be a really cool party," Morgan says, trying to convince me. There's no need; I already intend to go. I notice she didn't answer my question, though.

"I have to ask Harold about it, but I'm pretty sure he'll say yes," I tell her. Ivar and Shelby enter the classroom as I finish with the machine.

"You're going to the party?" Shelby asks with unconcealed excitement, confirming what Morgan said about everyone else being invited first. Ivar has his large arms around her spindly waist as she checks in, and her head appears almost doll-like with the clear brown skin and sleek curls.

"Yeah, if I can," I say.

"Good. We weren't sure if you got the SMARTtext," Shelby says. "But I didn't think you'd be excluded, since that just wouldn't be fair."

"Femi invited her personally," Morgan boasts, smiling at me proudly. I'm glad she approves of me, but I would appreciate less emphasis on that part.

"Of course she did! The rebel queen has to be

there for it to be a party," Shelby says, releasing one of her characteristic snorts.

"Rebel queen?" I ask. "What—"

"Talking about that damn party again, are you?" Lyle asks as he reenters. He grins at me, and I smile back as a weird sensation makes my stomach feel like it's sinking. I'm not unexcited about the party; it's exactly the opposite. But I wish I was invited because I'm wanted, not because of my apparent social standing. Morgan subtly nudges my arm again after Lyle smiles, and I resist the urge to sigh.

I haven't decided how to deal with that yet, I think in her direction, knowing full well she would still ignore me even if I spoke aloud.

The bell rings again, so we all hurry to our seats. Our instructor begins the arduous process of taking roll, and I don't have time to observe him further before I feel someone tapping on my shoulder. It's Shelby.

"No 'family meeting' today, huh?" she asks. The thought didn't occur to me, but I share her curiosity once I consider the idea.

"You're right, it seems weird that we're not having one," I say. "Maybe she thought it was too soon for another assembly meeting?"

"I don't know...she seems like the type who would want to flaunt her control as much as possible," Shelby says. I sense her doubt, and then I remember why Belinda probably isn't bothering with an assembly meeting.

The letter. There's a sinking feeling in my gut as I think of the neat, folded piece of paper with Harold's rushed penmanship decorating it resting innocently in my bag. I want to tell someone about it, if only to boast about how amazing Harold is. But at the same time, I don't want word to get out; the awful thing shouldn't even be required, or it shouldn't be a one-sided deal.

I don't desire further interaction with people like Katrina and Bryan, but a badly spelled, short apology letter from the human who insulted me wouldn't be unsatisfying. At least Belinda's handling of the situation would be equal.

"So...Lyle must like you, huh?" Shelby comments after Marlow Hynes concludes roll with a long sigh and moves on to announcements. There's never anything interesting for announcements here; important information would be relayed over the intercom system.

"What?" I ask Shelby incredulously, turning so I can see her face. She's smiling like it's a joke as she pats her dark hair, and I'm glad she's not manically happy— desperately cheerful, rather— like Morgan was when she brought up the same topic.

"Don't worry, I'm not going to harass you about it. Ivar noticed first, but I think I agree with him after what happened yesterday," she says.

"It seems like everyone is reading a lot into that moment," I feel like an idiot for not picking up these mysterious signs along with everyone else.

"It was pretty cool that Lyle stepped in and stopped Bryan once that other redheaded human followed you." Shelby doesn't realize it, but I'm more interested in the redheaded human who followed me than in whatever gallant action Lyle took. I choose my next words carefully.

145

"Oh?" I'm not sure how to question her about who else came after me without expressly asking. "He probably wasn't the only one...that was a pretty tense scene," I hope she'll explain further anyway.

"Yeah, but Lyle sucker punched him in the gut. Ivar had to step in after that; the humans got so mad. That's when the fighting really started," she says, rolling her eyes. "Most of the girls were just watching the men fight; it's so dumb. No one needed to get in trouble at all, but I guess they had to battle for their honor or something equally stupid."

"I know a good sized group of people got in trouble, but I'm glad that hallway was relatively under-populated," I say. I'm resigned to not getting any more information about the human; I didn't tell Shelby or Morgan about my encounter with Duncan, and I'd rather they not get curious about what I did during my run-away time yesterday.

Shelby wants to question me more about my thoughts on Lyle's interest, but I purposefully face forward in my seat to end the conversation. I need time to think about this relationship prospect on my own before I convey my thoughts to others. Plus, the first person I would want to talk to about a boy would be Hayley. Morgan and Shelby are nice, but I don't know them well enough yet to trust my feelings to them.

11

Bryan and Katrina's expressions turn from smug to shocked as I approach them right after Sociology; they were locked into a discussion, flirting expertly as Bryan leaned casually against his locker. Judging from their frowns, they thought I'd be expelled by now, or at least suspended.

Think again, I send the thought in their direction. Katrina crosses her arms and glares at me, every inch of her petite, narrow body screaming aggravation. Bryan stands beside her, stiff as a corpse.

I grit my teeth, telling myself to get it over with, and so far my nerve hasn't failed. My friends know about the "apology" letter, since throughout the morning classes I apprised them of what was going on. Morgan and Shelby were sufficiently horrified, and Lyle suggested I cut the drama and slip the stupid thing into his locker. I like to believe I do have a little pride about myself, so it's me handing it to him, or I'm not doing it at all.

If I have to do this, I want everyone to see it, I think. *I want everyone to know that I'm only doing this because the school required it. Then word can get out that I'm doing this to save their asses from suspension.*

Now I stand in front of the two people I dislike the most, wishing I could melt into the floor. The lights in the hall make me feel like I'm onstage again: everyone standing around conversing as they get stuff from their lockers won't ignore this scene for long.

"Why are you still here?" Katrina asks me.

"Same as you," I tell her like she's stupid. "School."

"It's not as if that matters for people like *you*," she says, glaring at me as if daring me to argue.

Difficult as it is, I try to ignore her; she's not the reason I'm within spitting distance of Bryan. I notice with relish that his face looks pretty bad; humans don't heal like M-DNA people. My slap yesterday left a good mark...along with the damage other fighting did, like random scratches and one very dark black eye.

"Here," I say to Bryan, holding up the letter. I feel like this is a silly, old-fashioned thing to do, which is infuriating. *Belinda probably wanted a physical copy involved so I couldn't get away with a private SMARTnote,* I think bitterly. I don't know if he'll take the document, but I make sure people see me giving it to him. "I'm required to give this to you if I want everyone to stick around Hostetler. Maybe you can use it to teach yourself to read."

At least pretend *you care a little,* I chide myself.

"That's it? You wrote a letter?" Bryan asks, incredulity coloring his words with disgust.

"Don't get all sentimental," I snap. Katrina glares at me and snatches the letter from my hand before Bryan can take it. Her skin brushes against my fur, but thankfully she's too angry to react beyond a shiver of repulsion. I predict the outrage she's going to feel, and I hope she'll voice it after she finishes reading. That way everyone in this hall will know I didn't give in, not really.

Bryan reads over her shoulder, but he keeps glancing up at me. I have to admit, he and Katrina make a good-looking pair; they're both smart, decent looking people. However, the angle of her profile is too severe to be truly pretty, and there's nothing about this human bully I find attractive or redeeming. Katrina's dark eyes narrow behind her thick glasses as she reads. Some of the half-breeds depart with the haste of those wishing to avoid trouble.

"*That* is utter rubbish, and if you think the school is going to accept this as an apology, you're as stupid as you seem," she snarls acidly, crumpling the paper in her fist. I shrug, showing how little her words affect me.

"I don't care what you do with the letter. I wrote it, he read it, and there are witnesses. That's all that matters," I say.

"You really think this is going to fly?" Bryan asks. "You can't just start a riot and then write an 'apology' letter as your only penalty." In some ways, I agree with him. It *does* seem too easy...while at the same time, it's too much. I resent Belinda for using this strategy to force me to submit, and I resent her for not punishing

Bryan at all for his part in the debacle yesterday.

"Take it up with Harper if it's such a problem. I don't make the rules," I feign nonchalance.

"We will," Katrina assures me, before grabbing Bryan's arm and walking away in a huff. I blink, surprised she just gave in—well, for *her* it was giving in—and left. I didn't have to do much of anything at all.

Thanks, Harold, I send him a mental message as I stomp down the hall to get my food. My friends wanted to wait for me, but I told them to go on. I didn't need anyone who was feeling particularly hostile—specifically Lyle and Ivar—nearby for that.

Maybe this means my semester will go well after all, I think optimistically. Hunger plucks at my gut, making my stomach growl; the leftover chicken spaghetti I packed last night is calling my name.

"Hey," someone addresses me, and my ears prick up in recognition of the voice. My tail quivers into a slow wagging motion, but I halt that particularly immature reaction. *Weird...*

"Hey, Duncan," I pause, turning to face my human ginger friend. I recognize his locker a second later and him standing near it. He casually leans his shoulder against the metal door with his arms crossed, the picture of teenage relaxation. The short sleeves of the school-issued sport t-shirt embrace the defined muscles on his arms handsomely, and his wide smile is friendly.

"What was that about?" he asks me. I communicate the short version of events. He's a good listener, very good; I almost feel like I'm talking to Eisen. As I speak, Duncan's eyebrows arch with incredulity; I'm positive that his outlook on the situation resounds favorably with mine.

"So let me get this straight: all that fighting went on yesterday, mostly among the guys, and the administration blamed you. Instead of a normal suspension, though, they made you the scapegoat and forced you to write an apology letter to the person who provoked you as your only punishment?" He's astonished and his smile has disappeared in favor of a scowl that makes his bright eyes darker.

"I don't quite understand it either..." I say. "I mean, I'm not complaining about not getting suspended along with half of my class, but still..."

"Any normal school would have suspended you for a few days for your part, but then everyone else would have received the same treatment," Duncan says, thinking aloud. "The whole thing is ludicrous...a letter? Really?"

"I know," I say miserably, plucking at a seam in the hem of my shirt.

"I'm sorry. You're probably tired of rehashing all of this by now," Duncan says. I'm glad he picked up on my feelings: dwelling on aspects of my life I can't change is frustrating. "It's good you're not suspended though. Your brother sounds like the coolest father figure ever, since he wrote the letter on his own." He lowers his voice a little so the few people left in the hall won't overhear, and I'm oddly distracted by the deeper tone his voice develops. I dare to meet his gaze, but then I have to work to concentrate on what he's saying.

Stop it! I firmly instruct my mind. *Why did I even tell him any of this?* I just gave away a secret that could get me in trouble, which isn't the best feeling.

"Um...I'd appreciate if you didn't spread that around—" I try to cover my mistake. The left corner of his mouth tilts up as he shakes his slightly shaggy head, cutting off my appeal.

"Don't worry. It's not like I talk to anyone in that group anyway," he says, shrugging. "I kind of prefer talking to people who are real friends," he says.

"Me too," I reply brilliantly, brushing my bangs out of my eyes. He reaches up and rubs his hand over the back of his neck with a quick swipe; I think it's a nervous habit. I feel horribly awkward again, but I don't understand how it can be so easy and yet so hard to talk to this particular boy. Aside from occasionally not knowing what to say, I feel more comfortable talking to him than I do when I'm talking to my new half-breed friends. I like our conversations the most out of anyone else here, even when I know this whole "friendship" will probably end in tears.

Time to tone it down, I think. *Much safer this way.*

"Anyway...where are you headed now?" he asks me before I can make my exit. We've begun walking in no particular direction without me realizing it. The hallway is virtually deserted by now, but some of the teachers take lunch in their classrooms. I hope they don't notice me and Duncan walking together, simply because I don't want any more hostile vibes today.

"Lunch with my friends. I'm pretty sure I know where they are, but it might take me a few minutes to find them," I reply. "I guess I'm directionally challenged."

"You guys don't eat in the cafeteria?" he asks, and I cringe; I'm not sure if he knows about the infamously

152

gross cafeteria meant for the half-breeds students, and I don't want to enlighten him.

"Not on nice days. It's still early fall and the weather's warm, so why waste the sun?" I sigh with relief when he nods and doesn't push the issue.

"True. I think we're going the same way, so do you mind if I walk you to where you're going?" He's being polite, and very carefully inoffensive. I wonder why he's making the effort, but I'm inexplicably happy that he's trying.

Precisely at the wrong moment, my mind travels back to when Morgan told me about Lyle proving his interest in me. I try to find any sign of Duncan perhaps being a little interested in me, but the more rational part of my brain attempts to block those thought trains before they leave the mental station.

As you've said about Lyle already, you've only known this human boy for three days, I lecture myself sternly. I've fallen silent for longer than I should have. A faint blush creeps over my cheeks, but I shake back my hair and ignore my shyness.

"That's nice of you to offer, but...my friends expect just me today." I don't know how to convey that if I walked up to my friends with Duncan in tow, the whole episode would probably end with snide comments and more fisticuffs. Also, I don't know what else to think of his offer besides how it was considerate of him to extend it...but I know what I *want* to think about it.

This scares me. *He may be a bit of a friend to you, but how does he feel about half-breeds in general? About half-breeds who obviously loathe humans?* I think with the faces of Lyle, Ivar and even feisty Shelby

153

in my mind.

He seems to understand, though. "That's fine. Maybe we can hang out some other time?" He's watching me, I can tell even though I'm not looking directly at him. *Well, this is an interesting development,* I think curiously as I gaze up at him speculatively.

"Seriously?" I ask. My ears perk up, as does my tail, and I'm intent on what he'll answer. I half expect him to laugh, or blow it off like he was joking, but he doesn't. However, he does look surprised at his own daring. He's blushing slightly—thank goodness I'm not the only one—but he doesn't recant.

"Yeah. It's hard to make friends only in school. The atmosphere is too..." he trails off, searching for the right word.

"...tribal?" I provide. He nods, looking a little more at ease.

"Yeah, that. Anyway...so could I see you sometime?" He asks again, seeking confirmation. My voice fails, suddenly unwilling to cooperate with me, so I confine my response to a nod.

We linger at the end of the hallway, facing each other and standing just close enough for our personal space bubbles to touch. My brain feels like this is the wrong place because we're too close to the main entrance for my preference; I feel nervous around this area because of the trouble I got into with Belinda. I assure myself that's why my voice isn't functioning correctly, and also why my face glows like the rising sun.

"What time works best for you?" Duncan asks. The sun shining through the glass of the main doors reflects on his red hair distractingly. His eyes are very bright green, but in this light they have specks of gold and brown that I missed before.

"I'm not busy the rest of this week," I say. *You really should've thought this through, Sierra,* I lecture myself. It doesn't do much good; my subconscious is dancing with delight. *This is not a date,* I remind it firmly, picturing a bucket of icy water pouring over me so I stop feeling so thrilled.

Duncan seems surprised by my answer, like he expected me to hedge around the issue, making him work harder to get any result. He's not displeased, though.

"All right," he says, relieved. Somehow, his excitement as he speaks is contagious. "Well, how about—"

"Sierra!" Lyle's voice startles me enough that I about jump out of my skin. My senses—enhanced thanks to my fox DNA—normally alert me when other people enter or exit a place where I am. But only if I'm paying attention, and I haven't been focused on anyone else since Duncan said hello.

"Hey, Lyle," I turn my back to Duncan as Lyle comes down the hall towards us. "What's up?"

My half-breed friend's customary baseball cap is missing right now, so I see his hair for the first time. It's shaggy and curly and very pale blonde, which contrasts his tan skin pleasantly; he doesn't have mountain lion ears after all. He looks wilder than Duncan, almost as wild as Wade does with his angular fox features.

"Shelby sent me to look for you," Lyle offers by

way of explaining his appearance. He looks confused as to why I'm socializing with a human as he prowls closer; his eyes flick back and forth between me and Duncan as we stand by the main entrance doors. I wonder if he's trying to catch a distress signal from me; for some reason I find his concern annoying.

I realize abruptly that Duncan and I are standing a tiny bit too close together. Flustered, I step back. Since normally I'm very conscious about personal space, the fact that I wasn't paying attention to that either...*stop*, I think quickly.

"Thanks. I'll be right down," I say. My voice functions, but it's too breathy. Lyle and Duncan stare each other down in a macho sizing-up match I don't care to understand.

This is silly. I fully understand masculine tension, thanks to being raised almost exclusively with my brothers, and I thought I knew how to deal with a situation like this outside of the family level. *I guess not.*

"Bye, Duncan," I say as I walk towards Lyle. I don't want to leave Duncan without finishing our *very* interesting conversation—and whatever plans we may or may not have been making—but I also don't want Lyle to say or do anything to cause trouble. I can't predict what Duncan would do if Lyle decided to act as hostile as he looks, but when I chance a look at the redhead's face, I'm pleased with what I see. He doesn't look angry or terribly offended by Lyle's presence, except in a way that's understandable considering how he and I were rudely interrupted. A bemused smile quirks the left corner of his mouth, distracting me again.

"See you around, Sierra," Duncan calls after me, and my lips betray me so I smile like an idiot. Lyle might still be gazing at me with those perceptive feline eyes, though, so I hastily conceal my grin before he notices.

"Sorry I took so long," I say to keep things light. I'm still disgruntled with the awkward scene that just passed, however, so I decide to let Lyle struggle a bit to keep the conversation going.

"It's fine. I just wanted to make sure you weren't in trouble," Lyle replies as we head for the stairs leading down to our hall. He sounds much happier than he did while he was glaring at Duncan, but I'm annoyed. *If he'd waited five more minutes...*

"So what were you and Ledford talking about?" Lyle asks me; to his credit, he makes an effort to not sound suspicious. I shrug nonchalantly, looking over at the wide, lion-ish shape of his face.

"Nothing really. Just school stuff," I say. My lie sounds hollow, and I cringe inside. Lyle studies me, but I keep my expression serene, and he changes the subject. But I'm not invested in the conversation, and I should be taking this short time alone with Lyle to consider what Morgan told me. But somehow my thoughts remain fixed on Duncan.

12

School ends without any further embarrassment, which feels like a big accomplishment for me. I'm outside with Morgan and Shelby, waiting for either Harold or Wade—Eisen is working late—to come pick me up. The afternoon sun shines strong on my hair and shoulders as I lounge on one of the three rusty metal benches lined up along the sidewalk. The weather has begun to release the barest tinges of cool fall temperatures, which I'm grateful for; I've always preferred autumn over any other season.

It's only been a few minutes since classes let out, but barely any students wander around outside. One or two unlucky half-breeds must stay late to finish cleaning up their lockers before they get in trouble with the establishment, but everyone else went home already.

This is proof that Belinda has honored our arrangement so far: I give the letter to Bryan, and no one else gets punished.

Morgan and Shelby also await their rides because none of us fit the age requirement for half-breeds to drive.

"Do you ever go home with Ivar, Shelby?" I ask my friend as she joins me on my bench and slouches into a more comfortable position. She hasn't been very happy all afternoon, not since one of the toxically pretty human girls walked by and told her she looked like a walking brillo pad. So far it's been hard to cheer her up, but this time she responds to the conversational tidbit I've thrown her.

"Sometimes," she shrugs. "We typically do better on our own, although it's nice to have a driver sometimes so we can go on actual dates. His family doesn't understand why he's dating me."

"Why is that?" Morgan asks curiously, echoing my own thoughts. She and I exchange glances as Shelby explains.

"Well...look at us. Mixing up half-breed DNA pairs is fine, but black bear and standard poodle DNA?" She doesn't seem aggravated about having
to spell it out for us.

"You'd think as long as he dated a half-breed and not a human, they'd be happy," Morgan says as she rolls her eyes. "Do they have any other problems, or do they tend to be negative?"

"Not really," Shelby replies, shaking out her head of black waves. "We've been going out for four months and a few days, so they're more accepting than they were at the beginning. It could be a lot worse than the random confused looks I keep getting from his little sisters and parents."

"Ivar has little sisters?" I ask. Shelby grins.

"Three little sisters. They're all under the age of nine and totally adorable," she says. Shelby doesn't strike me as the type of person who would be fond of children, but she's happy talking about Ivar's siblings. I smile too as I picture her boyfriend tossing a tiny girl with fuzzy bear ears and furry paws into the air.

"Anyway, I think there's enough judging based on appearances in this world, so I'm glad you two are fine," I say, changing the topic back to the original source.

"Yeah...Ivar and I don't really have problems in our relationship. Not serious ones, anyway," Shelby says. Morgan stands beside us rather than sitting, looking noble with her straight posture and doe aspects. The breeze feels pleasant as it teases the strands of my hair—liberated from its hair-tie hours ago—and glides through the exposed fur on my hands and the line of more red fur on my neck.

"So...Lyle?" Morgan asks. Her question comes out of the blue, but I'm not startled by it. She's been hinting around this topic all day, and until now I found excuses to avoid talking about it.

"What about him?" I ask. Morgan huffs, rolling her dark eyes and tilting her head slightly; the sun gleams off her handsome dark antlers. I almost hear Shelby perk up before her inquisitive squeak is audible.

"Oh, come on! He's been subtle, but not *that* subtle. I think he's interested in you; Shelby does too.

What do you think?" Morgan replies. Her manic cheerfulness has returned. I wonder what her real opinion on the subject is, and I wish she would be honest enough to tell me. I don't know her very well, but I *do* know when someone is trying too hard to push an idea on me.

I don't want to know what would happen if she was like this with everything, I think.

"I don't think anything about it," I say truthfully. *Except that I'd rather not discuss my feelings right now.*

"That's hard to believe!" Shelby exclaims. "Femi's and Hasida's party is tomorrow night, so surely you're curious about what might happen?"

"Faintly," I say this hoping it might appease my friends. I have been avoiding talking about this subject purely because I'm not sure how I feel. The one thing I do feel certain about is how I don't want something unstable like a sudden relationship with Lyle to jeopardize my budding ties with my new friends. I have a whole year stuck in this place, and I don't want enemies among the half-breeds as well as my rivals among the human students. I don't even know how Lyle really feels, but I'm sure I don't want that worry added to the mess in my brain.

It's been easy to forget about Lyle, though. My mind has been full of other things today, one of them being a certain redheaded human boy. Part of me wishes I didn't think about him so much.

I wistfully glance up towards the path leading to the main entrance. It doesn't matter which door I enter or exit since all the doors lead to the same place, but the main entryway symbolizes everything about this place I'm unsatisfied with.

Suddenly, as if materializing into physical existence from my thoughts, I hear Duncan's voice behind me. The fur on my neck bristles, but not in an unpleasant reaction; I've been around him enough to recognize his pinewood tinged human scent.

"Sierra?"

I rise to my feet and turn around right as he's coming out of the shabby doors of the half-breed entryway. He looks a little apprehensive about where he is, and I'm embarrassed for the messy, ramshackle hall he had to walk through; the students still inside must have given him very dirty looks. I wonder what he'll think about me and my kind being forced to use such a place when the humans have more access to the renovated facilities upstairs.

I don't say any of this, though; in fact, I'm so busy staring at him that I forget to say anything at all.

"What is he doing *here?*" Morgan exclaims, jolting me out of the reverie I'd tripped into. Her voice isn't loud enough for him to hear, but my ears droop slightly. *Why this hostility?* I think. Her words help me make a decision about what to do, though.

"Hey there," I say to Duncan, taking a few steps towards him away from my friends. I'm nervous, but not so much that I can't shake it off. "What are you doing here?" I ask. My tail is on the verge of twitching again, but I force myself to be calm so it obeys me again.

"I didn't get to set up a time with you earlier for me to see you...plus you said you had anytime the rest of this week free, so do you want to go somewhere?" he says. He's smiling, and I can tell he's nervous too, but

I'm very, *very* glad he asked. I can't help it; I smile back too, probably wide enough so the sharp little points of my canines are more obvious.

"Well, yes, but...my ride should be here any minute to pick me up," I say. I *am* slightly worried about what either one of my brothers would say about me abandoning them to run off with a human, but at the same time...I don't particularly care.

"I can drive you home if you want," Duncan says. I imagine this human boy who can legally drive before I can dropping me off at home. I picture him interacting with the masculine members of my household—especially capricious, overtly animalistic Wade—and I cringe. *Probably* not *the best idea*...I bite my lip, wondering how to tell him so.

"Or I can drop you off someplace where it's easier for you to be picked up?" My anxious expression must have made him change his mind, but it's a good suggestion.

"You must really want to hang out with me," I say wonderingly before my brain-to-mouth filter kicks back into gear. He shrugs his broad shoulders and chuckles mildly.

"Well I'd normally hate to be so abrupt, but I don't know how to contact you other than seeing you at school. Also...I didn't really feel like waiting," Duncan says, our eyes meeting just long enough for some kind of emotional spark to make my right ear twitch with what feels like happiness. My stomach fills with a few stray butterflies.

Maybe I'm really seeing him for the first time, with the sun reflecting off his bright hair and kind eyes.

Somehow in spite of his superior height, it's like he's looking up at me, like he really cares about what I might have to say. Disconcerted, I wonder if I can afford to trust this strapping, green-eyed ginger boy; thus far, this human has been kind to me. I've never known the word "kind" to go with "human" before.

I briefly consider what my brothers would say about trusting a human I barely know enough to get in his car and go somewhere with him, or what my two girlfriends would say to me or tell other people about me leaving with Duncan. I may be adapting to caring less and less about what other people think, but I do care what my brother's would say.

"How about we go to Omnium Beanery? It's a coffee shop my—" I pause; I don't want to give away all my information quite yet; he doesn't need to know I have a brother who works there. "One of my brothers can swing by and pick me up there once we're done."

"Great," Duncan says. "My car is near the east parking lot, so should we go?" I nod an agreement as we begin to walk away. I feel a little wild and carefree about going somewhere with this boy, even for a couple of hours at the most. My brothers probably wouldn't approve of this liaison, however casual it might be, but I dismiss the errant picture of their angry faces with a mental shrug.

"Sierra?" Morgan says, and suddenly I remember that she and Shelby have been standing by the entire time I've been talking to Duncan. I stop walking and turn around slowly; I probably look like a kid who got caught dumping rare books into a bathtub. (Something that I actually did when I was a kid. Thankfully Harold caught me before I got my tiny mitts on the Tolkien collection.)

"Sorry...I got caught up," I say lamely, trying and failing to excuse my rudeness. Duncan has stopped walking too, just a few steps ahead of me, and I feel caught in the middle as Morgan and Shelby stare at him with confused faces. I still don't want to jeopardize relations with my half-breed friends, but when it comes to Duncan...

"I'll see you tomorrow," I say, trying to give Morgan a look that promises more communication at a later time.

I'm the only one who has said anything the last couple of moments, and I resume following Duncan as hurriedly as possible. Morgan and Shelby haven't said a word.

That'll be a pain to deal with tomorrow...if they even bring it up, I think before pushing that idea to the back of my mind. I'm leaving this horrible school with a human boy I barely know, and that's quite enough excitement to be getting on with.

Carter Bowman's regulation vaccine accomplished a great deal in the name of peace for humans and M-DNA people alike, but two significant conflicts continue to take place in the present day of our culture.

1. Regional Conflict — The former United States of America, divided into numbered regions instead of states at the end of Century 22, endured most of the biological warfare trauma perpetuated by the pure DNA extremists. Region 5, comprised of the former states Kentucky, Tennessee, North Carolina, and South Carolina, was hit by attacks considerably more than any other region because of the concentration of M-DNA people who had gathered there to reside before the war. Thus, Region 5 receives most of the Governmental support as well as support from the SMART industry, which was founded in North Carolina.

2. Political Conflict — M-DNA people are still not widely accepted in many areas of the country and the world. Like dark-skinned people in Century 20 and previously, M-DNA people have been relegated to certain parts of the city and have areas they are unable to enter legally. Recent desegregation laws have been issued to right some of these wrongs, but politically the people are just as divided as they were

during the war.

A third conflict, social conflict, is yet to be determined. The results of the desegregation laws are pending, and only time will tell if pure and M-DNA people return to unity on all fronts.

13

Duncan and I have been talking for a little while now, although we were quiet during the walk to his retro car with the plain beige paint job. He has a nice walk: it's a confident, long-legged stride that is solely the property of young men.

We're driving now, and judging from the SMARTvan repair shops, strip malls, and boutiques we've been passing, we're not far from Omnium Beanery. He was courteously silent while I sent a SMARTtext to Harold and Wade, telling them not to pick me up. The excuse I gave them wasn't a lie; I said I was going to Omnium Beanery with a friend, hoping they wouldn't ask how I got a ride, or who I was with. I don't know how to warn Eisen that I'm coming, but I'm just going to wing that situation.

"Your friends seemed a little confused about me," Duncan says as he adjusts the angle of the steering wheel for a turn. So far we've discussed school and trivial matters, but I figured we would come back to the topic of friends eventually.

"That might be a bit of an understatement. I probably should have introduced you all, but I wasn't thinking about that at the time," I say, my half-breed friends' mystified expressions frozen in my head. "Actually, they were just short of being scandalized."

"Scandalized? That's an old-fashioned word," Duncan says. I quickly look at his face to see what he means by that, but he's been glancing at me periodically, so I direct my eyes to the window to avoid eye contact.

"I read a lot...or at least I used to when I wasn't working during the summer." I offer the information casually, wondering if he'll ask more or volunteer information about himself. I kind of want to hear more about his life, even if I keep telling myself it's just friendly curiosity.

"Where did you work? I had a summer job too, but it wasn't much. Selling SMARTtech at a warehouse kiosk probably isn't very exciting compared to what you did," he tells me.

"I wouldn't say that. I have a brother in the SMARTtech business, and he probably thinks sales would be a blast," I say, wanting to be reassuring. "I worked at Summer Greens, the little café and bakery in my town. It wasn't much, but I enjoyed the baking, and the work wasn't too demanding most days."

"You worked at a bakery? Really?" Duncan asks,

laughing. I can't help it; I have to look at him when he laughs because it's a warm, pleasant sound. He looks confident when he's driving, his large hands dwarfing the steering wheel.

"What's so funny?"

"I don't know...It's just easy to picture you working in a place like that, customer service and all," he replies. "I might stop by Summer Greens some time."

"Oh? Why is that?" My question falls during the moment we pull into the not-so-expansive parking lot of the coffee shop that is our destination. I exit the car quickly, but Duncan is faster at getting out. He comes around to my side of the car, and I have another fleeting moment of discomfiture when it occurs to me that he may have wanted to be chivalrous and open my door for me.

Stop it...stuff like that doesn't happen anymore, I tell my smug subconscious.

Unflustered by my haste, he waits for me to pass him as he locks his car. "Do I really look like the kind of guy who needs an excuse to find food?"

"I suppose not," I reply, feeling a smile creep over my lips. "But you probably shouldn't go there, it's...it's really not your kind of place." My smile fades as I consider this. I picture Duncan in my old workplace, the sunny-bright but *tiny* café with my eccentric, "bird-lady" employer.

"How do you know?" Duncan asks conversationally as we walk towards the main door. It's only a small door, yellow and wood-paneled on the side of the building; the designer for this establishment clearly pursued uniqueness over functionality.

"Not many...humans usually venture that far into half-breed areas," I confess. His mouth forms an O as he realizes what I mean, but he doesn't pursue the subject. I wish...for the first time, I really, truly wish that humans—at least *this* human—were allowed into the same places where I'm inclined to spend my time. It's not that it's illegal for a human to go to half-breed establishments...but it sure as hell is discouraged.

I enter Omnium Beanery with my human friend in tow. This is the only kind of coffee shop in the city or surrounding areas where everyone is accepted...or at least, where half-breeds are allowed to linger without being bombarded by glares, rude comments, or both. Thanks to the government desegregation policies, a few places like coffee shops and libraries have been designated as common grounds for all. Theaters, performance halls, churches, and some of the wealthier universities remain out of reach for half-breeds. I wonder if Duncan appreciates the value of this coffee shop to people like me.

As it is, Omnium Beanery isn't particularly crowded this afternoon: a few solitary patrons brood over black coffee in the corners of the room, but otherwise the area is empty. The air here smells different from a regular café: not so much coffee as spiced fruit, or cinnamon, or tangy citrus with the faintest undertone of rich, dark coffee; around Christmas, a strong pine scent infiltrates the shop atmosphere. It all depends on the day, or on how you breathe in.

"Do you spend a lot of time here?" Duncan asks me as we move out of the narrow entryway into the far roomier social area. The concrete floor space is filled with an eclectic, colorful collection of sofas, armchairs, and mismatched kitchen tables with chairs.

"I used to...have you never been here before?" I ask in response, and he shakes his head. I don't visit often anymore, but when Eisen started working here I used to come every day for his company and for the free beverage samples he was able to sneak out for me on occasion. He's moved up to almost assistant manager here now; I lean over to tell Duncan this, but he's too busy looking around to notice me—for the moment. Then I remember I didn't tell him I have a brother who works here.

If Eisen is working at the register today, he eludes my cursory gaze as I look around. I've always loved the beanery, even if I haven't been here much lately, and now I try to view this place like I'm seeing it for the first time. The path to the ordering counter is crooked, blocked in places by the assorted furniture set adrift about the room. As I breathe in the intoxicating and familiar aroma, I can't understand why anyone wouldn't enjoy an afternoon spent in here. Dark, secluded corners with smoky lighting and well-worn leather seats lure the more solitary patrons, while sunny work-stations strategically arranged beside windowed areas charm more social customers. I always preferred the wide open common area, cluttered as it is by tables and chairs of all kinds; the decorations are colorful and quaint, although a few pathetic lawn chairs pollute the mix.

Plus, the drinks are amazing. I idly wonder what Duncan is going to order—I've pegged him as more of the savory than sweet type—as we make our way to the ordering counter.

I've caught Eisen's scent already, familiar and clean with a tang of city-boy flavor, but it's not until he comes out of the green door leading to the back kitchen that I realize my brother has gone into camouflage too. He's actually deigned to wear a hat: a cobalt hipster beanie that makes his blonde hair whiter and his angled, expressive eyes more reflective. The beanie must be more comfortable than a baseball hat or flat-bill cap, but I sense the indignation my brother must feel about having to conceal his fox ears at all. We thought he'd have to pretend to be a human to work in this line of business, since humans might not want a half-breed preparing their food and drink, but the owner of this coffee shop is a decent person—when he's not drinking—and most of the patrons who come here aren't bad either. Eisen must be making the effort for Harold's sake.

Eisen recognizes me as we approach; ordinarily he would be more than pleased to see me at his workplace, but his eyes rapidly travel between me and Duncan in an attempt to understand why I'm with a human.

Alone with a human. A human *boy*.

Eisen opens his mouth to speak, eyebrows arched in disbelief, but Duncan misses the facial cue and speaks before my brother can say a word.

"Hey, do you have any recommendations? I'm looking for something with high caffeine but not much coffee," my redheaded, very human companion asks. I direct pleading eyes towards my brother, shaking my head slightly so he doesn't give me away.

"Probably..." Eisen begins, pausing as he gazes at me with one eyebrow still arched. "Probably our Shivering Whizard. The peppermint will wake you up long before the caffeine even kicks in."

Thank you, I mouth the words to my brother as Duncan orders the Whizard. I know that isn't the end of this, but I did buy myself some uninterrupted time with Duncan. I don't know why this is important, especially since Eisen will take me home as soon as he gets off his shift, but I'm glad anyway.

"Anything for you?" Eisen asks me next, playing the courteous barista perfectly.

"A small Rice Pudding Mixer," I say, recalling the name for my favorite treat. "No raspberry topping, extra cinnamon, and cinnamon infused whip on the top."

"You're very specific," Duncan remarks as Eisen taps my order into the SMARTpad register built into the counter. I shrug.

"I just know what I like," I say. I didn't mean anything by saying that, but Eisen chokes back a rude snort.

"S-Sorry...your order will be up soon. Why don't you two go sit by that partial stained-glass window? Best seats in the house," he rushes, scanning Duncan's pay chip as fast as he can. I was perfectly able to purchase my own drink, but my human friend paid for my order without fanfare...which I kind of like.

"Okay," I say. Anything to escape further awkwardness. Duncan and I head for the area our friendly barista so kindly indicated, and I have to agree that it is one of the best sections in Omnium Beanery.

I sink into a squishy pumpkin colored armchair that happens to have just the right amount of plush left in its soft cushions; my tail curves into my lap by habit. Duncan takes the seat across from me. His lean, muscular form fits comfortably in the wingback chair made of sun-faded charcoal leather.

"You seem to know the barista," Duncan says after a moment of silence. I'm glad he broke the ice—again—but I cringe with embarrassment.

"Was it obvious?" I ask, resisting the urge to reach up and make my fox ears stand up straighter. I think back on the brief conversation, wondering how Eisen gave us away.

"I have a younger sister, so I recognize the older brother type," Duncan informs me; I wonder if he's offended, but his eyes are curious. "I'm assuming he's your brother? That's the vibe I was getting."

"Yeah, that's my brother Eisen. He's the reason I come here sometimes...actually, he's my ride home when he gets done with his shift. Mostly I come for the drinks, though," I say. "You have a sister?"

Duncan glances over at Eisen, then back to me, so there's a delay of his answer. "Yes, I have a sister; her name is Ryella...sorry, I'm trying to catch a resemblance between the two of you," he explains as his gaze finally abandons the order counter.

"It's very subtle...mostly because he doesn't have much fox DNA, not compared to anyone else in our family," I say.

Eisen brings out our drinks: Duncan's Whizard releases a strong, pleasant aroma of herbal mint, and my glorious, calorie-intense Rice Pudding Mixer balances in the center of the tray. I bless my brother as he drops off our drinks without a word and saunters back to his station to continue working. No doubt he'll be giving us the evil eye whenever he's not taking customers.

I take a sip of my drink, humming as the taste of cinnamon and sweet cream fills my mouth along with small kernels of rice. My tail does that funny wagging thing again, but thankfully it rests in my lap so I can hide the tremor. *I hope this isn't becoming a habit,* I ruminate as I watch Duncan take a swig of his drink and examine the recycled cup appreciatively.

"I can sort of tell who the M-DNA people are, even if they wear hats or scarves to cover up the signs," Duncan says as he sinks back casually into his seat, holding onto his cold drink with one pale hand. "Hats are the easiest camouflage to spot though...speaking of hats, I take my hat off to your brother—Eisen?—for this amazing creation."

I smile at his praise for my brother. "There's a reason he's getting promoted soon. Eisen has a gift for the barista business," I say. I wonder what Duncan would think about the rest of my family, but this isn't the time for that conversation; besides, I want to know more about his family.

"How many siblings do you have?" I ask.

"Two: a younger sister and a younger brother. Neither one of them goes to Hostetler though, in case you're wondering. Ryella moved out as soon as she could, and Coby lives with our mom and her husband," Duncan says. He's not any less cheerful, but somehow I get the vibe from his slightly furrowed eyebrows that he doesn't want to pursue this topic any longer. I'm curious about his family, suddenly, if they all share the same red hair, or if they tend towards the same body type.

A distraction slips through the unique door of the café. My nose twitches, catching the scent before I turn around. Sure enough, it's human girl wearing the standard overpowering, fruity perfume.

Ugh. I want to pay attention to Duncan and forget this silly human, so I sit back in my seat and indulge in another long sip of my drink. The twiggy blonde loiters near the door with her friends, perhaps choosing where to sit or reading the confusing and tiny printed menu behind the counter, so Duncan and I talk in peace for a few minutes. But then they stride over to the order counter like they own every brick of this place. Eisen, bored and unconcerned, has been waiting to take their orders, and I stop speaking almost mid-sentence when I allow myself one more glance in their direction.

I already pegged the girl, who looks to be eighteen, as an overtly flirty type, and I wasn't wrong.

"I wonder what she'd say if she knew he was a half-breed," I say, thinking aloud with gritted teeth. *So much for trying to ignore her.*

Duncan, who was learning forward with his elbows resting on his knees, sits up slightly to observe what I'm staring at."She might not know, but I think her friends do."

He's right; while the girl is fluttering her eyes at my brother in a come-hither fashion, her three friends slouch around watching disapprovingly or composing texts on their SMARTcalls. They haven't ordered anything, and they aren't inspecting the menu.

I watch Eisen carefully, more concerned with him than with the pack of silly girls. He's fulfills the blonde's order with the bare minimum of responses to her dallying; I'm thankful for my animal senses that let me hear even from a distance.

"They must have been here before…judging by how hard this girl is trying, anyway," I say, perhaps with more venom than I intended. Duncan seems to understand, although I can't tell because he doesn't reply right away.

I didn't realize until now how little joy my brother apparently takes from human girls, if this interaction is anything to gauge by. Oh, half-breed girls he enjoys; I don't remember the names of all the girls he's brought home. I assume at this point that this girl's flirting is an offense, patronizing and spiteful; I'm glad her friends clearly disapprove of her behavior, even if their reasons probably aren't admirable.

"Sorry," I tell Duncan after one more moment of watching; I return my attention to my drink, taking another sip. "This is distracting."

"I bet….it's okay," he replies. "You and Eisen are really close, then?"

"Yes. Well, all my brothers and I are, so it's hard to watch them get harassed by…anyway, I'm surprised too," I say. "Eisen used to flirt right back when he started working here and getting attention, but now…" I struggle to summarize what I'm thinking. *Things changed. He's grown up.*

"Your ears flop down when you're focused on something," Duncan observes with a smile and cocked eyebrow...something about this expression makes the stray winged creatures jittering around in my stomach flutter again, and I clear my throat.

"Oh? Just a reflex, I guess," I say with a shrug, cursing my wit for abandoning me when I need it.
Now that he pointed it out, I notice one of my ears is flopped down, probably making me look more like a puppy than I prefer.

"What's it like being part fox?" Duncan asks abruptly.

I must seem astonished by the query, because his face colors again, and he clarifies. "I mean...what is it like being M-DNA? Are your senses super heightened? Sorry if the questions seem weird, I—"

"—don't talk to half-breeds much?" I cut in. I'm not offended; this boy seems genuine, which is alluring when I'm used to verbal abuse from humans, particularly human boys and men. I really want to trust my gut feeling of safety with Duncan. *Why?*

Duncan is still trying to cover what he thinks was a mistake. "I'm sorry. It's not usually like me to be this nosy," he says, then kind of smiles and holds up his drink. "Must be the peppermint."

"Must be," I agree, a responsive smile stealing into my expression too.

Careful, Sierra, my thoughts chime in again, warning me....but I don't listen. Instead, I begin to tell Duncan what it's like to be half-breed in a human society.

I don't know where to start or what to say at first, but the conversation becomes easier and more interesting as I continue. My mentions of segregation and the benefits of animal aspects—here I'm more careful with how I describe sensations; I don't know how Duncan will respond to half of what I say—get interrupted by frequent questions, and somehow we end up laughing more than a few times. I marvel at his interest, this attention that is confusing as well as flattering.

"So you can turn off your heightened senses at will?" Duncan asks me once I get around to answering one of his first questions.

"Yes...try to imagine how exhausting or how painful it would be to have all the higher senses that a fox might have cranked up in this noisy, smelly world," I explain as best I can.

"Gotcha. That does sound like it'd be pretty painful," Duncan agrees. I consider his expression, and something seems odd to me. I don't know why, but he looks almost *relieved*.

"It's worth it to keep the animal senses toned down most of the time. I don't need night vision very frequently, and I don't often need to run as fast as my fox DNA would let me," I say. Duncan's expression has returned to normal, and he absentmindedly rubs the back of his neck.

The afternoon sun, formerly drawing patterns on the wall through the stained glass window beside us, has sunk now, and the lighting in this coffee shop turns soothing and kind. I'm more comfortable in my squishy chair now, and both of our drinks are long gone.

"Am I the first half-breed you've ever asked about this?" I ask after a long pause.

"Yes. There's never been opportunity to ask anyone

else," Duncan replies; he leans back in his chair, absentmindedly toying with the recycled lid of his empty cup. "Humans are generally unaccepted in M-DNA circles, so it would probably have been a bad idea to randomly ask someone."

"I wish I could disagree with you, but I can't," I confess, shaking my head. My hair falls forward into my face a little, and I push it back with a hand. Around this one human, I don't feel as self-conscious about the fur on my hands anymore.

"You didn't check out any SMARTvlogs or blogs to find out about this topic?"

Duncan doesn't seem painfully shy, but I'm really noticing how he tends to blush. "I kind of wanted to ask you in particular about it," he says. "The information seems more authentic coming from a direct conversation, and...yeah. I wanted to ask you."

I don't need to keep pushing, but I do. "How long have you been curious about M-DNA life?"

"Probably as long as you've wondered about what it's like to have plain human DNA...so for a while," he admits. He's right again; I have wondered about human life since I've grown up in a mostly M-DNA community.

"Also true...however, you waited this long to ask someone about all this? I'm probably not the best person to ask about half-breed customs and our way of life. Other people can probably explain better, even if the source is a vlog," I say.

"Maybe...but since I met you, I wanted to ask you," Duncan says again. I feel the increasingly familiar swoop of something with the power of flight in my stomach as our eyes meet. I'm not sure if I like this feeling yet, but his eyes attract mine with an unspoken force. I hastily look away before he can notice how very animalistic my yellow eyes are, but I already know how hard it's going to be to get the shade of green his eyes are out of my head.

"Oh," I say wittily. "Well, I—" I don't finish my thought because Eisen waves at me from his counter. This is the signal we used in the past, when I would hang out here at Omnium Beanery waiting for Eisen to get off work.

"You have to go?" Duncan asks me when I turn my attention back to him; he's still lounging in his chair. Even though he's not a half-breed, I picture him as a large, warm-furred canine creature: comfortable for lying around but muscular with both brute force strength and athletic speed. Maybe he would have Rhodesian ridgeback DNA, if he was my kind; his large, gentle hands would be a good match for the paws of the huge dog that was bred to hunt lions. He's different from Lyle; in a feline way, mountain lions are more dangerous creatures with their sharp claws and teeth.

"Yeah, Eisen's going to take off his apron and check out," I answer. I don't know how to return to what I was going to say before I noticed my brother waving, so I busy myself with the arduous task of gathering my school bag up into my arms. It's silent for a moment as Duncan and I rise and walk to the recycling chute built into the wall beside the door to throw away our empty cups.

"Thanks for this afternoon," I finally say. I stand by the door with my human friend, waiting for Eisen to come around. Duncan's expression appears conflicted for a moment, confusing me as to what he's thinking, but then he responds.

"No problem...I enjoyed it," he says, then pauses. "Let's do this again soon? Like, tomorrow?"

I don't answer for a moment because I don't know what to say. My tail twitches again as my ears perk up. Something must seriously be wrong with me for me to be so happy about this, but I try not to think much farther than that.

He wants to see me again! Soon!

I think I forgot to voice my response again, because he resumes speaking again before I answer. "If you don't want to that's completely okay, I just—"

"It's okay, I'd like to," I say, breathless and surprising myself. On the heels of this delight, however, comes a memory that halts my grin. "But...I kind of have a party to go to tomorrow night. It would be really weird if I wasn't there." If I was excited for the party before, that excitement has been considerably mellowed.

"Okay, well—" I'm guessing it's Duncan's fate to be interrupted by other people in my life, because suddenly Eisen sprints through the back door leading out of the employee area and seizes my arm on his way out. I manage one very hasty wave towards Duncan and a breathy "see you at school!" as my brother practically drags me out of Omnium Beanery.

I catch one last glimpse of Duncan coming out of the coffee shop, walking in the direction of his own car. Thankfully he's smiling; I'm glad he's not offended. For some reason, I feel it might hurt if he was upset with me.

Careful, I warn myself yet again.

"That was rude!" I huff at Eisen as we get into the car; he's already torn the beanie off his head, and his hair and the fur on his ears sticks up hilariously. I almost have to laugh, but then I notice my brother's expression, and how his ears angle back with irritation. *Oh.*

It's going to be a long car ride home.

14

Some miracle helped me convince Eisen to keep quiet about what went on last evening at Omnium Beanery. He wasn't happy about staying silent, but he's never been a tattle-tale when it comes to stuff I've done. He'll keep my secret for now, but his grumpy sulking lets me know that he's unhappy about the whole matter. He did have a warning for me: *Don't trust too easily. Humans can be cool sometimes, but typically they only ever view you as a lesser being.*

His advice may have helped me keep my head, as well as the memory of that girl flirting with him, but the words have soured in my stomach. My only course of action is waiting. I want to see how things turn out before I tell anyone in my family beside Eisen about...whatever is going on with me and Duncan. It's not like I have a clue what's going on myself.

All Harold and Wade wanted to hear about when I got home was how the "apology" letter had been received. I didn't say as much as I could have, but they were fine with my information. I feel guilty about keeping secrets from Harold, but I know if he knew I would feel obligated to change my ways. Looking back on everything I know about humans and this one boy, I'm not so sure if I should trust Duncan. But I don't even know how to explain that I *do* trust him in spite of that. So for right now...I'll wait and see. Harold will understand once I work up the nerve to explain.

I have enough problems to mull over as I follow my standard routine Friday morning; the official administrative thoughts about the letter I gave Bryan and what my friends thought about me going off with Duncan after school yesterday are just two. I'm not sure if Morgan and Shelby spread the word, but I'll find out soon enough.

Plus I need to put together an outfit for the party tonight; after pawing through my relatively small wardrobe, I despair of this rather quickly.

My arrival at school is punctuated by the odd looks my friends give me as I arrange my light faux leather jacket on the hook inside my locker door and set my lunch on the top shelf. Lyle makes an effort at conversation with me, which I'm grateful for; Morgan is less chatty, and Ivar and Shelby aren't in sight. The odd tension in the air has set my teeth on edge, and I finally interrupt Lyle midsentence with a slightly over-loud voice.

"Okay, this is *really* dumb! If something is wrong, or

if you have a problem with yesterday—" My words,\
aggravated and sharp, dwindle into silence when I
notice Morgan frantically shaking her head at me while
at the same time trying not to get Lyle's attention. Her
antlers make this a comical picture.

"That doesn't matter, Sierra," she says, the pale
doe spots under her eyes standing out. This, along with
Lyle's bewildered expression, is her way of letting me
know that Lyle *doesn't* know about my adventure with
Duncan yesterday. I'm surprised she didn't tell, but glad
too; it's not really his business anyway.

Morgan's brown eyes study me with some emotion
I can't read, but then her eyes slide over in Lyle's
direction and her expression alters to something kinder.

"Look around," she tells me, and I do. I feel stupid
for not noticing the differences in my half- breed
classmates right away; this is bigger than any tension
that might be lingering between me and my friends
right now.

It's ironic that just as my brother deigns to go
camouflage and wear a hat to work for the first time in
his life, every single M-DNA student here has suddenly
decided to drop their disguises. The muted colors and
all the hats and scarves and jackets I've been seeing
for a few days are nothing compared to the many
shades of color my vision absorbs now. Vivid fur and
feathers and scales and skin patterns are on display
everywhere, and a slow grin creeps onto my face. This
feels like the community I've been raised in. *Home.*

It's an unofficial heritage day for the half-breed
population. Everyone has gone out of their way to
display their animal aspects: wings are folded neatly for

the few students who have bird or bat DNA, and paws and claws and tails and ears—some few with piercings—are on colorful display. Some girls have worn complimentary colors in all shades, and I notice some very outspoken make-up on quite a few feminine faces. I can hardly pay attention to anything else because of this spectacle; I feel underdressed. I made more of an effort with my appearance today and wore a short denim skirt instead of pants, but what I'm wearing isn't particularly stunning.

"Wow," I say, proud of my classmates for finally being brave. "What happened?" I inspect my friends closely. Lyle is still wearing his hat, but something about the lines near his mouth definitely looks more feral; he also hasn't bothered to hide his wiry tail. I look around;

Ivar and Shelby have also followed the new trend of standing out, and even if Morgan couldn't hide her antlers before, she's wearing a very woodsy colored dress to emphasize her deer features.

"Everyone decided to stop hiding," Morgan tells me.

"Why?" I ask. "I mean, why now?"

"Awesome response, Sierra!" someone hails me before my friends answer my question, and I browse the faces around me to find the source of the voice. Femi and Hasida are on their way to our homeroom, and I think it was Hasida who called me. She and her sister are perhaps the most outspoken with their apparel: Femi looks like she's dressed for a tropics-themed masquerade—minus the mask—and Hasida conveys a reptilian feel with her futuristic silver garb. The silver contrasts splendidly with her crimson hair.

"Thanks?" I call back, unsure what response they're referring to

"Bring a signed copy to the party tonight! You can read it to us all...if we can hear you over the music!" Femi says, laughing as her and her sister exit the hallway.

The subject of their praise dawns on me, and I remember my letter—well, Harold's letter—to Bryan.

How do they know what it said? I'm annoyed with my confusion as I speculate with Lyle and Morgan.

"Did Bryan publish the letter on the school SMARTspace page or something?" I ask. *I wouldn't put it past him...or past Katrina, for that matter,* I think.

"Not really," Morgan pipes up helpfully. "Someone in the half-breed class saw the note fall out of Katrina's bag, and they managed to salvage it."

"Why?" I sound like a little kid as I repeat this question.

"A friend brought the letter to me, so I kind of..." Lyle breaks in, pausing for effect. "I made sure copies of the letter were sent to the school SMARTpads of every half-breed here."

I'm stunned. *Why the hell would you do that?!* My thoughts shout at Lyle...then fly to Belinda and the administration. If this advertisement of that ridiculous letter has any effect on the student body behavior, I'll be blamed for it even if I wasn't the person who sent it out. *Rabble-rouser. Troublemaker.*

"And you did this because?" I ask once I'm certain my voice will remain steady and at a normal level. "It wasn't a big issue that needed to be publicized. It was enough that people saw me give him the letter and

191

knew I wasn't just submitting blindly. The letter was just rebellious enough to make a point without causing too many waves. And I did it so other people wouldn't get in trouble!" *That was the plan, anyway,* I think acidly.

Lyle smiles at me like I'm supposed to be happier than I am with this scenario. "Don't you see? This way, if Katrina was planning for Bryan to lie about the letter there are copies in several places for back up," he explains.

"I already planned for witnesses," I say, thinking of the people in the hall who already saw the nightmare of me having to do something so pointless.

"Look around, Sierra!' Lyle says excitedly. I do, and it dawns on me why all my fellow half-breeds so proudly display their heritage. *Oh. Oh no...*

I'm happy for the courage my classmates found in the face of all the social oppression from the humans upstairs; it's such a relief to be able to look around and see the familiar pattern of DNA matches in the people around me. I just wish my influence—my indirect influence—hadn't been necessary to get the ball rolling. I remember the way Hasida and Femi and even some of the other half-breeds looked at me when I came in: like I'm a leader, some sort of savvy and brave and coolly rebellious person.

Rebellious enough to throw caution to the winds? I think, hoping not. Harold would kill me, and then there's the administration to deal with. *People who make too many waves are removed from the water,* my thoughts hum ominously.

I have no desire to discuss this any further; the damage is done. "It's almost time for the bell," I say.

Since Lyle and Morgan stare at me curiously instead of moving, I lead the way to our homeroom. I check in and make it to my seat un-harassed, but my mind is too busy to pay much attention. I probably seem horribly moody to my friends, but I don't care.

As Marlow Hynes calls roll—he's slowly improving speed-wise—I wonder what Belinda will think about the passive-aggressive revolution taking place among the half-breeds.

You have enough to worry about already, S.

I'm very drowsy in between my first and second classes: Business Math followed by Psychology seemed good originally, but that must depend on the day. Some stresses of this past week are taking their toll; I walk out of the math classroom and into the hallway in a slight daze. But I wake up soon enough as my eyes notice the tall ginger coming around the corner. Duncan isn't looking at me right now; since he's with a few people, I assume they're his friends.

I forget not to stare because I want to see who my human friend spends his time with. He's debating something with a tall boy with round rimmed brown glasses and bright red jeans, and the girl with long, straight strawberry blonde hair standing beside them is short in comparison.

Another boy with brown hair under a hipster beanie with some obscure band logo decorating the fabric laughs with what I guess is another couple; he turns his head and I see he has at least four ear piercings. The boy the kid with piercings is speaking to has curly black hair, and a confident stride that bespeaks a distinctive blend of arrogance as well as healthy self-assurance. He has his arm around a tall, sunny-looking girl with a few freckles, short blonde hair with lighter highlights, and cocoa brown eyes.

They all look very happy and fun-loving. I allow my fox senses a brief moment of luxury so I can catch their scents on the breeze of the air conditioning; their aura is relaxed, comfortable, and the two girls wear simple floral perfumes which blend with their human scent. Watching even in a few seconds of this dialogue reveals that Duncan is more of a listener than a talker, at least with them, but he's clearly happy to be with this group. Some musky cologne tickles my nose, and I taste the air on my tongue so I will remember the scent later...

"What's up, Sierra?" Shelby interrupts my staring and I startle, hurrying away to my next class after almost dropping my donated SMARTpad.

"Nothing really...just looking forward to another day ending in a few hours," I blurt without much consideration for what I'm saying. She skips past the small talk and moves on to another topic right away.

"So...what was all that about yesterday? With the human boy?" Shelby asks me as we walk to Psychology class. I'm relieved she just came out and asked instead of beating around the bush.

"Nothing really. We hung out after school, got drinks from Omnium Beanery," I offer carefully. Shelby raises her eyebrows skeptically, dark lips pursed.

"Are you sure?" she asks.

"Sure about what?" I'm uncertain what she's going for with this talk, so I continue. "I don't think it was any more than that."

"Okay," Shelby pauses before continuing. "I just want to make sure you know what you're doing. He's a human, after all." Now I'm a little aggravated, and my fur is bristles with offense. *How are my friendship choices your business?* I want to ask.

"I'm aware," I say crisply. Shelby analyzes me; her arms are crossed, and her walk is firm enough for her smart fuchsia heels to click on the hard floor.

"Lyle asked me for your SMARTcall number earlier. He said he wanted to ask you for it, but he thought I might know already so he asked me," she says.

I blink at her, trying to figure out why she randomly changed the subject. "And?"

"I told him I didn't have it, because I don't, and he said he was going to get it from you later," she answers. Her tone makes the issue seem more important than it actually is, and ordinarily I'd be very interested in a situation where a boy was so keen on furthering contact with me. But now...

I haven't willingly thought about Morgan's theory regarding Lyle's interest in me. My mind, while it has been busy with other thoughts, keeps shying away from the topic.

"Thanks for telling me," I say with an anti-climactic tone. Shelby nods a few times. Her scrutiny grows more unbearable by the second, and I'm very glad to reach the Psychology classroom.

I've only been here a few days, but I feel like I need a bit of space from my friends. I hope this feeling wears off, but Shelby speaks again and I don't feel so guilty for wanting a bit of distance anymore.

"I don't know if you want to hear this, but a lot of half-breeds here look up to you, Sierra. Hanging out with humans probably isn't the wisest decision," she says. She means well; she may be serious, but her tone isn't condescending or authoritative. Nevertheless, I'm still aggravated.

Just as I sit down in the clean, minimalist lecture room, the high tech intercom buzzes into activity with a faint chiming sound. Periodically, trivial announcements reverberate through the halls via the intercom, so I don't pay much attention to the voice.

"SIERRA MAURELL NEEDS TO COME TO THE ADMINISTRATION OFFICE."

My name sounds smooth over the upstairs intercom, and everyone in the room spins around to gawk at me. People know who I am now, unlike my first day after the assembly meeting when Harper called me up to her office. I was hoping I'd never have to go back; it was just dumb luck that got me out of a visit on the day Bryan insulted me.

Frozen, I sit with a rigid spine as my thoughts race chaotically through my brain. A call to the principal's office in an ordinary school isn't necessarily a cause for alarm, but the way of life here at Hostetler is very different.

I guess Belinda read the letter, I think as I come up

with reasons why I might be in trouble.

I gather my bag and stand up, wanting to flee the classroom as quickly as possible, before anyone realizes the significance of the principal calling me in.

15

Once I'm in the hall, my thoughts settle down; it's easier to think now that my friends' concerned glances are absent along with the glares from the humans who were in the classroom. I work on calming my feelings so my fox ears will stand up straight again. *At least I don't have listen to another lecture about half-breeds not following "normal" psychological patterns,* I comfort myself.

By the time I begin walking, I'm more or less ready to face Belinda Harper. No one loiters in the hall, and my steps echo uncomfortably loud even with my high top shoes. I'm almost relieved to reach the less cavernous administration wing. The assistant at the desk has been expecting me: she motions me through with a well-manicured hand after giving me a cursory once-over. I nod, deciding to be polite; she personally has done nothing to offend me.

I don't have to knock at the principal's door: it glides open as I raise my hand.

"Come in, Sierra," Belinda speaks as if she's inviting me to share a friendly exchange of neighborhood gossip.

Perhaps it's because I haven't heard her voice since my first day at school, but I forgot how charitable this woman could sound. I don't know if it's on purpose, but her voice doesn't match her perfectly manufactured face and angular form.

She stares at me as I walk in, and I'm wary of her smile. Ironically, I notice we're both wearing the same color shirt, although in very different styles: hers is a silk peach blouse, and mine is a glorified scoop neck t-shirt with ribbed sides and three-quarter length sleeves.

"Thank you for arriving so promptly," she says, her posture rigid and her blinding smile cold. *Like I have a choice*, I think, wishing I could give this awful woman a piece of my mind.

"What's this about?" I ask as I slide into the seat facing her desk. I want to keep my distance, so I very subtly begin sliding the chair back with small pushes with my feet against the floor. It's only a small rebellion, but it certainly makes me feel better.

"This shouldn't take much of your time. We'll probably be finished in time for you to return to class and catch up on the material being discussed today," she says. "I had two subjects I wanted to chat about with you."

Here we go.

"Am I in trouble?" I ask. It's a stupid question—I'm here, after all—but I'm trying to gauge exactly how much trouble I'm in so I can call Harold after this meeting if necessary.

"Firstly, I want to discuss the letter I required you to write for your classmate Bryan," she says, acting like I hadn't asked a question at all. A surge of anger pulses through my head again, but I clench my hands into fists and mentally push it back.

"That was an...interesting method for handling the issue," I say delicately. Belinda's responsive smile is infuriating. I try to picture her as a half-breed, but I can't: it would be an offense to any animal I could think of, even a goldfish.

"Exactly. I really wanted to make sure you understood the seriousness of what you did, and why it was so very wrong," she tells me. I have no desire to reply, but she stares at me expectantly.

"Well, I did write the letter the same day you asked me, and I gave it to him after the morning classes," I say. She nods slowly, her dark hair neat in a sleek French twist.

"So I'm told. In fact, your guardian sent me a copy of your letter last evening. I'm thankful he did, because it gave me a chance to really *read* your letter to judge the content thoroughly."

I'm relieved Harold sent her a copy, but for a different reason: this way, she never felt compelled to search for another copy at all. I'm hopeful that Lyle's virtual publication of my letter will pass by unnoticed by the powers that be.

"I'm glad," I say dully, wanting this entire situation

wrapped up.

"I'm sure," she says in a tone that sounds like she wasn't listening. "However, as I was reading, I did notice the tone of your letter seemed to require a few observations on my part."

"Oh?" I ask, imagining just the sort of "observations" Belinda might have for me.

"I noticed what I believe to be a significant lack of *repentance* in your overall attitude," she begins, watching my face with eyes as cold as her voice. "I understand how difficult it might have been for you to lower your pride and admit your wrongdoing, but I am still very concerned about what the tone of your letter implies."

I don't instantly reply; it's become a norm for this woman to offend me. I'm amazed Belinda, principal of a huge and prosperous high school, has time to nitpick a ridiculous letter, but perhaps she was put here just for this purpose. After all, in spite of what the government's current party line is regarding equality, most of society would like to keep half-breeds shamed and cowed.

"I did everything you asked. I wrote the letter and gave it to Bryan. The apology message was clear in the content, so isn't that all that was required?" My voice is cold too now, not quite as silken as hers, but I hear the frigidness in my words. Belinda must be able to hear it too, because she pauses just a moment before replying.

"Why are you at this school, Sierra?" she asks. I blink at her, different answers rolling through my mind. I'm pretty sure "I sure as hell don't want to be" is not an acceptable reply.

"The latest desegregation laws required all half-breed students to attend human schools," I say, choosing the easy route of the textbook answer. She nods, a friendly smile back on her face.

"Very good. I note that you called this a *human* school," she says. "You are quite right; Hostetler high is an excellent academic institution that has been educating privileged human students for many, many years."

"How do you know all that, seeing as you got here roughly the same time I did?" Perhaps I shouldn't have blurted that out, but her repeated and pointed use of the word "human" is galling. Her smile slips into a tight line before making a quick return.

"I may be new to this particular school, but I did my research. I was formerly on the government education board in this district, so I do know what I'm speaking of," she says. *Whoopee,* I think acerbically.

"Attending this school is a recent advantage we have granted to your kind, Sierra. M-DNA students have been accepted in schools they were previously denied access to, and this is a considerable privilege." She pauses for effect. "But privileges can be taken away, you see. I have the power to arrange that, and if I informed the school board of all of your activities, or even read them your letter, they would agree with me in reconsidering your place at this establishment."

It isn't difficult to catch her meaning. I direct my gaze to her perfectly shaped eyebrows, thinking back to what Harold said about drowning this school in bad press. *She knows it's a virtually empty threat,* I realize with a sinking feeling in my gut.

"Is there something else you would like me to do?" I ask, entering damage-control mode. I'm nervous, and the urge to fidget in my seat is maddening, but I grit my teeth and think of my brothers. For all their complaining about how the desegregation laws are forced and ineffective, it would hurt them if I got thrown out my last year of high school. It would hurt the other half-breed students in this and other schools; I can't help but feel like this whole school-related desegregation act has been an experiment. There's not really a predictable outcome, but I don't want to be the one to bring everything tumbling down. Belinda warms perceptibly, apparently pleased with my response.

"This is the kind of attitude I like seeing in you. A willingness to comply with the rules can take a person—someone like *you*, Sierra—far in life."

It's not a question of bravery when I lower my gaze from hers; it's a struggle to not pick up the silver vase filled with yellow chrysanthemums sitting on her desk and chuck it at her head. "Someone like *you*" according to Belinda is definitely an expression of her opinion that half-breeds are less than people. It's not something she would ever voice in those words, but the representation of the thought is there in her face, her words, and the way she smiles at me like I can't comprehend ideas the same way pure humans can.

Finally, I can look up again. "Is there something else I'm required to say?" My voice is monotone; I almost sound bored. Belinda shakes her head.

"I won't belabor the issue with the letter. I am quite capable of mercy, so we can move on from this incident with the full knowledge that you admit your wrongdoing in attacking that boy, and that you must learn to control your nature," she says, leaning back into her rigid chair in what I assume is supposed to be a relaxed position. I would say she looks like a cat that's got the cream, but there is nothing animal in her posture or expression. I see nothing but cold, human calculation.

I nod curtly, unwilling to answer; my hair falls in my face again, but I toss it back with a quick movement of my head. My muscles are sore from tension, like I've been fighting, but I'm glad that heightened senses for half-breeds are optional; I don't want to smell her satisfaction as well as see it.

"Peach as a color becomes you, Sierra. You could be almost pretty," Belinda says randomly in a backhanded compliment. "You must have admirers among your kind." *Okay, this definitely took a weird turn,* I think warily.

"Maybe," I grunt the word, resisting the urge to slouch in my chair and stick my tongue out unattractively. My chair is pretty far from her desk now; I've pushed it back slowly but surely.

"I think you do. I think people here already look up to you...maybe as a leader?" Belinda's unwavering gaze settles into an emotion growing more hostile by the minute, and it's not difficult to read into the meaning behind her words. I'm adapting to this game, although I refuse to play it the same manipulative way she does.

"I don't make myself a leader here. I attempt to follow the rules," I say, struggling to keep the monotone in my voice. The principal bows her long, tan neck in a graceful, if skeptical nod.

"I have noticed that there seems to be a new dress style for M-DNA students as of today," she informs me. "I saw all these changes, and I admit that my mind came back to you when I wondered who originated such a forward change in style."

"You're worrying about our clothes?" I ask, and then amend myself to cover my growingly obvious loss of control over my emotions. "I mean, you want me to convince the others to go back into hiding?" I expect her to be affronted by my words—far bolder and more direct than hers—but her shark-tooth smile only widens.

"However you wish to phrase it, yes. Your popularity here should allow you to convince your classmates of the wisdom in staying under the radar," she says. "I wish you to be an example to the class of students you have influence over. If you are who they follow, then you should be able to convince them to cease flaunting their mutations." I want to run out of this room right now so I can be done with this close-minded woman with her sugar-coated smiles and false beauty.

"I see," I say. "Is there a new rule about dress code for M-DNA students I should know about? Perhaps another SMARTnote I missed?"

"Yes, unofficially," Belinda admits; she sits up rigidly in her fine, black leather chair. "I believe I have made myself perfectly clear already, Sierra, about what I expect from you. I will deal with this issue now before any more serious consequences are necessary for transgressors," Belinda says as she clasps her spidery hands together on top of her desk.

"Fine. Are we done now?" I ask. I picture what

would happen if I told Harold all of what was going on. He would go to the media, and I'd like to think the world would believe me and be on my side—there's definitely proof enough concerning the oppression of half-breed students—but I can't be sure. Everyone is so torn between support of humans and support of half-breeds...there's a distinct probability of me making circumstances worse and getting myself expelled. Plus, the side that is suddenly concerned about what they define as "equality" is most likely more interested in the great social experiment started by that crazy scientist before the war.

The principal considers me a moment longer.

"Yes, I think I've explained to you what kind of behavior I expect from now on," she says. I try not to hear the triumph or smugness in her tone. I feel defeated, and I have no idea what I'm going to do about "leading" the others back into hiding their animal traits. I don't know how to be an example, especially if I don't want to be, and I wonder if I even have a choice.

When I get out of Belinda's office, I expect the aide to ignore me once more, but this is not the case.

"I'm to show you back to your class," she tells me. Her grimace lets me know he doesn't want to, because we both know I can get back to class perfectly fine.

"There's no need," I say as I continue walking, but the assistant follows me anyway. She glares at me, and I stifle a sigh as I chalk her up as yet another person who wants me gone from this school. I assume this is one more power play on the part of Belinda Harper; she already thinks I'm mentally inadequate, so why not make the rest of the school view me the same way? Even making me look like I can't find my way around the school after almost a full week of classes is one small step in her evil plan.

I don't know what I'll do about what she expects from me as an apparent leader here, but I know that the last thing I want to do is comply. I still see Lyle as a leader, a hell of a lot more than me, but I'm also the last person who wants us half-breed students to go back to being cowed.

I wonder, as I tell my friends in a very brief summary what happened in the principal's too-neat office, if they are tired of hearing about all the authority related drama that seems to be haunting me lately. They haven't shown any signs of annoyance so far. Morgan is of course very sympathetic, and Ivar and Shelby have their own discussion about what's going on apart from us. Lyle keeps quiet, simply listening and considering my words. His anger is palpable.

It's about the end of Psychology now, and I'm excited for this whole hour to be done with. My face is still flushed from what just took place; Morgan, the only person among my quartet of friends here with my SMARTcall number, just sent me a text letting me know that she gave my number to Lyle. I'm embarrassed, but

I can't express why. I wasn't attracted to him to begin with, not as much as...well, a long-legged ginger, but now my thoughts solidify into a more of a denial.

The bell rings, releasing me to make my way to my next class: senior English. I can't resist the urge to look around for a glimpse of red hair, and I see it this time. Duncan strides down the hallway, again with the group of friends I'm beginning to recognize. Something about his gait is different from the other boys': confident, but not arrogant. He's also broader in the shoulders and heavier muscle-wise, which I see as I notice the way his shoulders taper down to a deliciously proportional waist.

Stop, I tell myself firmly...but my protests are weakening. I lower my eyes, looking away right when the girl with strawberry blond hair glances at me inquisitively. Morgan chatters about the party as she stands behind me, and I give her a few empty replies. I blankly follow her to our next class, and I wish I could make my thoughts focus on matters at hand.

My SMARTcall buzzes in my pocket, vibrating like an irritation. One of these days it's finally going to break, or leap out of my pocket from buzzing too violently. *Maybe then Wade will have to smuggle me a new one*, I think as I fidget to get the SMARTcall out of my pocket. I see the message preview on the little screen, along with the message
ID.

"Oooh, is that Lyle?" Morgan asks excitedly, and I try to restrain a grimace as I confirm her question with a nod.

LYLE ZEMAN: *Hey Sierra, I was just making sure your number works.*

I'm not sure what to say; there's not much room for reply.

SIERRA MAURELL: *It works, thanks for checking!*

"What did he say?" Morgan pesters me, craning her head over my shoulder trying to see my phone; I have to dodge her antlers poking me or worse, tangling in my hair. I experience a brief urge to shield my phone from her, but right then a reply blinks onto the screen.

LYLE ZEMAN: *So I was wondering...would you like to be my date for the party tonight?*

Well you sure move fast, I think. I consider sending this as a reply, but Morgan's gasp startles me and I nearly drop my phone. We've stopped in the middle of the crowded hallway, but thankfully people just step around us for the moment. I turn to observe my friend, and for a brief instant, I see a very hurt expression on her sweet, innocent face.

"Morgan—" I begin, wanting to say something to...to what?

"You have to say yes!" she says right away, cutting me off. Her voice is slightly higher than normal, and I now know for certain that she really, *really* likes this lion boy who is suddenly so interested in me. Guilt settles in my stomach again, even though it's not my fault that her crush is showing interest in me.

"Say yes?" I ask, timidly sliding my phone into my pocket. I don't know what to reply, but I know I don't want to hurt or block my friend. "Why do you think so?"

Morgan's dark eyes look so serene now; if it weren't for the slight tremble to her lips, I would think I imagined her hurt just a few seconds ago. "Yes, he really likes you. Three or four day's acquaintance or not, I think you should give him a chance, Sierra," she says.

I listen, internally debating my level of non-interest. Perhaps she can see this lack of enthusiasm on my face, because she cocks her head to the left.

"It might be worth it to give him a chance....he's a bit more suited for you than some of the other guys here," she says. My charitable feelings for her evaporate like water, and I tighten my fingers around the SMARTcall device in my pocket. I know full well who she's talking about, but she glances over at Duncan anyway, forcing me to as well.

Have I been that transparent? I think as I watch him laugh at something the sunny blonde girl said. *Well, running off yesterday to Omnium Beanery after school might have been a little obvious,* I answer myself. Something curls up in my heart, angry and a little hurt. *Maybe Lyle deserves a chance...*

I look at Morgan and pull my phone back out, toying with the red gel case enclosing the delicate device. She watches me to see what I'll do, and I look down at my screen to avoid her eyes. I'm trying not to do this out of spite for her comment—or spite for everyone else who is putting down a friendship I want to keep up with—but I confess that my hurt feelings, and my realization that I as a half-breed really can't be friends with a human, pollute my motives.

"He might be a fun party date," I admit.

SIERRA MAURELL: *Sure. I'll meet you there.*

I hit send before looking up at Morgan, who makes a noise of affirmation through her nose. She remains silent as we finally abandon our spots rooted in the center of the hallway, and I'm already looking for the relief of Shelby and Ivar's or even Lyle's company to ease the tension.

16

My SMARTcall flashes with new messages the entire next period, and I try to be as unnoticeable as possible as I answer the texts.

SHELBY JEAN: *U said yes! I'm so happy for u. What r u going to wear tonight?*

LYLE ZEMAN: *So what kind of music do u like? I hear the Reis girls have good taste.*

I may not appreciate Shelby's enthusiasm as much as Morgan's willingness to let me have a date with a guy she *clearly* adores, but part of me is glad that I have friends who are interested in my life. Back in my private school, I did have a circle of friends, but something about them having parents and growing up together did keep me a little isolated. No boy was ever interested in me before, either; there are times when I get really sad and miss my mother a great deal, but now more than ever I wish she was here to share some wisdom on what to do about boys and my feelings about them.

Would she tell me to try things out with Lyle, or would she say back off for Morgan's sake? I know I would rather Lyle be interested in Morgan...but he's not, and I'm no matchmaker. Perhaps I should really give things a go with the lion boy who looks at me with so much interest.

But Duncan... I don't know what I want there. I've had a crush before, and I do admit that I'm starting to want more than friendship—however ashamed I am that I want this after only a few days acquaintance—and I want to get to know this human boy who doesn't avoid half-breeds at this hell of a school.

I decide to text Hayley in between my conversations with other people. It'll be a miracle if the English teacher doesn't notice my texting, but at least it's fairly easy for me to type without looking at the screen.

SIERRA MAURELL: *I have news on the drama front.*

HAYLEY MANCHESTER: *Ohhh? Do tell.*

SIERRA MAURELL: *I got invited to a party for*

people at school, and Lyle just asked me to be his date.

HAYLEY MANCHESTER: *Well that's not really a surprise. Go on.*

SIERRA MAURELL: *However, I just confirmed my suspicion that Morgan is a lot more interested in him than I am.*

HAYLEY MANCHESTER: *Ouch.*

SIERRA MAURELL: *I'm not sure what to do. I told him he could be my date because Morgan really wanted me to, but I'm not sure where to go from here. I'm not as excited as I think I should be.*

HAYLEY MANCHESTER: *You are wise to come to me for counsel. My medical opinion is that Morgan wants you to go out with Lyle because Lyle likes you better...she wants Lyle to have fun. I'm not saying she's not hoping you'll bomb the date so Lyle will fall into her arms, but that's what it looks like to me.*

SIERRA MAURELL: *That...makes some sort of sense I guess. Thanks, doctor. Anything to add to that diagnosis?*

HAYLEY MANCHESTER: *Don't do more than you're*

comfortable with.

SIERRA MAURELL: *Thanks Mum.*

HAYLEY MANCHESTER: *Who knows, maybe this will get you to not carry a torch for that Duncan boy.*

What? I never told Hayley any of my thoughts on Duncan...we've talked since my time with him in Omnium Beanery, but I know for a fact I never said anything to her about my increasingly confused feelings for a forbidden human boy. *Is he even interested in me?* I think next, my silly brain rapidly reviewing every interaction with him since we met. Duncan isn't repulsed by my kind, that's true...

But he may not want to be in a relationship with someone like you. I feel stupid now and I want to break something. I don't bother lying to Hayley.

SIERRA MAURELL: *You're right. We'll see...let's hang out soon and catch up, I'll have to tell you how the party goes.*

HAYLEY MANCHESTER: *You got it kiddo, I better hear from you tomorrow about all this stuff.*

The bell rings, so I'm unable to compose a reply. I sense the eyes of my friends on me, and I want to escape the pressure. I don't know how I suddenly got to be so popular, but I'm solitary by nature—except when it comes to my family—and so much pressure to communicate might drive me batty.

It's our morning break between classes, so I dodge Shelby and Ivar and head towards the lower wing where the bathrooms are. It's not necessarily a rule for half-breeds to use the bathrooms downstairs, but it sure feels a lot safer down there: the human students don't go down there at all. At least there I can park on the bench by the sink and have some peace.

"You look frazzled." Duncan's voice shocks me into slowing my pace, and I turn to my right to see him walking next to me. "Care to share?" He smiles slightly, and I feel the tight muscles in my neck relax as a responsive smile creeps towards my lips.

Then I remember: I promised to be Lyle's date tonight. *It might be better if I stay away from Duncan for now*, I think, and the thought dissolves my smile.

"It's nothing worth talking about," I say carefully. "Just a full day for me, that's all."

"Academic stress?" he asks, continuing to walk with me; his arms swing free at his sides, and I direct my eyes away so I'm not tempted to touch his bicep. *Damn. Is it really necessary he looks good just walking?*

"No...social drama," I say, purposefully vague. I pause in the hall, my nose clogged with human smells as waves of students pass us by. "Listen Duncan, I've got to—"

"Hey there fox girl!" One of Duncan's friends comes

up behind Duncan and whacks his back in what I recognize as a friendly male greeting; he's looking at me though, this boy with the black curly hair, and wide, mischievous smile.

"Hey?" I say back uncertainly. I haven't interacted with any more human students besides Duncan and the couple from hell, Bryan and Katrina. Duncan's friends or not, I don't want to get set up for any more ridicule.

"It's Sierra," Duncan corrects the curly-haired boy and faces me. "Sierra, this is my best friend Aaden...please keep in mind that no, you don't want to know anything about the medicinal benefits of legal and illegal herbs. It's hard to stop him once he gets going. "

I can't help it; a grin sneaks up around my lips, although I'm still nervous. My hackles rise from my alertness; I hope no one notices how jumpy I am, especially not the rest of Duncan's friends who are confidently approaching as well.

"Nice to meet you," I say politely to Aaden, determined—and probably failing—to act natural. Duncan watches me from his peripheral vision, and I wonder how he feels about this scene. I'm not sure why he would be anxious, but for some reason I want him to be comfortable.

"I'm Sierra," I introduce myself to the group who scrutinizes me almost expectantly. Going out on a limb, I extend my hand to see if anyone will be polite and shake it; if I feel like I'm being tested, then I want them to feel under scrutiny as well.

"Hello Sierra. I am Bari," the tall boy in red jeans and glasses says solemnly in a voice that was definitely deeper than I expected from such a skinny build. "This is my girlfriend, Mabel." Mabel, the hourglass-figured girl with a ready smile, light eyes, and long strawberry blonde hair extends her hand to shake mine. I try not to cringe as I wait for her to recoil from brushing against my fur. But she doesn't, and I watch her face. *She must be used to half-breeds,* I conclude.

"This is my cousin Truman and my girl Kylie," Aaden says, pulling in the laughing sun-haired girl with one arm and giving her a quick kiss on the top of her head. Truman lingers at the back of the group, looking benign. I don't know what else to say; my eyes flick over to Duncan again, assessing before I speak. He's watching me too, and we both realize it; he smiles at me encouragingly.

"Nice to meet you," I repeat, sending him one more questioning glance. *Did he arrange this...?*

"Your hair is absolutely gorgeous," Kylie says, approaching me to finger a few strands. My instincts are in revolt, and I want to step back; perhaps Mabel senses this, because she pulls Kylie back with a laugh.

"Kylie, chill. Personal space bubble, remember?" she says.

"Never," Aaden laughs, and Kylie huffs good-naturedly at him; I notice now they're closer that she's as tall as her boyfriend. In fact, Mabel and I are the only ones around average height.

I recall as I'm watching them interact that I was going to use this fifteen minute break to find a place to recover from the morning. I imagine my friends looking for me right now, and hope they haven't seen me with this fun looking group of humans.

"I have to go," I say, "I-I forgot some stuff in my locker, and I should go—" I take a few steps back, but Duncan follows me.

"Gotcha. I'll see you guys in a bit," he says, giving them a clipped farewell wave.

"Nice to meet you, Sierra," Mabel says with a mysteriously wry smile. Feeling stupid, I walk off with Duncan following me.

"Your friends seem...nice," I say. While I still want some peace and quiet, I also want to keep talking with him. I'm under no illusions, however, not any more. The crush I'm developing isn't going to go anywhere, so I'd better get used to that idea right now.

Duncan shrugs. "They're all decent people. I think you and Mabel would get along; your personalities seem similar."

"Oh?" I question. "She did shake my hand..." I notice my hands are clenched into fists with fur bristled, and I sigh, attempting to relax.

"Lucky," Duncan mutters, surprising me.

"Lucky?" I repeat stupidly; I notice he's looking at my hands. His eyes return to my face, and I realize he might not have meant to say that out loud.

"Oh...I forgot you have super hearing," he says, color seeping into his face under the attractive stubble.

I look away quickly, towards the stairs. I feel myself blushing too as I imagine this boy touching my hand, even in something as casual as a hand-shake...then I wince. Mabel may not have shown any repulsion she felt, but I don't want to take the chance Duncan won't like the feel of my fur.

"Sorry...did I offend you?" he asks after a second, and I blink to shake myself out of the reverie I'd stumbled into. He's in my personal space bubble now, hovering just on the edge. I don't mind...though it would probably be better if I did.

"No...I just...I have this party tonight," I say stupidly. *What the hell does that have to do with anything?* I think. Duncan raises an eyebrow at me, perhaps thinking the same thing.

"Oh?" he asks. "I think you told me this yesterday...is it troubling you?"

I sigh again, shaking my head. "Just...it's at Femi and Hasida's house, and I've heard they only invite important people." This is only part of the problem, but I'm reluctant to tell Duncan about Lyle's interest. Their interaction yesterday seemed a little too tense for me to feed with new information.

"Femi and Hasida Reis?" He asks.

"Yes...why?"

"I know who they are," he shares. "My dad is a security guard, and their parents hired him before for random details around the house because of some vandalism and theft issues."

"Understandable. Even if they live in a good

neighborhood, stuff like that still happens to us," I nod, a little more sympathetic with the Reis twins. For all their flashy dress and apparently splendid parties, they're still in the same boat with the rest of the half-breeds who struggle for acceptance.

"You should cheer up: if they invited you, they must think you're important," Duncan says. I shake my head before explaining.

"Ordinarily that would be great. However this time...people who think I'm important could get me into trouble. I'm already in Harper's bad books," I say. Duncan nods seriously, leaning his shoulder against the doorframe of the stairway; half-breed students pass us with questioning glances, but I ignore them and my discomfort from their stares.

"You *are* kind of a rebel," he tells me, one corner of his mouth hitching up in a smirk. "I don't think you should get in trouble, but I think everyone at Hostetler knows you rule the M-DNA students."

"That's what people assume," I sigh. "I'm sure I'm very flattered, but I just want to finish senior year and get the hell out of this dump." Suddenly the one minute bell rings, and I startle, almost throwing my school SMARTpad down the stairs. Duncan laughs, and those butterflies in my stomach rattle like crazy.

"Your ears were drooping, but they just stood up straight really fast," he says, chuckling. I know he's not making fun of me maliciously.

"I don't appreciate loud noises," I say, then add: "We should go; Sociology calls." I lead the way back, only regretting a little bit that I didn't have some time to cool down. Duncan calmed me, somehow.

"Can I see you again?" he asks. His tone makes me look up, and our eyes meet once more. I can't look away, nor do I want to.

"Yes," I whisper. He smiles, and I forget why I would have said no in the first place.

"Tomorrow?" he requests. "It's Saturday, so we might have more freedom as to what to do."

"Okay...do you need my number?" I ask, and he nods. I rattle off my SMARTcall number rapidly, hoping his memory is good.

"See you later," he says once he's got it, and then he saunters off to class, leaving me to wonder what I'm going to do about this situation. Strangely enough, I'm more excited for tomorrow than for the party tonight.

The nation—indeed, the world—is divided on the issue of the rights of M-DNA citizens. In many places, the conflict is still violent as M-DNA people—who still refer to themselves as "half-breeds" amongst their own kind—fight for their freedoms.

In the Regional United States, disagreements are still solved by committees and SMARTvision televised talks. The committee of senators who manages the country has recently passed a controversial law regarding the future of our nation. That is, the future of the peace between M-DNA people and pure DNA humans: most of the senators believe that the only way to preserve the peace is to teach our youth to cooperate and live with each other fruitfully.

According to the polls SMART industries has provided to the general public, the desegregation laws have had mixed success rates. Only time will determine the future of blending pure DNA human lifestyles with M-DNA life, but the general agreement thus far is that the way into a successful future is by removing the barriers between pure DNA and M-DNA young people.

17

My brothers wait in line at the bottom of the stairs after I finish preparing for the party tonight.

"Guys, this isn't prom night," I say jokingly, fluffing my freshly curled hair as I come down. "I might not even be out that late, depending on how things go."

Now that school is over after this long week, I feel ten times better. It was much easier to prepare for a party knowing that I don't have to deal with humans or with Belinda Harper for a couple of days. I cranked up some loud music and rocked around my room for a while, enjoying my improved mood and looking forward to partying with some friends.

There's still the problem of Lyle's interest and how I might be encouraging it just to get my mind off someone else...but that was more convenient to ignore.

"Doesn't she have a curfew?" Wade asks as I walk past the three of them to the shabby full length mirror hanging on the wall beside our non-working fireplace. Harold chuckles.

"Yes, but it's later than yours was. Sierra is a lot less likely to cause riots than you boys were," he says, surprising me.

"Oh? What about the fight I got into this week?" I ask.

"Yes, perhaps you forgot that Sierra is currently the queen bee at Hostetler," Eisen has planted himself behind me, arms crossed and legs belligerently apart. "If we had to be home by eleven, shouldn't she?"

"Jealous, much?" I say teasingly, smoothing a smudge of neutral but flattering lipstick away from the corner of my lips. I took a lot of effort with my make-up tonight; the smoky-winged eye will never go out of style, and I like to think the foresty eye shadow I used compliments the yellow and gold of my irises. I won't have to hide anything about what I am tonight: this is a half-breed party, and I plan to luxuriate in my own me-ness.

"You both have fair points, but you forget that Sierra hasn't been a trouble maker for at least two years...not until this week anyway, but she was provoked," Harold says reasonably. "Her curfew is one a.m. because she earned it, as you two might have if you'd partied more responsibly." Harold is definitely enjoying this more as an older brother than as a parent figure, and I smile at memories of younger, wilder versions of Eisen and Wade when they cared about

228

rules a lot less.

"Plus, I'm the baby of the family," I tease, rubbing salt into the wound.

"Baby gets what baby wants." Wade huffs, genuinely annoyed, but Eisen stalks forward and grabs my waist, finding the points in my ribs that are the most ticklish.

"Harold, make him stop!" I gasp between giggles as Eisen laughs at my squirming. "He'll mess up my outfit!"

"You're such a *girl* sometimes, S," Harold chuckles, letting Eisen carry on for a bit before breaking us apart.

"Not much of that outfit to mess up," Wade mutters, still standing by the stairs with his arms crossed.

"What?" I ask innocently once Eisen backs off, glancing at my outfit in the mirror again. I'm wearing a flowy dark green skirt that falls right below the middle of my thighs as well as vintage grey fishnets to match my petite faux leather pumps. My shirt isn't terribly low cut, but the scoop neck shows off a pleasing amount of my collar bones and some of what I've been endowed with; the cool black fabric hugs my torso flatteringly. This is definitely more formal than what I would have thought to wear to a party myself—what happened to jeans and t-shirts?—but I consulted with Shelby and Morgan, who'd been to a Reis party before, and they said this was more acceptable. I even took the effort to brush my tail and ears, so I thought I looked nice enough. Plus, here I can focus on enhancing my animal aspects; at school, I'll have to start downplaying them to please Belinda. The thought turns my stomach, so I push it away.

However, while I understand my brothers being a little leery about what I've chosen to wear to my first real party, Wade's grumpy attitude about the whole affair strikes me as odd. It's not like him to be antagonistic about something like this.

"Something wrong, Wade?" I ask, shaking out my hair so the hairspray continues to dry correctly. Our gazes meet in the full length mirror, and I know from the weird golden sheen in his eyes that my brother is troubled.

"It's nothing," he mutters, looking away. "Bad day at work."

"Sucks, man," Eisen says, moving over and manfully patting him on the back. I turn away from the mirror, glancing at Harold to make sure he notices Wade's troubled mood. His familiar frown settles at the corners of his grey eyes. He gives me an *I'll talk to him later* look before manufacturing a smile.

"Cheer up, Wade. Your curfew is one a.m. now that you're out of high school, so at least that's something," he says, striding to the front door to grab his keys out of the metal dish.

Harold knows where the Reis house is, since he's worked as their attorney in the past—one of his more important cases—so he's driving me. Suddenly Eisen comes and gives me a hug; I like hugs from all my brothers, including Harold's bear hug and Wade's hugs that are sneaky from behind. Eisen gives a kind of reassuring hug that somehow embodies family loyalty, which I've always found comforting after a hard day or after an upsetting incident.

"Be safe...stay away from boys with unidentifiable

drinks," he tells me quietly so no one else hears. I notice his ears droop when our hug ends. I don't mind my brothers being protective, but it does bother me when they psych themselves up with worrying.

"I'll be fine...it's just a party," I try to reassure all three of them, smiling. "Besides, we just had a discussion about how responsible and mature I am."

"Did we? I thought your words were 'baby gets what baby wants'..." Eisen says, ears slowly perking back up. Harold laughs and takes my arm.

"Okay, okay, we're going to make her late. Let's be gentlemen and escort the lady to the vehicle," he says, leading me towards the garage.

"Gentlemen, sure. We'll be the only ones she'll encounter tonight, then," Wade says darkly, grumbling further as he retreats up the stairs to his room. I'm very glad that I didn't mention Lyle—or even Duncan—to anyone else.

I'm sure human teenagers would be mortified to have a guardian drop them off at a party, but this is very normal for half-breeds. Most people our age can't even afford a regular SMARTvan, not to mention the fact that human leaders don't trust young half-breed drivers. Supposedly our instincts might go haywire and we'll crash the vehicle...at least, that's what they tell the public.

I gawk at the fabulous house and the surprising number of people lingering on the lawn; I can see into the front door, which keeps opening and closing, and it looks equally crowded inside. Blending in will be easy, but I'm still nervous; I'm not good at meeting new people, especially not in large quantities.

I continue walking up the brick sidewalk towards the house, wondering how Femi's and Hasida's parents managed to get into a house that is clearly old money material. *Probably illegally,* I think. I'm right outside the ostentatious brick house when my SMARTcall buzzes twice in my small red leather wristlet. I tug the device out of its pocket and glance at the screen.

LYLE ZEMAN: *Hey there, where are you? The party is awesome.*

You said you'd let this play out, I think, telling myself the fluttering in my stomach is from nervous excitement about this sort-of date instead of plain old uncertainty. *He is a nice guy and he's confident and outspoken.* I look at the next text.

MORGAN CHEPI: *We've gone around back, if you want to look for us. Lyle already went towards the front room to look for you.*

I enter the house, passing several half-breeds I don't recognize. So far my outfit doesn't look out of place...not that anyone would notice. The room is dark with perfect lighting for partying: smoky with roaming colored lights installed in the antique arched ceiling. Deafening music—which might be overwhelming if I had my animal senses cranked up—pounds through the entire house. I hope the walls have been sound-proofed; we don't need angry neighbors calling the police to complain about the raucous party noise jarring through the bricks.

"Sierra!" An excited female voice calls my name close behind my head, and I jump, startled. Femi's tanned face beams with satisfaction as I face her. "It's great you're here!"

"Thanks," I reply. Femi is beautiful in the way a real parrot would be: exotic, colorful, a tropical creature with bright yellow eyes, glittering make-up, and clothes at the height of fashion. She must be feeling the heat in here, judging from the faint sheen of sweat beading on her forehead. I expect to see Hasida nearby, but Femi is alone this time.

"Aren't you glad this week from hell is over?" she yells, shaking out her spiky blonde, chin length hair; her feathers gleam scarlet under the roving lights. "It's nice being able to chill with a few cool people on a Friday night after all that garbage we had to deal with."

"Just a few?" I query as she expertly leads me through the masses of people. She laughs.

"What can I say? My sister and I come into contact with a lot of half-breeds. It's definitely worth having most of them at a party. Now come on!" She turns and grins at me, then gives a guy who looks like he's got some hawk DNA a flirty wink and a wave. "Lyle already asked me where you were, so I said I'd help him find you."

Apparently getting to where Lyle is involves crossing the huge living-room-turned-dance-floor, which means Femi and I have to dance our way across to avoid getting tangled up during the crossing. Or perhaps the point *is* to get tangled up; there's a wild atmosphere in this house already. As I'm rocking through the masses I feel more than one body pressing up against me in a way that can't be accidental. True, half-breeds don't do vulgar butt-grabs and all the groping I've heard humans do—a lot of times half-breed women are strong enough to discourage unwanted attention, not to mention the boys who don't want their "territory" infringed upon—but it's not really a dance party unless there's a lot of physical contact.

Not that I speak from experience. My experience only covers worrying about a noise complaint and the fortune this party must have cost.

One particular face in the crowd seizes my attention; another Egyptian-looking man— absolutely not a high school boy—with expertly gelled black hair and a long, sophisticated nose observes the crowd with some distaste as he leans against the massive doorframe of a room that looks like an office, from what little I can see behind him.
His eyes are the blackest I've ever seen: glittering, intelligent onyx.

Jackal, I think, sensing his animal DNA without trying to catch a scent.

"Don't mind him," Hasida joins us right as Femi and I come through the crowd. "That's just our brother, Issachar. He and some of his college buddies are having their own private soiree in his office tonight."

"That seems like poor planning on his part," I remark, gesturing to the air vaguely as music pounds through the room. The sisters laugh, and I see Issachar's sculpted lips curl with dissatisfaction. He turns away, and I notice as the lights gleam on the shining black fur on his ears and tail that a gold piercing has made one of his jackal ears jagged. Then the door closes behind him.

Hasida and Femi are a pair, one fluttery and gleaming golden, and one in sleek, tight garb of burning silver and shocking shades of violet. I feel plain beside these striking siblings. Their eyes appear strange as well, even for half-breeds.

"It's fine," I say. "I'm kind of amazed we made it through there. I've never been dancing in a crowd this big before." I feel like a backwoods girl saying this, but Hasida flips her hair back and smiles with teeth that gleam under a blue light.

"This is your first real dance party? Are you enjoying yourself?" she asks, and Femi gasps beforel can answer.

"Not yet she's not!" She exclaims, whirling me around to face her so she can inspect my eyes; then she grins mischievously. "You're still walking human, right?"

"Walking...human?" I ask. There's a brief spell of quiet as the song blasting over speakers in the ceiling transitions to another. My throat is parched already, but judging by the crazed atmosphere here, it might not be safe to drink anything.

"Yeah...your senses are still toned down?" Hasida

asks.

"Yours aren't?" Now that I understand, I'm surprised; I would've thought the sounds and smells and other stimuli would've been overpowering at this level of action.

"Oh honey...our kind doesn't do drugs, not recreationally, but if you haven't tried going full half-breed, that's no kind of life," Femi clarifies. I've never thought about it that way: in a human world, it's been easier to just stay as human as possible unless it's a matter of immediate survival.

"Is that why everyone else is so...out there?" I ask, curious. Call it peer pressure, but I'm so intrigued that the excitement in my stomach becomes real. I've already started cranking up my fox senses; every bit of my fur on my body bristles, but in a good way this time.

Hasida nods. "Parties are much more...*enjoyable* when everyone lets the animal out to play. Instinct mode just feels so...natural," she says with a slow wink that makes her eyes appear more reptilian than ever. This sounds dangerous, but I don't think I mind. I wonder if my pupils are sharpening too as I allow all the nearby stimuli to trickle in.

Here goes, I think. *Let's see how the fox likes being in control...*

"Sierra!" Lyle's voice startles me, but not as much as the music. It's so loud that I want to run and hide, or at least cover my ears. My skin feels sensitive, like when you have a fever and every bit of skin is raw nerves. My tail thrashes back and forth as my nose tingles from the human and animal scents dispersed through the air I can almost taste. A few beads of sweat trickle into the fur lining my spine.

Wow. I think, impressed; it's been a long time since I've let the other DNA take over, and definitely my first time letting it go without feeling stressed or endangered. *This has to be better than just being human.* Maybe something about both sets of DNA enhances whichever part that I give dominance.

"Hey there," I say to Lyle once he comes closer. I see the features of his face better, and I have to admit that—without his standard hat, which ironically hid his lack of animal ears—he really isn't bad looking. The wide planes of his face aresymmetrical, aside from the healing bruises from the fighting; I'm glad half-breeds heal quickly. His eyes are blue, but very feline, and the way his hair falls in his eyes is admittedly attractive. He's not taller than me, but he's very fit and his jeans and the cut-off sleeves of his shirt show off wiry muscles I'm sure he's proud of.

Easy now, I tell myself. *You weren't thinking about him this way earlier.* The thought of Duncan slams back into my mind, and I forbid a frown to creep onto my face. My phone burns in my wristlet, niggling at my mind, making me wonder if Duncan ever messaged me.

"You look great, S," Lyle says to me, and I am grateful that his gaze only flickers down from my face to my chest twice. *You're thinking too hard,* I tell myself before my anxiety can stress me out again. *Fox, not human.*

"Wanna dance?" I ask boldly, reaching forward and taking Lyle's hand.

"Sure," Lyle replies, leading me back onto the

dance floor where at least a hundred bodies come together and part to the beat of the outrageously loud music pounding through the house. Femi and Hasida are probably mixed in there now, since they tactfully disappeared when my date found me.

Now that I'm thinking fox, my insecurities fade. I've never held a boy's hand before, but my enhanced senses don't mind the hot touch of Lyle's palm on mine. I see in his eyes that he isn't walking human either.

What a strange concept. It's easier to push away thoughts of human troubles and human boys with kind eyes and red hair when dancing is involved. Lyle and I exchange a few words in between several songs, but there's not much time or inclination for talking. Right now he's more lion than boy, I'm more vixen than girl, and that's fine with us. I even forget about Morgan and the rest of them, although one of my passing thoughts hopes that they are enjoying the party as well.

"You're a good dancer," I call to him in the middle of a retro punk rock song from the pre-2020's. "I thought boys weren't fun when it came to dancing."

"Maybe human ones," Lyle clarifies. "Music is part of the jungle, and I've learned to go with it."

"The jungle? I thought your kind lived in the mountains," I tease, the fox in me acting the vixen. Lyle grins and his hands find my waist. He's been doing this more, tentatively at first, but more frequently as the music reaches sultry points and as I dance a little closer. The DJ is an angel; he or she plays all the right songs, perfect for shaking my curly hair around and performing the moves I can do.

"Sometimes we come down from our mountains to the villages," Lyle quips.

"What for?" I glimpse my reflection in his eyes as the lights installed overhead flicker over us briefly. My eyes are hypnotic and smoky, and I can tell he definitely noticed that as well as other things about me.

"To hunt." A sly grin steals over his mouth and my heart does a funny swoop downwards as his eyes burn into mine. We continue dancing...

...but right then the music changes to something with a lower, sexier beat. My cheeks are already flushed from dancing, but I sense the couples around me instantly moving closer and lower toned laughter sounding around the room. Several people cheer.

"What song is this?" I ask, giving myself time to decide if I want to be closer.

"It's another old one," Lyle tells me, "It's been popular lately since the retro stuff started to come back." His eyes burn, and suddenly his hands are on my waist again, a little tighter, sliding down more towards my hips. It's not unpleasant; this both-hands grip makes me feel tiny and fragile in the best way.

But... the human part of me interjects. *Why are you doing this, Sierra? Do you really want to? What about Morgan? And Duncan...*I reconsider for a split second, a human face flashing to the front from my recent memory.

Hush, I tell my thoughts sternly before shutting them off as best I can. *Fox, not human...fox.*

My hands are cold and shaking, even if the rest of me is warm, but even in this unusual state I feel like something is off. I smile invitingly anyway and move closer, mostly ready for this dance I'm planning to engage in. But someone bumps into me really hard, almost knocking me off my feet. The song pulses ahead in spite of my separation from my dance partner.

Damn! I think as I'm lost amidst the host of couples tangled up with each other on the dance floor. Everyone can see in the dark with our DNA, sure, but the point of the moving lights is to make it so our eyes won't adjust properly to the dimness. I won't find Lyle by sight, and there are too many smells to pick out him out. Quickly...before the song ends and the moment passes.

Maybe this is a good thing, my responsible, human mind hums smugly. *You were getting carried away.*

So what? I think, but I'm relieved. Without Lyle around I feel, if not more human, more *me*.

My confusion disappears as an appealing scent floats past my nose, and another pair of strong, large hands settles firmly on my waist from behind. If I thought Lyle made me feel petite and tiny, these hands make me feel like a fairy. I'm so busy trying to recall the oddly familiar scent that I don't look turn around. Besides, my new partner and I have to keep dancing: we're on the dance floor, and it's easier to dance than be crushed by everyone else.

"Hi," I say weakly, but I'm not sure if my partner heard me. A warm, spicy canine scent fills my nose, along with a flavor of that pleasingly masculine cologne that settles on my tongue. Temporarily powerless to resist, I lift my arms up in the air as I dance. He's a good dancer too; I don't want to turn around and break the spell as his hands move *slowly* down to my hips before sliding back up to settle on my waist.

A gentleman, but not too much of one...who is this guy? I think, gliding my hips in a circle before dancing away slightly. I know it's not Lyle: his scent I recognize, and it's definitely not canine. Plus he doesn't wear cologne...

Half-breeds don't wear cologne, my thoughts chime dizzily. My fur was already standing up from the unadulterated *animal* chemistry passing in tiny electric shocks between me and this guy, but now I feel a sense of alarm zip through my skin.

I whirl around quickly just as the lights settle on us long enough for me to recognize Duncan Ledford holding on to my waist.

18

"Duncan!"

I'm too stunned to react, so my fox senses analyze the situation for me. Duncan looks *amazing* this way, I have to admit: his eyes are very bright and that kind of piercing green you only read about in books. All of his freckles are pleasantly defined along with the fine-boned structure of his face and stubble-covered jaw-line and neck. He's so tall compared to me, and I can't shake off how his hands felt on my waist.

But if I can tell Duncan is human by a whiff of his cologne, others might notice too. That would be a huge disaster.

Now that the spell is broken—I tell myself that even though Duncan's hands slide very slowly from off my waist—I notice the grey beanie he's wearing, with holes cut in for a pair of overly-fuzzy white wolf ears to poke through. *Probably a fake costume headband,* I assume.

"What are you doing here?" I ask in a strangled voice. Both of us stand still now as the sexy song continues to play, and various couples give us dirty looks as we don't move along. "*How* are you even here? Are you *stalking* me?"

Duncan grins sheepishly; I smell his anxiety. "I told you, my dad worked for Reis senior once. I went with him on the job at the time, so I remembered where the house was. And no, definitely not stalking. Well, I mean, *technically* it is, but—"

"Way to give me a heart attack, Ledford!" I say, peering around anxiously to make sure Lyle or anyone else isn't paying attention to this scene. *We need to go,* I think, determined.

Not considering the action before I do it, I grab Duncan's hand to tug him with me so we can get as far away from these party people as possible. This is the first time our bare skin has touched: something shocks us both, probably static from my fur, and my face turns pink as his hand drops from mine. Still, he gets the point and follows my lead.

Why is he here? I'm thinking, questions bouncing around my brain as the two of us maneuver between all the people crammed into this house. Trying to get out before anyone notices how human my companion is will be difficult.

"What's the rush?" Duncan asks as we finally reach the front door and head outside. I want to pull the ridiculous beanie and fake ears off his head, but that will have to wait.

"You're a *human*. At a *half-breed* party. After a week of us being mistreated by other humans," I explain curtly. "Do I really have to explain how it'll go if someone in this menagerie notices you're a human?"

"It's definitely a menagerie," Duncan speaks at an appropriate volume now that our words aren't overpowered by the beat of the song inside. "What are you all *on* in there?" His tone is more curious than derisive, so I'm not upset with him assuming that everyone here is high.

You're only upset that you had to stop dancing with him, my thoughts smugly point out to me, and I resist the urge to growl.

"Apparently we don't use our human senses a lot at these kinds of events," I say.

"That explains a lot of the behavior I was seeing—" I suddenly notice Shelby approaching with Ivar, although she hasn't seen us yet.

"Go get your car, now!" I hiss at Duncan, stepping in front of him. Maybe he got the idea that I don't want Shelby to see us together and possibly recognize him, because he swiftly obeys so she doesn't see him hurrying away from me.

"Hey, Shelbs!" I say with my absolutely brightest smile. "This is some party, huh?"

"How is the date going?" she asks with a smile, looking up adoringly at her boyfriend. "You look great"" she chortles. I don't know how long it will take Duncan to get the car from wherever he parked it, but I need to get rid of her. It's easy to fix a worried expression onto my face.

"Thanks. The date is going well...but I just got a text from my brother, and something is wrong at the house. Harold or Eisen is coming to get me. Plus I lost Lyle during the dance, and that seems like a bad thing to do on a date. I haven't been able to find him, so I came out here hoping—" I begin; Shelby understands and pats my arm in assurance.

"Don't worry, Shelbs and me will go find him for you," Ivar offers generously, looking fairly nice—if still enormous—in a grey jacket and faded jeans.

"Really?" I ask; there's no need to fake my relief.

"You can text him in the meantime and let him know you have to go, perhaps make plans for another time? Problem solved!" Shelby smiles fondly, adding the sand-papery feeling of guilt to my drama. She looks very different from me as she flounces away, around to the back of the house to find my not-boyfriend: she's wearing white to compliment her Arabian-esque skin and make it bronze, and somehow the overall effect is very sweet. Ivar lumbers after her, surprisingly quick for a boy his size.

I anxiously look around for Duncan's car, willing him to hurry. I wonder why he even came in the first place. *There's nothing for him at a half-breed event,* I muse. The only person he knows here is me, and not even that well.

Maybe it was enough that he wanted to see you sooner than tomorrow, my next thought whispers. I quash this mental rumor before my subconscious latches onto it too tightly. After a night of freedom like tonight, though, my reasonable thinking won't last long. Part of me still wants to be back inside, dancing with

Duncan under the strange lighting. Maybe it was how he looked at me when I turned around, maybe it was the spicy scent that surrounded him, or maybe it was how big his hands felt on my waist...all I know is that I really wish I'd just danced with him anyway.

Finally, I see Duncan's beige car pull up, and I hurry to climb in on the passenger side. He looks at me before we drive away, a side-ways glance with a close-lipped, smirking grin bespeaking great confidence.

"Hey," he says. I don't say anything as I settle as primly as I can in the passenger seat, trying to keep calm.

"You look good as a fox, by the way," he adds after another moment of awkward silence.

"I wish I could say the same about you as a...a wolf, right? But those ears are a little too puppy-ish to be real," I say roughly. I've curved my tail around into my lap, and I stroke it nervously.

"Then why were you so eager to take a drive with me?" he says before noticing my determination to not be amused. "Listen, Sierra—"

"Why did you come here tonight, Duncan? It doesn't make sense that you'd do something so stupid," I begin; he's silent this time, and I try to smooth over my harshness. "You're my friend, and you should know that it was a pretty bad idea for you to pick this party to crash." *Not that I regret it,* I think, and I'm tempted to fidget as I consider the mixed feelings punctuating my thoughts. Lyle didn't and couldn't affect me this way, I definitely know that now. *Perhaps it's a blessing Duncan came in when he did...*

Duncan sighs, both hands gripping the steering wheel as we drive. I tentatively allow my fox senses to return; it's hard to repress them so soon after giving free reign. I sense from my ginger friend a paradoxically nervous confidence, like a kid who's successfully stolen a desired toy from a high shelf. The scent of alluring cologne mixed with the unfamiliar canine scent lingers in the air, and I make a note to ask him about this along with my other questions.

"Okay, Sierra," he begins in an ominous tone, "I...a lot of what I want to tell you is going to be fairly hard to say, and even tougher for you to believe, I think. You seemed pretty unenthusiastic about this party tonight, and since I knew where it was and that you would be there, I decided to go. Maybe it was a bad idea?" His last statement is a question which produces more questions, and my eyebrows arch in confusion.

"Maybe?" I say. "You would've gotten beat up if you hadn't found me soon. Did you forget my kind can actually *smell* any human who approached the house?"

"I didn't forget," he says quietly. "That's part of why I'm here. And part of where we're going." I take the time to observe my surroundings.

"Where *are* we going?" I ask; I thought we were aimlessly driving nowhere.

"See, I figured if I went and found you, you might be...eager to get me out of there before someone found me. Sorry if that was a dick move, it just seemed like the best plan at the time," he says, turning to look at me with a semi-apologetic expression. I nod, wanting him to continue justifying his appearance. "So I prepared some stuff so you might not miss the party so much. I-I kind of got the impression that you liked hanging out with me, so I didn't think you'd be too mad."

"You're kidnapping me?" I look toward the back seat he gestures to. There's a shopping bag full of marshmallows, chocolate, and graham crackers. My stomach grumbles, and I realize I'm hungry after all the dancing. Speaking of dancing...

"I was on a date," I say, wondering how this curiously assertive version of Duncan will react. He doesn't disappoint me: there's no arrogance I have to snap back at.

"Gosh, I'm sorry...I didn't know that," he exclaims with real repentance. "I did see you dancing with the lion kid, but I didn't put it together. If you want to go back I can turn around—"

"It's fine," I cut him off. "You brought s'mores. I might forgive you if you explain." I meant to make him feel better—it was important that he not feel bad for some reason—but I might have made him feel more awkward.

"Was—was your date going well?" He asks after a moment while I try to figure out where we're going. I realize I need to answer this for myself as well.

"I guess so. We were flirting, but it didn't really feel like—" *Like when you and I were dancing together. Like when your hands were on me instead of his.* I finish the sentence in my head, but not aloud. "I was pretty much over the party," I admit to him and myself.

"That's good, I suppose." He looks relieved.

"So where *are* we going, actually?" I ask again as

we exit the large, ordinarily sleepy neighborhood. My eyes pick out random details passing us by now that the elegant antique houses have given way to an un-crowded stretch of highway. I glance at the clock on the dashboard, and it surprises me that I was at the party for at least two hours. *All that time dancing with Lyle. I wonder where he thinks I am?* At least Shelby will cover for me; I'll have to think up some family emergency worth leaving a party for.

"I happen to know of a nice lake closer to the mountains that isn't more than twenty minutes from this area," Duncan says matter-of-factly. "As far as kidnappings go, this isn't much: if you demanded I take you back to the Reiss' place, I would. Plus, this area isn't really too secluded...I didn't want to seem like too much of a creeper."

"It's a good plan," I admit. "You engaged my curiosity, so I can't leave until I find out what all this is about."

Duncan looks over at me with a slightly lopsided grin. "That's not much incentive to start explaining right away."

"Please," I snort. "I think it'll take you more than a twenty minute drive to explain this." I suddenly find the ears perched atop his head more amusing than annoying. I didn't realize it would be easier to relax away from all those people.

"How's this: question for question. You ask me something, I answer, then I get to ask you something," he proposes as we change lanes and go on one of those circular turns on the road that make me a bit dizzy. So far, we haven't gone on any back roads yet, but I'm watching. I can't explain how I trust Duncan, but I *am* keeping an eye out for my brothers' sake. Besides, even if Duncan did have bad intentions, I'm stronger than him since I'm half-breed; it wouldn't be too difficult to fight back or run away.

"I'm not the one crashing parties and taking risks, so what could you possibly ask me?" I ask.

"Well if that's the question you want to ask first, I'll answer, but—"

"Hey! No, that's not my first question!" I exclaim. "Let me think of a good one..." Now that I have the opportunity, my questions avoid my tongue like shy toddlers.

"Five...Four...Three..." Duncan counts down teasingly.

"All right! Why do you smell like dog under whatever cologne you're wearing?" I blurt; turns out my words aren't shy at all. "I mean this in the least offensive way, of course."

"You can smell that?" Duncan asks, sounding interested and surprised. We pass under a streetlight, and I notice he's wearing a green, three-quarter sleeve t-shirt that looks very, *very* good on his chest and arms. He's more muscular than I thought he was now that he's in something a little more flattering than what he wears to school. *Focus.*

"Is that your question?" I ask, turning the tables on him with my own sharp-toothed smile.

"No, of course not...but I'm surprised you noticed that. Or, I guess I'm *not* surprised. It makes sense, considering you're part fox and had your senses cranked up." He reaches up to absentmindedly rub his hand over the dark red stubble covering his jaw, making me realize that perhaps my desire for closeness didn't fade once I left the party.

"Let's just say that question will have to wait until I can show you in a few minutes...you wouldn't believe me if I just told you," he continues. "But so you can't say I evaded answering...it's the same reason I chose this particular costume to wear." He gestures to the fake wolf ears on his head.

I blink, confused; the only thing I can think of is that he let his pet dog sleep on the clothes before wearing them to get the scent. Perhaps he notices this, because he sighs in frustration.

"Sorry...I'm being cryptic and annoying. Let's move on, and I promise, all will be revealed soon," he says.

"Your turn then," I say, relenting.

"Okay, I'll start with something easy: do half-breeds have to be vegetarians? Or, are most of them vegetarians?"

I can't help it; I laugh. "That depends on whether or not the DNA they share is of a prey or predatory nature. My friend Morgan has deer DNA, so she mostly sticks to salads and fruit. My other friends and I don't have problems with eating meat because it's part of our nature to need and desire meat," I say. "I don't know if there are lions and bears who confine themselves to bunny-food out there, but I would say it's a rarity, and they'd be healthier if they just ate some chicken or beef now and then."

"That's a relief," Duncan mutters, probably thinking I won't hear. "Your turn!"

His questions are maddeningly interesting, but I

know how the game works now, so I don't dig into why he asked what.

For the rest of the drive, we warm up by each asking a few silly questions—things like "why are you so tall?" and "how often do you give in to the urge to hunt squirrels?"—but then we fall into a rapid-fire pattern of question-answer to get the most relevant information across.

"Why did you come with me tonight instead of just making me leave the party?" he asks when it's his turn.

"I wanted to make sure you actually got away, and it seemed like you would need my help," I reply. In hindsight, he probably would've been okay on his own if he managed to get in there without setting off any alarms, but I don't regret leaving. I keep telling myself it's not the same, but this feels more like a date than the whole arrangement with Lyle.

"Why did your friends act like they knew me already when we met earlier today?" I ask.

Even though it's dark, I see Duncan's ears go pink. "I told them about you...I kind of had to, since I blew off some after-school plans with Aaden and Bari when I went to Omnium Beanery with you. Are you and Lyle going to start dating soon?"

"What? No!" I say; if Lyle was in hearing range, I'd be embarrassed. "Why would you think that?"

"It...it seemed like you two were having lot of fun dancing," he says quietly.

If I'm willing to admit I'm starting to really like Duncan in spite of nothing being able to come of it— nothing productive and nothing he would want to work for—then I understand why it's important to me that he knows I'm not interested in anyone else.

Especially Lyle, I decide in a flash. There's no point trying to force something that won't work.

"How long were you at the party before you ran into me?" I ask for my next question.

"Only a couple songs before I found you...I kind of stood to the side, looking around and taking everything in before I got up the nerve to try dancing," he confesses. "I did...I did watch you and lion boy for a little while, but that was because I was trying to figure out how to get near you without hurting anyone by trying to dance."

"You're a good dancer, let me tell you," I say, thinking back to when I grabbed Duncan's hand and how his skin felt. It's flattering that Duncan did watch me dance for a little. *Was he jealous?*

"How—"

"You might want to hold that thought, since we're rapidly approaching our destination," Duncan interrupts me as we pull into a small parking lot.

The scent of the lake breeze drifts under my nose as we park. We're several feet away from the gleaming, crystal clear lake reflecting the slanted moon dangling in the atmosphere. There are wooden picnic tables closer to the lake set up with grey plastic solar lanterns already charged and lit from being in the sun all day. My night vision already makes my eyes glow an ethereal green, which I can see in the rearview mirror of the car.

"Wow," I say as Duncan comes and opens my door, letting me out of the car like a gentleman. "I'm impressed. We don't have a lot of areas like this near our half-breed neighborhood."

"You don't?" He asks incredulously as he shuts my door and opens the back so he can get the s'mores materials. "That's a shame...I think your kind might appreciate views like this more than humans."

"Maybe," I hedge. The last thing I want to do is whine about how few breaks my kind gets when it comes to living space. "My family is lucky; we have a decent sized townhouse instead of the apartments and houses scattered around less savory neighborhoods. Comes of having a lawyer for a guardian, I guess."

Duncan and I discuss more trivial things as we walk towards one of the tables closest to the lake and farthest from the parking lot. I'm sensing his nervous confidence again, but I don't comment on it. He promised to communicate, so I'll wait until we're set up and he feels more comfortable.

Still, I'm so curious I could burst, and anxious as well. *What could be so important that he'd risk and plan all of this?*

"So I bet you're wondering why I summoned you," Duncan says after skewering three marshmallows on a poker and holding a torch lighter to each one.

"I'm madly curious," I say as I watch blue-tongued flames lick at the dusty surface of each marshmallow. "If those are for me, I prefer charred rather than brown."

"So you like the taste of ashes in your mouth?" he asks with a laugh only a little flavored with nerves.

"I suppose I'm used to it since that's what I taste whenever I walk into school," I quip, sniffing the heavenly smell of smoke on the air and cooking

255

marshmallow. Duncan hands me the skewer and I sit on the bench of the table facing the lake, blowing out the flames when my treats attain the blackened appearance marshmallows need for perfection. I'm so hungry I don't wait to eat as Duncan takes his time browning his own marshmallows.

"Do you think of yourself as gullible, Sierra?" he asks once we both sit down to eat; none of us bothered with the chocolate or the graham crackers. I shake my head, knowing that if I speak he'll only hear the sound of marshmallow gooeyness muffling my speech. "Good...if you believe me, that means I'm not crazy after all."

I swallow my second marshmallow with a gulp. "Seriously Duncan, what's this about?"

He takes a deep breath, blowing on his marshmallows to cool them. "I have a couple things to tell you and ask you, and it took me a while to figure out in which order to present the material."

"You sound like a student teacher," I say, stress responding. Blessedly he ignores my word vomit, and I listen as I brush the ash out of the fur on my hands.

"Okay...so...right. Sierra, have you ever heard of someone human developing half-breed traits?"

"Yes, we all have. Didn't the entire war start once enough humans began developing animal traits that the humans felt threatened?" I say, remembering the pictures in every single history class I ever took.

Duncan nods, also wincing: the last war was the worst because it was more like an attempted extermination. For once, all the humans were allies in what they perceived was a global pest control situation.

"Yes. And as we know, didn't they find a scientific reason for why humans would stay human and why M-DNA people would always produce half-breed offspring?" he says, still speaking like he's teaching a lesson. He eats one of his marshmallows whole, chewing while I think. In the back of my mind, I worry if I have marshmallow goo or ash stuck to my nose, and I casually brush off any residue that might be on my face. My senses are all human now as I try to think.

"Yeah. The scientists managed to modify the contaminated DNA so we half-breeds would stay mostly human except for our senses and certain physical mutations, but you have to have a specific genetic code for the animal DNA to latch on to," I say. "No human can just develop animal DNA out of the blue, not anymore, not if they were already born human." A canine scent drifts right under my nose as I finish speaking: familiar, emanating from Duncan's direction. It's not unpleasant, and it actually overwhelms the cologne that had me so distracted at the party.

Suddenly...

No, I think. *There's no possible way...*

"Well, this is me breaking the mold," Duncan says dryly, looking right into my eyes as he blinks and the unmistakable glow of night-vision gleams in his eyes that have turned tawny brown.

19

I don't know how to respond. I sit frozen like a rabbit, my tail and ears quivering as I stare into Duncan's sepia eyes; they're brown, but tawny gold rings the outer circle of the iris. Irrelevant to the moment, I wonder if he has fur like any other half-breed.

He's silent, but he's trying to show me further proof: his scent is stronger now, like he whipped a covering off a food dish—unfortunately it's equally appetizing—and I think if I tried hard enough I could determine what breed of canine DNA he has. Ridiculously, I focus again on the ears on top of his head. *He can't be a wolf,* I confirm, *he doesn't have the personality.*

"Please say something," he pleads. A dozen responses flood my mouth, rushing towards the front, but the weirdest one makes it through.

"You have marshmallow on your chin," I say woodenly. "You should probably get it before it sticks in your fur...I mean, your beard."

Duncan blinks, and now that my eyes have adjusted to the dim lighting of the lantern on the table and to the moonlight, I miss the peridot green I'd learned to enjoy.

"That's not quite the something I meant," he says, brushing the marshmallow away with his fingertips. I self-consciously brush at my nose again, hoping there's nothing on my face.

"You're right...I don't believe you," I say. "But then...I do. You wouldn't risk sharing this knowledge with someone you've only known a week unless you had proof." I don't want to be the silly girl who goes into denial with all the proof right in front of her.

"You're right," he says. "I do. I...Sierra, you're the only half-breed I can trust right now. I've been going out of my mind since this began months ago, wondering if I've gone crazy, or what all this will lead to. But...never mind that. I have more proof."

I nod. "So far, I can see your eyes have turned, and you *reek* of dog," I don't mention how much I actually *like* his smell. "I don't know how you mask your scent against half-breeds, but any proof you can give me that your DNA spontaneously mutated would be helpful." I'm proud of myself for not shouting or bolting away from this strange boy with his strange mixed scents and the voice that makes me want to nuzzle against his neck and trust more than I should.

"Okay," Duncan says. "I should thank you for your

open mind, but I know your instincts are going absolutely crazy right now. If it's any consolation, mine are too. I've never told anyone else about this."

"Just…explain. I believe you, I can't deny it, but…" I squeeze out the words haltingly.

"Okay," Duncan says, and then he smiles. It's not the real smile I like, but it serves a purpose: I see how sharp his canines are now, how they're a little bigger than even my slightly pointy teeth. He stands up suddenly—well, suddenly to me—watching me very carefully, and moving slower than usual to make sure I don't startle.

"This part is a little weird…but bear with me," he says with a strained chuckle.

I haven't moved, and I clutch my tail tightly as it rests in my lap, my eyes probably gleaming green in the dark. Duncan doesn't take his eyes off my face as he slowly grabs the bottom of his t-shirt and pulls it up and over his head. Ordinarily, two reactions to this would be my excitement that I get to see the bare chest of the boy I reluctantly have a crush on, or complete confusion over why this boy I hardly know is stripping his shirt off purely for my benefit. However, the situation being what it is, I can guess why he's doing this.

Sure enough, once his shirt is off, he tosses it on the table beside the s'mores supplies and turns around to show me his back. I see what I expect: a ridge of sable and chestnut fur, thick and raised like hackles. It goes all the way from the middle of his neck, down his spine to below his belt where I can't see it anymore. I take another sniff of the breeze carrying his scent, slowly opening myself back up to my fox senses.

Not Rhodesian ridgeback, despite the huge hands...not wolf either, I think, puzzling over what breed of canine Duncan's genes melded with.

"Do you know what kind of animal you are?" I ask him as he slowly turns back around. I've seen the brown and black tones of the fur, and also by the scent, I think I know for sure what he is.

"Obviously I know I'm a dog of some kind, although it's hard to tell for sure without animal ears and a tail," he confesses, walking back over to grab his shirt. "I don't know if those will magically grow in as my DNA continues changing, honestly."

The scent of him is almost overpoweringly attractive now, which confuses me. Even as a fox, I don't have any battles to fight with hounds, but it's not like me to be this attracted to the spicy, homey smell of my friend who is apparently a canine.

"You're part German Shepherd," I tell him, watching his chest in the moonlight. *Even better than you dreamed, hm?* My girly subconscious, enamored of Duncan, purrs in my head; if it was a person instead of a figment of my imagination, I'd smack it into next week. My breath catches in my throat a little, and I'm glad Duncan is occupied with re-clothing himself so he won't notice me ogling the play of the toned muscles under his smooth, gleaming skin. There may be a thick ridge of hackles on his spine, but his chest isn't furry at all, except for a little down by the V of his hipbones. The freckles sprinkling his skin are more endearing than off-putting. I clear my throat, more to distract myself than to get his attention.

"German Shepherd, hm?" He pauses, considering; finally, he removes the beanie and the costume ears off his head, and his messy red hair poofs out. "Not what I expected...it would've been cooler and more sensible if I was a wolf. Wolves can have red fur," he thinks aloud.

"So do some German Shepherds. I've known wolves, and trust me, you don't have the personality for that," I inform him, shivering as a chill comes from the lake. "German Shepherds are loyal and a lot smarter than people give them credit for. It's not a bad choice, if you'd had to make one."

"I wish I had," he says. "I'm not saying that I wouldn't choose this...but if you had the chance to change to a human, would you?"

"I might have a few years ago...but now I wouldn't. I like being what I am," I say, smoothing my skirt over my legs so I won't have to look at his face after staring so long at his body. "But I don't blame you for wishing you'd stayed human."

Duncan plops back down next to me, leaning forward so his elbows are on his knees as he looks pensively at the lake. We're both silent for a few minutes, and I'm sure both of our thoughts whirl around chaotically.

"Thanks for...understanding. I didn't know what response to expect from you, but I had to—I had to tell someone," Duncan says, his voice low; there's a new tone to it now, something deeper, pleasant, and more like a rumbling growl in the chest. I wonder if that's a product of his new DNA. "I had to tell a half-breed, and I'm glad it was you."

Instead of asking how any of this even came to be, or how he's been hiding all of this from friends and foes alike, I ask: "Did you befriend me just because you thought I'd be sympathetic, or just because I'm a half-breed?" *Please be honest,* I add in my head. It would hurt me more if he lied than if he told me it was purely selfish motives.

"Sierra...no, I didn't. Those motives were in play, but they weren't the main ones. If I had needed a half-breed to tell, it would have been a lot easier to find someone to talk to when all of this started the end of my junior year," he tells me. He regards me earnestly, his irises back to the pale green I missed. His hand twitches towards where mine are folded on my lap, but then he mirrors my posture, folding his own hands together.

"Why me?" I ask quietly.

Duncan still regards me intently. "You showed up to school this week, not hiding a thing like rest of your kind was, and you were kind to me when I expected more of an attitude against humanity than friendliness. I talked to you because you caught my interest, and even though I pursued you for my own reasons, I would still want to be around you even if you had rejected all of this tonight." I look up at him for a few moments, waiting to catch a lie in his eyes or from his face. But I don't, and my shoulders relax when I decide to trust him.

Careful, Sierra, my thoughts remind me yet again, and this time I decide not to listen.

"Okay," I say simply.

"You sure?" he asks.

I nod this time, still looking into his eyes. I'm not afraid of him being repelled by my animalistic eyes or by my fur or my fox features. *We are the same*, I think, and I wonder what my scent is like for him. Hope blossoms in my silly heart, and I don't have the strength to squash it while I'm daydreaming about running my fingers through Duncan's hair.

"We've known each other hardly a week, I drop a bombshell on you like 'Hey, just so you know, I'm secretly a half-breed too! Even though I was born human with no history of animal in my bloodline, and I just stole you away from a party to take my shirt off and show you the new German Shepherd fur I grew over the summer,' and you just say 'okay'? That's it?" He rattles off the naked details, crazy as they sound, just to contest my simplistic response.

"It does sound nuts when you say it like that. But...you showed me kindness too, Duncan, in a place and in a time where my kind is almost worth nothing. You might have had a few selfish motives, but somehow...it's not in your nature to be cruel, and that makes me trust you," I say, to myself as much as to him; a sideways smile edges the corner of my mouth. "Must be that fox DNA kicking in, responding to human—well, semi-human—kindness. One week or not, if you were a different sort of person, I think you would have manifested a different kind of DNA. I know there's no science to back that particular statement up, but we half-breeds do know that the animal DNA does often depend on personality." I take a deep breath, hoping I didn't say too much and scare him off. He gapes at me incredulously, almost in shock that it would be so easy to persuade me that's he's telling the truth and means well.

"I...now I'm the one who doesn't know what to say," Duncan says in that low tone of voice again. I inhale his scent through my nose as surreptitiously as possible.

"Well, you just explained why you had so many questions about half-breeds while we were at Omnium Beanery," I say. "I guess this time it's my turn to ask all the questions, about your speculations and what you plan to do about your increasingly dominant half-breed DNA." Duncan grimaces, opening his mouth to reply, but I cut him off.

"Really, do you have any idea at all how this happened? How have you been hiding it, since normal half-breeds can't hide their scents from other half-breeds?" I ask, curious and fascinated now that my instincts stopped telling me to run away. I wonder if Duncan will suddenly grow ears and a tail, or maybe fur on his hands; I wonder if he'll be as animalistic as Wade.

"I think it's because I started out human. The part of DNA that keeps me human—in spite of however the serum in that damn mandatory vaccine failed—helps me *seem* human if I want, at least when it comes to having a human scent," Duncan explains rationally. I kind of expect him to elaborate further, but he falls silent. I think he's lost in thought, but the way he's looking at my face draws heat to my cheeks and keeps me from speaking for a moment.

"Duncan, what—" I begin, but he shakes his head.

"Would you be horribly upset if I asked for your

other questions to wait for when we meet tomorrow?" he asks. "That is, if you still want to."

"I'll wait, if you want...but you don't have to keep me curious to keep me around," I say; the high-pitched quality of my voice makes me wonder if I sound desperate, so I modify. "We're friends. I'll keep your secret, and I'll still be around."

Duncan nods, self-conscious as he runs a hand through his hair. "I know...but it *is* getting pretty late, and I don't want your brothers to attack me if I drop you off past midnight."

"Really? It's almost midnight?" At this I go to reach for my SMARTcall, but I remember I left it in Duncan's car, so I pause. It's almost like time doesn't matter after a night of discovery like this...but I know if I push the limit and show up late, Harold might actually cut my curfew to what Wade and Eisen had during their high school years.

"We both lost track of time, I think," Duncan says, stating the obvious.

"After what happened tonight...first that whirlwind party, then this," I marvel at how I expected this night to go and what actually happened.

"Do you regret it?" Duncan asks. "Me telling you any of this, I mean?" I shake my head in a negative.

"No. I don't regret leaving the party, and I don't regret you trusting me enough to share this impossible information with me," I reply. To avoid sounding too sappy, I stand and turn to the table to gather up the torch and marshmallow skewers. "I don't have a clue how to help or what to do about it, but I'm glad you're not dealing with this on your own."

"Me too," Duncan says, and then I freeze as his hand gently rests on top of mine, his palm on my fur as I clutch the coarse handle of the cookout skewer a little too tightly. "I have one more question."

I'm still frozen, hardly able to think with Duncan's hand on mine. Part of me, the most inconsequential part I'm not listening to, tells me just how ridiculous I am for being so enthralled when a boy touches my hand; but the rest of me is absolutely thrilled, and I have to work to keep my expression from showing my inner turmoil. The fact that he's willingly touching me is captivating, and I kind of wish he'd hold my hand a little tighter.

"Ask away," I say, pleased my voice doesn't crack.

"This was what I didn't know how to ask without sounding like an idiot...but...Sierra," Duncan says, his voice a little lower. "Is there...is there any tendency in the M-DNA strain that makes us bond to one person very quickly?"

I tear my gaze away from our linked hands to look at his face, my heart thumping erratically. "Not...not scientifically," I say, too quietly; I clear my throat and try to explain. "There are theories, of course, and varying degrees of proof...but how would you know about that? I didn't tell you." Duncan nods like I confirmed something, his eyes closed as he thinks.

What...? He opens his eyes and they're that canine dark brown again, too deep for me to read. Then he smiles, a genuine smile that makes the fur on my spine stand up pleasantly.

"Looks like it won't be so bad to be a half-breed after all," he says cryptically. I'd chastise him for his vagueness, but he runs the pad of his thumb over the auburn fur covering my knuckles and I struggle to remember what I was going to say. He's looking up at me with something like wonder coloring his expression, and heat rushes to my cheeks from the pounding of my bewildered heart. I want to lean forward, close enough to...

"We should go," I say instead, not knowing how else to respond. I remove my hand—reluctantly—from under Duncan's and finish gathering the stuff. He helps, and we walk back to the car in silence. I sense that weird confidence from him again, and I sigh, glad at least that I'll have more information tomorrow. I'm also glad that I see him so soon, more than I'd admit to anyone else, even Hayley.

We're silent on the way back, except for me giving Duncan directions to my house. That silly hope blossoms within me again, and I hope that my determined silence will keep me from making any mistakes tomorrow.

I don't check my phone until I'm back inside my house. Upon my request, Duncan dropped me off half a block down the road; I didn't want him seen by my family, in case someone was waiting up for me. Eisen was waiting for me in the living room, his long legs sprawled out across our somewhat battered brown corduroy sofa. I'd decided not to wake him, but right when I finish removing my dusty black pumps and head for the stairs, his eyes snap open.

"You almost missed curfew, little sister," Eisen says in a drowsy voice filled with gravel. I glance at the digital clock built into the wall above our chipped green front door.

"It's only just now 12:45, Eisen," I say. "You should go to bed." I turn to go up the stairs again, glad I don't have to flick any lights on to see in the dark, but he stops me again.

"Who dropped you off? I thought you were going to text when you needed to come home," Eisen asks casually; I hear him stretching as he stands and grabs his blanket for his bed off the couch to drag back upstairs. I bite my lip, not wanting to lie, but knowing that I might be in big trouble if I don't. I decide to fudge some details.

"Some guy from the party I met, one of Issachar Reis's college buddies...he's of driving age, and he knew some of us in this area needed rides home, so he took us," I say. It sounds like a lousy plan, and I'm not one to willingly carpool, but it's the best excuse I have for right now. *I can tell the truth once I know more about Duncan and what's going with that,* I think to appease the acid feeling of guilt slithering into my stomach.

"There were college guys there? Damn, S, that might not have been the best plan to take a ride from one. Plus, since when do high school parties end before five a.m., and since when would a college guy—a friend of that dick Issachar Reis, no less—leave a party early?" Eisen questions, sounding a little irritated now he's thinking through my plan. I shrug innocently, secretly longing for my shower so I can climb into bed and digest all the information I learned before I sleep.

"A lot of high school students have curfews, Eisen. Just because you constantly broke yours and worried Harold to death doesn't mean everyone else follows the same pattern," I say, knowing full well that the party is still probably going strong and will for a couple more hours. "How do you know Issachar Reis?"

Eisen grimaces. "We'd be the same year in college, if I'd been able to go. He's one of those privileged rich kid brats, and I was glad to see the back of him after graduation...but still. You shouldn't be taking rides from college boys, Sierra."

"It wasn't exactly a dangerous situation, Eisen, there were more people than me in the car," I say, brushing off his concern in spite of knowing he's right. All I want to do is escape before Eisen smells the marshmallow smoke and the lake breeze coming off me along with lingering party sweat and my own scent.

"Okay, goodnight then," Eisen capitulates to my reason easily, probably because he's half asleep. I reply with my own goodnight and escape to my room to prepare for my shower.

My phone feels like it's burning a hole in my wristlet, and I just know there will be frantic texts piled up for me to read and respond to before I can sleep. The mirror in my room catches my attention, however, and I take one last look at my appearance before responding to

271

the summons emanating from my SMARTcall. My hair isn't as curly anymore, and I look like I danced a lot, but my clothes don't look any worse for the wear. Maybe I expected that after all of the information Duncan gave me I'd look more exhausted, but I look much the same as I did when I left the house with Harold.

My latest text message reads:

DUNCAN LEDFORD: *Thanks for tonight. I really appreciated your cooperation with the whole kidnapping gig. See you tomorrow!*

I smile before I can help it. *Why is it so easy to like this boy?* I think. My other notes don't look like they'll be as pleasant.

SHELBY JEAN: *I found Lyle and explained what's going on. Let me know how things are with your family!*

MORGAN CHEPI: *Lyle is looking for you! I thought you were having a good time??*

FEMI REIS: *Hey Maurell. Are you in the bathroom with a drink or did you leave with a boy? I get it, just please say you're fine, or tell your friends you're okay.*

I can't believe I forgot to tell my host I was abandoning her party, but I quickly text everyone back to let them know I'm fine. I embellish a little story about how Harold was having a bad time with a case and wanted me home safe, knowing that they won't ask a lot of details about lawyer business.

Finished, I look up into the mirror and grimace; I'm not used to having my whereabouts questioned so thoroughly, and I know that sometime I'll have to get back to Lyle and let him know we're not going to work out after all. Shelby and Morgan will want to know why, but female confidentiality isn't really my thing. At the most, I'll confide in Hayley, or even in her mother if I really need advice.

This is going to be one hell of a weekend, I think, excited but nervous about tomorrow.

20

Sleeping didn't seem within reach when I finally climbed into bed, but my slumber refreshed me after all. I awoke this Saturday with the sun shining in through the grey and white curtains on my window, and it seemed like it was going to be a very good day. I hummed and took my time brushing the waves of my hair and my fur, and selecting what clothes to wear—jeans as dark as Duncan's were last night and a purple shirt with flounces at the collar—came easily to me. I purposefully ignored my phone: I checked only for my new half-breed friend's name before closing all the text windows.

Now, eating breakfast with Eisen and Harold is relaxing, except for the need to fudge some of the details of the party last night. I answer their questions absentmindedly as I eat some scrambled eggs sandwiched between two pieces of perfectly browned toast, wondering when Duncan will contact me again today. Wade is still snoozing, we assume.

"You know, it's really lucky all three of you have Saturday off," I say as I grab a sausage link off the platter Harold set on the table. It occurs to me that I haven't cooked as much as usual lately, and I bless my brothers for being so willing to help me out on top of their own obligations.

"A rare but welcome occurrence," Harold says, everything about him proper except for the messy black fur on his ears and tail. "The office didn't need me this morning."

"For once the boss didn't spend his Friday night drinking...I heard his wife was having an anniversary party and he was dreading the arrival of his sister-in-law....so I get this fine day off as well," Eisen leans back on his favorite kitchen chair, and he stifles a yawn as he speaks. He finished eating first, of course, and I notice that he doesn't have any spilled food on his bare, lean chest. *Good to know he's not a messy eater anymore,* I think with a nostalgic smile.

"Maybe when his majesty arises from his beauty sleep I'll wash all of your bedding and do some laundry," I say, deciding I might as well get a few things done before donating the rest of my day to Duncan. Harold gives me an odd look, abandoning the observation of stock stats on his SMARTpad.

"You're in a positive mood today, Sierra. How good was that party last night?" he remarks, and I'm glad he sounds more curious than suspicious. I open my mouth to reply, but Eisen cuts me off.

"Good enough she got a ride home from a college friend of Issachar Reis's," he mutters, giving me a sideways look of mischief before taking his dirty plate and fork to our tiny but clean metal sink. Harold sputters, choking on the sugar laced sip of coffee he'd been about to swallow. I wince.

"You took a ride home from a college boy you don't even *know*?" he exclaims in a loud voice, benefiting me with the full front of his worried, stern expression. I glare at Eisen, hissing "troublemaker!" under my breath. His shoulders shake a little from laughter as he meekly washes his plate.

"It's not a big deal, Harold, it was only a carpool with a few others," I explain, directing dagger eyes at my golden brother's back to avoid the scowl on Harold's face. I really wish I wasn't lying, but I don't appreciate Eisen's droopy-eared mischief when he's trying to get me in trouble.

"That was a bad idea, Sierra," Harold begins his lecture. "The Reis family can make very good friends, but sometimes their associates are affiliated with...less than savory characters, which—"

"He means the whole family is mafia royalty," Eisen cuts in with a dark laugh. "So watch out, or they might end up taking the cannoli and leaving the gun, if you get what I'm saying—" I cut him off this time before Harold can, annoyed.

"Since when do you make jokes from old movies?" I say indignantly. "I don't even see how this is any of your business, brother."

"It is when you come home smelling like—" I'm very

relieved Wade decides now is the time to make an appearance. I shamelessly dodge the tail end of Eisen's coming accusation to greet my grumpy looking brother with a smile and a hug.

"Hi, Wade! Happy Saturday!" I say, enjoying the sleepy smell of Wade's pajama shirt even if I am using him to avoid trouble. Eisen snorts behind me as Wade gingerly hugs me back.

"Do not be fooled by this subterfuge, my brother," Eisen begins, striding forward to pry me away from Wade. "This is merely a ploy meant to garner your trust—"

"Let it be, Eisen," Harold interjects, apparently tired of the conversation. I loosen my grip on Wade, surprised as Harold relents in lecturing me and Eisen consequently stops trying to separate me from a very confused Wade.

Why are my brothers acting so weird? I think, bewildered. It's not like Eisen to sell me out to Harold, it's not like Harold to suddenly relent mid-lecture, and Wade...

...It's not like Wade to be so quiet. I pull back from hugging Wade, which probably allows him to breathe better now that I've relinquished my death grip on his torso. Something is wrong, and I sense it as well as see it in Wade's sharp fur and limp tail. I always know this, like I always could tell he was in trouble from the way he'd have a devil-may-care smirk on his face and a bad attitude when he was hurt. I turn around to observe the rest of my family; Harold scrutinizes Wade as well.

"Wade? What's up?" Eisen asks, speaking first. Harold is silent, knowing an explanation will come soon.

"Bound to happen eventually, we knew," Wade starts, and I hear that he is more angry than sad. *Must not be Emilee, then,* I think with some relief. My brothers don't really date much, but the event of Wade and Emilee has been a long time coming, and I don't want it to end so soon.

"What happened, Wade?" I ask quietly, attempting and failing to pull my brother over to a chair. He shakes me off and stands rigid, a disgusted curl hovering at the edges of his lips.

"They fired me. They waited until I'd be home on my day off, then they sent me a SMARTnote letting me know I'd been laid off for 'reasons we cannot disclose at this present time.'" He speaks each word distinctly, like each and every syllable personally offended him. The four of us are silent, our thoughts directed with confusion and frustration towards the SMARTfactory we thought liked Wade.

"Morons," Eisen growls, glaring up at the ceiling. Harold still doesn't speak, but he wordlessly walks to our fridge and grabs one of our very few beers from the back of the refrigerator. He pops the top and hands it to Wade, who allows his stiff posture to break long enough to give Harold a tight nod of thanks.

"Beer at ten in the morning?" I question, trying to break the tension a little. Wade shrugs, also shrugging off the knowledge that the drinking age for half-breeds is twenty-five instead of nineteen.

Once again, my thoughts don't know what to do with themselves. *It was supposed to be a good day,* they whine plaintively before zeroing in on the problem of Wade being fired. *Of course, it's obvious why they fired him...look at his face!* Perhaps especially when he's angry, Wade looks more fox-like than human, and in a sick way I understand why the humans would care about that more than Wade's talent with manipulating technology.

"That can't be legal, can it?" Eisen breaks our silence as we ponder what we're going to do about this situation. "Not saying why they fired him, I mean. With all the half-breed regulations in place, something about that can't be legal. We should complain."

"I think we all know why they fired me," Wade says bitterly, taking another long swig from the dark brown bottle in his fist. I want to hug him again, but I don't.

"Oh, we're going to go in to complain, I promise you that," Harold says in a tone so cold I'm exceedingly glad I'm not on the receiving end of his censure. "I don't know if there's anything we can do about it, but I know your boss does like you, even if he fired you from peer pressure, or because someone went over his head. Either way..." He frowns, trailing off as he drums his fingers on the hard surface of our cheap wooden table. Abruptly, he gets up and walks into the living room towards the stairs; I assume he's going to get dressed in lawyer attire.

"I'm sorry, Wade," I say at last, now that a plan of action is on the table. "Like Harold said, I don't know how much can be done...but I hope if you talk with your boss, he'll re-hire you."

Wade snorts. "Like I'd actually want to work there again...still, not like I have a choice, right?"

His bitterness is contagious, and I look around at my brothers, thinking of the injustice that surrounds our lives because of what we are. *Harold, overworked and underpaid half-breed lawyer...Eisen, overworked and socially abused at Omnium Beanery, too poor to go to college because of taxes...Wade, still in debt from a year of trade school, fired because of his appearance...and me, harassed at a human school I don't even want to be in with no future plans to speak of.* I tally up the grievances in my head, my own bitterness seeping out from where I store it in the corners of my mind. *When will it end? Will it ever end?*

"What will you do if they don't take you back?" Eisen asks bluntly, getting up and walking to the tiny laundry closet behind our kitchen. He comes out after a moment, pulling a wrinkled blue t-shirt over his head and mussing the fur on his gold ears. Wade shakes his head, still stiff.

"I just got the note this morning, so I don't have any new plans yet," he confesses. "Honestly...I had my life planned out for the next few years, and now the entire thing got overturned by one act of bigotry." A rumbling sound fills the kitchen, and it takes me a moment to realize that it's all of us, growling softly and deep in our throats.

"I can imagine: factory work for life, marriage with Emilee, the whole apple pie life?" Eisen sounds so bitter that Wade offers him a swig of his beer, and Eisen tips back the bottle with a sour look on his face.

I'm not surprised by Eisen's deduction; half-breeds marry fairly early if they can, and it's not uncommon for strong bonds to form within very short periods of time. As I think this, my heart skips forward and then back a few beats; Duncan brought this subject up yesterday, and just thinking back to his hand on mine is distracting. *Not the time!* I mentally hiss at the sappy feeling tugging the heart strings of my memory.

"Yeah, right," Wade says, startling me back into the present. He reclaims his beer from Eisen and grabs a sausage link off the chipped yellow platter before departing to get dressed in his work uniform. "Here's to hoping Harold can wheedle my boss into taking me back."

Eisen and I look at each other, mirror expressions of worry and frustration coloring our eyes.

Eisen departs as well, called into work very shortly after Harold and Wade march off to do battle with the bigots at Wade's SMARTfactory. I confess I'm a little relieved: I don't want to hear what Eisen thought I was doing last night, at least not yet. My happy Saturday still has a chance to recover somewhat, but the whole day has been tainted by my concern for Wade and my disappointment that he was fired in the first place. I know Harold said it was going to get bad for us again, but I suppose I was living in denial that it would happen so soon.

True to my word, I get a few things done as I wait for news from my brothers or contact with Duncan about today. I clean the kitchen and prepare a cold pasta salad with cheese, summer sausage, and minced vegetables for tonight's dinner, munching on a snack of ham and cheese croissants while I clean and cook. My worry for my brother and my anxiety that Duncan wasn't serious about today after all—silly as that is, since I'm fairly certain that Duncan won't ditch our plans after what he said last night—teeters back and forth at the forefront of my mind as I strip the sheets off all our beds and start a load or two of laundry.

By the time everything is cooked and the last load of laundry whizzes around in the washer, it's almost one in the afternoon, and I haven't heard from anyone about anything. My SMARTcall hasn't buzzed this whole time, although I know I've put off answering the texts from last night long enough. With a sigh, I tug the elastic hair tie out of my hair and shake it out before slumping into Wade's kitchen chair with my SMARTcall.

HAYLEY MANCHESTER: *Hey! Call me soon. I want to hear all that transpired after your debut party as the Queen of all half-breeds. *chortle**

SHELBY JEAN: *I'm going to the mountains with Ivar and his family Saturday, so we can't chat then, but Sunday we should talk! I want to hear if your family is okay!*

I'm more than happy to hear from Hayley, and I kind of want to call her now to talk about everything that I found out last night. However, I don't want to tie up my phone just in case one of my brothers tries to call, and I also doubt Duncan wants me sharing his story with anyone right now. As far as Shelby goes, I'll have to grit my teeth and call her tomorrow...but that's tomorrow, and I have enough problems now. I don't have any more texts from Morgan, and I wonder if she's mad at me. Lyle, however, is a different story.

LYLE ZEMAN: *Sorry about your family emergency! I enjoyed being your date for while you were at the party.*

I literally don't know what to say, except that the difference in my mindset now is that I no longer want to force myself to try things out with Lyle. I remember dancing with him too, and the feeling of his closeness was not unpleasant at the time. But now I know there's not a chance for anything there.

Morgan needs to win him over, I think determinedly, deciding to have a chat with her at the next opportunity. I move to the next message instead of replying to Lyle, and the sender surprises me.

EMILEE CHIRZA: *Hello, Sierra? I'm Emilee, your neighbor. We've not SMARTtexted before, but I'm sure your ID will pick up my name. Wade gave me your number for emergencies, and I haven't heard from him for a couple days. Could you ask him to check his SMARTcall for me? Sorry to bother you.*

Wade, sometimes you're a drama queen, I think with a little sour amusement. Emilee sounds sweet to me, and I don't appreciate Wade not letting her know what was going on, since he cares about her enough to give her my number as an emergency contact. I send a quick *TEXT EMILEE!* message to Wade, and reply to Emilee.

SIERRA MAURELL: *I let him know you wanted to talk to him, don't worry. You're totally fine, I don't mind you texting me!*

Right as I hit send, my phone buzzes with a call flashing on the screen, and my heart spasms with an audible THUMP.

"Hello?" I say, my voice a little high as I answer Duncan's call. Instead of the casual greeting I expected in return, Duncan is terse and a little concerned.

"I just saw what's going on, and I can't believe it...how are you handling it?" he says, and I hear in the background noise that he's driving. I'm confused, wondering if perhaps Wade being fired was publicized knowledge.

"It was a surprise that he got fired...but Harold and Wade are trying to fix that now," I say, walking to click on our SMARTvision screen built into the wall of our living room. *Maybe there was a news story after all,* I think, *or maybe Wade beat up his boss and now he's getting arrested. I can see it now: M-DNA AGGRESSION STRIKES SMARTINDUSTRY EMPLOYER.*

"What? I didn't know your brother got fired...but I suppose it makes sense," Duncan exclaims, and I hear the sound of his car accelerating. "You should turn on the news. I'm on my way over, assuming of course that my presence is acceptable."

"Of course," I say, perhaps reassuring him a little too quickly; I can almost hear his smile on the other end of the line.

"That's good...honestly, Sierra, I can't wait to see you," he says, making my heart tap dance against my ribs.

"T-That's nice," I say; my voice squeaks. "Make sure you smell like dog and not human boy...my brothers aren't here, but they'll recognize a human scent."

"Gotcha," he says. "I'll let you go so you can watch what's going down on the news before I get there. They keep replaying the same broadcast over and over, so you should still get to see it."

"Okay, bye," I say before hanging up. I quickly press the gel button right above the screen on our wall for our SMARTvision and take a seat on the couch; I forgot that I could've turned on the SMARTvision with a voice command.

It looks like an official speech is going on: the typical slightly over-weight human senator stuffed into a shiny suit poses on a stage in front of a silver curtain, speaking loudly and emphatically to the camera as he gazes into the lens with cunning grey eyes. I recognize this man: it's Abel Denmann, the senator Harold has been complaining about for almost a year. According to Denmann, half-breeds should be rounded up and tagged like cattle—he says this in more politically correct wording, of course—and according to Harold, Denmann should be assassinated someone from the Reis family as quickly as possible. Harold never had much patience for people with antiquated beliefs, like those before the war who were intolerant of our kind.

The sight of the senator on screen makes me sick, but I turn up the volume with a voice command and listen to the message.

"As you all know, a major change is on the way. Some senators don't want me to tell you this, but you people with uncontaminated DNA are the true citizens of this country, and I believe you have a right to the truth, and a right to vote," Denmann begins with an inveigling but serious expression on his stone-hard face. "Your government and your country both suffer, and there isn't any point pretending that they aren't. We went through a war several years ago, a war that was both global and civil, and it nearly tore our society apart irrevocably. As you know, we reached a truce with the growing population of M-DNA subjects, and our scientists found a way to limit the pollution of the gene pool so only M-DNA people could produce more of their own kind, and humans would continue to reproduce pure human DNA."

Fat lot of good that did, I snort, picturing Duncan's new attributes in my mind's eye. *You failed in fixing the government just like you failed to stop the "pollution of the DNA pool," apparently.*

"I believe this was wrong, good people, and please allow me to explain why," Denmann begins again, and the unease stirring in my heart travels down like poison into my gut. "Ever since we made peace with those who were sadly contaminated from birth with the DNA of certain animals, our government has suffered. We have had to provide and sacrifice too much for these subjects; just think of what we have spent and given up in food, shelter, energy, fuel for the M-DNA members of society! The war alone cost Europe and Asia trillions of dollars, not just in defense costs, but in the unsuccessful attempt to develop a cure. We sacrificed the most, and while we didn't find a cure, we did develop the solution I mentioned a moment ago."

"Maybe you shouldn't have dragged us all into the war then, dumbass," I growl, too angry to keep my thoughts to myself. I expect to hear shouts of derision and protest from the crowd Denmann addresses, but the surroundings of the senator are ominously silent; they probably had this filmed at a hidden location to avoid rioting and similar violence from both sides.

My father died in that war, and the rogue factions you refused to punish killed my mother in a bio attack at her workplace, I think, knowing I'm shaking with anger and furious tears are in my eyes. It dawns on me that this broadcast was part of the reason Wade must have been fired, and why I might not have heard from Harold or Eisen yet. Apprehension sets my teeth on edge and I can hardly sit still.

Abel Denmann is still speaking, and I want to take a sledgehammer right to his smug face. "We have not recovered from these expenses, and if no changes are made, we will not recover for at least a century. As I said, certain senators—the same type who wished to make peace with the M-DNA subjects near the close of the war—would not wish me to share these things with you, just as they tried to keep me from pushing forward this chance for you all to vote on our rights as pure citizens," he says, his voice precise and grave just like a

288

senator's ought to be. I'm getting an inkling of what's coming, and I feel almost faint.

"I am also risking my safety in telling you this. No doubt, some misguided M-DNA subject will take offense at my speech. The whole community may lash out in a typical case of the aggression that we regrettably encounter so often, now that these so-called citizens have nested in our once flourishing society. Regardless…an opportunity has been put forward. I believe we should be working on a vaccine to ensure that M-DNA people produce only pure DNA children, if they refuse to be sterilized.

"If you true citizens vote positively, we will reclaim our jobs, our living spaces, our schools for the future of our children, and our very way of life so that we can replenish our country—our world—one step at a time. You, my dear people, for the first time in many years have a choice put before you about two weeks from this approaching Wednesday: a choice *you* can make, not a decision made for you by fat regionalists who don't know what it's like to live among the people. You can allow the M-DNA subjects to drain our society as they have for so many years, or you can join me in reclaiming the beautiful country and way of life we enjoyed for centuries." I sense that his carefully prepared speech is drawing to a close, and with the change of the militant, commanding tone to his gravelly voice, the hypnotic spell of horror is broken. I call out a hoarse voice command to the SMARTvision, turning it off so the smooth face of the senator dissolves into a black void.

Questions zoom around my brain: did the humans

know about this earlier? Is that why the boss who used to like Wade turned on him so quickly? How is this even happening?

We fought a war for the right to live as a people among humans! It can't just go backwards! Panic and frustration makes my fur bristle and my hands shake from helpless fury.

I know already that we M-DNA "subjects" won't be allowed to participate in the vote, and if humans are allowing this unfair vote to be put up in the first place...what happened to all the politicians who gave us rights in the first place? What about all these "desegregation" policies the government has been enforcing? We don't know why they helped us, even though their tagline was equality. But if they're resigned to lose to the never-ending bias against my kind...*do we even have any hope?*

I imagine a world where me and my loved ones would be treated as animals, like they tried to do to my parents' generation. A world where I would be forced to choose between a vaccine—or worse, a poisonous tester for the vaccine—to make my children unlike me, or sterilization. I can't even imagine.

Swiping away the infuriated tears decorating my cheeks, I check my phone again for something from anyone who might have seen this. No one has contacted me except Duncan, not even Eisen with the SMARTvision built into the wall of his break room at work; I wonder if he'll return jobless as well. Harold might be the only one who has a job by the end of the day: half-breed lawyers will probably be in high demand right up until the vote.

Wednesday: the day only a couple weeks from now when everything might go sour. Then the war will start again, including the nightmares Harold once told me about with a white, tight-lipped face.

I'm panicking now, hardly able to breathe as I imagine my brothers—and even me—caught up in the absolutely brutal guerilla warfare my parents went through when Harold was a child. *The humans might even have the upper hand this time...how can anyone stand for this? Even the humans? Doesn't anyone remember what it was like back then?* The humans have memorial services and a day in the summer set to celebrate the end of the terrible war, and we half-breeds have our own memorial rituals that we practice.

I imagine the faces of all the students I encounter at school every day, and try to picture us all literally fighting to kill each other. I can't. I may not like a single person there, but I don't wish any of them dead.

Duncan's knock on the door startles me, and I'm out of my faded violet suede chair to open the door before he even finishes knocking. I'm having a panic attack, like I used to when I was a toddler, and I can't stand being alone right now. Hell, I almost fall into his arms once I open the door, but I manage to maintain my dignity long enough for him to see my face.

"Wow," he murmurs softly. "Pretty bad, huh?" I nod, willing the moisture in my eyes to dissipate. Now that he's here, his scent fills my nose again and I am weirdly comforted by his presence. I hardly know what to say except one thing.

"Let's go," I say, brushing past him to walk to his car. I thank him in my head for following me silently.

21

Conversation isn't an option for me for about ten minutes, and Duncan is kind enough to drive around aimlessly while I gather my thoughts and calm down. Perhaps he sensed my distress was too much to handle alone, because after two minutes of cruising through the half-breed neighborhoods around my house, he tentatively held out his hand across the retro bench seat of his car. I took it, hesitant but grateful for his compassion. His hand is pleasantly dry, and the calloused ridges on the top of his palm from working out feel good against my skin. I wonder if dark fur will ever decorate the back of his hand like auburn fur decorates mine.

I don't know what is coming for us, but Duncan feels like more than a friend now, and not in a one-sided way.

"Where would you like to go?" he asks after we've exhausted the main and back roads of the little town where I live. I shrug, turning away from listlessly gazing out the passenger window to observe him.

"I had a few ideas this morning, if the opportunity presented itself, but unless your ridiculous costume is still in the car, we might not have access to the areas I was thinking. Not after—" I hesitate to mention Denmann's speech, loathing the memory already. I wonder if Duncan will even want to venture into the strictly half-breed populated areas I'd thought of while laundry and cooking were occupying my time.

"I have it in the back seat, since I didn't have time to clean out my car last night," Duncan assures me, and I'm distracted as his thumb glides down my sleek-furred hand. "Just tell me where to go."

"All right," I concede. "Turn left out of this subdivision, then follow the signs to the center of downtown Thymes Ridge. Once you're in the middle, go right: there's a nice trail for walking, if you want to see it." My directions might be a little vague, but I can help him along the way if he gets lost. We fall silent again. Now that I'm calmer, I can show interest in the curiosity that is Duncan.

"So," he speaks before I can compose a proper question in my mind. "Humans, huh?"

The corners of my mouth fold downwards. "Humans. All of them are insanse," I say, then reconsider who I'm speaking to. "I mean—"

"Please don't worry on my account," Duncan says, his voice deep and growly again in that way I'm drawn to.

"Humans aren't all bad, but today I'm glad I'm not one anymore. I...I have no clue what to say to you or to any half-breed I'd meet after this debacle. It's shameful, this whole 'voting' process."

"I don't know why it's so hard for everyone to understand that our kind is human too, and worth equal treatment. M-DNA makes us stronger, better; we live twenty years longer than most humans, and look only about sixty when we pass on," I muse aloud. Duncan nods, agreeing with me; I notice the hand that isn't holding mine grips the steering wheel awfully tight.

"I've noticed. I didn't have a problem with being human, but however this new DNA got into me, or went active, whatever...it's made me stronger, faster, and possibly a little smarter. That may sound arrogant, along with me saying I wasn't totally stupid before, but my schoolwork seems a whole lot easier. I actually have to hold myself back in senior P.E. now," he says as we get close to the first turn I told him to make.

"At my school, P.E. was actually fun. Everything was more competitive, but at the same time you could use whatever animal attributes you had however you wanted. It was chaos, and we loved it," I reminisce. "Thankfully I don't have to take anything like that at Hostetler, since my credits panned out in my favor. I can only imagine how they'd react...Harper would probably fail me out of spite."

"True...you're public enemy number one, and we're barely into the school year," Duncan says, then coughs self-consciously. "Sorry, sorry...I'm trying to be encouraging. It's not easy to cheer someone up after watching a scumbag like Denmann humiliate your race on SMARTvision."

I grow bolder, squeezing Duncan's hand as a tiny smile creeps onto my lips. "It's okay...you're helping. Wanna know how you can help more?"

"Do tell," he says, giving me a side-ways smile and a look just flirty enough to make my heart pump a little faster.

"I have more questions, and...something you said last night made me think..." I say, wondering if he'll know that I'm referring to the part where he brought up half-breed bonding.

"Ask away," he says more casually than I'd like, calming the butterflies in my stomach; I shy away a little. "I imagine a lot of what I said last night made you think."

"What are your ideas about how this happened?" I ask. Duncan shrugs, briefly seeking eye contact as we reach a traffic light. There aren't many cars out today, understandably: the half-breeds are either storming human neighborhoods in a mob, or they're staying out of sight to avoid heckling and general aggression from humans.

"I've had several theories since all of this started a while back...some of them are nuts; I thought I'd been poisoned or contaminated by contact with a half-breed person. None of those panned out, obviously," he explains. "Right now, the working theory is that the government serum they inject five-year old humans with isn't a permanent solution. I'm thinking it was a temporary solution they sold to the public to stop panic, and I'm pretty sure I won't be the only one turning now that the gene pool has been changed this much already. It doesn't make sense for it not to affect more people than just me."

"That sounds very plausible; I'm impressed," I say after digesting his information. "It sounds like something the government would do, especially after today."

"Agreed...I mean, they're talking about a mandatory sterilization process or DNA cleansing vaccine. That's got to show some desperation, right?" Duncan says before shaking his head to clear it. "Anyway, shall we play the question game again? Because if we do, it's my turn." I pretend to deliberate for a moment.

"Sure, but you have to swear that you won't put me off anymore," I say, and he shakes his head with amusement.

"So what is the best perk of being a fox, and what is the biggest downside?" He asks, surprising me again.

"Hm...no one has asked me that before. What do *you* think the best and worst things would be?" I know I'm not playing the question game right, but he is forgiving and answers.

"Biggest perk is that you are a very attractive fox, and biggest downside is your irresistible draw to pillage chicken coops, I imagine," Duncan teases me, and I laugh as his compliment cheers me.

"We have to fix some of your stereotypes for sure—oh, here's downtown TR, make sure you're not blinded by all the city lights as you find that right turn," I say, sarcastically mocking my quaint town as it takes us all of six minutes to drive through without any traffic. "I would have to say the biggest perk is the inborn cleverness, and the biggest downside is the general mistrust of any birds in the nearby vicinity."

"Yeah, because that's not a stereotype at all," Duncan chuckles as we head toward the trail. He lets go of my hand and reaches in the back seat to rummage around for the beanie and wolf ears headband he wore last night. I stop him before he puts on the too furry ears.

"You don't need those after all; the beanie is enough. People will think you're just hiding your ears, and after today they won't blame you," I say. "Your turn for a question, I think."

"Okay," he says through a mouthful of marshmallow; he grabbed the leftover bag of those as well, and I suppose he doesn't mind eating them raw. "What is your current favorite hobby, besides pissing off anyone in the administration of Hostetler High?"

"Hey now! That's not a hobby, that's an occupation," I insist, fishing a marshmallow out of the thin plastic bag. "My interests include but are not limited to reading, writing some middle quality poetry, baking, and going on the occasional run with my brother. I'd include shopping in that list, but there's a stereotype that goes with that hobby, so let's pretend I didn't mention that."

"All of those sound well-rounded and balanced...you should be proud," Duncan says pompously, making me laugh; his efforts to cheer me up are working well enough that I don't have to focus on the bad parts of today. I consider my next question.

"What was it like when you first showed signs of having mixed DNA?" I ask after hesitating briefly;

Duncan doesn't seem like he's offended, but his eyebrows draw down and his hand tightens on the steering wheel.

"Well...it was really slow at first. I didn't realize it for a long time, because apparently when the dormant DNA matures, you never feel sick. At least, not more than a few little illnesses that went away in a day or two," he says, looking thoughtful as he traverses back to the time when he still was completely human. "After about three weeks of that, my allergies kicked in like crazy for a day, and then I felt better than I had my entire life. I could see and hear better, I felt stronger and had a ton of energy, which I used at the gym and playing soccer and small local games of summer football with Aaden, Bari, and Truman. I think I drove everyone nuts for a little while; I must have been like a puppy for most of the summer. Even when I started showing other signs, like a disturbingly improved sense of smell, I didn't pay much attention—"

I interrupt him long enough to give one more set of directions. "We're going to come up on a grassy, gravelly area near the trail that we use for parking in a little bit. Make sure you turn right up here." He nods, continuing as we pull in and park.

"I guess the wake-up call after the growth spurt and burst of never-ending energy was the fur on my back...it seemingly grew in overnight, and then my teeth and eyes changed. I couldn't believe it, and like I said last night, I thought I was going crazy. I knew enough to hide everything from my family—they wouldn't handle the knowledge well—but I don't understand completely *how* I can hide my other traits.

One time I went for a run with Aaden and Bari after a game and almost blew my cover. This group of three half-breeds stops us and starts talking trash, asking why I'm hanging around a bunch of humans. We almost got in a fight—them more than me, since I was trying to figure out how they knew I was half-breed—but I talked them down and we got away. My friends were curious, but...they never knew. No one knew until I told you last night, thankfully. The hardest part was learning how to curb my scent, but...it worked."

"That sounds awful," I say with sincere sympathy as we pull to a stop in the grassy area I told Duncan about. "It must have been hard to keep this hidden. Plus the change..."

"It was worse because I couldn't and can't risk looking anything up directly in case my SMARTspace track record gets selected for a random review," he says, removing the key from the ignition once he haphazardly parks wherever there's room. It's a nice day, so normally this place would be busier, but as it is only a few cars pepper the mashed down grass of the makeshift parking lot.

"Once I figured it out...it was easier to manage. Well, except for being able to smell absolutely everything...how can anyone even get used to that? But until I found you, I was in the dark and utterly confused about what to do. Well, with this new version of myself anyway." We're both thoughtful as we exit the car; Duncan tugs the beanie down on top of his ginger hair.

"And now?" I ask, walking around to his side of the car after smoothing my pale purple shirt down and quickly checking my make-up in the side-view mirror. He glances in the mirror on his side as he adjusts his hat; then he straightens and looks at me. He has that curious smile that makes his eyes gleam just the way I like, right before faint spots of color appear on my face.

"Not your turn," he says with a mischievous grin. I notice how well his casual dark blue button down shirt fits and matches his black jeans, just as I notice how his collarbone looks appealing right where he's left the top two or three buttons undone; he's rolled his sleeves up almost to his elbows, and I try not to stare at his muscular forearms.

"Ask away, then," I say, self-consciously trying not to stutter as I look up into his face; his eyes are the German Shepherd brown again, which is growing on me almost as much as his more human green eyes.

"Let's start walking first," he suggests. "I'm going to assume the little pathway leading through that grove is the start of the trail, so shall we?" I nod, and he gestures for me to lead the way. We're silent as we start on the path, and I allow us both some time to observe the scenery.

The trail rests completely under an arch of trees, most of them still covered with ivy from the summer. The pesticides the self-appointed groundskeepers spray keep the bugs to a minimum, and they repave the black trail often enough so that there aren't a lot of holes in the ground.

"Whatever people say about half-breeds, you sure do take care of the areas the government designated for you," Duncan says as we leisurely explore the winding trail; the weather is so perfect I couldn't have asked for better.

"It's all we have, so it's better to take care of it so we can enjoy it," I say with a shrug.

"True," he agrees. Now that I'm here, memories of sunlit spring and summer days resurface in my mind. Pretty much every memory I have here is pleasant.

"I've been coming to this trail since I was young," I reminisce aloud. "Harold brought me here after school when I was little, shortly after my mother died. He knew I was having a hard time, and since he was my new parent figure, he wanted to make sure I was going to be okay. It was spring then...the whole trail was lined with either honeysuckles or lilacs."

"Sounds like a good memory, in spite of the circumstances," Duncan says, and looking at me long enough to make my stomach butterflies quiver.

"Are you ever going to ask your question?" I query, a little nervous with him focused on me this much.

"I suppose so," he says, and I can smell that he's a little nervous too. Funny, I'm more attuned to the variances of his scent than anyone else I've known besides my brothers. "Do you remember what I asked you last night?"

"Is that your question?" I tease, allowing myself to bump his shoulder with mine. He smiles a little.

"No, but I think you remember. So here's my question, since it relates to that: I've known you almost a week, Sierra, which means I barely know you. So why do I feel like I've known you a lot longer than that?" His voice deepens again, and some intimate quality about it makes me check for observers; we've come a good way along the trail, and both of us would have scented the approach of another person. It feels deliciously forbidden to be alone, but also...*right*, somehow.

"I..." I begin, unsure what's going to come out of my mouth next. "I don't know...but I feel the same way. It's kind of silly, I guess, because it has in reality been such a short time."

We've stopped walking, and we stand a little closer than normal in the middle of the path. My heart speeds up as I look up at Duncan's face; a wave of shyness washes over me, so I level my gaze with his shoulder. He nods, and suddenly I want to sense him more as a fox than as a human. As he speaks, I slowly allow my fox senses to mesh with my human ones.

"I asked you that question last night...about half-breeds bonding to another person very quickly, almost before reason can catch up...because I think I came down with whatever is in my genes that causes that to happen," he says. The scent of him is spicy and good and absolutely intoxicating; I hear his heart race as quickly as mine, and the hope I've been trying to crush with logic nearly bursts its bonds.

"You feel this for me?" I ask quietly, my voice too soft. The vulnerability in my question is nearly too much to stand. I lift my gaze back to his face, analyzing his eyes for some proof of truth or emotion. The look he gives me is intense, hopeful as well as wary.

"I strongly believe...hell, I don't know. You just...you just showed up in my life and, regardless of whether or not it makes sense, I can't get you out of my head. I don't think I'll ever be able to, and I don't want to fight it."

"We're different," I make a last ditch effort to control what I can't predict. "So different. You might be like me now, but you were raised a human, and I wasn't. Our backgrounds may make our differences too much to cope with, and there are still so many questions…"

"…I'm not sure if that matters, not when we feel this," Duncan says gently, trying to persuade me without discrediting my words. "Do you have a name for this…whatever it is that caused what I feel for you?" he asks me. We're closer now; I want to reach out and touch him so much that it's hard to breathe normally, but I resist.

"No…there's no official name for this, since it's not scientifically based, as I said before," I explain; it's a little difficult to think clearly. "I just know I felt this when I thought you were human, even though I tried to tell myself it was nonsense."

Duncan sighs, tilting his head a little to the left; the angle of his neck briefly snares my attention. "I don't blame you. I gave up ignoring it sooner, though, because I knew I had to get closer to you before I could let you in on the whole canine DNA thing. And honestly, I'm really glad to be here with you right now. I'm glad it's you."

"I'm glad too," I say in a voice barely louder than a whisper; he inhales slowly, a reverse sigh of relief. "I'm happy that you're the one to make me feel this way, if this is the way life works for us." I look down at my shoes, suddenly more shy than I was when I met him. Duncan reaches forward and takes my hand, giving it a slight squeeze; I'm so relieved that we finally have physical contact that it's like some sort of pain I've not noticed until now went away. He opens his mouth to speak, and for a second I don't think he can; then the words come.

"Sierra, I think I—"

"Don't," I say, surprising him and myself. "Don't say it yet." My eyes close briefly, and I bite my lip as I savor this moment. Just for another excuse to touch him, I hold my finger up to his lips to stop him from changing my life too fast.

"Too much?" he asks. The uncertainty in his voice endears him to me further.

"I think I know what you're going to say, but...wait. We have time, so let's see where this goes first." I don't know how I can be the voice of reason, not with my heart caught in my throat and my hands trembling from an emotion I hardly know how to define, but somehow what I'm saying makes sense.

Duncan's eyes are still green, but the burnt umber tint of half-breed nature seeps into the iris, not drastically, but enough to hypnotize me. I wonder why he's struggling to decide which set of senses to give control, but he speaks before I can ask him about it.

"You're right," he says, taking the hand I held to his lips in his other hand and lightly kissing my knuckles. My heart simply can't keep up with this scene; it keeps stopping or racing or turning my cheeks pink. "I can wait."

His closeness makes me want more, and I secretly wish he would kiss me; it's not time for that yet, though, even if all it would take is a small movement forward for me or him. I try to concentrate on other things so I don't

305

act too fast either; my reactions are strengthened by my fox nature. My tail slowly sweeps back and forth, showing my alertness, and my fur feels sleek. My eyes must be burning gold; in a moment, I close the minimal distance between Duncan and me.

"I—" I don't know what to say as I look up into the rugged planes of his face; there's no human way of explaining I want to memorize this boy, so I never forget anything in spite of the uncertain future before us. Worrisome thoughts form storm clouds at the front of my brain, but it's easy to push them away. My elation that I finally have the boy I've wanted since I met him helps preserve this moment in my mind.

"It's okay," he says, releasing one of my hands to push a few strands of my hair away from my face.

I stand perfectly still, caught up in my human insecurities, but he acts when I can't. Very slowly, he leans forward, his eyes warm brown. His cheek brushes against mine; his five o'clock shadow rasps pleasantly against my face. I breathe in the same time he does, both of us drawing in the other's scent. His mouth hovers close to my neck, and I barely manage to recover from that thrill when his right arm snakes around my waist.

"You smell like fresh laundry and some sort of floral-like spice I can't describe," he says, a laugh caught deep in his throat; the sound so close to me makes goose-bumps pattern my skin, and I wonder if he'll notice. "It's kind of light and sweet...and oddly edible. I knew your scent from earlier, but now that I can finally examine it, describing it is a lot harder."

"It's the same for your scent, kind of," I say,

enjoying his amusement as he holds me; he nuzzles my hair and a breathy laugh escapes me. "I got to know your human scent, but then you changed to a half-breed on me. Now I need to absorb your new smell, minus the cologne."

"What's the difference?" he asks, distracted; his hand falls from caressing my face, but then he has both arms around me, so I don't complain.

"You should know this, since you've been a half-breed for a few months now," I tease, hesitating before I slide my hands up to his shoulders so he can hold me with more ease. "Humans...their scents are more subdued, except for the unhygienic ones. Half-breed scents are more diverse because we have more variations than simply the human aspects of our DNA."

"Oh," he says, huffing in a very dog-like way; he pulls back to look at my face and I regret the loss of closeness. My hands explore his shoulders; when they reach the back of his neck and I feel the ridge of fur on his spine under his collar, I remember more troubling reasons we should be concerned about our new relationship.

"Duncan," I say, beginning with a question. "Since you hide your animal aspects so well, everyone still thinks you're a human?"

"Yes...oh," he says, his distracted expression focusing and his irises settling on pale green; I want to count the cinnamon freckles on his perfect skin. "I see. That could be...problematic," he concludes, and I'm glad he knows where my thoughts are headed.

"I don't mean to be all melodramatic, but we might need to keep...whatever this is a secret," I point out, already sad about how the people in our life won't let us live as free as we would wish to. He frowns too, a pensive expression troubling his face.

"I'd rather...not," he says, making me rally my arguments to explain why it would be dangerous not to; however, he continues so I don't need to speak. "I understand why, and for the time being, we can be more subtle instead of putting it all out there too soon. I just want you to know...I don't like it, and it's not what I would choose if I had a better option."

"You're sweet," I tell him, trying to muster the motivation to pull away from him. "If it's any consolation, we might get wildly lucky...if this whole vote goes in our favor, we might be able to publicize our...value to each other soon enough."

He concedes with a nod, but I can tell he's not thrilled with the arrangement. I'm not either, and I probably make it worse when I extricate myself from his arms and step back.

"We should probably go soon," I say, smoothing out the creases of my shirt and self-consciously straightening the fur on my ears. "Just to be safe..."

"If you say so," Duncan sighs. "However, since I'm a half-breed in a half-breed neighborhood with a half-breed girl, it doesn't seem like there's much risk here." He smiles and takes my hand again, drawing another shy smile onto my lips.

"I guess we can take our time on the rest of the trail," I yield, wanting to spend as much time as possible with him. For now, we have a whole trail before us, and I want to take my time before reality returns.

22

Duncan slowly pulls into my driveway around eight in the evening. We've spent hours together learning everything we can about each other. It's easy to agree on the fact that, strong feelings or not, learning the other person's personality quirks and related subjects has to be a priority.

We finished our walk on the trail, and then went for dinner at the retro diner Cygnet's, the primary fast food carrier in downtown Thymes Ridge. He enjoyed that, mostly because half-breed food is—whenever possible—prepared better and with more healthy materials than human food.

Now that I'm home, staring at the cheerfully glowing windows which prove that all of my brothers have returned home by now, I'm glad I have today's happy memories to keep me stable. Basking in Duncan's interest has been the highlight of the year already.

Harold did text me earlier, which is why I know that once I go in the house, this includes returning to the reality that life won't continue as normal once the vote is passed.

HAROLD MAURELL: *Wade will not be re-hired in the same position, but we bullied the boss into hiring him for a different department. Wade could spit poison, fair warning. I'm assuming by now you've heard about the mockery set to take place Wednesday, so if you could, you should go to a friend's house or to Mrs. Chirza's so you won't be alone.*

Well, I kind of went to a friend, I thought at the time, ignoring a faint guilty twinge before returning to my conversation about music. Now that I'm home, Duncan senses my anxiety and takes my hand again. I'm normally not so affectionate, but I'm thrilled that he's barely stopped touching me in some way since our fateful discussion on the trail in Thymes Ridge.

"Will you be okay?" Duncan asks me. I shrug, unwilling to get out of the car.

"I will be, and I need to talk things out with my brothers anyway," I say. "Wade might need more calming down, Harold will definitely assume I need calming down, and Eisen..." I frown.

"Eisen?" Duncan prompts carefully. I sigh.

"Eisen is already suspicious of my activities, and in a very short time I have to figure out what to tell him. Plus, he's already seen me with you in Omnium Beanery...and he knows you're a human, so I can't exactly lie," I say. "He wouldn't be fooled."

"What's wrong with telling him the truth?" Duncan asks, studying me.

"What?"

"I mean it...what's the harm in telling him the truth? You told me he's the cool brother, less conservative than Harold and more reliable than Wade...it might not hurt to have another person on our side," he says reasonably. I pause, picturing Eisen's pissed-off face once I finish telling him what I've been up to lately.

"You mean just tell him I'm kind of in a relationship with a human boy who's turned into one of us?" I query incredulously.

Duncan considers before he shakes his head. "That might be a little too much truth. But he might be accepting of the human part, eventually at least. I'll leave it up to you though...I trusted you enough to tell you about me, so I'll trust you to decide who to tell. You'll be able to win him over."

I snort. "Sure I will...if I can get him to stop yelling and persuade him to wait and listen before telling Harold. Eisen isn't a snitch, but having three older brothers can give the whole house a...protective instinct when it comes to me." I mentally wince at what Eisen's going to say about my latest adventures, even if by some miracle he keeps his voice at an indoor level.

"You won't know until you try," Duncan says, reassuring me. I notice I've been taking shallow breaths, so I take one deep breath and release it slowly.

"You're right. I'll try it...but you should go. If we linger any more, one of the musketeers might come out and investigate—"

"Gotcha. I'll leave," Duncan agrees, sitting up and subconsciously leaning closer to me. "I...I had a really good day, Sierra," he says in a quieter voice that makes my tail want to wag again. I clutch it tightly in my lap before pushing myself to exit the vehicle.

"Me too," I say in a near whisper. "One of the best, actually, once you showed up."

Duncan smiles, and I love how his smile crinkles his eyes and makes his entire face light up. "See you Monday," he says as I close my door.

Definitely, I think, ridiculously wishing I could go back to school tomorrow just so I could see my half-breed boy sooner. In spite of what might happen next, I have a silly grin on my face as he drives away.

I try to slip into the house quietly, but not so quietly that it looks like I'm sneaking around. Everyone lounges carelessly in the living room with the SMARTvision humming in the background. I know it's been a bad day, because all three of my brothers have an empty beer bottle sitting beside them. At this point, I'm not sure if the booze will mellow them out or make them touchier.

"I'm home," I announce needlessly, clutching my phone tightly in my hand as I walk to my lavender suede chair and perch on the arm. A brief memory of all the phone calls I have to make soon—Shelby, Hayley, and probably Lyle as well if I want to keep the new developments in my life concealed from the general public—flits across my mind, but I push it away.

No one has contacted me since the news report, so I assume everyone is in shock and trying to cope with their families. The calls can wait until tomorrow.

"Who dropped you off?" Harold asks me, peering anxiously at my face from his peripheral vision in an attempt to be subtle.

"A friend from school...we went out for a while," I say, grateful that this is the truth. Wade snorts from the far end of the couch, obviously ready to rip into an available target.

"Since when do you have friends?" he asks nastily, a growl lodged in his throat.

"Apparently since you have a girlfriend," I retort, although my heart isn't in the snappiness. Wade's going through a hard time, and the last thing I want to do is fight with him.

"Shut up, Wade, don't be a dick," Eisen says, unexpectedly defending me. "It's not her fault humans are total morons." He's got a snarl stuck in his throat too, but he's more under control. Wade huffs, absently tracing his finger around the mouth of the empty bottle beside him.

"Sorry, S," he grunts, and I lean over to pat his arm in a silent reassurance that we're okay.

"So aside from all of that, how was your afternoon?" Eisen asks, giving me a shrewd look. I try not to wince at the subtle judgmental tone to his voice, but even Harold notices the tension between the two of us. He tears his focus away from the SMARTvision—which merrily continues to broadcast the scene of a riot in a city one or two counties over—and flips his gaze between the three of us in the living room.

313

"What?" Wade asks, throwing his hands up in the air. Harold nods his head towards the door, gesturing for him to leave, and Wade rises to his bare, furry feet with a hostile sigh.

"Damn kids," I hear him grumble on his way out, nearly making me laugh. Harold's stern expression stops me, however.

"I don't know what the hell is going on with you both, but I'm going to go work on some new cases in my office before it gets too late," he says, also standing. "By the time I come down here for the rest of the pasta salad, I expect you two to be on good terms again." Eisen sniffs sarcastically.

"If by office you mean your bedroom, okay, Harry," he says, and I see Harold's patience wearing much too thin as my blonde brother speaks. I glare at Eisen, wondering why he's being such a jerk.

"We'll be fine," I assure Harold. "Go on up, and I'll bring you the pasta salad later if you want."

He does, leaving me alone with Eisen, who continues to glare at me as he reclines on the couch. His arms are crossed, his ears flattened back on his head, and somehow he's peering down at me from his long nose even though he's sitting in a lower place than me.

"Suck up," he mutters, his cerulean eyes a lot harsher than I'm used to. I'm annoyed with his hostility, but if I get him too angry before we get to the meat of the matter, he might be less willing to keep his voice down.

"Well, one of us had to be. It's not like this has been the best day for everyone, so you should give him a break," I say, glancing up the stairs to check if Harold or Wade is within hearing range. I'm reasonably certain their fox senses are tuned down right now, but I keep my voice low just in case.

"It may not have been a good day for the rest of us, but I don't know if you had a bad day at all," Eisen says accusingly.

"What's that supposed to mean?" I demand. "You've been moody lately, so if you have a problem, spit it out." My hands shake; I absolutely hate fighting with Eisen, because he usually wins all the arguments if we're left to our own devices.

"Sierra Candra Maurell, if you think you can lie to me all the day long, you have another thing coming—"

I interrupt him. "Shhh! Can we please try not to make this a household affair?"

"Maybe it needs to be," Eisen growls. "If you are choosing now of all times to be a rebel and sneak off with a *human boy*, then maybe the rest of us should hear from you about it!" I knew this was coming, but my pulse still quickens unpleasantly.

"Why would you think that?" I ask, stroking my tail anxiously. Eisen laughs derisively before replying.

"I know this because you're a bad liar, at least when you're trying to lie to me. I don't like snitching on you, little sis, but something like this is *serious*. Especially now that the human mood towards us has become so appalling," he says, and I stay silent.

Duncan told me to tell some of the truth so maybe Eisen would be on our side, but that doesn't mean I walked in here knowing what to say. I can't even explain our attachment: it's a half-breed thing that started it all, and describing it sounds foolish.

"Well?" Eisen challenges, breaking into my musings on how to respond.

"How did you know?" I ask softly. Eisen huffs, launching to his feet so he can pace in front of me.

"No way in hell did any of Issachar Reis's 'college buddies' consent to carpool a bunch of high school kids home. If one of them had, it would've been just you and him, and you definitely would have broken curfew," he snarls; from what I saw of the Reis heir, I can't disagree with that. "When you came home last night, you smelled like a lake, and I happen to know for a fact that the Reis twins don't live near a lake. Plus, Sierra, I have my wits about me, and even I can look out a window to see who dropped you off."

"You saw who it was and didn't say anything?" I ask. I'm surprised he still covered for me now I see how angry he is.

"I saw the human boy you brought to my coffee shop, yeah. Generally I'm not a nark, so I didn't say anything. I thought I'd give you a chance to explain yourself to me before I told Harold you needed a transfer pass out of that damn school," Eisen bursts out, running his hands through his silky hair. He releases a frustrated sigh, and I feel another guilty pang over my deceit.

"Come on," I say impulsively, walking to Eisen and tentatively grabbing his hand as it hangs loosely at his side. "I'm going to make some warm milk with cinnamon and honey, and I can explain while we drink."

"I want mine laced with brandy," he grumbles, but

he follows me anyway. Perhaps to give us both time to think, we brood in silence as I prepare our nighttime drinks. Once we sit down at the kitchen table with two hot mugs in our hands, I take a deep breath and try to explain.

"I'm sorry I lied to you, Eisen. Honestly, it's no excuse, but everything just got carried away this week," I begin, selecting my words the same way I would choose good fruit from bad in the grocery store. A muscle near his mouth twitches, revealing his annoyance, but he doesn't speak.

"I did bring Duncan to Omnium Beanery, but that was because I thought it was a good place to test him out. I didn't know anything about him, except that he's one of the kinder humans who asked to talk with me," I say. "That went pretty well, and you and I did talk about this. Like I said, I'm sorry for lying about yesterday...I did go to the party, but—" Here I don't know how to continue. *Duncan crashed the party to see me so he could tell me his deepest secret?*

"You bailed on the party to hang out with your human?" Eisen assumes, mirroring Wade's earlier action and tracing his index finger around the rim of his mug. *Well, that's simple enough,* I think, hesitant to follow this easy way out.

"Yeah. My new half-breed friends are a little...clingy...and I needed to get away. The all look up to me as some sort of revolutionary leader against the administration and I didn't want to deal with that anymore," I say cautiously, trying not to ramble. *More truth, at least,* I think.

"So...you meet this human boy, he's nice to you a

couple of times, so you go out for coffee. That sounds fine. Well, not fine, but understandable," Eisen growls deep in his chest, obviously winding up for a rant. "Then you decide it's all right to bail on a party where you could be having fun with your own kind, just to go somewhere alone with this human boy you barely know. On top of that, the very next day you do it all again, and spend the greater part of a day—a day when almost everything in relation to our kind is in uproar—with this kid. How is this smart, S?"

"The bare details are a little...sketchy," I say in a small voice, because it's true: aside from the missing detail of Duncan's true nature, and our consequent bond springing from the connection in our mixed DNA, my actions sound similar to what any other empty-headed teenage girl would do. *At least I haven't mentioned anything about love...*

"Sketchy? You sound like an idiot, Sierra, and it's a miracle you're okay after making one stupid decision after another!" This stings, and I blink as hurt worms its way into my system.

"I understand that times are crazy right now, Eisen, but I *am* capable of making educated decisions about people—" I begin, my voice already stiff. Eisen cuts me off.

"Educated decisions? Our world is going to hell, and you decide now is the time to cozy up to a human? Are you some kind of pet, responding to human 'kindness?' Really?"

"That was a really awful thing to say," I murmur, taking a sip of my cinnamon-crusted milk instead of saying anything else. I'm hurt, but I'm angry as well. I don't want a shouting match.

"It's true though, isn't it? You get to a new school, everything is overwhelming and you're the center of trouble, then one human boy is nice to you, and you fall for the act right away," Eisen says. I want to be like Duncan, I want to be the anti-racist one who can say "they're not all bad" and push for equality. But part of me wonders, even after such a splendid time with Duncan, how he acted towards half-breeds when he thought he was just human.

"I don't know all of what's going on, Eisen, I just don't," I say. "But I do know making a hasty judgment based on someone's race probably got us into this mess in the first place...sure, the humans started it, but why should we continue it?" I don't know where this message is coming from, but I feel a tiny bit better once the peaceful words fall from my lips. Eisen stares at me like I've lost my mind.

"You think you love him, don't you?" he remarks, seeming more stunned than angry. I almost choke on a sip of my drink.

"What?"

"You barely met this kid and you've already got stars in your eyes from just a few days," Eisen speaks his perceived knowledge like it's the end of the world. My hands shake, so I clench them into fists.

"That's what you picked up with all your grand perceptive abilities?"

"It's the only answer that makes sense," Eisen insists stubbornly. "I don't normally think you're a fool, but you're young, and you've never dated before...making you easily accessible for a boy to take

319

advantage of, if you ask me."

"Who asked you?" I snark again. "Thanks so much for assuming that I don't know how to take care of myself, or that any human boy who likes my company is a pervert with a fetish!" I set my mug down hard on the table, angry and ready to escape this scene.

"I just don't understand...you don't lack the qualities you would need to captivate a boy. Why does it have to be a human? And, if it's so wholesome, why do you have to sneak around to hang out?" Eisen backtracks as he tries to reason with me, perhaps employing argument techniques he learned from Harold. I try to be reasonable in return, as much as I can be; but then I remember Lyle, and dislike churns in my stomach along with my hurt that Eisen apparently thinks I'm a fool.

"If the case is like you think it is, shouldn't you trust me enough to believe anyone I chose would be worthy of me?" I say. "Even if it's a human, would I pick someone who was a complete jerk?"

"Others have before you...and the fact remains that *he's a human*. I know you've heard the horror stories of what's happened to some half-breed girls before, and—" I cut him off this time, irritated that he'd bring up those nightmare stories of dark allies and girls left for dead.

"I don't have anything else to say about this, Eisen," I say in what I try to make a clipped, cold voice. "Are you going to tell Harold or not?" I squeeze the stone handle of my mug tightly, hoping that the answer will be no. Sure enough, Eisen is furious, but his shoulders slump, and he's quiet for a moment.

"I don't want to. I want to trust you, S, I do...but you aren't the problem here. It's him. Humans do not mean us well, and they never have," he says at last. "If I don't try to stop you, will I find you later on in some ditch all bloody and bruised, if I find you at all?" My heart softens, but I try not to let it show.

"Are you going to get Harold to enforce a ban on talking to humans?" I press for a definite answer, sensing that I'm winning.

"No. I'm no snitch, like I said. But there are conditions," Eisen says, and a small breath of relief escapes in a short exhale on my part.

"Yes?"

"Every single time you're with him, I want a message telling me where you are and how long you're going to be. When you come home, I want you to look me in the face and tell me how you spent your time, and if anything weird happened. I don't want to be a jailer, but if you're going to pursue this, and if you want my cooperation, you'll obey my rules." Eisen rattles off his conditions, waiting for me to object. I'm silent, weighing my options...would Harold impose the same restrictions if Eisen did tell him?

"They'd be worse, believe me," Eisen says, guessing what I'm thinking. "You know he's more traditional, and it would take hours to talk him through this so the results would end up in your favor."

Finally, I nod. "Okay. But you don't tell anybody about this. It's between us." Eisen growls as I finish speaking, perhaps because I closed the loophole of him sharing any tidbits with Wade.

"Deal," he grunts. Before I can say anything else,

he's taken off towards his room upstairs. I sigh, sitting still for a moment before taking both of our empty mugs to the sink. Abruptly, weariness washes over me, and it's all I can do to drag myself out of the kitchen and up the stairs to my own room. Duncan was wise enough not to message me while he knew I'd be dealing with my brothers, but before I head off to shower I send him a quick message.

SIERRA MAURELL: *We're okay. Eisen's a drama queen, but I think he's fine. I only told him the necessary parts and saved the rest for another time.*

DUNCAN LEDFORD: *Glad you're okay. I'm dealing with a friend who wants to know why I've been so nuts lately, so I'll get back to you tomorrow about that.*

After this, I shut off my phone with a determined click and place it on my dresser instead of on my antique white bedside table. My recycled red journal, rare because it's made of physical paper, attracts my notice, and I decide to write in it after my shower. My thoughts don't seem to be in order, though, because they keep repeating in a loop and echo my doubts.

I hope I'm not wrong about him. Please don't let me be wrong...

23

"Sierra!" Hayley exclaims through the phone, nearly making me drop the device on my bed. I'm in my room trying to work on my math homework while carrying on a conversation at the same time, but so far our dialogue has taken precedence over boring equations.

"Why are you always so loud?" I ask, holding the phone away from my ear. "It's not as big of a deal as you think it is."

"Not a big deal?" Hayley squawks again. "You should be glad all of your brothers are working today so they don't hear my effusions of joy!"

I blink, unsure how to handle her reactions. "I wish we were having this conversation in person so I could read what you're thinking a little better," I say.

"Well yes dear, that would be nice, but I can just tell you what I'm thinking! I am *thrilled* for you!" Hayley's excitement is palpable even over the long distance, but I'm not sure she understands the import of what I told her.

"Hayley, I just told you I'm in a relationship with a boy who used to be human, and now he isn't, and I'm not even sure I should've told you that secret," I say, ticking off the details as I tap my stylus against the surface of my school SMARTpad. "Eisen will be watching me like a parole officer from now on, and all my friends at school are on my back about crap already."

"Heavy the head that bears the crown," Hayley intones with a mockingly ponderous voice. Then she laughs, and in spite of my troubles, the sound lightens my heart. "Boo-hoo...you're a leader at school, so if your new friends keep bothering you, use your usual blunt honesty and tell them they need to get over themselves. You should be elated over the fact that you have a boyfriend—who, not to be weird, might end up being your eternal soul mate, since that's how these things usually transpire—and *I* happen to know just the right way to get Eisen back into his place."

"Oh? Share," I say, ignoring her advice to tell off my friends. Since Hayley has been home-schooled, she might not realize that getting on the bad side of new friends when the year has barely started isn't a swimming idea.

Hayley hums indistinctly into the phone before sharing her plan. "Look, Eisen's card is that Harold doesn't know about Duncan yet, right? You don't want

Eisen to tell Harold, who will panic because, as far as Eisen knows, Duncan is human. Now, you know you're eventually going to have to tell your brothers all about this. You told *me*, for crying out loud, and you know I'll keep your secret—I'm having this conversation in the woods behind my house so my family won't overhear, after all—but I think you should trust your brothers with this."

"You think I should've come out with this last night?" I ask. "Hayley, Duncan hasn't even told *his* family about this yet, and you want me to tell everyone in my family about this?"

"Duncan basically gave you permission, which was decent of him. But instead of telling Eisen, you told me over the phone. Let's pray the government isn't listening in..." Hayley trails off, suspiciously listening for white noise in the background of our call to let us know if anyone is spying on our dialogue. "I agree that last night was not the time to discuss your budding romance, not after a long, bad day for everyone but you, but this Tuesday might be the day."

"Why Tuesday?" I ask.

"Tuesday evening, all of you Maurells and Duncan are going to make the drive to my house for a nice family dinner. We're going to conduct a little experiment, my child." Hayley sounds entirely too gleeful about this whole affair.

"That sounds risky," I point out.

"Great leaders take risks," she says; my silence prompts her to continue in a more serious vein. "If Duncan walks into your house before the dinner as your boyfriend and as a half-breed, only you and Eisen will

325

know the difference. We can see how he reacts, but I'm going to make an educated guess that he'll wait to talk to you again before freaking out. This will give him the entire dinner to cool off and think...and the rest of your family will have ample time to adjust to the idea that little sister has a boyfriend."

"That...kind of makes sense, but at the same time it doesn't," I say, completely abandoning my homework as I recline on my bed. "Eisen might not keep quiet, but if by some heavenly act he does, there's still the fact that my brothers now think Duncan's a regular half-breed."

"Exactly! Your brothers will meet Duncan as an unassuming half-breed, which means when you eventually tell them that there's more to the story, they won't have anti-human bias in the way," Hayley speaks like she's presenting a magnificent hand of poker before an audience. "Eisen, upon meeting your future lover, will be able to analyze your attachment for himself, and when you talk to him after the whole event, it will be easier to calm him. You'll have taken away his trump card for causing Harold to freak out and put you under house arrest, and after a rousing argument, your whole family will be on your side."

That's a lot of pressure on Duncan, I think, imagining how he'll respond once I explain this plan to him. My brothers will look forward to the dinner at Hayley's, since the Manchester family has always been our version of extended relatives, but Duncan would be walking into a situation where he has to be under the close scrutiny of half-breeds as a M-DNA person himself. *I think he can do it, but I don't know how psyched he'll* be for the whole event.

"Okay," I say at last. "Let's do it...and see if you can get your mom to make some banana pudding."

"Done, and done," Hayley says, the volume of her voice rising with her excitement again. "The best part of this plan is that I get to see you in a couple days, *and* I get to meet your first boyfriend before anyone at your school does."

School...

"That's a whole different breed," I say, imagining the general student body and faculty reactions if Duncan and I started dating publicly. *It's kind of silly that one high school couple would even matter in the grand scheme of things,* I muse.

"Well...we don't need to deal with that problem yet," Hayley hurries to soothe me. "Just keep your head down as much as possible, don't let your friends guilt you into stuff you don't want to do, get Morgan and Lyle to realize they are meant to be, and wait everything out until the vote in a couple weeks. You can do it."

"Hope so," I sigh. I'd love to keep talking to Hayley, but responsibilities like homework and dinner preparation call me away. "Listen, I have to go—"

"I know," Hayley sighs too; I hear a breeze blow past the speaker of her phone as she walks around outside. "I have to go too. My dad's work dinner is tonight, and I have to help around the house."

We say our mutual goodbyes and I end the call by tapping my nail on the screen of my SMARTcall. I have my stylus in my hand to continue my homework, but a few minutes of staring at one problem without seeing it

327

makes me realize that I definitely won't get a good grade if I force myself to work on this now. I lay back against the pillows on my bed, sighing as I allow memories from my walk with Duncan yesterday to fill my mind.

Suddenly, a call from Duncan makes my phone buzz violently. I startle, jolting to an upright position as I fumble for my SMARTcall.

"Hey," I say in greeting once the device is in my hand; my voice sounds happier and more relaxed than I feel.

"Hey," he says back, and I can tell he's smiling. We exchange trivialities; I'm a little awkward at first, hesitant to be so casual after the intense conversations we've had over the past couple of days. But Duncan is as kind as always, and we get to the meat of the matter quickly.

"So how did your issue with your friend go?" I ask. Duncan exhales, perhaps to dispel any lingering feelings of annoyance.

"Let's just say that since I told you about me, this whole thing is harder to keep a secret," he says. "I've got the half-breed identity hidden still, but...Bari isn't normally perceptive, but I've blown off plans he made two or three times now to be with you."

I'm flattered, but I wonder if his friend will be a problem. "So you told him about...us?"

"No. I tried to put him off, in fact, but apparently my 'suspicious behavior' made him speculate about what was going on...and when directly confronted, I'm a lousy liar," he says. "That's why I called, actually. I just wanted to give you a heads up that my best friend—

and probably his girlfriend—are unashamedly enthusiastic about us being a couple."

"Um...wow. I don't know what to say to that," I say, my eyebrows high on my forehead from my incredulity. "That's..."

"Unexpected? I know," Duncan admits. "He told me that the rest of my friends—the ones you met the other day—have seen this coming since we met, because evidently I can't keep my eyes off of you, and it's distracting."

"Sounds like a real problem," I say, knowing he'll hear the smile in my voice. *Can't keep his eyes off me...* "But they're okay with the whole thing? Like...no one's reporting to the police or selling the story to the media?"

Duncan laughs. "No. Even if they didn't approve of us, they're not losers. Not all human teens are like Bryan and Katrina...but anyway, they want to get to know you better, so they think all of us should have lunch together at school tomorrow."

Caution presses me to decline that suggestion, but then I remember the plan Hayley concocted, so I bite my lip and try to keep an open mind. "What did you say?"

"I didn't commit...although I don't think it's a bad idea if it's done properly. If you don't want to for the sake of the plan to hide our being a couple, I'll get them to understand," Duncan says. I wish he was here so I could see his face.

"I don't think I mind, but I know my friends will talk if I don't sit with them," I say. "It's kind of ridiculous and juvenile but...if I don't keep up a certain image, life would get messier than I need right now." Imagining the looks on my friends' faces, well-meaning as they usually are, isn't pleasant. I rise from sitting on my bed to pace around my bedroom.

"So we can all sit together and call it lunch for equality or something," Duncan says, and I picture him shrugging. "I can pretty much figure where you all usually sit, so we'll just come and join you, maybe..."

"Okay," I say after a few seconds of pondering the outcome. "It's crazy, but we'll see how it goes." This subject is clearly closed, but I don't want to end the call.

"How are you doing?" I ask vaguely.

"In regards to my regular health, never better," Duncan says with a small chuckle. "If you mean how am I doing now that I have a girlfriend and an insanely uncertain future, I'm doing great. More or less excited."

"Neat," I say, a distinct feeling of pleased embarrassment surfacing with Duncan's flattering acknowledgement that I'm his girlfriend. I'd say more, perhaps continuing this feeling, but my phone vibrates again with a huge shudder.

"Hold on a sec," I say as I glance at the caller ID on my SMARTcall. *Damn*, I think as I see Shelby's name.

"Not good news?" Duncan asks as I sigh.

"I have to take this call...like you said, secrets are hard to keep when friends interfere," I say. I could promise to call back later, but I'm not sure how much of my time Shelby will claim before my brothers get home. Besides, I have to tell Duncan that I told Hayley about us—only because I seriously trust her and needed her advice—and I'm nervous about what he'll say.

Here goes nothing, I think as I hang up on Duncan and take Shelby's call.

Monday morning dawns with its typical lack of cheer. It's becoming a habit for my mind to avoid sleep, so my eyes have tired from spending at least three hours lethargically gazing at the outdated popcorn ceiling of my room. It's a relief to wake up and get ready for the day, since my night was so unsatisfying.

My thoughts wander listlessly as I stare into the breakfast pan of eggs, bacon, and mostly fresh bits of tomato. Part of me contains excitement for the day, true: Duncan is the one good part of the school I despise, even if we won't have too much interaction. I hope his friends will be discreet and not sell me out in front of my own friends. Shelby at least might act decently, and Ivar as well if she indicates that he should be calm.

This could all go up in flames, my brain warns me as if it's an old woman sitting in a rocking chair in the corner of the room with a sour face and her cane.

I asked Harold if all of us could go to Hayley's for dinner tomorrow night, and now all three of my brothers anticipate tomorrow as the high point to an otherwise dismal week. The overall mood in the house remains foul, and breakfast passes in silence. I think back to my ridiculously long conversation with Shelby as I eat and go get dressed for school.

She was very accepting of my "family crisis"; she had called to talk about her date with Ivar and his family. It looks like I'm her new confidante, because now I know more than I ever wanted to about the foibles of Ivar's family and their interactions with her.

All of this seems so inconsequential with the prospect of the life-changing vote coming up all too soon, but when I tried to change the subject, Shelby's winning reply was: "The world is going to hell anyway, so I don't care about that."

So, heading to school this morning isn't something I dreaded as much as I did the first day of classes, but my stomach knots just the same. Eisen drives me to school; I wait for him to bring up Duncan again, but he is curiously mum about the whole affair as we weave in and out of traffic. I'm left to my own thoughts as we arrive and I enter the school without much interaction from my peers. I half expect Duncan to be waiting by my locker, but then I remind myself that he wouldn't be so unwise as to wait for me in a half-breed hallway.

"You, my girl, have a lot of explaining to do!" I startle, almost dropping my school tablet as Femi's loud voice catches my attention. I've set my lunch in my locker, and when I turn around my parrot DNA friend stands with arched brows and her delicate hands on her narrow, denim-clad hips. I remember that I never clarified to her exactly why I bailed on the Reis party.

"Oh gosh," I say with real chagrin, "I'm so sorry I didn't get back to you, it's been a crazy—"

Femi grins, her serious demeanor melting. "Don't worry about it. Lyle told me you had a family crisis of some kind. Being related to a lawyer can have its downsides, especially these days," she says sympathetically. I remember that she must know Harold from the mysterious case he worked for her family a while back.

"Yeah," I reply uncertainly. "Sometimes work interferes with a lot of stuff in my life..." Femi nods understandingly, her eyes skimming the corridor, probably searching for her sister or my friends.

"Did you hit it off with Lyle, though?" she asks. The muscles in my face twitch.

"Well enough...I'm not sure if we had much chemistry, though," I say truthfully. Now that I know how to recognize true chemistry, I can admit that it's is something Lyle and I do not have.

Surprisingly, Femi looks relieved. "It didn't seem like it. At least..." she doesn't finish her sentence, and the absentminded pat she bestows on my shoulder is uncharacteristic of her.

"Fai?" Hasida appears, stalking towards us from the direction of our homeroom. She and Femi wear slightly more subdued clothing than the day when all the half-breeds decided to stop hiding their animal aspects, and I hope this might be enough to pacify Belinda without me getting involved.

"Just be careful, Sierra. Boys think with their dicks," Femi huffs, her eyes narrowed in sudden anger.

I blink, unsure what to do with this information.

Which boy is she referring to? I wonder, panicking for a second in case she might know who I left the party with. Hasida nods to me in apparent agreement with her sister's statement.

"You should have lunch with us sometime," Hasida's voice is warmer than I've heard it before; maybe she decided she wants to be friends too. "There are more half-breed seniors in this school than Lyle's group."

"Sure," I say, bemused with this whole conversation. Hasida nods to me, glancing over my shoulder, and the two leave.

What was that all about? I wonder as Morgan approaches. She's smiling, but it's tinged with a manic edge that worries me. *We really need to have that talk soon,* I tell myself sternly. She needs to know I don't like her obviously long-time crush before events get out of hand.

"How are you?" she asks, making the effort to be nice. I shrug casually.

"Fine, I guess. A little shaken up by the whole vote thing coming up...but let's not talk about that," I say. "I've heard enough about it to last me a lifetime."

Morgan doesn't look like she paid attention to what I said. "You never told me, how did your date go with Lyle? Before you left him, that is."

"It's not like she wanted to leave," Lyle's voice startles me, and I chastise myself for being this jumpy so early into the day. "Duty called."

"All that turn out okay?" Ivar slouches behind Lyle, and suddenly I get the sense that he's the most genuine of the bunch. Morgan is sweet, but confused and probably bitter against me, judging by her stiffness; Shelby is too out there to trust, and Lyle looks like he expects too much from me.

"Thanks for asking...it's fine," I say, noticing that my bear friend has real dimples on either side of his smile. The bell twitters before anyone else can speak, and I'm glad for the excuse to hurry to the half-breed room before anyone can say anything else. It may just be me, but Femi's cryptic warning has made me feel more on edge than I'd like.

24

Lyle hovers a lot closer than I'd like most of the morning. I attribute this to his view that, when I left the party, it was reluctantly and only because Harold told me to. Lyle takes pains to pick up where we left off, but I want no part of his attention as we maneuver between classes; it's more annoying than anything else. I can't even speak to Duncan, though we've been watching each other as surreptitiously as possible. All the self-control in the world wouldn't be enough to keep our eyes completely away from each other. Lunch seems days away.

In fact, everyone lingers much nearer than normal. I try to be equal with where I bestow my attention, but while Morgan and the rest stand close by and are willing to engage in conversation, it's almost like they're the court, and Lyle and me are king and queen of our clique.

It's nauseating.

The moment I finally have enough is when Lyle and I debate the vote, in spite of my earlier admittance that I want to avoid thinking about Abel Denmann's decree. We're leaning against the wall beside our classroom, and I try to be as casual as I can while his lion eyes analyze my face.

"I don't understand why this is happening in the first place," I huff, irritated as I remember the smug face and shiny of suit of the senator I despise. "Supposedly everyone was boarding the equality train, but now this happens, and here we are…"

"It was only a matter of time," Lyle interrupts, scowling. "They were playing with peace, probably biding their time and using our labor to build up resources again."

"I don't know," I combat his cynicism in spite of my own mistrust of humans. "I'd like to think they were making an effort, at least for a while. But now…"

"Now it looks like they really should have donated a continent to us. At least then we'd be free to have our own way of life," Lyle's opinion surprises me, but I don't comment; he's distracted me by reaching out and pushing a strand of my hair out of my face. I nearly flinch, alarmed by the touch of his warm fingertips brushing against my cheek. I look away, down at the still-gleaming floor of the hallway. Lyle clears his throat. *How awkard.*

"Sorry…your hair was in your face," he says, shifting

his weight awkwardly. I nod, not trusting my voice; my gaze finds Duncan where he's been standing across the hall, conversing with Truman and pretending he doesn't notice me. But his eyebrows have drawn down into a glower, and I remember that German Shepherds score high on protective instinct.

"Thanks," I say robotically. "I'll be right back." I march away from the English classroom, careful not to make eye contact with anyone except Duncan. I hope he knows to follow me, or at least check his phone in a minute.

SIERRA MAURELL: *Lunch isn't a good idea. The amount of tension in the air could set off another hallway brawl.*

I make my way towards the stairs again—the other stairway I'm not supposed to use because it leads to the human cafeteria—and it strikes me once again that the students are all behaving strangely. I thought the upcoming vote would have had everyone snapping at each other's throats, but the usual heckling and frustrated whispers have disappeared. Each side, human and M-DNA, seems content to ignore the other, as long as no one breaks the peace. One small spark—like what happened after I backhanded Bryan—could set everything on fire, and then we half-breeds would definitely end up worse off. We might prove ourselves to be animals, even if humans have no right to treat us the way they do.

It takes two to fight, my thoughts arrange themselves into a phrase that makes me feel sick.

I reach the stairwell in good time, although I'm still worried I'll be late to class. Hell, after my record, being late seems like a small thing...but I don't need more marks against me.

As I'm wondering whether Duncan bothered to follow me, he bursts through the doorway of the stairwell with a glance over his shoulder.

"Did you—" I begin, but he cuts me off with a stern look before taking a few steps down and peering into the area under the metal lined stairs.

"What are you doing?" I ask instead. He exhales, his hands gripping the railing as he leans back to look at me. A lopsided grin graces his mouth, the kind that makes me smile too.

"I think you forgot what usually goes on in high school stairwells," he says, taking the few stairs separating us in a couple strides. This time I do blush, but I decide that this conversation is less awkward than Lyle

touching my hair with awkward affection in front of Duncan.

"You could have just smelled for them, or listened for breathing," I remind him, referring to our animal senses.

"True...but I'm glad no one's here," he says. "You're a hard person to stay away from."

"And you're really difficult to ignore," I reply as he joins me in leaning against the wall. We stand parallel to the stairway, watching the laser numbers built into the wall right above the doors click down to class time. I catch his scent again and, inexplicably, my mouth waters.

"It's...challenging to watch another guy flirt with you," Duncan says, chagrin in his eyes as he rubs a hand over his jaw line. "I guess it'll be harder to keep this under wraps than I thought. It's like I've just noticed how many people are going to try to get between us."

"Tell me about it," I mutter, the faces of my friends, the principal, and even my brothers filling my mind. Duncan frowns, a look similar to the scowl I saw when he noticed Lyle tucking my hair back, and I know who he's picturing.

"Maybe we should just come out with it...what's the worst that could happen?" he says next. I shudder.

"Only that we're both arrested or assassinated in the streets under the feet of an angry mob." My ears arch down, and my tail sweeps the wall behind me. "That's why I called off lunch...even if we manage to avoid raising suspicion, there are too many variables. Lyle and Aaden might attack each other in two seconds flat."

"But how do you know that for sure?" Duncan asks.

"What?"

"How do you know that for sure?" he repeats, cocking his head to the left in a very adorable way. I can't resist; I take his hand as I answer.

"You know how we are...there's literally going to be a vote on whether or not half-breeds have basic human rights." I wonder at his optimism, watching his face as a muscle twitches near his mouth; I think both of us have decided being late is worth this conversation. "Do you really think humans are going to settle and let a half-breed girl and a human boy date?"

"Suppose I reveal myself?" he asks, squinting in concentration. He's serious.

"And cause mass panic and end up a figure on a government experiment chart? I don't think so, at least not until we have more facts," I say. "Besides...not to be selfish or anything, but I'm unbiased enough to admit that it wouldn't just be humans in the mob. The half-breeds would be furious: I'd be a traitor for dating you, and probably get my whole family in a lot of trouble."

Duncan huffs with frustration; his eyes have turned brown now, which oddly makes me notice how much stubble he has on his face. I reach up to touch it, half-expecting him to pull away, but he rubs his face against my palm, successfully melting the tension in the air. Well, one kind of tension, anyway.

"I don't see how our relationship should be anyone else's business. Even if it was an issue, two teenagers dating against the rules of our culture shouldn't be a matter of national security," he says, meeting my gaze and touching his warm lips to my palm. Distantly, I hear the bell ring for class.

"It shouldn't be. But it is, and I don't want you hurt because we can't handle the secrecy...and to be honest, I don't want a scarlet A painted on my chest either."

Impulsively, I stand on my tiptoes and kiss my boyfriend on the cheek; we're close enough for me to hear his heart accelerate, if I cared to listen...which I do.

"Fine," he gives in right away. "No lunch. I can handle watching lion boy flirt with you all day if I get more of your time than he does."

Evenings...Tuesday evening...Hayley. My thoughts ricochet off random memories, and I remember I have to tell him about my plan to get my family on my side tomorrow. I have to tell him I told Hayley about us in the first place, and that she's the only one I've spilled Duncan's furry little secret to.

"I have something to tell you..." I begin reluctantly, my tail still swishing back and forth nervously. Duncan's momentarily dreamy expression—which made me really want to know what he was thinking as he looked at me with glazed eyes—snaps back into focus.

"What is it?" he asks. I open my mouth to tell him, but he stops me by placing his index finger over my lips.

"Hm?" I query; his eyes glimmer bright green now, staring at my lips. His expression and features suddenly look like he's a hound on the hunt that I freeze up. However, one thing I'm sure of is that I like this side of him already, even if the pounding of my heart is a sign of danger. The *good* kind of danger.

"Tell me later," he says in a low voice. "I haven't seen you all day, and I think I—" he doesn't finish this thought. My eyes partially close, and I realize I expect to be kissed. I've never been kissed before, so maybe it's some human instinct kicking in at the last minute.

"Yes?" I prompt, breathless. His face is so close to mine, and I hold my breath as his warm fingertips brush feather-light over my jaw line and the pulse in my neck. I look up at him, willing him to go for it and kiss me, and his eyes burn so warm that my lips part in anticipation...

He pulls away, breaking us apart with a few inches space; he had me pressed back against the wall with his body aligned with mine. We hadn't been touching, but it still felt like we'd been in a very intimate position.

"You told me not to say it yet, S," he murmurs. The inviting lips I'd been focused on curve into a familiar smirk. My heart trips in annoyance—I dislike being made fun of, a weakness my brothers often exploited—and I'm briefly tempted to push him away.

"I did say that," I admit ruefully; my mind hadn't been on certain declarations, but now I realize he must tie kissing and love together pretty strongly. Somehow, even though I was denied my first kiss by a boy I'm very attracted and attached to, it makes me happy to know that Duncan is still careful about taking advantage of me. Even in something seemingly insignificant.

"I was just going to say I think we're late to class." Duncan proves his lie by laughing. I can't help but grin as I punch him in the arm.

"Aren't you a high school boy? I think it's your job not to care about being late or missing class," I say. He shrugs, opening his mouth to speak again, but then he stiffens. My hackles lift, and my nose twitches as I catch the scent of a human approaching from downstairs.

Before I can think beyond *we're in trouble*, Duncan has seized my arm, opened the doors leading to the main hallway, and shoved me through. He's so quick I believe his canine senses activated by instinct, and for a moment I stand speechless as I stare at the solid steel fixtures of the doors dividing us. *What...?*

Duncan peers at me through the small pane of glass near the center of the door, his eyes dark brown; it's only a moment, but he waves for me to go as we hear the steps of the person coming up the stairs.

"What are you doing here?" I hear the voice of an older woman as she reaches the top of the landing and sees Duncan.

"I'm skipping class, ma'am," Duncan says in a comically matter-of-fact fashion.

"Is that so?" the woman says in a stern voice.

"That's right," he replies. Duncan clearly got in trouble so I wouldn't, and I'm grateful his quick action kept us from being seen together. I'm a bit peeved that he had to be the one to get in trouble, and part of me wants to march in there to keep him from taking all the blame, but that wouldn't be wise.

He's a human, so the worst that would happen is that he'll be sent back to class or to the principal's office, I tell myself as I muster the will to head back to class. A late is better than a skip, after all, and I resolve to make it up to my boyfriend—be still, my heart—later.

I don't know when later will be, especially since Eisen has his little decree hanging over my head, but at least Tuesday—*tomorrow! Crap!*

I missed my chance to tell Duncan about Hayley's infamous plot to get him in with my family.

I'm not quite sure how I lost total control of my Monday evening. The afternoon slipped away from me, true; my teacher didn't expect an excuse for my lateness, but my classmates did, and I had to say I'd felt sick. A lame excuse, but I was worried about Duncan, and incapable of coming up with something better.

Lyle backed off somewhat, perhaps realizing he spooked me by touching my hair earlier, and Morgan and Shelby swarmed and expected a bunch of girl talk during class when I wasn't paying attention. When I wasn't worrying about Duncan—that mostly stopped when I saw him back in classes by next period—or going on autopilot during conversations with my two friends, I continued to ponder Femi's words about boys. *"Just be careful, Sierra. Boys think with their dicks,"* she'd said. I wondered which boy she'd been concerned about, and why she'd felt the need to pass on the vague warning. What did she know?

"Sierra, do you think I could come over after school today?" Morgan asked me out of the blue as we lounged near the soccer field during lunch. I'd wanted to ask Femi and Hasida to join us, but I couldn't find them before Morgan accosted me in the hall. *At least I'm well accepted,* I'd restrained myself from grumbling as I munched on some blackberry tart.

"I'm not sure," I'd said, chagrined to admit that I didn't want Morgan's unstable friendliness any closer to me than it had to be. "I might have a family thing tonight...my brother Wade isn't working the hours he used to, so I'll have to go home and make dinner."

"Oh, okay," she'd replied, and I made the mistake of looking up into her sweet doe eyes.

"Maybe for an hour though, if you don't mind

watching me cook?" I caved too easily, and I should've known then by the way her face lit up that this wasn't the best idea.

Wade came to pick me up from school today, and I courteously gave Morgan the front seat. If all else fails, I am a wonderful hostess. As I'm thinking about how I'm not going to call Duncan until later tonight—I can't tell him the dinner plan over SMARTtext—I try to drown out Morgan's happy chatter with Wade about various sports teams I don't care about. *I didn't even know Wade knew how to talk to girls,* I grumble internally as Morgan releases a high-pitched laugh. *Still, he's dating Emilee, so that has to count for something.*

Finally we reach my house, and I manage to take Wade aside to tell him to stay away from the kitchen if he knows what's good for him.

Now I assemble the ingredients for a simple taco casserole in a large plastic bowl, listening to Morgan's idle chatter as she perches on our biggest kitchen chair. Two icy peach lemonades condensate on the table, but she's already sipped the foam off of hers, and I could tell she liked it.

"How have Femi and Hasida been recovering from the festivities at their house?" I ask, tactfully interrupting a soliloquy about a hot actor who starred in the latest teen film craze.

Morgan shrugs, continuing without missing a beat. "Their parents were okay with the party, and Femi and Hasida are usually good with keeping any alcohol consumption hidden. I assume they had a cleaning crew come through afterwards since they can afford it."

"That's convenient," I reply, picturing the sisters picking up trash in an empty house; I can't imagine why parents would knowingly sanction a party where teenagers might get wasted and have premarital sex, but the Reis family has always been eccentric to my memory.

"And how have you...recovered?" Morgan asks in a timid voice; I decide not to face her as I grate a block of spicy cheese for the casserole.

"I'm fine. I wasn't there long, so there wasn't much to recover from. Everything worked out in the end," I say. *Too true...I snuck out with Duncan and my life got a whole lot better.* I can't explain my feelings yet, but I know they're worth all the trouble we're going to go through.

Morgan sips her peach lemonade; I hear her delicate slurps and her appreciative hum. "How are you and Lyle doing?"

"We're good," I say too quickly, and too vaguely. "I mean...there's nothing to report. Lyle and I are friends, and the dancing was fun. It was great until I had to leave."

"So what happened to giving him a chance after all?" Morgan asks; instead of sounding annoyed with me, her voice sounds hopeful. "I think he remembers how things stood between you differently."

"Did he say that?" I ask, dumping the contents of my bowl into a glass cookware pan and sliding it into the oven; the heat smacks my face, perhaps reminding me to be kind.

"Gosh, Sierra, I understood you not wanting to see the signs at first, but it's silly that you're ignoring his major crush on you at this point," Morgan groans theatrically, rolling her eyes.

"I'm not ignoring the signs," I say carefully, "but I don't want to make him feel something I don't return." Now that dinner is in the oven, I take a seat at the table with Morgan and sample my own glass of cold lemonade.

"Didn't work out, huh?" she says after a long moment when both of us are silent. I sense a feeling from her I can't quite define, although the hopeful feeling is tinged with a sour scent I can only call jealousy.

"No," I speak firmly, wanting this dealt with once and for all. "And I don't know what's between you two or what happened in the past, Mae, but if you have a crush on him you need to go for it. Regardless of how he feels about me, we don't run in the same leagues." I sound like a snob, but better that than I make an enemy or hurt a friend.

Trying to force an attraction to Lyle was the dumbest idea you've had all year, my subconscious cheerfully informs me, and I take another swallow of my drink to keep from growling.

"I told you, Sierra, that wasn't going to work out...especially not when he's head over heels crazy about you," she replies too quietly, her eyes fixed on my face in doubt.

"Crazy or not, that will go away in time if I don't return his feelings. For frick's sake, we've only known each other for a week or so, it's not like we've bonded over soulful discussions," I assure her, wondering why it's taking me so much effort to explain my lack of attraction to the mountain lion boy. "He'll be over me in a week, and if you play your cards right, he can fall into your arms for 'consolation' and maybe notice how you're the one he's wanted all along!"

In response to this wisdom, Morgan continues to stare at me with something like wonder mixed with confusion. "How can you *not* like him?" she asks.

"It's easy...you're my friend, you *like* like him, and since I'm not interested, it doesn't make sense for me to hold on to something that won't happen," I say. "I try to be fair when I can, and setting you and Lyle up is as fair to you as it is to me."

"Then you really don't mind?" Morgan cocks her head to the left, which is a comical look with her majestic antlers.

"Not at all," I admit sincerely.

She sighs, and we both sip our drinks in the quiet. I feel awkward having this conversation, but I'm relieved it's out of the way. Shelby will be upset she missed it, but I for one am glad her enthusiastic protests have been absent from this scene.

Morgan's SMARTcall rings shrilly; she fumbles in her pocket to answer the device. Her greeting for the person at the other end is chipper, and I glance at the clock on the outside of her battered device. *Exactly four o'clock...how convenient.*

"It's Shelby," Morgan says, tilting the speaker away from her mouth to talk to me. "We had sleepover plans of some kind, and her Mom is ready to pick me up now."

"Sure, go ahead," I say, since she's acting like she's asking for permission. "I have to catch up on some stuff around here, but I hope you have fun."

I sit in awkward silence as she chats with Shelby over the phone, and I feel I served my purpose by getting out of her path to Lyle's heart. Morgan smiles at me, and I choose to believe she's grateful. Honestly, I thought she was very sweet when I met her, and her virtuous expressions haven't entirely dispelled that impression. *When it looked like it would be best for Lyle and for you, she* did *back off and encourage you to go to the party as dates,* I remind myself to dispel my annoyance.

Still, me and my subconscious both know that Morgan's not as sweet as she wants me to think; I *am* a fox, and I can read people well when I try.

After Shelby and her mother pick up Morgan, I continue to ponder events as I clean the two empty glasses we left on the table. Now that I've rescinded any and all claims to Lyle, I hope Morgan will go back to being how she was when we met: fun, sugary, and not prone to think too deeply or pry too much into my personal life. *This is why I don't have many girlfriends,* I muse.

"You seem tense," Wade grumbles as he pads into the kitchen barefoot; this is usually a little harder for him, since the fur on his feet can be slippery on our clean but stained linoleum floor.

"You think?" I sigh, knowing he can sense my anxiety from across the room. "Don't worry: I'm taking my frustration out on the lemonade glasses instead of on people."

"I could tell you didn't like your guest from the minute she got in the car," Wade acknowledges as he sets something down on the kitchen table with a thud and shuffles to the fridge. "What did she do to piss you off?"

I rinse the glasses and set them on the towel beside our tiny metal sink to dry. "She thinks I like someone she has a crush on, and I don't."

"Bet she's still psycho about it, right? Girls...let one guy get between you, and best friends become mortal enemies," Wade chortles as he removes a container of horseradish from a shelf in the back.

"We aren't best friends, but yeah I—" I pause, noticing Wade's white-bagged prize on our wobbly table. "What's in the bag?"

Wade avoids facing me; his ears droop as he stares determinedly into the fridge. "A sandwich...or two."

"I just put dinner in the oven!" I protest, my hands automatically resting on my hips.

"Mrs. Chirza invited me over for dinner," my brother grunts, abandoning his sanctuary by the fridge and approaching the table. "I know she and Emilee don't have much to spare...and I don't want to eat them out of house and home...so I have to scarf these down and leave in about ten minutes."

"My my," I say, my anger evaporating. "You're turning out to be a sweetie after all." Wade isn't a boor, but sometimes he can be inconsiderate. His showing respect to Emilee is endearing.

"Don't count on this being a trend," Wade looks up at me, embarrassed but pleased at my praise.

I dimple at him and go about my business, cleaning up the kitchen and waiting for him to leave. I have just enough time to call Duncan before Eisen or

Harold gets home.

25

My bottom lip feels worn from my stressed-out nibbling. I have to remind myself to stop so I don't accidentally draw blood from the chapped skin. Still, it's hard to quell the anxiety: my conversation with Duncan wasn't disastrous, but tonight's the night I find out how my family will act about Duncan.

I'll also find out how Duncan acts around my family...but judging from what I already know about his mellow personality, I think we'll be okay on that front.

Sociology class becomes more interesting as the days go by, but it's still not enough to hold my attention. Especially since this is my class with Duncan; he's only a couple of seats away, and the sight of his tantalizing skin and his wonderfully scruffy hair is immensely distracting.

I picture him as I imagined him last night when I told him my news; serious, worried with distinct frown lines between his eyebrows, and pacing his room as he considered my words. Sure, he was willing to follow the plan, but he has his doubts. Who wouldn't? Forcing a human who suddenly has to completely pass for a half-breed for a few hours in front of my three shrewd brothers isn't the nicest thing to do, especially since he has to reveal it's all been a lie—to some extent—by the end of the night. He has more right to be nervous than I do.

FEMI REIS: *You. We need to have lunch today! Hasida and I usually eat up on the bleachers on the field outside, if you want to join us.*

I scan the SMARTtext without really considering it; multitasking usually comes easy to me, but paying attention in class, ignoring—or failing to ignore—Duncan, and desperately making the attempt to show Lyle I'm not interested by not talking in class is a lot to keep up with. I really want to text Duncan, but if we get caught the teacher might read our message out loud and address the recipient. That seems like a dumb way to come out to the public that we're dating.

Lunch with the Reis sisters might solve my problems, or at least a couple of them. It's a bit of a gamble, but a plan formulates in my mind, so I act on it.

SIERRA MAURELL: *Sure! I'll be there. I might have a few tag-alongs though, if you don't mind.*

I imagine this isn't what she wanted to read, because her reply is terse.

FEMI REIS: *Not Lyle and Morgan. Trust me, we'll have a lot more fun without that drama.*

Femi's perceptiveness surprises me again, but I'm not displeased. *Trust me,* I think grimly, *we're not thinking of the same tag-alongs.* I already figured Lyle and the group of friends I need distance from will have to make plans on their own.

As I look up from my phone, I notice Duncan is looking at me. It's subtle, a sideways glance barely indicated by a turn of his head. But our eyes meet, a faint smile plays around his mouth, and he returns his attention to the teacher after a couple seconds. I struggle to keep a goofy smile off my face as the fur tracing my spine tingles.

SIERRA MAURELL: *Don't worry, I wasn't talking about them. See you later!*

I'm not sure why this feels like a good plan, but I feel bold today in spite of my worries for tonight. I want to have lunch with my boyfriend—even if I still have to be careful as to how I go about it—and I'm damn well going to do it. I'm tired of all the inequality drama, and for some reason I have a strange feeling that Femi and Hasida aren't as hostile to humans as the rest of my classmates. My attitude about this plan yesterday doesn't matter, and I'm willing to try again now that the friends I'm tired of won't be involved in my plans.

We'll see, my subconscious whispers snidely.

"**W**hat are you up to?" Hasida asks me as she waits for me to grab my container of food from my locker. She sounds suspicious, but her pointed teeth show in a smile to dissipate any worry I might have.

"You'll see once we get to the bleachers," I say. "Let's just say I'm using my rights as the rebel queen of Hostetler to my advantage."

"That's terribly vague of you," Hasida shrugs, waving to her sister as she approaches from the end of the shabby hall. "But good for you for sticking up for yourself."

"Thanks," I reply, thinking how good it is that they don't know they're the test subjects of this plan. *Let's hope they don't mind a few humans hanging around instead of my other friends.*

"Yes," Femi inserts herself into our conversation as we amble outside and begin the relatively lengthy walk to the bleachers at the other end of the school. "Good for you for escaping your clique. I wasn't sure if you had it in you, but I'm glad you did."

"Femi!" Hasida chides, whacking Femi's bony shoulder with her teal designer lunch bag. "Don't be rude!"

"It's fine...they're definitely a clique since I got so much grief for not spending this hour with them," I admit wryly. My strange boldness helped me weather the displeasure of my first friends, and it also helped me notice the weird clinginess of the group. I got Morgan on my side simply by giving her a significant look and nodding my head towards Lyle: she got the hint and latched on to him before his attention could return to me. *Thank goodness.*

"I don't know how you put up with them, especially with the little love triangle that's been going on," Femi snorts derisively, stomping on the spectacularly green grass in her dainty grey wedge heels. "It's only been a few days, and I'm tired of them already."

"Does everyone know about the...the love triangle?" I squawk; I don't say it, but I'm tired of the immature clinginess of the group as well.

"Yeah, but I'm doing my best to quash the rumors," Hasida says, pausing to pluck a purple clover from the ground and tuck it into her bright cherry-colored hair; she styled it in an attractive fishtail braid today. "Femi said you told her you and Lyle weren't going to work out, so I've stopped the rumors as I've heard them. Hope you don't mind!"

"I don't," I say truthfully. "I wasn't even aware someone was spreading rumors."

"They are," Femi is still stomping the ground as she walks, and I notice she's been crushing fluffy weeds instead of plain grass. "Hey, it's not like we have much influence aside from our party throwing skills, but we can certainly set a few half-breed students straight when we overhear gossip."

Hasida laughs suddenly. "Well, us and any of the six junior boys who have a crush on us. Between us we can usually control the rumor factory."

"The first thing I heard about you both when I met you was that you throw the best parties and only invite certain people personally," I say.

"Morgan told you that, right?" Hasida sighs. "That's what comes of staying isolated in human communities."

"We used to do that, sure: junior high was a popularity contest, after all," Femi explains; the bleachers are in sight now and my stomach rumbles from hunger as we approach our spot. "But not anymore...we typically invite people in person that we haven't officially met yet. It simplifies things, gives us a good look at who will be at our house or club or whatever."

"Oh," I say brilliantly. It may be fickle of me, but Femi and Hasida look like better friends by the minute. The lack of pressure is kind of refreshing.

"Basically, we keep to ourselves and use our aloof rich-kid status to manipulate the masses. Here we are," Hasida announces, stalking up the bleacher steps to the top row; her boots clang loudly against the metal surface. I follow, noticing as well the crowd of humans at the far end of the rows. *Good, humans hang around here too,* I think. *That will make it easier.*

"What are you staring at, Sierra?" Femi asks curiously.

"I didn't know there were humans in this area," I admit.

"Of course there are! These are the best seats, after

all, except when it's raining," Hasida seats herself grandly at the edge of the top row, composed as she takes a gourmet sandwich out of her lunch bag.

"Do humans bother you too much?" Femi asks, taking a seat on the row below Hasida and patting the space beside her for me to sit. She scrutinizes me with her yellow eyes, and I suddenly struggle to not spill my story about Duncan. *How wise is it to blurt out you're dating a human? Not very,* I remind myself as I sit.

"I did mention I'd have tag-alongs..." I begin as I slowly sink down on the seat beside Femi. "I hope you don't mind, but I'm making a move for equality here, so—"

"Equality my ass," Hasida says, but her tone is light instead of accusing. "Sierra, if you wanted your human friend to have lunch with us, you didn't need to hide or make excuses."

"Although we appreciate your efforts, and we're sure you really do support equality," Femi cuts in, grinning.

"Wait, what? How did you know?" I ask before realizing I just removed any doubts they might have had.

Why are they okay with it, if they did know? I wonder, my ears slanting down. I cock my head to the left as Femi sighs long-sufferingly and shoos a mosquito away from her salad.

"Surely you've heard that we Reiss don't exactly hold the law in the highest esteem?" she asks. "We know things. I can't say exactly which things we know, nor can we give too many details about *how* we know, but we never go into a situation without owning the facts beforehand."

"What she means," Hasida explains after aiming a good-natured kick at her sister's shin, "is that we've known of your...friendship with Duncan almost since the beginning. Of course, we never *dreamed* of it advancing very far until he showed up at our party in that ridiculous wolf costume. Even then, we expected you to reveal him to the rest of the group or send him away...but you surprised us by leaving with him."

"But we don't judge," Femi winks at me, causing my face to heat up with embarrassment. Alarm contributes to my flushed skin as well: the possibility that these two know about Duncan's dual nature fills me with panic. My tail twitches madly, and I take a deep breath to calm myself.

"You don't mind?" I ask. "Like...it doesn't bother you that I'm friends with a h-human?"

"If we were the type who did mind," Hasida says darkly, "Trust me, you wouldn't be here or still at this school right now." Then she smiles, reaching down to bestow a friendly pat on my arm. "Don't worry! Your secret is safe with us. We've been lucky enough to know several good humans in spite of all the bad ones, so we don't see why anyone should interfere in our two races bonding a bit more."

She doesn't know he's not human, I stop myself from exhaling in relief.

"That's not to say your timing isn't bad," Femi points out. "What with the vote coming up, any friendship—or something more, judging from the reports of your dancing—will be absolutely trashed if you let anyone less tolerant find out. You should be careful."

"We are. That's why he's bringing a few friends with him today, just to keep off speculation that anything weird is going on," I assure them, slowly relaxing; I'm able to enjoy the breeze sifting through my hair and fur. I don't know why, but just like I knew I could trust Duncan, I believe that the Reis sisters might be on my side after all. At least, they'll be more reliable—and so far more trustworthy—than my other friends.

"Femi, why were you warning me about boys thinking with their dicks yesterday?" I ask one of the questions bubbling at the forefront of my mind. Femi chokes indelicately on a crouton, but she recovers quickly as Hasida pats her on the back.

"That was a little vague of you, dear," she reproaches. Femi looks up at me apologetically.

"Sorry...I wanted to wait and see if I could read your feelings with more success," she confesses with a pained expression. "Now I know for sure you don't like Lyle, this is easier."

"Explain!" I command. I want her to tell me before my human friends arrive: they're probably in line in their own cafeteria now, or perhaps they decided to eat lunch inside. Duncan might find it easier to persuade his friends to come out here over food.

"Well...Lyle likes you, as you well know. He's been interested in you since the moment you came in the front doors of the school, and especially since all of the half-breeds here look up to you so much," she complies, and I can tell by her breathy speed that she wants to get this over with quickly. "But some of my...assets overheard Lyle bragging to some of the other boys about his intentions towards you."

"This is sounding more and more like a gothic novel," I remark dryly, drawing a snort from Hasida.

"Sadly yes, your gentleman's attentions are not honorable. I'd credit that to your famously good looks and bewitching character," Femi grins, teasing me. "But from what it sounded like, it's more for your status as queen here."

"Honestly, you two seem more like queens to me," I retort, slouching as I pick at my food. "I'm a thoroughly middle-class girl from an isolated half-breed neighborhood, and you are from—"

"—a notorious crime family, yes, we know. We have the connections, but it's not prudent to overuse them," Femi waves her fork in the air, gesticulating to the clouds above us. "But you have a seemingly sweet, relatively honest disposition with an iron backbone, and you're not afraid of standing up to Belinda Harper or anyone else here. Accept that you are popular and well-liked for now, whatever the reason."

"Fine," I concede, not churlish enough to combat her praise. "The point?"

"Lyle was boasting to the guys at the party—a few hours after you left—that he can't wait until you guys are officially together so he can persuade you to help him take over the school and such," Femi says with an expression on her face like warm garbage has been shoved beneath her delicate nostrils. I blink, not totally surprised, but unsure why this would be a big issue.

"That sounds like something he would come up with," I say. "It wouldn't work, especially not now since I don't feel the same way about him, but he was drinking at a party and all guys like to brag."

"Tell her the rest," Hasida encourages, eating faster so she has more freedom to speak. Her diminutive size led me to believe she would be health conscious and not prone to eating a lot, but she sure can pack away a sandwich.

"I am, I am!" Femi shakes her head impatiently. "It's true he'd had a fair amount to drink, but he wasn't drunk enough to excuse his bragging and the other comments he made about how much you'd...er...enjoyed dancing with him. Horizontally as well as vertically, if you catch my drift."

"I catch it," I say disgustedly. *How much I enjoyed dancing with him?* I think back to dancing with Lyle: I *had* enjoyed it, but it was nothing to the brief moments Duncan had danced with me. But Lyle didn't know that, and why would he spread suggestive rumors about me?

"That's..." I struggle to voice my befuddled thoughts. "He's boasting all that? What for? I could easily refute it, and if I'm as popular as he thinks I am, everyone here would believe me."

"This is why I warned you about boys thinking with their dicks. He probably got a rush from the attention you gave him, decided to take over the school and bully the humans with night raids to graffiti the school or whatever—which, knowing Lyle, I doubt he walked in here without a plan involving some sort of human subjugation—and decided to humor the guys with details about your...ehem...*allure*."

I don't know what to say. "That's...incredibly petty. And wrong. And...what?"

"Perhaps we should finish this conversation now," Hasida suggests wisely. "I see your tag-alongs coming now."

Giving myself time to think, I turn around after she announces the approach of my human friends. They're good at looking inconspicuous, all except the sunshine girl dating Aaden; she's obviously trying to stop herself from walking ahead impatiently. Duncan is casual as well, striding with the cavalier grace belonging equally to teenage boys and confident hunting hounds. My injured feelings about Lyle's careless words evaporate for an instant as I see my redhead fighting to hold back a grin...but they return the moment I drop my gaze from Duncan's face. *Better he doesn't learn about this today,* I decide.

"Are you sure your asset was right about what he overheard?" I ask Femi, wanting to confirm her story as best I can before I steer clear of my former friend.

"Absolutely. He's kind of my boyfriend for now, so he wouldn't lie. Hell, he'd do a lot to curry my favor," she tells me, shamelessly staring back at the humans approaching us; I notice how predatory her eyes are as she sees Duncan's friend Truman, and I don't suspect her current boyfriend will last long.

"How about we make this lunch a regular thing, then? I won't relish the company of my other recent friends anymore," I say. "Shelby and Ivar might be fine, but between Morgan's jealousy and Lyle's arrogance...I'm not going to be Lyle's trophy girlfriend, that's for sure."

"Just say the word and they'll be dealt with," Hasida speaks in a silky smooth voice that makes me shudder; I look at her strangely, noticing how very metallic and cold her irises appear.

"Er...no thanks, I think I'll just keep my distance," I say, and she smiles angelically, eyes returned to normal.

"As long as he keeps his stupid plans to himself, I won't interfere," Hasida sings, her dangerous aura dissolving as my human friends approach.

"Mind if we join you?" Bari calls up to us as they ascend the bleacher steps; their feet echo on the metal with more noise than my friends and I made coming up.

"Sure," I call down, giving my friends one last questioning glance to make sure they approve. The strawberry-blond girl—Mabel—doesn't wait; she marches ahead of everyone and plops down beside Hasida, who regards her with shrewd surprise. Facing me, I notice how bright her huge smile is.

"You guys are together?" Mabel asks me in a stage whisper; I'm glad the humans at the other end of the bleachers can't do anything but watch.

"He told—?" I begin, but Kylie cuts me off as the others casually arrange themselves in the available seats around us.

"Gingers tend to blush when they keep secrets. Aaden saw through him right away," she says.

"I guess foxes blush when they have secrets, because we're in on the scheme too," Femi says, craning her neck up to look at tall Truman as he takes a seat with the guys lining the seats to our right. "So the answer is probably yes, even if she won't tell you so."

"Thanks for your input," I grumble, but my heart

367

soars as I see how well everyone is interacting. Hasida was wary, as well as Aaden and Truman, but they're quite willing to try this out and see what happens.

"Any girl Duncan likes is welcome around us," Mabel confides happily. "Now if we can just get Truman to date, our group will be perfect!"

"I might be able to help with that," Femi winks, and though she's cheery I can tell she's testing Mabel just like I tested these friends before by offering a handshake.

"Good luck," Kylie snorts. "If you can distract him from his rock band, I'll plan a parade for your first date."

"Wonderful, a challenge," Femi grins in Truman's direction, waggling her eyebrows like an arch villain, and somehow that's the card she needed to play to help everyone relax and laugh. I'm shocked, but in the best way possible.

Maybe we have hope for getting along after all, I muse, absentmindedly eating my food. It may be silly to base the fate of my race on one just-begun interaction

between high school students, but I can't help but be encouraged as introductions are passed around like a new and interesting candy meant for sharing. I know that one of my weaknesses might be trusting too soon, but as far as starting friendships go, this seems like a good place to begin.

Duncan's gaze warms my face like the perfect early autumn sunlight streaming through the sky. We're not sitting next to each other since, in spite of the apparent outing of our budding relationship to the perceptive group around us, we don't want any outsiders to observe anything but an unusual mix of human and half-breed students enjoying a lunch hour together. I smile at him, looking around at the group and back to him, showing my pleased surprise.

"Thanks for working this out short notice," I tell him once the others are caught up in interaction and asking absurd questions. I keep an eye out for a conversational lull, desperate to avoid awkwardness, but so far I haven't been needed.

"No problem. I'm glad your friends don't mind us party crashing," he replies, snatching a bite of my food; I'm reminded of Morgan's habit of always bringing Lyle lunch, deciding I might do the same. But only once in a while.

"They didn't mind you party crashing on Friday," I tell him, grinning at the thought that Femi and Hasida are actually okay with my choice of boyfriend. It's unexpected and refreshing: no one has been on our side yet about dating.

"They knew?" he asks, glancing towards my half-breed friends as they point out their unique animal traits to the others upon request.

"They're Reiss: they always know trouble when they see it," I shrug. "Speaking of trouble, how much did you get in when that teacher caught you in the stairwell earlier?"

"Not much, since she told me to go back to class...I went out to my car though, since if you came in late right before I got to class a few minutes later that would look weird," he says, reaching up to rub his neck again. I'm distracted by the hot memory of Duncan's proximity to me in the stairwell, but I clear my throat and calm myself before I blush again.

"Oh...well, don't get in trouble on my account again," I say before remembering the shouting fest that's probably going to happen tonight after Hayley's dinner. "Not school trouble, that is," I clarify.

"Ah, it's worth it," Duncan says, and his tone is so warm he might have said "you're worth it" instead. The appealing canine scent drifts briefly through the air again and I wish I could capture the scent in my fur.

It is worth it, I think as Duncan gives me another reassuring smile before rejoining the conversation.

26

It's still worth it, I remind myself as I listen to Eisen rant in the car on the way back to the house. Contrary to Hayley's opinion about whether or not I should tell my currently bad-tempered brother about the real reason for tonight's dinner, I decided it would be wiser to warn Eisen about Duncan's presence before he showed up. The excuse would be that Duncan's dad dropped him off about a block away on his commute to his night shift, but since I'd be revealing Duncan's identity tonight anyway, Duncan could walk the few blocks to his parked car and drive away on his own after the dinner.

"Why the *hell* did you think this would be a good plan, Sierra?" Eisen shouts at me, gripping the steering wheel so tightly as we turn that I'm afraid the whole thing will snap off.

"You told me to tell you whenever I was with Duncan," I mutter grumpily; I just put up with an afternoon trying to avoid everyone but Femi and Hasida, and Lyle's attention discouraged me after my lunch pow-wow with the Reis girls. "This is me telling you."

"I hardly meant you should parade him around the family and bring him with us to the Manchesters' house for Tuesday dinner!" he exclaims like Tuesday dinner is a white tie event.

"Hayley invited him," I insist. "So it's not like I'm being rude and dragging an unwelcome guest into things. Besides, her mom invited him as well, so it's not like Bernette would care."

"That is not the issue!" Eisen swells up, prepared to spout more useless reasons why I shouldn't bring my boyfriend along, but I've had enough.

"You're right, Eisen! The issue is that Duncan is actually a half-breed, so if you shut your trap for two minutes, I could explain what's going on!" I shout, my voice ringing in the tiny space of Eisen's beat-up car. Before I can react further, Eisen slams on the breaks at a traffic light; I have a feeling he would've slammed on the breaks anyway, regardless of traffic.

"What was that?" Eisen asks. His voice sounds eerily soft as he swivels in his seat to regard me. The atmosphere seems to crackle like thunderstorm is nearby after my shouting. I look out the window, unable to meet the piercing blue gaze of my older brother.

"You heard me. I understand if you don't believe

me, but I think you know I wouldn't lie about something like this," I say. My voice feels like it should be hoarse, but my words come out smooth. Eisen stays silent for too long; the light changes and we sluggishly turn the corner.

"Well?" he says right when I open my mouth to ask him to say something.

"Well what?"

"Explain. You just told me that your boyfriend who I thought was human is actually a half-breed, and you also told me to shut my trap and listen. I'm trying to do that, so please explain before I explode," Eisen says, each syllable armed with a painful edge.

"It's a secret...only you, Hayley, and I know. Hopefully Harold and Wade will know by tonight, if they accept Duncan accompanying us to the Manchester's for dinner," I begin haltingly. "Only trustworthy people know, which is why I'm telling you, Eisen. I think...I think this explains some of why I'm unwilling to give my feelings for this boy up."

"If that's true, then I'm sorry for what I said when you got home the other night. This...this changes everything. I..."Eisen is speechless. He doesn't know what to say, like I didn't when Duncan revealed his German Shepherd DNA to me by the lake.

"It shouldn't," I say quietly, finally directing my gaze to Eisen. "It shouldn't matter one bit whether he's human or half-breed. I...I don't know what love feels like, Eisen, but my feelings are...very strong. Strong in spite of the short time that's passed, strong in ways I can't describe."

Eisen sighs, perhaps in frustration. "But what you're

telling me changes everything. It *does* matter. Half-breeds find mates young, Sierra, typically under twenty-five. That's because something in our DNA recognizes a match and...attaches, bonds, whatever. Our human feelings play a part and follow along, but his half-breed DNA changes this into something more serious. And the fact that he can be human or half-breed at will..."

"I know it's scary," I say as another wave of confusion and worry crosses my brother's face; if he wasn't wearing his hat from work, I know his ears would be trembling. "*I know*. It's unexplainable and weird, but it's true. He was a human, and now he's a half-breed, and I—"

My thoughts fragment apart, repeating a phrase my logic refuses to back up as Duncan's face and shifting eye colors and his calming voice resurface in my brain. I'm still learning his personality, but I think of his loyalty to his friends and his curiosity about everything, and I know I'll love learning about him for as long as possible. I put my hand over my mouth to keep from admitting feelings I can't yet accept myself.

I think I love him.

Eisen remains silent for the rest of the drive; we're both stiff in our seats, lost in thought as the afternoon sun I appreciated earlier beats oppressively through the windows. My fur stands on end, and excess moisture gathers in my eyes, though I'm not unhappy.

"Harold needs to know," Eisen speaks gruffly, passing the responsibility to decide on the issue to my eldest brother. "If he makes a decision you don't like, you'll be more willing to listen to him instead of me."

I don't deny the truth of this. "I will tell him, but not

until we get home after dinner. The whole point of this exercise is so Wade and Harold get to know Duncan a little before the human stigma comes into play," I say. I don't add that Eisen is the main reason I want my brothers to meet my boyfriend as a half-breed: I can't afford to have the bias my kind has against humans working against me.

"Fine," Eisen grunts as he pulls into our driveway and garage. I grab my school bag and open my car door to exit, but he stops me by laying a clammy hand on my arm. When I look at his face, I see his eyes are closed and his lips are white. Guilt knots in my gut.

"Do you know what this means, S?" he asks me in a voice barely above a whisper. "He's a human born half-breed. Are you sure you want to go on with this?" I consider the warning, the plea for this to go away. In some ways, life might be easier if I could pretend Duncan had never come into my life. The world would resolve itself into clear lines again: half-breed versus human.

"He's not dangerous, Eisen. I'm sure," I say, my voice the same volume as his. He opens his eyes, staring at me with a wariness that hurts. Perhaps desiring to say more, he moves to speak, but then he closes his mouth with a snap and practically leaps out of the car. I follow at normal speed, suddenly exhausted from the short conversation with my brother. At least I know Eisen won't sell me out; I can tell Harold about all of this on my own terms.

I send a message to Hayley as I enter the house; Harold and Wade still aren't off work, although they will be in time for us to leave for Hayley's about five o'clock.

SIERRA MAURELL: *Phase one of the plan is complete. Better so far to tell Eisen beforehand.*

HAYLEY MANCHESTER: *Excellent. How long did he yell?*

SIERRA MAURELL: *Not very long.*

HAYLEY MANCHESTER: *That sounds suspicious. Keep an eye on him.*

SIERRA MAURELL: *I plan to. You're still sure about us bringing our drama to your house tonight?*

HAYLEY MAURELL: *Please...I can't wait to see you!*

This conversation encourages me, and the tension making my muscles tight eases. I have other reasons to be nervous or excited for tonight, but I do miss my best friend; I don't have anyone else like her in my life. Femi and Hasida seem more like promising friends, but friendships take time to build, and Hayley and I have known each other since before my mother died.

Glancing at the clock as I get ready, I think of my mother as I select the right clothes to wear. I don't want to be too fancy, so I settle for a grungy pair of plum corduroys falling just above my knees, a turquoise colored t-shirt with cute buttons, and the leather rose choker Wade bought me for my sixteenth birthday. I wonder what she'd think of my life right now: she would be pleased with my close relationships with my brothers, but I'm not sure what she would think about the Duncan affair. Miraculously, none of my brothers got sick from the toxins she brought home by accident and I did. I survived, although I was weak and panicky for a long time, and she died before we could really get to know each other.

What would you think, Mum? The thought zips past the boundary where I store painful memories, and suddenly I'm conversing with someone who isn't on this earth. *You married Dad when you were young, so would you understand why I feel this way about Duncan? Would you like him, or would you be on Eisen's side?* My questions don't get answers, not from the porcelain-skinned, dark-haired woman with the warmest grey eyes I've ever known.

One question I don't dare voice: which side of myself should I give more power in this case? The fox whose instincts scream for more of Duncan in spite of the approaching turmoil caused by the vote, or the human who can't logically explain why her feelings are so strong? I've always believed that balance is the key to happiness, but these two sides of me have become increasingly tricky to reconcile.

I do know what my mother would say about the vote: she lost my dad to the fighting, raised her sons and daughter as a single mother in a post-war city, and I doubt she'd be anything but livid about the very fact that the vote is allowed in the first place.

I spend the rest of my time getting ready alone, and I empty my mind of anything stressful as I shower, blow-dry and curl my hair, and perfect my make-up.

It's not easy: I keep picturing Harold's and Wade's faces once I tell them I'm bringing my new boyfriend to Hayley's, and then again as I reveal Duncan's human side. Worse, I picture Duncan's discomfort around my family and pseudo-family, and my stomach plummets.

So, by the time 4:55 rolls around, I'm a nervous wreck as I pace our living room floor. Harold won't have time to change before work, but Wade just dashed upstairs shouting about a two minute shower. I hear Harold's car pulling into the garage; Eisen should be down here, but he's nowhere in sight, and I worry that maybe I misjudged his willing silence about my secret. He could be up there right now, spilling the beans to Wade as he hunts down a mildly respectable t-shirt...

"Sierra? What's wrong?" Harold's voice startles me so much that a loud squeak escapes me, sounding a lot like someone stepped on a mouse. My plan all along has been to tell Harold and Wade at the last minute that I have a boyfriend, and he'll be here any minute to come to the Manchester's with us, but I'm horrified as the words burst from my mouth at top speed.

"Harold, I met this guy at school who I really like, and I invited him to come to Hayley's with us...he'll be here in a few minutes."

Harold drops his scuffed and worn leather briefcase on the table with a thud; he was in the process of loosening his tie when I spoke. Eyebrows raised, he gives me a careful once-over before removing his tie and re-tucking his shirt into his pants.

"Yes, I could have guessed as much from what

you're wearing. Don't you normally wear sweatpants to Hayley's house?" He chuckles, shaking his head like I'm a child wearing my mother's antique wedding dress again. "Bernette called me at work and asked if your gentleman friend would prefer barbecue ribs or Italian beefs. I told her you would prefer the less messy option."

"Oh, I—Good call." My voice is too high-pitched; I swallow and clear my throat before continuing. "I was planning to tell you myself, but I guess Hayley's mother beat me to it."

"That's what I was hoping you'd say," Harold sighs, shrugging his angular shoulders like he shrugs off the fatigue from late nights at the office; he strides over to me from the kitchen and abruptly envelopes me in a strong hug. I feel Harold's thinness as I wrap my arms around him, and I sigh as he pats my hair.

"You're not eating enough again," I say softly into his chest, an old guilt squeezing my heart again. *If I was working instead of finishing school, he wouldn't have to spend so many hours at the office.*

Harold grumbles and gently tugs my right fox ear. "Don't change the subject, S. I regularly eat enough for three people, as you well know," he says, but we both know he works more than he eats. "You know you can talk to me, right? I would have liked to know you had a boyfriend and wanted to bring him to meet our friends, just as any older brother would."

"I know," I reply, reluctantly taking a step back and out of the hug. Harold's strong but long face possesses that dog-tired look many people in his generation seem to have, and I wish the people he works with

379

gave him more appreciation. I might have misjudged my brother when it came to telling him the truth. "Harold…"

"Yeah?"

"I have something I need to tell you," I begin, taking another breath to tell my story; perhaps he notices my serious expression, because he shakes his head to stop me.

"I've been betting you're holding something back, S, but now isn't the time. Maybe tonight after dinner you can tell me, but right now I hear your boyfriend walking to the front door."

He's right: I'm familiar with Duncan's step already, and I recognize his footsteps coming to the door. I'm partially glad Harold stopped me because Wade thumps down the stairs now, his brushed auburn tail waving saucily behind him. *Eisen has been tolerable, Harold might even be kind, but Wade?* I think, deciding Wade will barely accept Duncan as a half-breed boyfriend, never mind a human.

"I'll get it," I tell Wade before Duncan's knuckles rap on our front door. Wade's expression as I see it before the door opens is confused.

Duncan looks nervous, but not as nervous as I feel; the mellow aura that always seems to surround him is charged with tension, but I'm grateful he's brave enough to face my family of brothers.

"Hey," he says; his voice sounds a little huskier than I expected, but then I remember that his canine DNA affects his voice slightly. Of course, it might just be me who hears that quality.

"Hi," I reply, my lips twitching into a fleeting smile.

He looks so good standing there, dressed up in a pale grey button down shirt with rolled-up sleeves and fantastically well-fitting jeans that make strange thoughts pop into my head. "Come in."

"Thanks. My dad dropped me off a couple blocks down the road on his way to work," he speaks his lines of our script carefully, and I notice his tawny eyes looking to me for approval. He really has tried to blend in, even if he can't use the wolf-ears headband for a disguise: he's enshrouded by the distinctive half-breed scent I love about him, and I notice how he's turned his collar so the fur on his spine is clearly visible.

I nod, shutting the doors as he enters and avoiding Wade's eyes. "I'm glad you could find our house," I finish our performance with my lines, impulsively taking Duncan's dry hand as he stands by me.

"Um...could someone explain what's going on?" Wade questions, standing back by the bottom of the stairs with his yellow eyes narrowed in suspicion; his gaze rests on my hand in Duncan's, and I cough delicately to get him to snap out of it.

"This is Duncan, Wade. My boyfriend." My face colors as I say the words, and Duncan takes a step forward to shake my brother's hand. It's a very smooth movement, and I remember that Duncan said he was a salesman for his summer job. He must be used to greeting people, even if they're staring distastefully at his open hand as he offers it. Harold, ever the peacemaker, swoops in and shakes Duncan's hand before Wade's rudeness can extend to action.

"I'm Harold Maurell," he says, suddenly every inch the successful lawyer instead of the affectionate older

381

brother I know best. "I'm sure Sierra's told you a lot about us already."

"Duncan Ledford. And yeah, your family is a main feature in a lot of our conversations," Duncan says as Harold steps back.

"We were planning on leaving right about now, if Eisen ever comes down the stairs," Harold tells him after they make small talk for a few seconds. I probably should be intervening more, smoothing the semi-awkward conversation with my support, but I'm busy glaring at

Wade to ensure he doesn't make an ass of himself in front of someone I care about.

He does anyway. "You're awfully human looking for a half-breed, aren't you?" Duncan looks down at my brother—who stands shorter than my redhead—and I see a smart reply forming in his eyes. Eisen, racing down the stairs and tugging a battered comb through his hair, beats him to it though.

"And *you're* rude, Wade Hampton. Hasn't Emilee taught you any manners?" Eisen flicks Wade's scruffy ear as he tucks the comb into his pocket and approaches Duncan with the stride of an arrogant prince.

"Eisen," he introduces himself, thrusting his hand out towards Duncan with an expression that looks more combative than welcoming. Duncan calmly takes his hand, accepting one of those rough handshakes that males competing for supremacy hurt each other with.

"Duncan. I'm dating your little sister," Duncan speaks in that deep tone of voice again, staring Eisen down as they release each other. *Ugh*, I think, exasperated. *Did you have to deliberately bring up the fact that I'm the little sister?* I shake my head and stand next to Harold, impatient for this awkward scene to end so we can get in the car for the drive to Hayley's country house.

"You know, Wade," Eisen says, his lips stern even if he's keeping his eyes wide and innocent of suspicion. "He can't help if his human DNA is the strongest thing about him."

Eisen, you ass, I think angrily. He and Wade both deserve a good kick to the shins. *Is he trying to give hints that Duncan is more human than Harold or Wade thinks?*

Duncan's focus flits to me for the briefest second, and I remember I forgot to tell him about Eisen's foreknowledge of the plan. Perhaps sensing my distress, he wisely chooses to leave my brother's jibe unanswered.

"Time to go, all," Harold cuts in, leading the way to the door. We're taking Wade's van so we can all fit; his car usually stays in the driveway, since it can't fit into our garage. I notice the humorous tone to his voice, and realize that he thinks this whole scene is amusing. If Harold and I hadn't had that nice exchange before Duncan arrived, I would be inclined to kick his shins as well.

27

The Manchester house is in uproar when we arrive.
I'm well used to the chaos of Hayley's younger siblings
playing before supper, as well as the ensuing disorder
of Eisen and Wade—who enjoy children far more than
me or Harold—joining in with reckless disregard for the
value of the surrounding furniture, but I'm not sure
about Duncan's acceptance of this scene. Harold
abandons us to visit Mr. Manchester in his office.
Ordinarily, this is the part where I greet Bernette
Manchester as she puts the final touches on dinner, or
when I run upstairs to find Hayley if her assistance
wasn't needed in the kitchen.

Instead, Duncan and I linger in the doorway, taking
a moment to catch our breath as Eisen scoops up tiny
Arabella and bodily tosses her to Wade; the girl

squeals, cat tail waving and whiskers twitching, and tabby-furred Kami latches onto Wade's legs with a loud meow.

"Is this all okay?" I ask Duncan anxiously, peering up into his face as he scans the room. "It's bad enough Harold had me sit up front so you were in back with Eisen and Wade...and I forgot to tell you the Manchesters have kids..."

"It's fine," Duncan says, his gaze returning to me; the brown makes him look more intense, but it's in a way that makes my heart squeeze up with pleased recognition for his canine DNA. "Everything is...better than I expected, actually. Don't worry."

"Better than expected?" I query, smoothing my clammy hands over my corduroys. Duncan nods, looking meaningfully at Eisen and Wade.

"I was expecting a lot more hostility from your brothers, judging from the way you spoke about them whenever they came up," he explains, taking my hand. "But so far they don't seem any more resistant than normal older brothers should be...except for Eisen."

I wince sympathetically. "Yeah...I told him about you beforehand, guessing that would be better. Maybe I shouldn't have, if he's going to drop hints about you all evening in front of everyone."

"I'm glad you did," Duncan says, looking at me like I'm the only person in the room; perhaps realizing we're having an only-two-people-in-the-room moment, he self-consciously re-tucks his shirt into his pants with a surreptitious glance at the surrounding mayhem. "The fact that he didn't spill the story to your other brothers right away proves that he's more likely to be on our side…you're handling this well, I promise."

"Oh, you," I say, grateful for his reassurance. *I'm glad you're here, and that you want to be here,* I want to say, but the words don't come easily to my lips. "What's the title of the book you used to teach yourself all the right things to say?"

"Ouch," Duncan laughs. "You don't think I can learn boyfriend skills on my own?"

"Well you learned so quickly I thought…" I don't finish my smart comeback because he's taken my hand again, looking into my eyes as he brings it to his lips and kisses my knuckles. I swallow, my knees feeling weaker than normal as my heart drums forcefully in my chest. *Wow…*

Suddenly a small stuffed animal that looks like a badger wearing a scarf sails towards Duncan's head from across the room. It wouldn't cause any damage if it hit him, but Duncan lifts his other hand in the blink of an eye and snags the missile before it hits him. I'm startled by his reflexes, since they're quick even by half-breed standards.

"Nice," I say as Duncan drops my hand and chucks the badger football style towards Eisen, who was examining a potted plant in the corner with too-innocent interest. It hits him before he can turn around, and I realize with a thrill that Duncan can not only pass for one of us, but truly *be* one of us. No human has that speed, nor do they possess the excellent reflexes that accompany animal DNA.

"You didn't tell me your boy was a jock, Sierra!" Hayley's voice startles me out of my momentary reverie, and I hear her fluffy grey tail swishing against the stair banister as I turn to see her perched on the stairs behind us.

"I'm not," Duncan says, examining Hayley curiously. She too is like Wade in that her animal features are very prominent: her hair is long, but it's a sleek iron grey color that compliments her tufty cat ears and the whiskers on either side of her petite nose. She's wearing a pale blue peasant top with her floral patterned jeans, and her hands are strong looking under the layer of fur that extends to her elbows. Her feet are more like paws as well, so she rarely wears shoes around her house.

"Well you'd blend in just fine," Hayley says, and from the mischievous way she's smiling, I can tell she's not referring to jocks when she talks about blending in.

"Hayley!" I exclaim in greeting, feeling in a rush how much I missed my best friend. She bounds up to hug me, smelling like clean cat and faintly like laundry detergent, and it feels like I'm hugging a sister.

"You took too long getting here…did your brothers harass him on the drive?" she asks me, smiling at Duncan amiably. "That is, did they give you a hard time?"

Duncan shakes his head. "Not really…Sierra talked too much for that."

"I was trying to help!" I whack his arm playfully, knowing full well that I did chatter most of the drive to keep my brothers from asking more stupid questions.

"I'm inclined to believe Duncan in this matter, sweetie," Hayley grins, her sea colored eyes bright in her round face; she takes my arm and leads the way to the kitchen. "Let's not linger by the front door; it's boring. Besides, my mother wants to meet you,

Duncan." Hayley is the one talking a lot now, so I sense rather than see Duncan following us.

"He does smell good," Hayley whispers very quietly. "Very canine...but in a good way."

"Yeah," I say, not wanting to gush about Duncan's attractive qualities when he's so close to me. Fangirling in private isn't an issue, but it's not exactly wise to feed a boy's ego so early in a relationship.

We find Bernette in the kitchen, artlessly finishing the last touches on a homemade banana pudding that she knows I favor greatly. She smiles at me as we enter; the soft lines on her face enhance the depth of her dark eyes. Bernette is the closest thing I have to a mother now, and I wouldn't trade our relationship for anything.

"I escorted the rabble," Hayley announces dramatically, hopping up to a countertop to sit precariously on the edge.

"I see that," Bernette says dryly, coming over to give me a hug. She's a very unique person: content with being a stay at home mother, but as independent as she can be sassy at times. It's a trait that runs in the family, judging by the banter Hayley and her sisters keep up constantly.

"Hi, Mom," I say, accepting the hug Bernette offers me. She has a wonderful, clean linen closet smell mixed with the nice cat smell associate with her meek tail and cat ears, and it's one of my favorite things.

"I've missed you," Bernette says sincerely, smiling at me before she looks up at Duncan. He's lingered awkwardly in the wide doorway of the kitchen, although he tried to be cool about it by slouching casually against the doorframe."Who's this?"

"Duncan, Mum. I told you this," Hayley grunts as she snags a vanilla cookie from the box sitting beside the bowl of pudding.

"As always you are as polite as you are successful with your math skills," Bernette says, but her tone is light. "Nice to meet you, Duncan. You look like you and Sierra will be good together."

That's a positive sign, I think, swishing my tail back and forth as I relax. *If she thinks he's okay, then he must be.* Bernette is a good people-reader, although when she doesn't like someone she's been known to inflict verbal blunt force trauma. In this case though, she seems willing to talk to Duncan in a subtle mom-interview way; Hayley motions me over while they talk.

"She's going to ask how you two met, why he's interested you, that kind of thing," Hayley confides in a whisper as I hop onto the granite countertop beside her. "Of course, she'll be as subtle as she can about it, but she'll still do the good cop thing. My dad will probably do the bad cop routine, just a memo."

"Excellent," I groan, although I have an ear cocked so I can attend to Duncan's conversation; he's telling her about school, already making her laugh with a description of our stern Sociology teacher with her pursed lips and clip-on earrings. 'It's not like my brothers are doing their best at the bad cop routine on their own."

"Cheer up, it's not as bad as it's going to be later when you spill the beans about the...*furry little secret* once you get back to your house," Hayley says optimistically. I grimace, covering my face with my hands. "How is your faith in The Plan So Far holding up?"

"Well enough," I intone. "If I'm reading Harold right, I think he'll be reasonable; he was nice enough when I dropped the boyfriend-is-coming-to-dinner bomb. It's Eisen and Wade...Wade is going to *freak*, and I don't know how Eisen will play his cards."

"At least you look pretty," Hayley pats my arm affectionately. "And at least tonight is going well so far. Just try to relax and enjoy yourself for now, so your brothers can see how comfortable you are around Duncan."

I exhale slowly, then take a deep breath to fortify myself for the next few hours. The kitchen—indeed, the entire house—has an aroma of garlic and tangy pepperoncini from the spices mixed in Bernette's classic Italian beefs. My mouth waters, my stomach snarling with hunger; I've been so anxious I forgot to be hungry until just now.

Duncan catches my eye as he chats with Bernette and leans on the island countertop; he's good at this, the easy conversation with people he's just met. I smile encouragingly at him, letting him know I think he's doing well. His answering smile is endearing, and I decide tonight is going to be okay after all.

The dinner plates rest on the smooth wooden surface of the dining room table, full of bread crumbs swimming in the leftover juice from the beef sandwiches we just devoured. Duncan is seated to my left, Hayley to my right, and the dinner conversation has evaded any awkward lulls. Hayley's little sisters are absent as well: they ate their dinner early, and Hayley set them up with the SMARTvision in her parent's room upstairs. Mr. Manchester cuts an imposing figure, red faced and rotund with a whitening goatee and a distinct lack of any animal attributes but small cat eyes and a hidden tail, but thankfully he conversed more with Harold and my brothers than with Duncan. Right now he discusses the merits of good coffee with Eisen while Bernette asks Wade about Emilee Chirza.

I'm full and contented, although when Hayley asks me about school today, I remember what the Reis sisters told me about Lyle and that group of friends. I repeat the story to Hayley, knowing she'll want in on the drama.

"So Lyle is a skeezebag after all," she sniffs disdainfully, munching on a bit of the leftover mozzarella cheese.

"No surprises there. At least Sierra's lunch plan was a success," Duncan chips in helpfully; he's the only one still eating, packing away three whole sandwiches, which is one more than all three of my brothers consumed. "I confess I was worried that her friends wouldn't like having mine around, but they—Femi and Hasida?—were pretty welcoming."

"Kind of gives you hope for the future, doesn't it?" I

ask quietly, nudging Duncan's knee with my own under the table. I catch him blush, but I can tell he's pleased.

"Y'all are ridiculously cute," Hayley must have noticed our little exchange, judging by the smirk that angles her kitty whiskers up. "I don't know if any of the peasants have told you this yet, but it's true."

"Thanks," Duncan says, giving me a sideways humorous look. "We try."

"No one's told us that, so you're the first. Congratulations," I laugh, but another troublesome thought occurs to me. "You might be the only one, actually. I don't know if we'll get much support...later on."

"Probably not," Eisen's voice breaks into our conversation as he sticks his neck around Wade to butt in. "Make room, little brother. My turn to talk to the little kids."

Wade, busy listing the merits of his new girlfriend to Bernette—the best listener here—switches seats without complaint, and Eisen leans around Hayley to continue speaking. "Once the secret gets out, you'll have a lot of drama on your hands for a long time."

"Thanks for stating the obvious," Hayley makes a face at him; she and Eisen get along fine, but he did use to tease her horribly when she had braces on her sharp little teeth, so she's perfectly content to snap at him whenever the occasion arises. "I think they can handle it."

"Do you?" Eisen snorts. "Sierra's a tough kid, but that's just it: she's a *kid*. She's a teenager who doesn't know anything about the outside world. The fallout from this story is going to be incredible."

"I don't see how their relationship is anyone's business, including yours," Hayley defends me with a coarse meow obviously stuck in her throat.

"Is that what you really think of me, Eisen?" I ask, slightly embarrassed that my brother is putting me down in front of Duncan. I expect Eisen to soften, but he still has that arrogant, hard look in the flash of his eyes and the scornful lines around his mouth.

"You've got guts, Sierra, but it's really not in your best interests to continue this fiasco. Hayley, their relationship wouldn't be anyone's problem in an ideal world, but here...have you ever heard of a half-breed-human couple before, presuming the ginger here doesn't want his secret going public? Have you ever heard of—" Hayley slaps a hand over his mouth before he can spill the rest; he's already said too much, and we can't count on the other dinner conversations to grant our dialogue privacy.

"The ginger here," Duncan interjects, surprising me by doing so and by the faint chill in his voice, "doesn't care if the word gets out and causes trouble. I'll be there for her and protect her when it's needed. Like Hayley said, it's not anyone else's business, and I'd rather go through the muck than just give up on...what Sierra and I have for public reasons." He's staring Eisen down, not with narrowed eyes, but with determination and something like annoyance in his voice. Eisen, surprised, closes his mouth against arguing more and studies Duncan, a hard look on his face.

"Let's go get the bowls for dessert!" Hayley chirps nervously, breaking the tension in the air. Grabbing my arm, she practically drags me out of my chair; I think about summoning Duncan as I go, but he and Eisen continue to size each other up.

"Whew!" Hayley exclaims once we escape the tense bubble by sojourning in the kitchen. "At least you got one that can defend you from your brothers."

"I'd say that's a strange concept, but we both know you're right," I admit, checking my reflection in the patio window to make sure I still look presentable.

"Of course I'm right," Hayley snorts as she reverently lifts the bowl of pudding out of the fridge and sets it on the island; I help by gathering the appropriate number of bowls from a cabinet near the stainless steel sink. "Honestly, you know I am very fond of Eisen, but he can be such an *ass* sometimes!"

"We knew he was going to be an ass about me dating anybody," I reason as I line the bowls up on the counter for Hayley to fill; she huffs as she opens a drawer to pull out a large wooden serving spoon. "It's no surprise that he's an ass about this issue either."

"That's no excuse!" Hayley scoops hefty servings of creamy banana pudding into each bowl, scowling at the dessert. She's always been fierce on my behalf, and I'm grateful for her support now.

"I miss the reasonable Eisen, you know?" I say as I grab several spoons out of a different drawer. "The one who'd always be willing to listen and wait and see before jumping to conclusions or letting bias cloud his judgment."

"He's still a young, hot-blooded male, so I suppose we shouldn't expect a lot of decent behavior from him when it comes to his little sister. Nevertheless, I'll be sure to send him a SMARTnote later detailing his rudeness to our dinner guest."

"You do that," I smile when her long fluffy tail bristles in indignation as she slides the depleted dessert back into the fridge. Undoubtedly, she *will* message Eisen before the day is done.

"At least you have Duncan to protect you...not that you need protecting, of course, since you are a strong woman and the equal of any man," Hayley sighs. "The only guy who's been interested in me was that Jansen dumbass who turned out to be a drama queen with masculinity issues. He could give my psycho cousin Jenifer a run for her money...the two of them could take her prescription meds and go mess up other people's lives."

"Yeah...at least I have Duncan," I say, wondering if he and Eisen have stopped glaring at each other by now as I ask about Hayley's semi-existent love life and help her escort the bowls of pudding to the dining room table.

28

Our drive back to the house is quiet, mostly because all our stomachs are completely stuffed from Bernette's delicious dinner and dessert. My fingers tap against the fabric of my seat as anxiety over coming clean to my brothers fills my mind. Post dinner, Hayley and I enjoyed a good amount of conversation as we slouched on the sofas in her furnished basement like the teenagers we are, and I admit that I've missed talking to someone who knows me so well. Duncan joined us once everyone else at the table had interviewed him—Wade found out he plays a champion game on SMARTspace, so they discussed that for a long time—and I felt...comfortable. I was relaxed around people who weren't judging me or wanting to use me to do something for them.

My brothers were surprisingly kind—Eisen especially so, since I guess he and Duncan have decided to be civil—by letting me sit in the back with Duncan, although that could be residual mental dullness from the food coma we're all suffering. I hold Duncan's hand, strangely peaceful in spite of what's ahead. He has that calming effect on me, and I hope he's not too keyed up. They probably won't, but he could possibly think that my brothers might attack him once they know the whole story. I wish we could talk, but not while my brothers would listen in immediately, all three pairs of fox ears swiveling to catch the slightest murmur.

After the long, quiet journey, we arrive home in fairly good time, and groans about being so full get passed around by all the men as we pile out of the van; Wade in particular ate so much banana pudding that Bernette won't have more than two spoonfuls left. Duncan squeezes my hand as we head inside before letting go.

Here we go, I think grimly, uselessly trying to string together a magic combination of non-chaos-causing words.

We loiter in the kitchen for awhile, standing around in the shadows cast by the outdated, plain chandelier hanging above the table. Duncan and I lean back against the sink, our arms crossed in a subconscious mirrored position; Wade has thrown himself into a chair, and Harold takes a seat with more dignity. Eisen, glowering slightly, angles himself with the door frame, leaning against it. He catches my eye and nods significantly towards our brothers.

"What time did you say your dad would pick you

up?" Harold asks after we exchange more small talk involving casual questions about Duncan's life. He says it kindly, but I can tell he wants my boyfriend to go home so we can all sleep.

"Actually," I say, seizing the opportunity. "He's going to drive home himself."

"Sure he is," Wade laughs mirthlessly. "That would be great, I'm sure, but until you're twenty you should accept your fate as backseat baggage."

"That's true," Duncan says, casual as if we're still talking about his family or school. "If I was a half-breed, of course I wouldn't drive until it was legal." His tone is courteous, like he's quietly letting Wade know he made a social faux pas. Meanwhile, I inspect the linoleum tiles of the floor, deciding I need to sweep again soon...but I feel prickles on my skin as my family registers the content of Duncan's words.

"If...you were half-breed?" Wade asks.

"What do you mean?" Harold's voice is suddenly stern, since his lawyer sense lets him know that Duncan's apologetic face isn't amused.

"Show them," I say quietly, not daring to look up from the floor; I'm going to have to do battle shortly, so maybe my unhelpfulness now can be excused as mere preparation.

Duncan obliges: his irises lighten to green again, and the animal alertness I've grown used to over the evening fades from his posture. Whatever weird trick he uses to turn off his half-breed senses switches off his warm, wood-spice canine scent; a less pure, all human whiff of Duncan glides through the room.

The effect on my brothers is instantaneous: Wade

leaps out of his chair with a profanity, clearly freaked, and Harold rises to his feet with anger in his dark eyes, although he keeps his fists clenched at his sides. I'm proud of him for keeping himself from flying off the handle as he surely wants to, but my eyes go to Eisen next. My look pleads for him to be on our side in spite of my wish for a poker face, but his expression is fathomless; I can tell he had hoped I was somehow wrong, but now without a doubt he believes me. I resist the need to step in front of Duncan to protect him from whatever they might do.

"He's human," I explain before anyone else can speak, "And he's half-breed. I know it's crazy, but it's real, and it's also not his fault. We all knew this day would come...the vaccine had to stop working or something..."

We *didn't* expect this development, that's for sure, and Wade calls me on it.

"Seriously? 'We all knew this day would come?' What is *wrong* with you, Sierra?"

"Nothing is wrong with me!" I take Duncan's hand, perhaps a little aggressively, and hold it tight as I speak. "It shouldn't matter what he is, right? Humans and half-breeds are supposed to be equal!"

"In an ideal world, sure, but not in a day and age where you'll get lynched just for going outside if anyone finds out you enjoy...*fraternizing* with a human boy!" Wade shouts, his ears almost flat on his head and his furry features transformed into a furious, frantic expression. "That is, if he's not dragged into a lab never to see the light of day again!"

"Do you think I would endanger her that way?"

Duncan demands, obviously no longer calm even if he's not as near to hysteria as Wade. "People think I'm still human. We're keeping this under wraps for now."

This wasn't the best thing to say, but Duncan's protective aura makes me feel a tiny bit better...until I really look around the room and see my brothers' pulled back ears and their arched, combative tails.

Are they afraid? For me, yes, but are they scared of me too? I wonder sadly. *Scared that I'm insane for fighting for something with too much baggage?*

"They think you're still human, hm?" Wade growls, hardly able to get out the words around the snarl lodged in his throat. "Fat lot of good that does her! You might get off with your kind assuming you have a fetish, but Sierra? Do you even *know* how people treat half-breeds who sleep with humans?"

"Wade Hampton Maurell!" I'm angry now, my voice rising as I stalk towards him, abandoning Duncan's comforting hand over mine. "That is the biggest load of *crap* I've ever heard come out of your mouth! You know no one has ever heard of another half-breed and human couple! Besides, where did your 'push for equality' attitude go, out the window with the rest of your brain?" Eisen chortles and I whirl on him, glaring.

"What's funny, Eisen? Is it perhaps your complete and utter *uselessness* that you're snickering at?" I need to avoid losing control, but the feelings I have for Duncan and my own self-respect interfere with my determination to make this scene go my way by being mature. My hands shake and I indulge in a slow, calming exhale.

"*YOU KNEW?*" Wade roars, turning on Eisen faster than I expected. "You *knew* and you decided to keep something this stupid a secret?"

Eisen is still cool somehow, the calmest one in the room besides Duncan. "Sierra told me earlier. I was as disbelieving as you, but I knew she wouldn't lie about something like this...besides, if it was one of her pranks, it's not one she could carry out to satisfaction."

"Why the hell didn't you tell us before we let him in the damn door?" Wade's hands are clenched into fists now, and I can see he's losing it.

"She said she'd tell you tonight...if she hadn't, I'd have told you myself at the soonest opportunity," Eisen shrugs, inspecting his nails like he hasn't a care in the world.

"Thanks for your secrecy," I snarl, stung.

"You never swore me to it, S," Eisen sighs long-sufferingly before striding forward and throwing himself into the chair Wade vacated. "As it is, I'm a generous soul, so I decided to wait and see what would transpire of our sister's unwise dalliance. I wanted to meet the knave she was willing to risk so much for," Eisen speaks arrogantly, like he's a scholar settling down to advance his academic proposal before a school board; I am instantly annoyed. "So far, aside from the obvious physicality factors, I—"

"Enough," Harold speaks for the first time since this whole episode began; our heads snap around to observe him, comically in sync. "Not a single person here is in the mood for your games, Eisen, so why don't you stop showing off and get to the point?" His tone is dangerous, and I repress a shudder. Harold could rule out of favor with my wishes, and this possibility suddenly feels very real. Even Eisen looks properly cowed.

"Basically," he begins again as he shakes back a few stray strands of hair out of his eyes, "I regret to say that aside from what he is and what my sister is, I don't see any problems with Duncan. I believe he values her...but if he's truly half-breed, it's not like that's much his choice anyway." His vote of confidence catches me off guard, and my ears swivel up to listen for the ensuing laughter, for Eisen to confess he was joking, there's no chance in hell I should be with Duncan.

He doesn't, though, and when I dare raise my eyes to look at Harold's face, he's nodding and rubbing his now stubble-rough chin with his hand. *Lawyer face,* I think, wishing I could tell Duncan that this is what my eldest brother looks like when he's working. But maybe that wouldn't be reassuring...

"Not my choice?" Duncan asks, his eyes lingering briefly on me before he meets Eisen's speculative gaze. "How is not my choice?"

"Half-breeds mate young, younger than humans," my golden brother explains. "I'm sure you've heard this before, but it's not in our nature to date around or fool around unless a certain...*connection* takes place. Having not felt this bond with anyone, I can't describe it fully."

"Are you saying that I'm not...I'm not in control of how I feel about Sierra?" Duncan's face is flushed, and I don't know if it's from embarrassment that he may have overestimated his feelings, or if he's upset that whatever value he's placed on me is under scrutiny.

"You're in control," Harold assures him, speaking

academically. "The human part very rarely lets the half-breed nature rule unchallenged. That is to say, your instincts play a huge part in all of this. The animal DNA enhances your feelings, no matter whether it's biological factors or matching personality types that would coordinate well together over an extended time period. Still...if you felt distaste or repulsion for Sierra's company, your animal nature would eventually follow your human wishes and naturally decrease the attraction. As it is...I think you feel more deeply than you seem."

"That...makes sense," Duncan is embarrassed now, as any guy might be when having a conversation about his emotions with another guy, but he doesn't deny the truth of Harold's theory. My heart swoops into my stomach as I realize that theory applies to me as well. *You feel more deeply than you seem...*

"You both aren't seriously considering this, are you?" Wade questions in a furious voice, interrupting the softening of my heart. "This is the stupidest idea known to man, and you're both condoning it?!"

"It's my decision Wade," I say, weary instead of angry; I want to hug Duncan, bury my face in his chest so I can re-memorize his scent, but I refrain. "Of course, I value your input, but—"

"—thanks, but no thanks," Eisen cuts in sarcastically. "'It's not you, it's me' kind of deal...bad luck, brother. Little sister won't obey."

"Shut up," Wade snarls at him viciously. "This is more than some silly crush, Eisen, and you need to quit being an ass and realize that Sierra might ruin her life with this—"

"Would you like me to stop you from seeing Emilee, Wade?" Harold cuts in smoothly, inserting his wiry frame in the middle of an argument like a skilled parent. Wade looks shocked, then wounded like Harold struck him.

"Like you could...but how is that relevant?" he asks gruffly, his tail angling down with his ears in a sign of retreat.

"It's the same thing as what you're asking Sierra to do, essentially—no, don't give me that look, just listen," Harold explains, closing the distance between him and Wade and placing a calming hand on his shoulder. "I've been a half-breed lawyer for a long time, Wade, and do you know what I've seen? I've seen humans mistreat half-breeds, and mistreat them cruelly, but I've also covered cases where half-breeds attacked or maligned humans with no cause at all. The problem with our world is that we—our two races—do not see each other as equals. If you and Emilee feel the...connection Sierra and Duncan do, would it be fair for me to deny either one of you a chance at happiness?"

"No," Wade says grudgingly, one of his ears twitching with irritation.

"Now you reached the point I got to earlier today," Eisen boasts, looking over at me with a barely strained smile. "I was as angry as you...and as intolerant...but it wouldn't be right to stop something like this just because of race."

"Exactly," Harold smiles like he won a case, which I suppose he did.

"Besides, aren't there *so many* other ways we can

give her grief about dating?" Eisen saunters up beside me and slides his arm around my shoulders possessively, although I can tell he's joking...a little. "She's still very young, and it's too early to be thinking about a serious relationship, obviously...plus there's the rights of passage Duncan will have to go through to be considered worthy, and he could easily fail!"

"Hey!" I exclaim, embarrassed as Eisen ruffles my hair with his hand. "That's not fair either!"

"Children," Harold sighs indulgently. "We are still in the middle of a very serious conversation, so if you want this settled before midnight—"

"I thought it was settled?" I ask as I firmly shove Eisen away and step closer to Duncan. "You three decided it wouldn't be fair to keep Duncan and me apart just because he's half-breed as well as human."

"Maybe not *fair*," Wade interjects, his tone unaffected by the brief spell of humor. "But perhaps necessary."

"Even if you don't care about race, the rest of the world does, and if rumor of this gets out and enough people believe it, both of you could be in a lot of danger," Harold explains; his voice is gentle, but the content of his words is still worrisome.

"Bull," Eisen cuts in. "They're young, but I think they both know enough to be careful...and so what if they did let the chips fall where they may and go public? Maybe it's time someone crossed the bridge about this." I blink at him, subconsciously pulling my tail in front of me to hold it as a personal security measure.

"I agree with Eisen," Duncan chips in helpfully, although his tone is also serious.

"You would," Wade snorts, his fur bristling again as he shakes his furry head. Harold makes a quieting gesture towards him before addressing Duncan.

"Explain your reasoning, then," he challenges, although far more calmly than Wade might have. Our kitchen has been divided into sides now: Duncan and I stand beside each other, leaning back against the sink with Eisen fidgeting nearby, and Harold and Wade sit uncomfortably at the wooden table with the knowledge that they are outnumbered.

Duncan looks taken aback when he's asked to explain, but he takes a moment to ponder his answer before he speaks. "I...I want to think I understand better how this whole thing works now. Initially, when I was just becoming half-breed, I wanted nothing more than to go back to being a normal human...but over time—and thanks to Sierra, since I've known her—I've come to terms with what I am, and I wouldn't change anything. In my case, the danger of becoming a lab rat doesn't seem likely as long as I keep quiet until I come out with the truth on my own terms," he says, his eyebrows furrowed as he speaks.

"As far as...how far I'd be willing to go to stay with Sierra, I haven't been able to say what I feel because I didn't understand the bond. For a while, I thought it was just a half-breed thing, the attraction I felt, but that went away quickly once we started talking more. Now, I still can't voice what I feel because to a human mind it doesn't make sense to feel such a link so strongly. Feelings aren't all what goes into it...like you said, Harold, my actual instincts want me to hang on and not let go. I don't know how anyone could resist that, and once regular emotions come into play..." He looks down at me, turning his head with a look of concentration still on his face; the anxiety and slight awkwardness he's shown around my brothers is absent, replaced with a clear-eyed, determined emotion which brings up a responsive flutter in my chest.

"It's been a short time, and I know feelings aren't the only important thing in a relationship...and if she felt endangered by me and asked me to keep my distance, I would...but I just know I'd go to hell and back for this girl. I don't see this...this focus in my life ever diminishing." His face has suddenly cleared as well as his eyes, so the expression gracing his features is strong but gentle as he meets my gaze. I'm so moved I can hardly speak, and three little words hover at the tip of my tongue...but I don't say them.

"Duncan..." My voice is barely audible, but I lose the opportunity to say anything as Eisen slow claps for Duncan's speech.

"Well, you won me over," he grins, "I'm a romantic at heart, folks."

"You weren't the one who had to be won over," I tell him as he skips around the kitchen pretending to toss flower petals everywhere. *Way to ruin the moment,* I grumble internally; but Harold doesn't seem perturbed by Eisen's antics.

"Well done," he says quietly, meeting Duncan's gaze as he stands. Then he's silent for so long, I can't predict what his response will be; the lines around his mouth are stern, although his eyes are kind. Finally...

"I can tell that Sierra feels the same way...and in the face of that, rules don't exactly apply...Wade?"

"Yeah?" Wade is still surly, and regards Duncan with angry suspicion as he responds to Harold's thoughtful address, but his antagonistic frown has mellowed somewhat.

"Let's see how this plays out," Harold still looks thoughtful, but when he looks down at a slouching Wade, I know this is the kind of executive order Wade won't be willing to combat.

"Fine," he growls, releasing the tension from the snarl he's had lodged in his throat. "Who am I to interfere with something so pure?"

"Only my brother...I'd rather you helped us figure out problems as they come instead of making trouble," I say before I can remind myself that Wade is uncooperative when he doesn't get his way. *I'm sorry I snapped at you*, I add in my head, regretting my initial outburst at the beginning of this discussion. *This is hard to come to terms with.*

Wade studies me, analyzing my sincerity with his bright eyes narrowed and his ears swiveling forward and back. "I never said I wouldn't help, S..."

"Just that you thought that her soul-mate wasn't worth a bit of risk," Eisen snorts, shrugging as he heads for the pantry for snacks; none of us are surprised at that, since it doesn't take my brothers long to recover after eating a heavy meal. Wade opens his mouth to argue, and I gear up for more drama, but Harold lifts his hand and passes it tiredly over his face.

"Enough, you three...we've had enough sibling issues tonight, don't you think?" As usual when Harold reveals how tired he is by some small action, the three of us are instantly contrite.

"Sorry," I say; my expression of regret is undoubtedly mirrored on the angular faces of Eisen and Wade. "Thanks for dealing with this...well..."

"...in the best way possible, considering the circumstances," Eisen chips in, emerging from the pantry with a small snack in his hands. "Thanks to you, we can all sleep peacefully in our beds, content in the knowledge that our little sister brought her boyfriend into the open instead of sneaking around."

"Speaking of sleep..." There were any number of responses Harold could have made to Eisen's words, but he ignores that and after a little more argument, my brothers leave so only Harold and me and Duncan remain in the kitchen.

"Thank you," I tell Harold sincerely. "I—" Harold interrupts me before I can swear eternal servitude.

"It's fine, S. Just be careful and don't let me down," he says, passing a hand over his face to disguise a yawn. "As for you..."

"I will do everything in my power to make this go our way," Duncan swears seriously. "Thanks for backing us up."

"Ah, you crazy kids," Harold sighs, and for a second I imagine how cool it would be if Duncan developed good relationships with all of my brothers. "Don't stay up late, S... and he stays in the kitchen until he leaves."

Harold exits, leaving Duncan and me alone in the dim light of the kitchen chandelier. The soft glow seems gentler now that the strained atmosphere of my brothers' company has gone. Duncan's returned to his half-breed self, and he looks down at me with a serious expression still troubling his eyes.

"We did it," I say to reassure him, taking his hand in mine.

"I'm shocked it went so well," Duncan says, absentminded as he rubs his neck thoughtfully. "But that's three more people on our side now...can't complain."

I wince as I remember Wade's clear desire to attack as we were arguing. "They'll come to like you soon enough...you'll have to stick around, though," I tease, trying to lighten the mood so Duncan doesn't have to leave on such a serious note. He smiles, but he's still distracted, and a look in his eyes makes me pause.

"I intend to," he says, glancing to the doorway my brothers disappeared through before stepping in front of me with both of his hands on the counter top on either side of me. We're close again, close like we were in the stairwell not long ago, and a delicious tension sizzles between our bodies.

"Thanks," I say. My voice is soft as I look into Duncan's face. His bright eyes captivate me, and I study the planes of his face as well as the many freckles decorating his skin.

"For what?" he asks, studying me like he doesn't want to stop.

"For enduring all of this. For being willing to deal with my family and friends and for—"

"Stop. I don't mind any of that, and the hard part of getting adequate permission to be with you from your brothers is over. It's a worthy exchange." He suddenly kisses my cheek, so lightly I would barely feel it except for the pleasant heat of his lips on my skin. "I honestly don't care how much trouble you get me into." He laughs, kissing my other cheek.

"I thought you were the one who was going to get me in trouble?" I ask; his easy humor is contagious, a good mix with the light kisses he's bestowing on my face. One time he kisses so close to the corner of my mouth that I forget to breathe.

"Right, I'm the instigator...I forgot," Duncan says, his smile as beautiful as his eyes and as confident as the rest of him. His voice is so quiet that no one but the two of us could hear it, and the kitchen aura is cozy and velvety quiet.

"I..."*What was I going to say?* I can't remember.

"Sierra..." Duncan begins again, once again serious even though a smile plays about his mouth. "Love you." I know I'd asked him not to say it too soon, but this moment is... *right*. It's time, and I don't regret his confession; I feel the same way, so how can I deny him when he admits to something we both can't deny we share?

"Love you too," I reply, hardly able to breathe.

Duncan nods once, like we satisfied a very important ritual, and his lips press down on mine once, twice, three times. His kisses are feather-light, like he's scared of hurting me, and my responses are tentative once I recover from the shock that I'm finally getting my first kiss.

Too soon, the moment is over, and I find my hands laced into Duncan's hair while his hands gently hold my waist.

"Wow," I say softly before I catch myself. Duncan seems contemplative, like the confessions we made need to be preserved like fragile glass.

"Thanks for letting me say it," he tells me, holding me to him like he's reluctant to let go. "I didn't want to freak you out by saying it too soon, but really...I love you."

After all that's gone on, it feels like years since I met Duncan, and I wouldn't trade these minutes of him holding me for anything.

29

The following weeks before the vote pass with alternating speeds. There's the too slow pace, with days and minutes stretching on for years...then everything races ahead with bits and pieces of moments preserved like insects in amber. I was never deluded that my worst problem would be persuading my brothers to accept Duncan as something like my soul-mate, but perhaps I didn't realize how much upheaval the upcoming political change was going to cause.

The calm at school hasn't lasted, although I've miraculously managed to keep out of the mayhem. Belinda Harper has been watching me, studying my movements during Hostetler's once weekly assembly meetings, during which she subtly infuriates every half-breed in the room with her slick-tongued talk about "changes to come." She's been awaiting my reaction in the form of a student-organized rebellion against the system, but no one I know would be that stupid...except perhaps Lyle.

I finally gained the distance from my old friends that I craved the week after the dinner at Hayley's. To get through telling a very smug Morgan that I wouldn't be eating lunch with them anymore to give her a better chance at Lyle—who still pursues me, although he's backed off to focus on trying to whip the half-breeds around him into some form of revolution—I imagined how Duncan looked right before he kissed me the first time. The serious, quietly joyful light in his fathoms-deep eyes lingers in my mind, a warming thought for when life brings me down.

Strangely enough, in spite of having to keep on the down low about our relationship, Duncan and I have grown very close the past weeks. I still have to follow half-breed rules—which means no dates on human territory, since I can't pass as human—but the support I've been getting from Femi and Hasida as well as from Duncan's friends has been invaluable. Bari or Mabel has helped me smuggle iced coffee in a thermos or decent lunches into Duncan's locker on random days, and I see them and Duncan every lunch hour. Femi and Hasida showed great enthusiasm about continuing our little "lunches for equality," and I think it's by their influence that any harassment we might have experienced is kept to the bare minimum.

Harold is tolerant of us, Eisen is occasionally hostile whenever I get too close to Duncan, and Wade has been very busy making himself absent to spend time with Emilee when he's not at work. I try to be fair: Duncan can't be the only thing in my life, and I don't want to push my close family away for a boy. Never mind how I feel closer to this boy than I have to anyone else; it's hard enough to pay attention to other things when Duncan is in the same room with me, and the urge to reach out and take his hand when he passes by in the hall is nearly unconquerable. It's not easy to remember to take things slow, to give ourselves time, when it feels like life as we know it will end on a particular Wednesday coming soon.

September passes into early October, and my heart turns with the leaves. Society may be descending into a battlefield again, with rumors of revolution, open human hostility, and general fighting in the streets...but when I'm laughing with my human and half-breed friends at lunch, or walking on our trail with Duncan, the rest of the world seems far away.

Six days before the vote, Duncan and I spend our Thursday afternoon walking the same trail we'd traversed the day we decided to listen to the instincts prompting us to be together. The weather is getting cooler, but the sun shines golden through the orange-tinted leaves on

Duncan's red hair and my ginger fur. Because it's right after school, no one is around except for us, although various pedestrians might meander across our path on this breezy day.

"Has it been worth it?' he asks me, my hand in his as we amble on the trail. "The secrecy, I mean."

"Yes," I reply, breathing in the air just starting to

gain a flavor of autumn crispness; I snag a bright yellow leaf from a bush as I pass, studying its veins in the sunlight. "I mean, it would be ideal if I could see you without the necessity of ignoring your presence so no one notices me noticing you...but for now, I suppose I have to be content."

"It doesn't seem like it's in your nature to like keeping something like this secret," he points out. Abandoning my scrutiny of the leaf, I let it fall as I smooth my hair over my shoulder so the waves sit properly.

"It's not," I admit. "But if it keeps you safe...if it keeps us safe...secrecy is not a high price to pay. Besides, enough people are in the know and help share the burden—not that my feelings for you are a burden—so I think I'm managing pretty well."

"That's very...stalwart of you, Sierra," Duncan remarks, something like an edge to his voice. "It's okay if you're unhappy with the arrangement, and to say so."

"What?" I lift my eyes, almost halting our walk so I can read him better. "I'm not...unhappy, Duncan. Are you?"

"No, of course not, not with you," he says, impatiently lifting my hand to his lips to leave a kiss there. "I...I don't think it's right for this to be a secret." When he looks at me, his eyes are brown again, prompting my next question.

"This meaning your canine DNA or this meaning us?"

"Us. I feel...I love you, Sierra, and it's not fair to you or to me to pretend that the feelings we have aren't there," he says, pausing and turning me to face him. "Sure, everyone who matters knows...except my family, and except everyone who sees you as just a half-breed who spends too much time around humans."

I'm distracted by the mention of his family. "Do you want to tell your family? Is that it?"

"Yes and no...that's part of it..." Duncan huffs in frustration, sounding very much like a dog unable to crack a bone. "I'm not explaining this correctly."

"Deep breaths," I say, trying to dispel the tension between us as I trace my fingertips across his jaw line.

"Try again."

Duncan gives me that look that's like he's looking up at me even though he's taller. "Contrary to popular belief, we're not doing wrong by being together. According to your brother and most of your—our—race, it's more natural that we should be attached. Our DNA literally increases our natural desire to be together."

"I know that," I say, my face immaturely heating at the word "desire." "We know that. And yes, so far the people who've known have supported us after a little persuasion, but...is it worth it to you to risk being made a complete—possibly unemployable and uneducated, if the law goes through against us—social outcast? Really?"

Duncan looks up at the tree canopy above us, perhaps asking heaven for strength before he returns his gaze to me. "How many people do I have to tell this? I *don't care* about all of that, and the future isn't set against us yet. Really, Sierra...you're worth it."

Then he kisses me, and I forget for a while. He's still

gentle, cupping my face in his hands as our lips softly meet over and over, and I'm grateful that he's not pushing me. The feeling that someone is content to just be with me and enjoy me without pressing for more too soon is intoxicating, enough to warm my skin and electrify my heart. When we part with the warm honey taste of his kiss lingering on my mouth, I simply study his face as he studies mine.

"You're worth it too," I say, wishing I could articulate the bubbly-warm but very solid feeling I get around this boy. "What do you want to do?"

"For now?"He smiles, a strange, amused look in his hot chocolate colored eyes. "I want to do this." His hands were caressing my face, but he slides them up into my hair towards my ears with careful slowness until he brushes them against the fur with a lightness that gives me goose bumps. He's petting my ears, stroking them with his fingertips as he judges my reaction; I don't think either one of us realized that fox half-breeds as well as regular foxes liked being petted.

"What are you doing...?" I ask once I wake up enough to resume thinking consciously. Duncan laughs, the lightheartedness reaching his eyes as he answers.

"I haven't done this before, and it's something I've been thinking about trying. You have to remember, I don't know anything about half-breed culture, and I've been curious about what your fur really feels like....and if you'd like it being touched or not." His face reddens slightly, but even if he did have another motive in mind, it's not like I wasn't thinking of the same thing.

"I don't mind," I confess, my cheeks turning pink from my wayward thoughts. "It *is* actually common in half-breed culture for the animal aspects to get some attention: mothers nip the ears of their children if they're misbehaving while very young, and when siblings fight, tails and feathers are often pulled. Harold used to kind of scratch behind my fox ears to make me relax whenever I was antsy as a child...it's kind of embarrassing to admit now," I laugh self-consciously.

"This is what I'm missing," Duncan says ruefully. "Because I don't belong to your world, and haven't belonged as a child, I miss out on the great aspects of your kind...things I could share with you."

"You could let it be known that you're half-breed, or..." A wild idea crosses my mind, one where Duncan and I leave our region and run away to a place where no one knew he was ever human; it's so close to a real solution that I almost say what I'm thinking.

"Or?" he queries.

"Never mind." I'm glad I caught myself before I voiced something that wasn't a real option; still, a strange sense of disappointment fills me. "What do you want to do, Duncan?"

"I want to...to claim you, or whatever," Duncan's answer catches me off guard. "Not like I own you, obviously...call it the protective instinct, but I want everyone to know I'm with you. You...you're worth everything to me, and I don't think you deserve to be a part of my life I have to keep hidden from everyone else."

"I can't say I don't feel the same way," I avoid looking at Duncan, resuming our walk so we can move along the trail. "But if it's not safe..."

"Is it ever going to be totally safe? I'm not trying to

be aggressive about being a couple...but why shouldn't we be the ones to take the leap?" Duncan reasons, following me. "If...if it's true that the vaccine keeping humans human is no longer working, then might there be other half-breed humans out there experiencing the same thing I am? Perhaps even the same thing we are?"

The thought hadn't occurred to me. "Possibly."

Duncan sighs again, making me worry if I've upset him. "I'm not saying we let everyone know tomorrow...but...we shouldn't need to worry about word getting around. I love you. I love how you're clever and careful and reckless all at the same time, and I don't mind everyone knowing."

My heart softens, even though I feel sure that this is a hasty decision to make right now. "I will think about it. Perhaps after the vote; after we see how much life changes once the humans decide to kick the M-DNA branch to the curb."

Duncan doesn't deny this, but his broad presence is reassuring, and my peace with this golden afternoon hasn't been interrupted. "I love you too," I say, nearly inaudible. Duncan squeezes my hand, and we continue on the trail and discuss pleasanter topics.

That was one of the better afternoons before the vote; after that, Harold forbade me to go out after school anywhere except Omnium Beanery when Eisen would be there. I didn't blame him, and neither did Duncan. Something about the weekend before the vote made everyone realize that this would be the week where everything would change and half-breed rights would be reduced to basically wartime measures. This meant a lot of robberies, a few very public shootings, and most likely more than one murder that was hushed up by the SMARTvision media.

So much for them being afraid of us, I would often think whenever Katrina would call out an insult, or whenever Bryan's cold gaze fell on the back of my neck. Their presence had become threatening, and I'd begun avoiding places I knew where they'd be.

Looks like we're more scared of them than they are of us. In spite of all of Lyle's rabble-rousing and fight starting outside of school—which I frequently heard stories about, since I couldn't shake off Shelby's tenacious friendship—nothing serious had come of the aggressive, human-hating half-breed group's plans.

The worst scare took place the Monday before the vote: Harold didn't come home from work until nearly four in the morning, and when he came in he was staggering from exhaustion, hunger, and a nasty cut above his left eyebrow. By the time he walked in the door, I had nearly convinced myself that he wouldn't, and Eisen had had to catch me before I collapsed at the base of the stairs. Then I'd half tackled Harold, hugging him fiercely before dragging him to the kitchen table under the light so I could treat his cut.

"What happened?" Eisen asked once the manic look went out of his eyes; Wade was standing by the front door, listening to our conversation but also making sure Harold wasn't followed home; this was the best task for him, since whenever Wade was really stressed, he would revert to a more animal state of mind where problems were easier to handle.

"There was a shooter...in the firm..." Harold

grimaced as I cleaned the crusty blood from his wound; I pressed my lips together to keep my pathetic soothing words back so he could explain. "You won't have seen it on SMARTvision; they kept it hushed up, and it wasn't important since it was only a human holding up the top lawyer in our firm."

"That'd be you then, right?" Eisen said, grabbing random condiments and leftovers from the fridge so Harold could eat as soon as I finished with the bandage.

Harold laughed grimly. "Obviously not. But that's a good thing: the guy the shooter was after is in the hospital now with a few shattered ribs and a bullet near his lung."

"What did he want? The shooter?" I asked, my voice cracking so I was barely able to speak.

"His version of justice, I suppose," Harold growled, holding his hair back so I could finish treating his cut. "It doesn't matter...he's dead now, thanks to law enforcement when they *finally* arrived on the scene. I only stayed so long because they wouldn't let us access our SMARTcalls. They spent most of the night interviewing each person and making sure we wouldn't talk about the event with anyone."

"But how did you get hurt?" Wade snarled as he came in, standing in the doorframe with his fists clenched to whiteness.

"I got a little mouthy with the shooter for smacking around that top guy's assistant, and he introduced my head to the desk a little more forcefully than I would like." Harold grimaced again before motioning Eisen over with the food. "That's part of the reason I'm so late...by the time I came to, I was last in line, and the officers took extra time with me because I was injured and a possible liability."

Harold spent the rest of the wee morning hours right up until I had to get ready for school reassuring us that he was fine and not in trouble with the law just for being present at a crime scene...as long as he didn't talk, that is. His reassurances were a little helpful, but my eyes met Eisen's over Harold's head as he spoke. *If it's this bad now,* I knew we were both thinking, *how bad will it get after the vote?*

30

Dear Students:

It has come to my attention that threats of violence have been made against students in this school. Therefore, all M-DNA student classes and lunch periods have been relocated to the lower wing until further notice. It is for your own safety that students will be separated by DNA class beginning this Wednesday. Trespassing between the upper wing and the lower wing will be a punishable offense. 50 demerits and two weeks of detention will be dispensed to students who disobey this rule.

In addition, the local SMARTvision media crew will be present Wednesday morning to interview students about the vote. It is a great honor for our school to gain publicity this way, as we are the biggest institution in *our area with the most sizeable population of M-DNA students. I expect each of you to behave in a manner befitting your school.*

Your Principal,
Belinda Harper

I don't know how I wanted to wake up this morning, but reading this SMARTnote from Belinda Harper has been a bad start to a day already bloated with the collective anxiety of a nation. I dress woodenly, but the clothes I have laid out are a bit nicer than my regular school clothes. I like looking prepared for an event, even if I'm dreading it the entire time. The day isn't nippy, but I feel cold; brown skinny jeans with slender caramel colored boots rising to my knees and a teal long-sleeved top make me feel cozy in spite of my fear for the future.

My brothers hover around the kitchen, equally prepared for their work days and brooding in total silence. My heart saddens at the stony expressions on their kin-related faces, and I try and fail to consume the lukewarm eggs and toast Wade made for us. We've been taking our breakfasts in the living room lately, watching the news for any change in the vote schedule or in case a new story of violence escapes the SMARTvision media muzzle, but I know none of us can stomach the smug, flabby face of Abel Denmann today.

DUNCAN LEDFORD: *I'm here.*

The message from Duncan wakes me up long enough to say farewell to my brothers. I give each of them an extra-long hug, just in case I don't see them until very late in the day. *Who knows,* I think miserably as I walk out to my boyfriend's car, *there could be another war by three p.m. today, and they'll go off to fight just like Dad.*

"Morning," I grunt at Duncan, my voice rusty from lack of use since last night. Wade probably isn't watching at the window, so I lean over to bestow a brief but sweet kiss on Duncan's lips.

"Morning," Duncan replies once I settle back in the passenger seat. "Are you ready for today?"

"No," I speak honestly, "But I will be." I notice the two drinks resting on the bench seat in the space between us; Duncan must have made an Omnium Beanery run, and he brought me my rice pudding drink as well as his peppermint Whizard.

"Thanks," I tell him, pleased by his thoughtfulness as I stir the cinnamon into the milk with my peach colored straw.

"I thought we'd need caffeine fortification for this morning," Duncan explains, but he smiles at my praise.

We don't talk much for the rest of the drive; Duncan holds my hand, and when I'm not sipping my drink I balance it in my lap and respond to Hayley's message.

HAYLEY MANCHESTER: *Are you still going to do it?*

SIERRA MAURELL: *Yes...it feels like it's time. Besides, Duncan already picked me up, and people will see us* *arrive at school together even if I wanted to back out.*

HAYLEY MANCHESTER: *I can tell you don't...besides, marching in the front doors hand in hand will be a real statement.*

SIERRA MAURELL: *That's the point: too many witnesses to say it didn't happen, and it helps that the local media will be there. It's too public to cover up...and go big or go home, I say. Besides, this will gauge how the reception will be if Duncan ever decides to let his furry little secret go public.*

HAYLEY MANCHESTER: *True...but wait, a news crew will be there? That's encouraging and sad at the same time...*

Tell me about it, I think wryly. Last night when Duncan came over, and I told him about Harold's dangerous adventure at work, and the consequent media cover-up, he was silent for a few minutes as he digested the information. Of course he was sympathetic, and he held me as I endured the short thirty seconds of a panic attack.

"I almost lost my brother to a crazy shooter," I told him once I could trust my voice again, "And I have a funny feeling that even if he had been...more seriously injured, no one would have ever known about it."

"They would've," Duncan assured me, smoothing his hand over my messy, un-styled hair. "You and your brothers would have spread the word in your own special way."

"I could've always hired the Reiss to prosecute somebody, or take someone out." I felt a bitter laugh clawing at my throat, and the tail end of it came out sounding strangled.

"Next time call me, okay?" Duncan said as my brothers pattered around the kitchen hunting for more food; we were sitting alone in the living room, since for now Duncan isn't allowed to sit with me in my room. "I don't care what time it is, I want to be there for you if something crazy is going on. Even if I'm asleep, keep calling until I answer."

"I wasn't thinking clearly," I mumbled, sleep gradually overpowering my senses. But an idea formed in my head as I snuggled beside Duncan, and when I brought it up, he listened and was willing to go along with my plan.

It's not right that our lives are treated as shameful, and bad things that happen to us shouldn't be covered up. I go through my reasoning process again to give myself courage for this morning's plan. *Good or bad, we have a right to live openly, and if I can show my kind how to do that and give them courage, it will be worth it.*

"Have you ever thought that no one will notice?" Duncan interrupts my reverie as we pull into his usual parking space at the school; our drinks are gone, and we leave the cups on the seat as we exit the vehicle. I give him a sideways look, making sure he's joking before I answer.

"They will...did you forget I was the half-breed queen for the first two weeks of school? Lyle displaced me as king, but I can still draw attention if I need to," I say, walking beside my boyfriend as I nervously regard the school. In some ways, Hostetler looks less intimidating than when I first saw it, but the increased population of students milling around the front steps with their necks craned to observe the sharp SMARTvision news crew does make me reconsider my plan to anger pretty much everyone.

"Let's help them out, shall we?" Duncan slides his arm around my waist, tugging me closer so that it's very obvious we're a couple as we walk. Very few half-breeds are present—most of them probably arrived early to avoid the news crew rush—but I do see a hostile looking Lyle and Ivar arrive on the scene. I wonder if they'll bother entering by the front door and risking punishment, but I don't particularly care.

"Last chance to back out," I say as one or two students I don't know do a double-take in our direction. "I could fake an ankle sprain, and you could be the good Samaritan—hey!"

"What?" Duncan tenses beside me, alert for trouble, but I ignore him as I regard the spunky blonde reporter interviewing a bored looking student at the base of the white brick school steps. She has the hungry look of a media worker about her thin face, and the smart blue business suit with the gold scarf gives her the look of someone desperate for public approval.

"That's Thea van Asch," I tell him, "Don't you recognize her? She's been in Abel Denmann's pocket for years, so the rumor goes."

"Oh yeah," Duncan says as recognition dawns in his eyes. "She did that interview with the senator a few days ago, didn't she? The one where all she could talk about was how half-breeds have stolen decent jobs from everyone else, and how mandatory sterilization could be the greatest step forward for our country in a hundred years."

"That's her." I glare at the back of van Asch's head as she shoves a microphone into a sleepy looking student's face. "Ugh. I didn't realize Belinda had invited her."

"Maybe this is a good thing," Duncan coaxes me into resuming our approach to the school. "She'll be sure to get the word out."

"Yeah, along with all the other biased crap she'll spew on every SMARTvision network she can reach," I grumble, but my annoyance is easy to maintain as a defense against my fear.

This is the best thing to do, I tell myself as student heads turn in our direction. They don't seem to believe what they're seeing; Duncan's arm around me is a dead giveaway, and I see many eyes zero in on the place of contact between us. I realize my face with its furrowed brows and pursed lips must make me look like an angry hostage, so I look up at Duncan to distract myself. His expression is calm, far more so than mine, and he looks content to be with me, like this is an everyday thing. Just a boy walking his girlfriend into school.

That's what it should be, I think, my fears dissipating as Duncan gives me one of those sideways smiles I love. The sun gleams on his brilliant red hair and reflects the sparks of gold in his peridot eyes. I feel golden too, filled with my purpose. *The whole point of this is making our relationship a normal thing. This is what I'm fighting for.*

"Hey," Duncan says as we purposefully ignore the incredulous expressions of the many people who've spotted us. I'm not sure I want to see those looks turning into dawning expressions of realizing the truth. "I'm glad it's you, if I haven't mentioned this before. Of all the half-breed girls around, I'm glad everything in me chose you."

My heart leaps, and I experience that rare feeling where Duncan and I are the only two people on this whole campus; we've stopped walking, and we face each other as we stand close together. We're near the news crew, but not too close.

"Yeah...I think you've mentioned it before...but I wouldn't change anything about us. You've made my life exciting just by existing, and I have a feeling it's going to stay that way."

"Sierra...can I try something? I really think it would complete this high school ideal we're setting up today." Duncan is serious, but he has a light in his eyes, and he reaches up to brush my bangs out of my eyes with his fingertips. He stares at me like he never wants to stop, and it's impossible to look away.

"Go for it," I say, my voice soft. In my peripheral, I see Thea van Asch looking our way as a human student points at us, probably telling her that Duncan isn't a half-breed, but then none of that matters. Duncan's mouth lands on mine, gentle at first before something crazy happens, and I can't think of anything else.

Duncan's never kissed me like this before, not in all our tender, soft practices where we were more focused on learning how to be together instead of just *being*. My eyes flutter closed as he slides his arms around my waist, his hands holding me to him and inviting me closer. He's kissing me like he wants me, and for the first time I truly get the sense that there's nothing he wouldn't do for me.

The world disappears, dissolving into swirl of color behind my eyelids as my lips match the pattern of Duncan's, moving in sync to a tuneless melody only two matched people like us could understand. The sunlight beaming down from the autumn sky is heavenly and warm, like it's a sentient spotlight preserving this moment. My skin feels like each nerve is awake and singing as I tangle my hands into his hair and press myself against him. Kissing Duncan has always been good, but I didn't realize he was holding back until now. *Amazing...*

It feels like a long time before we break apart, and when we do, everything else is silent. We're still very close together, holding on as we study each other like it's the first time. Duncan looks as awed as I feel, his eyes on fire with an emotion I must be mirroring.

"Wow," I whisper, my face warm as Duncan brushes his lips against the tip of my nose. "I think I love you." Duncan grins handsomely, his eyes crinkling at the corners. My reflection is mirrored in his eyes: flushed cheeks and lips still damp from our first real kiss.

"Yeah, I think so too," he quips.

When I break his gaze and look around, everyone is staring at us with a variety of expressions, and the babble of conversation swells like a balloon about to burst. Thea van Asch drags her news crew our way,

435

and behind her I glimpse Lyle glaring at me with something like hate in his icy lion eyes.

Everyone else must be too stunned to react, I think, deciding that I won't step away from Duncan as Van Asch finally reaches us.

"You!" She calls in a surprisingly masculine voice. "Are you doing this as a protest—"

BANG.

BANG.

I don't understand why she didn't finish her question, or why Duncan's arms have tightened around me so that I can barely breathe. My ears are ringing strangely, and someone seems to have pushed the slow motion button for my surroundings. Thea stares at me in horror, looking to where Duncan's hands press on my waist. Then she's gone, shouting and screaming at her news crew to chase down a boy who's carrying something small and black and running in the opposite direction. I catch a whiff of ocean-scented cologne...

"What happened?" I ask, shouting to be heard over the uproar that the entire student body has erupted into. The ringing in my ears won't go away after the shots, and everything seems layered in fog. Abruptly, I realize I've fallen down, or been knocked down to the ground.

Shots... I'm slowly putting it together.

"Sierra!" Duncan calls, and he's staring at my waist as well. I look down too, my heart nearly stopping as I see blood covering Duncan's hand.

No... I've never seen blood before, not more than Wade or Eisen might have spilled in a fight. That was a small amount, and Duncan's hand is sticky with the red substance. My stomach turns as my heart races erratically with panic. *Duncan! Was he shot too?*

"Are you okay?" I ask stupidly, but the fog thickens, and my voice sounds like it's echoing through a tunnel. Duncan responds, his face the brightest thing in my world, but I don't understand him. I feel myself folding, collapsing. He lets me down gently, holding me tight, and my eyes lose the fight to stay open.

Duncan, I think as the chaos around me melts into murky fog.

Acknowledgements

I published *Vixen* for the first time in 2014. I was still in college, and writing between school and work wasn't easy. I'm publishing this new and improved edition of *Vixen* in 2018, and while everything was said in the acknowledgments of the previous edition, I have a few new people to thank.

First, to Daniel: you've been supportive all the way through, whether I'm skipping dinners or leaving the house a mess so I can write, and I can't thank you enough. Also, thanks for the cover design assistance. I couldn't have done it without you. When I wrote this book for the first time, we were only dating. We've married since then, and you know I love you and all of that.

Next, to everyone who supported my somewhat failed previous writings and even now still manage to show interest in whatever I happen to be working on next. Every comment counts, and I'm grateful for your uplifting messages.

To you, reader, I wish you the absolute best. In its own way, this book is for you.

Catherine Labadie

About the Author

Catherine Labadie lives in the mountains of the picturesque Carolinas with her husband and her two hellhounds, Fannie and Heidi. *Vixen* was her debut novel, and her next novel will be released late 2018.

Follow Catherine on

http://authorcatlabadie.wixsite.com/catherinelabadie

Don't miss Catherine's next novel!
Autumn 2018

LONG GROWS THE DARK

BEFORE

Glenna, court sorceress and friend to the ascendant Princess Jael, nurses a secret ardor for Leland, her best friend's betrothed. Yet even as the land approaches its golden age, an unforeseen enemy rises to corrupt the princess and take power for himself. Fate may lead them all down a path too painful to contemplate, but are Glenna's choices enough to dispel the inevitable darkness set to veil their future?

NOW

Gwendoline Hallewell, a Starford University student in a land where magic is commonplace, has always been unusual. When her casting book summons a man from the past to intervene with her dangerous new present, she has no choice but to trust him. As she and her friends Colt and Everleigh reconcile what happened before with what must happen in the present, Gwendoline must decide what it means to make her own choices, suffer her own consequences, and if free will is really within her grasp.

25124158R00245

Made in the USA
Columbia, SC
31 August 2018